PRAISE

If you only read one thriller this year, do yourself a favor and make sure it's Best Seller! *April (USA)*

... likening Susan May to Dean Koontz, Stephen King, or Robin Cook, I realized is a false concept. She steps outside any known author and creates a voice all her own. *Lisa Ensign (USA)*

After reading horror for over 50 years I'm excited by Susan May's book as I haven't been since I read Stephen King's *The Stand*. *Michelle Hummer-Kindig (USA)*

It's absolutely brilliant and I couldn't put it down! *Amanda (USA)*

Susan May now ranks right up there with Stephen King and Brandon Massey on my list of fave thriller/horror authors! *Shannon Gray (USA)*

This book just kept getting better and better. *Jane Culwell (USA)*

This is a suspense filled thriller with a Holy S*%^ great ending! *Diane Lynch (Bookmeetsgirlblog USA)*

Few authors successfully make the leap from short story to novels as fluid as King, Jackson and Poe. But, damn May did it again and she keeps getting better. *Judy Clay (USA)*

A twisted story of jealousy and greed and paranormal happenstance plays off into a thrilling finale that will have you gasping in surprise. *Manie Kilian (South Africa)*

I've read almost all of Susan's books and for me this one is the best. *Faouzia (Germany)*

Susan May brings a fresh perspective to supernatural speculative fiction by mixing reality with subtle hints of otherworldliness. *Madelon Wilson (USA)*

She's been said to be the next Stephen King, which certainly shows in her newest novel, Best Seller. **Victoria Schwimley** *(UK)*

What a fun and fulfilling read! *Walter Scott* (USA)

I love the premise of this book **duffythewriterblog (Australia)**

I just finished reading Best Seller, boy what a ride! *Craig R. Newberry (USA)*

...the pace was breathtakingly fast which had me finishing the almost 500 page book in two sittings. **Kim By Hook or by Book (USA)**

This is one of those books that you end up finishing late at night (in my case it was 12:28am). *Cathy Weber (USA)*

With twists and turns that keep you captivated from start to finish. *Kaye (USA)*

... you may read way past your bedtime and not even know it. *Shannon Gardner (USA)*

I was like an addict waiting for their next fix, and became quite resentful of those annoying little things like eating and sleeping as they interfered with my reading! *Debbie Hauser (USA)*

This book blew me completely away. Just couldn't stop reading. *Angela (USA)*

I felt like this could have been written by Dean Koontz in the early 2000's ... more like the mature King, as in "Duma Key" and not "Carrie" or "Pet Cemetery". *Bill Schmidt (Holey One) (USA)*

"Best Seller" is the ultimate page turner that will keep you on the edge of your seat. *Sue May (Australia)*

This was a really good read, with some truly heart pounding moments. *Maureen (United Kingdom)*

Susan May really has really written a Best Seller! Anyone who reads it will not be disappointed. *Debra (Canada)*

You can get whiplash keeping up with all the twists and turns that are slowly revealed throughout the plot. *Debbie Hauser (USA)*

Best Seller is Susan May's best work to date and there aren't enough positive adjectives to describe how much I enjoyed this novel. *Peg McDaniels (USA)*

Another great book by Susan May! The end was a surprise; I didn't see that coming. *Alicia Maryweather (USA)*

It's like Hitchcock meets the Twilight Zone. *John Filar (USA)*

This is a book you don't want to put down. You have to see what is going to happen next. *Sharon (USA)*

I can honestly say if it were possible to give 10 stars I would! Possibly the best suspense novel I have read in a year. *Doreen Keele (USA)*

I love this author, although her mind and creativity scares me a little bit, I do understand why her style has been referenced as similar to Steven King. *Teri (USA)*

The story is fast paced yet full of detail. *Bill Craig (USA)*

One to read & highly recommended. *Joy Rockey (Australia)*

The storyline was imaginative, intriguing and, at times, heart-stopping. *Paula (USA)*

It has a story line that kept me reading late into the night. *Kandy (USA)*

I didn't want to go to sleep because I didn't want to put it down. *Sandy (USA)*

What an amazing story. *Jackie (USA)*

A book I found difficult to put down, full of twists and turns. You won't be disappointed... *Richard Tamer (USA)*

Susan really knows how to tell a great, gripping, page turning story. *Mike Rice (UK)*

I really did enjoy this story and... I read it in one sitting. *Peter Rouse (UK)*

Susan May has created some more characters you love to hate! *Diane Lybbert (USA)*

This is a very intriguing novel with a surprise ending. *Kenneth Lingenfelter (USA)*

... a fascinating look into the publishing world. *Carol Sidoti (USA)*

I was hooked by this book. *Ola Adamska (Poland)*

Like revenge? Dislike vengeance? Enjoy a little Twilight Zone? Read this one! *Steve Peterson (USA)*

Well done, Susan May. Very well done! *Beenish Arif (USA)*

I loved reading it and hated for the reading to end! *Beth Baskett (USA)*

A truly exceptional story that I highly recommend. *James Phillips (USA)*

What an insane read! It was unputdownable! *Mandie (USA)*

I enjoyed every page of this novel and need to read it again. *Ashok (India)*

Susan May keep writing the best suspenseful books I have read, and this is just another proof of that. *Claudia (Argentina)*

... at its core seriously creepy. *Anne Kasaba (USA)*

Great book, hard to put it down. *Cheryl Behrens (USA)*

... truly enjoyed the story from beginning to end. *Carrie (USA)*

... a fascinating tale that has more twists and turns (and is twisted) than you can imagine. *Ami (USA)*

A marvelous piece of writing for a book group, it raises questions of cause and effect. *Barbara Harrison (USA)*

I had to remind myself that I had work the next day and needed to sleep. *Robyn Lee (USA)*

Solid storytelling, good plot, interesting characters which contributed making a fantasy novel a believable thriller. *Jean-Charles Garaud (Canada)*

Very absorbing storyline. *Pamela Fries (USA)*

I wanted to continue reading late into the night in order to get to the end. And what an ending! *Camille Macchia (USA)*

AWESOME book. *Nicole Burns (USA)*

... definitely a unique & imaginative story as are all of Susan May's books. *Loretta (Canada)*

I don't usually read books with paranormal elements but I really enjoyed this one. *Shari Gross (Canada)*

This book kept me riveted from the opening page to the last page. *David Place Jr. (USA)*

... deep and dark... *Cath McTernan (USA)*

It's been a while since I've read a thriller, and this book reminded me of how much I love them. *Meghann (USA)*

A truly exceptional well written story that I highly recommend. *Jim Phillips (USA)*

Towards the end I didn't want to put it down. *Sherry Martin (USA)*

Another great read from a great author. *Dominic Lagonigro (USA)*

I haven't read a book I enjoyed this much in a long time. *Heather Hackett (USA)*

Susan May's incredibly taut thriller keeps the action going fast enough to take your breath away. *Rosemary Kenny (Wales)*

Loved the book. A great read...well done. *Suzanne SingletonBrown (Australia)*

Best Seller

INTERNATIONAL BEST SELLING AUTHOR

SUSAN MAY

BEST SELLER

ALL THE LUCK IN THE WORLD WON'T SAVE YOU!

A girl with power over luck. An obsessed author consumed by envy. Two nemeses drawn down a path from which only one will return.

Ten-year-old Nem has just witnessed her mother's brutal murder and her life appears destined for tragedy. Until, that is, she finds her mother's old green journal which holds an incredible secret.

This innocent looking book seems to contain the power over luck. As she uses it, Nem discovers the diary keeps a strange kind of karmic balance, that in gifting someone good fortune she must steal another's first. All it takes is a simple entry. There's dangers though, and not just for others but also for Nem.

. . .

Decades later, the literary world hails William Barnes' debut novel as a masterpiece. For some inexplicable reason though, his best seller success doesn't survive his next two books. What frustrates and infuriates William even more, is that while he loses everything his undeserving protégé Orelia Mason enjoys a meteoric rise up the charts. And this triumph of hers coincides suspiciously with his fall from grace.

So, William embarks on a plan, several actually, to take back the life he's certain she has somehow stolen. If people get hurt along the way, well, tough luck for them. What he'll discover though is that battling fate when luck is not on your side can be a dangerous game.

You won't know who to hate and who to cheer on, and the ending will surprise, maybe even shock you.

This is **A Star is Born** meets **The Picture of Dorian Gray**, and the consequences are not pretty. In fact, they're darn well ugly.

From Susan May, the international best selling author readers are calling the new *Stephen King*, comes a dark and twisted tale of jealousy, revenge and an extraordinary, unique power.

You won't know who to hate and who to cheer on, and the ending will surprise, maybe even shock you.

⭐⭐⭐⭐⭐ "As a fan of Stephen King's, I can honestly say I enjoyed this story as much as any of his."

★★★★★ "What an insane read! Unputdownable!"

★★★★★ "Wow! I loved listening to this through Audible. So many twists... and the ending... wow!"

★★★★★ "It's Hitchcock meets the Twilight Zone."

★★★★★ "I thought I had it all worked out... about five times... turns out I didn't. An incredible read."

★★★★★ "Best suspense novel I've read in a year."

DEDICATION

O, beware, my lord, of jealousy;
It is the green-eyed monster which doth mock
The meat it feeds on; that cuckold lives in bliss
Who, certain of his fate, loves not his wronger.

William Shakespeare from Othello

DEDICATION

To my husband, who always told me I'd write a best seller.
Honey, you were right!

$\mathcal{N}$em had named the kitten Patch even before she knew whether or not she could keep him. The black mark surrounding the little creature's right eye reminded her of a pirate, and she liked the idea of sailing away on a ship looking for treasure.

Earlier that day, on the way home from school, she'd found the tiny animal in a shadowed alley. The kitten's mewling stopped her. She squinted into the scattered-garbage scene, as Patch appeared from behind a dumpster. He crept toward her as if they were old friends, pausing at her feet, before curling his body around her ankles.

"Oh, you cutie!"

She picked him up, delighting in his softness as she ran her fingertips along his fur. How could she leave the darling little thing? Without food or someone to care for him, he might die. No, Patch needed to come home with her, and that was that.

Nem had hidden Patch in a box in her bedroom. She feared her mom might take him away before she had a chance to convince her having a pet was a great idea. But her mom wasn't easy to persuade. Nem should have listened and then what was to come may have been avoided. Instead, they stood in the kitchen arguing, neither backing down.

"You must take him back where you found him. It might even have a disease." Her mom sighed. "Besides, the building superintendent won't allow animals."

"Mrs. Klein, the lady in Apartment Fourteen, has a dog."

She begged some more, and though her mom seemed to soften, it became clear she may not get what she wanted without bringing in the tears. Her mom always said she hated to see Nem sad.

She'd just worked herself up to crying, when the smack came from nowhere. This caused her to jump in surprise and she knocked a glass from the table which shattered on the floor. Her hand went straight to the side of her face, patting at the stinging skin and the throb of her right ear, which had caught most of the force.

The slap didn't come from her mom. She had never hit Nem; barely even raised her voice to her daughter. Alan, her mom's boyfriend, was a completely different case. She'd grown accustomed to slaps here and there when her mother wasn't around.

But what was he doing here in the afternoon? His normal routine was to leave early in the morning to return well after eight. She hadn't heard him re-enter their small apartment today.

He'd been in their lives for six months. At first, he was a great addition to what was already the best school year so far. Grade Four was when she found her confidence in reading and had fallen in love with stories. Her mom had collected books to give her since before her birth.

But the book she wanted still wasn't hers yet.

The beautiful green-covered wonder would be hers one day. At least that's what she'd been promised. "Only when you're old enough," her mom had said.

What age *old enough* might be drove Nem crazy.

Her heart's desire lay hidden in a locked closet in her mom's room. On occasion she'd spy her mother looking through the mysterious book, with its ornate gold-etched design on the cover and spine.

Whenever she asked to see the contents, she received the same answer. "There're secrets inside these pages. And magical words."

Despite Nem's pleas, her mom always replied with a smile, "Ah-ah, it's only yours if you study hard at school."

She hadn't seen the book in a long time, not since Alan had arrived. He was okay at first and theirs was a happier household than it had been in forever. Her father died when she was a baby, but she knew her mom missed him. Missed him very much.

Before Alan came, Nem's mother cried at night and talked to somebody who wasn't there. Through the thin walls she caught snatches of words.

"You're to blame. You killed something, something... danger... something."

When she slipped into her mom's room though and climbed into her bed to offer comfort, there was nobody.

"Who were you talking to?"

Her mom had wiped the tears from her own eyes and kissed Nem's cheek. She'd make an excuse of exhaustion, from looking after them both. Without a dad, life was hard.

When Alan arrived in their lives, Nem felt happy at first. He smiled and shook her hand. "Aren't you the cute little one? You look like your mom and she's a cute big one."

Then they all laughed. Nem thought he must be a funny man who'd tell jokes and be kind, and she hoped he could stop her mother from crying. They might even become a family.

Something went wrong a month ago.

Alan's sense of humor disappeared. He often shouted for no reason. Then he began hitting her. She couldn't understand why, except that her just being in the apartment seemed to make him angry.

She'd tried hard to be a good girl because when he got mad, she wasn't the only one to suffer. Her mom had started crying in her bedroom again, and that broke Nem's heart.

Alan arrived home late every night these past weeks, and he didn't eat dinner with them much anymore. The evenings when it was just her and her mom were the best. In fact, she prayed he might stay away and never come back again.

She'd thought today might be one of those best days, until he appeared behind her, as if possessing superhero invisibility.

"Alan, don't!" her mom said. The words muffled and distant. Nem's hands flew to cover her head as she cowered against the kitchen wall.

Alan raised his palm, and she knew to run, dodging around him to get beyond his reach. She felt the air movement as he swiped at her, and yelped as his hand connected with her arm.

Twisting to the right, she slipped out of his clutch and ran to her room, where she slammed the door behind herself. She whirled about to fumble with the lock. When the mechanism clicked into place, a sense of relief flooded through her. She backed away, her gaze never leaving the door, gulping in mouthfuls of oxygen to fill her heaving chest.

Within seconds, Alan was knocking and banging so loudly she feared the door would crack and he'd smash through any second.

"Don't you run 'way from me brat. Lem-ee in!"

Nem stared at the only entry and exit to the bedroom. Her body shook as if she'd entered a freezer.

What should she do? Hide!

She scanned the room, but there was nowhere except her wardrobe or under the bed.

"If you don't open this fuckin' door I'm smashing it in, you little shit."

She looked at her arm where his hand had connected. A darkening bruise had formed around the red welt. He'd never been this angry, and she had no intention of letting him in.

She rushed across the room to pull out the cardboard box she'd stowed beneath the bed. As she peered inside, her galloping heart felt as if it would burst from her chest.

But everything was fine. Patch was there, curled in a tight ball of white and black fluff. He lay sleeping on the blanket she placed there earlier to keep him warm.

Nem planted a reassuring smile on her face and said, "Are you okay, little one?"

She reached in and stroked her small friend, who opened his eyes at her touch. He arched his neck to stare up at her, as if to say, Why d'you wake me?

She picked him up and snuggled the kitten beneath her chin. With Alan's shouting and banging, she feared the noise would terrify the poor thing.

"Hey you. He'll go away soon and then I'll talk to mom again. How could I leave you in that nasty lane? We're meant to be friends, aren't we?"

Patch replied with a loud purr, his body vibrating at the pleasure of Nem's touch. In return, his sounds of pleasure relaxed her. She stood up and sat on the bed, continuing to stroke and whisper to him.

"We'll be okay. Trust me."

As she said the words, she imagined their friendship in the years ahead. Despite the jam in which she found herself, for that small second the world felt perfect.

She would love Patch and Patch would love her. Alan would leave, and their lives would be mom, her new furball friend and her. But not just yet.

Alan's banging had grown louder, more insistent, tearing Nem from her happy reverie. Her focus now became keeping the kitten calm.

"We'll have a wonderful life together," she said, staring at the door, as if sheer willpower might stand between her and the crazed Alan.

Why didn't he give up and leave her alone? Why did he turn into a monster? And where was her mom?

Oh no, she's on the other side. With him!

Now the kitten noticed the ruckus, and he too stared in the door's direction; eyes wide, ears rigid and twitching. He'd stopped purring and struggled in her arms, his claws scratching at her skin. She resisted letting go and instead tried to calm him.

"Shh, don't be scared little baby. Everything'll be okay. I promise."

When Alan's fist came through the door with a shattering crack, Nem realized she couldn't have been more wrong. Nothing would ever be okay again.

2

New York Times Review
FLYING TOWARD THE SUN *by William Barnes*
Reviewed by Anthony Shadley March 4, 2014

I'll keep this review of Flying Toward the Sun on point, a skill of which author William Barnes hasn't the faintest concept. Barnes imagines we've all the time in the world to indulge in insufferable, hackneyed writing and derivative, basic storyline threads mashed together in a bowl of rotten prose.

Two years ago this reviewer waxed lyrical over Barnes' debut novel Suffer Them to Come to Light, regretfully in hindsight, likening him to the greats of Miller, Fitzgerald and Hemingway. Those authors must be slamming their heads on their ghostly typewriters now.

The promise in Barnes' first book led to disappointment in his next, Hidden in the Shadows, but we gave him a chance at redemption.
After this monstrosity of a novel, filled with ricocheting clichés and leaden languishing characters, I won't be conned again. This is cream cheese left

somewhere hot for a week, blended and offered up as a tasty smoothie. Rotten it is and rotten it reads.

The author's publishers canceled his four-book contract and are cutting this book's print run. Who could blame them?

Dear Mr. Barnes, after chewing on the tough, tasteless gristle of Flying Toward the Sun, please do continue past the sun and give my regards to Uranus, which is where this reviewer suspects you've been writing these past few years.

William Barnes stared at the wretched article. The newspaper's fibers seemed to have sprouted poisonous thorns; minute needles of pain pricked his fingers as they held the page edges. A dark, terrible toxin slid inside his body, traveling through his veins. Any moment now, he expected the venom to reach his core and explode his heart. Everything that was him would then become nothing but spinning particles lost in a black space.

Except those words on the page. They'd survive. Those awful, bitter, horrific words would live on forever while he crawled away and died in the corner of his office.

And nobody would care.

He lived on Uranus!

What a disgraceful thing to write. The vile New York Times reviewer had it in for him. That's what William thought. The only planet he'd inhabited was *work-your-butt-off* third rock from the sun. Hardly reeking of wit! That living on Uranus line had been around for a million years. Now look who was clichéd!

Six years of work went into his three books. Six years of turning up every morning to his laptop. Jotting. Writing. Typing. Musing. Backspacing. Deleting. Inserting. Pulling out his hair. Facing a taunting blank page demanding greatness of him.

And those sleepless nights when plot eluded him, well, he'd

suffered those beyond counting. All this dedication, day in-day out, only to be ridiculed by this half-wit in a newspaper. Damn it, a newspaper read by millions. Those millions who might have bought his book before reading the vitriol spewed in this article.

Anthony Shadley—he thought of the reviewer as the *Great Shitley* —didn't know him, or understand his work. He certainly had no right to tell the public to not even give his book a chance.

Shitley was wrong. His opinion wasn't William's truth. No, his story was of a hardworking writer who believed in the words on the page, just like his namesakes': William Faulkner, William Shakespeare, William Golding. He'd hoped to write books that would stand the test of time.

His first novel took off right out of the gate. The Great Shitley had loved that one back in 2012. He'd kept the review in his online scrapbook. He had been so proud, occasionally even reading it to encourage himself when he felt stuck. He read it again now.

New York Times Book Review
SUFFER THEM TO COME TO LIGHT by William Barnes
Reviewed by Anthony Shadley July 27, 2012

William Barnes is a shining light in what has been a glum literary year. Comparisons to F. Scott Fitzgerald, Henry Miller or Ernest Hemingway, though paying Barnes the highest of compliments, fall short. In a landscape filled with duplicates, derivatives and doppelgängers of these great writers, this author can hold his head high as a true original.

Barnes' debut Suffer Them to Come to Light travels where most authors fear to tread. The narrative delves into a wondrous story, horrific in its violent imagery and yet breathtakingly nuanced and satisfying. Where a reader might doubt the value of the explicit portrayal of insanity and life views delivered via his colorful characters' language, in the end you are left understanding the necessity of 'going there.'

The novel is a masterpiece. This reviewer will be holding his breath for his next release. Hurry up Mr. Barnes, your fans await your genius.

Even a year previous, with his second book, Shitley remained on William's side. Although a little harsh, his article gave hope that the literary world still loved him. Every author had a bad book, the one that hadn't taken off. Authors were human and sometimes they just didn't quite hit the mark. Or the readers missed the point, which is what William presumed.

That second book's review from Shitley hurt, although it hadn't stopped him. He'd even told himself to treasure the bad reviews because they kept him grounded.

New York Times Book Review
HIDDEN IN THE SHADOWS by William Barnes
Reviewed by Anthony Shadley September 15, 2013

Call me disappointed and color this critic annoyed with William Barnes' follow up to Suffer Them to Come to Light. I adored his debut, but now struggle to imagine how an author can fall so far, with such an alarming, excruciating fail.

Where his previous literary masterpiece scaled the heights of eloquence and imagination, this book falls from these same statures with boorish and clunky prose to land with little grace.

Here's to not holding my breath for the next! Mr. Barnes, what's left of your fan base awaits your comeback.

Yeah, blah, blah, blah, William thought at the time. *You'll see, Shadley. They would all see with the release of his next novel.*

So he'd imagined. He absolutely, utterly believed that, and believed in himself until this third book. He'd never for a second thought this would be his last. But that's what frightened the hell out of him. His *come-back* might very well be his *get-going* missive.

After the negative reviews of *Flying Toward the Sun*, all mimicking Shitley—because everyone paid attention to the Times—his books would be lucky to stay a month on the retail shelves. Some parts of Shitley's rant had already proven true. Damn him!

The publishers *had* canceled his contract.

"Not to publishable standard" was the term in the official looking letter for his fourth submitted manuscript. The writer from their legal department quoted from his contract—which he'd never read, that's why you have agents. It contained confusing clauses, sub-articles and gobbledygook worse than anything he had ever written.

What they meant was "get lost." We've fallen out of love. No more free lunches, tours or signings. No publicists will call anymore to check if you'll be ready for the limousine arriving to whisk you to an interview at this station or that studio.

How insulting! He, winner of the Aubery Award for a Literary Debut, dropped by the same publishing house selling *Twenty Shades of Green*, the pornographic fictionalization of the lifestyle of some tree-hugging nymphomaniac.

William had thought for certain, take-your-royalties-to-the-bank certain, that another publisher would pick him up. His next book was completed to second draft and, if he did say so himself, the storyline and his writing were top notch. The night before, he'd fallen asleep imagining the publishers' bidding war over his masterpiece. In his dream, his previous editor begged him for forgiveness, assuring him the termination letter was just a silly mistake.

That was until today.

Today, William finally heard back from his agent. God knows what had happened to the man. After countless calls and an armada of emails, his messages growing increasingly irate, his expectation was a profuse apology.

Upon hearing Morris' voice, he'd drawn a deep breath, ready to play the role of the bigger person and excuse his agent's tardiness, once the shirker said sorry.

Morris, though, hadn't given him a chance to even say hello and as the call progressed William grew bewildered by his aloof tone.

This same person had assured him only five years ago of "a long career filled with awards." They'd be "toasting dozens of best sellers on a tropical island," he'd said often.

Now Morris didn't sound like that man at all. There was no excuse or apology, and William sensed his agent might be typing something, unrelated, while talking to him. He couldn't even pay attention for a lousy five minutes.

"No need for you to keep calling William," he said. "I'll call when I've news."

He'd begun to ask himself what he would do about the agent's nonchalant attitude, when Morris insisted he must hang up. His excuse? He needed to rush off to the bathroom. "A stomach bug." Well, that sounded like fiction.

As he reread the horrible, despicable, ugly review for the third time, he suddenly felt alone. Totally and miserably by himself with nobody he could trust. He reminded himself that solitude came with the job and that's what he'd created. He made his life about the work and not about people or relationships.

This little gem, along with all his other catch phrases, he'd repeated in dozens of interviews. He had his go-to quotes, which in hindsight he regretted, in light of his diminishing success.

Diminishing success!

Failure. Let's be honest and frank.

Setback, he corrected himself.

His go-to quotes seemed a touch arrogant now.

"I don't know from where the words come. My muse just loves me."

"I turn up every day to a job I love. Luckily the job, which it seems is all I'm good for, pays the bills."

"If I knew the secret to writing a best-seller, I'd bottle the magic and make a fortune, but I'm just lucky."

Those lines now haunted him, and he wished they could be

wiped from history. The dreadful reviewers discovered them in Google searches and included many in their commentary using a mocking tone.

The muse grew bored and left the building.

Shame you didn't bottle that secret, Barnes, because you're clean out of luck.

When the magic evaporates all we're left with is an empty hat and a dead rabbit.

On some obscure blogger website, which probably now boasted more readers than William, he found a quote that would be funny if it wasn't about him.

"An ability to be alone comes with the job," claims Barnes. Now his books will never be alone as they lay in the bargain bins looking for a home.

William wanted to curl up in a ball and die, to be reborn and start again tomorrow. He'd tried making himself small, but it didn't work. He didn't intend to hurt himself or give in to the feelings of worthlessness, but the emotions caught up with him without warning.

Last week he ended up under his desk, coiled in the dark hollow along with the dust bunnies. With his arms wrapped about his legs, his head resting on shaking knees, he'd sobbed tears of utter despair. At some point, sleep had taken him, or he'd passed out from the pain wound around his heart.

He'd like to indulge in a *pity party*. According to Queen Oprah and her clichés this was okay occasionally; then you'd snap back stronger than ever. Wrong.

He didn't feel better at all. His mouth felt *yuk* with whatever disgusting fibers he'd inhaled. Saliva dribbled from a corner of his mouth. His knees ached as if someone had taken a sledgehammer to them, and his legs cramped and hurt like heck. How long he'd slept he was uncertain, but his head had begun to throb, announcing the imminent arrival of a migraine, threatening to become a major-graine.

He may as well eat M&M's as take painkillers. They might dull the pain, but every time he thought about his career, the headache crept back.

Tomorrow he had a physiotherapist appointment because his right arm had begun to throb. There was something terribly wrong with his back too. A pea-sized lump had grown from nothing to a mass embedded between his shoulder blade and spine. Shards of stringy pain radiated from the spot. Every time he pressed on the swelling the thing felt connected to a flaming-red agony button.

He'd tried drinking, but his constitution couldn't handle alcohol. Hemingway, Kerouac and Foster Wallace's addictions somehow sounded romantic, but he couldn't master the ability to drink more than half a glass.

The publisher had sent out early ARCs of *Flying Toward the Sun*. Advance Readers Copies, as they were known in the biz. William had renamed them Asshole Redneck Crapshoots, once the reviews started appearing.

He thought the negative responses were just a few random idiots who were too stupid to see the quality of his work. For a week or so, he'd held a slim hope they'd received uncorrected proofs, which had since been improved in the final edit. But no, even normal readers—and he used that term loosely—seemed to take joy in tearing his work to shreds, just like the professional vampire critics.

Reads as if written by a teenager. I got halfway through and gave up.

Don't waste your time reading this.

You need a lot of stamina to get through the middle of this book. I did not possess it!

He'd taken to checking his online reviews daily, just on the chance their tone might turn around, that some wonderful, sensible person would deliver him five stars.

And three readers did last week.

His joy knew no bounds. He liked that cliché; made him think of kangaroos, the ones that box people. In his mind he saw them punching critics and those sour-reviewers.

Happiness was short-lived, seemingly like his career. One reader had mistakenly placed an opinion for an entirely different novel on his book's page. The other was hardly encouraging, because despite the five stars, he'd written.

I'll never get the time back I spent reading this crap.

And some pea-brain claiming to be six years old left him five stars but wrote ...

Even though i am only six i love horror storys and all of the killing. i sound like a cycopath but i am really not.

That one he'd pondered for days, clicking through and checking the kid's other reviews. Could he really be six? Certainly, he spelled as if he'd received no education. He took the score though. Five stars helped bump up the overall ratings from two stars to two and a quarter.

William kept refreshing the book's Amazon page on his phone browser whenever he thought of his predicament, just in case his ratings improved or new positive comments appeared.

He almost convinced himself his book's rating was okay, that he was only a quarter off an overall three stars.

Three wasn't terrible, right? In an exam that meant a pass.

But that little filled-in quarter of a star was so close to two that a few more bad numbers and the sliver would disappear. Then his book would be back at two.

Two was a fail in any test.

The reviews, the publisher cancelling his contract, or his agent developing diarrhea during their call, weren't really why his heart had turned black. This was simply an appalling moment in his career. It would get better.

As a writer he had tough skin, although in his imagination this sturdy hide now flaked across his keyboard in dried, salty tear-drop specks.

No, another reason curdled his stomach and made him scream, causing him to smash a hole in the wall of his rented apartment. Said damage, which he could ill-afford because there wasn't money in only one best seller or a canceled contract. All these deals were loaded at the backend. You needed to sell a lot of the third book to really make your money. In the publishing world a million dollars wasn't necessarily a million.

He sat in his gloomy kitchen staring at his damaged wall, in which he'd stuffed pages of what had once been a perfectly lovely book. The only image in his mind was that of Orelia Mason.

This disaster was her fault.

To put things right all he needed was to come up with her punishment. For there was only one thing which would lift him from this pit of despair. He must find a way to serve that woman her just deserts.

3
———

Whenever Nem thought back to the moment Alan smashed into her room, overwhelming sadness engulfed her. That moment was a turning point. What followed changed her life. Later she'd learn that a normal future was not her destiny. But on that afternoon a frightened child faced something terrifying. When Alan's fist exploded through the door, two things happened.

Nem screamed. That scream caused Patch to scratch at her so that she had no choice but to let go. The kitten fell to the floor, but like all cats, landed as if gravity didn't exist. He disappeared in the direction of the bed.

Wild with fear, she reached for the nearest object to defend herself. A pair of scissors. Something told her Alan wouldn't stop at smacking her; he wanted to hurt her. Badly. She clutched the pathetic weapon in her hand, as a pirate held a sword, and thrust her arm toward the door.

Despite the damage, the door's lock held firm. Alan's fist disappeared back through the gaping, jagged-wood hole and for a few hopeful seconds Nem thought he might give up and leave her alone.

She scanned the room looking for Patch and saw a tiny paw

peeking out from beneath her bed. She needed to hide him. Should Alan get inside, she wasn't sure what he'd do to the tiny creature.

The carton in which Patch had slept now sat near the closet. She must have bumped it in her panic. While keeping a grip on the scissors, she kicked at it with one foot, bringing it closer to the bed. She was careful with her weapon because her mom had explained they "weren't a toy."

The kitten must have understood this was for his protection, because when she leaned down he allowed her to pick him up. At her touch he purred as if nothing had happened, and she gently nestled him into the box.

"Good boy Patch," she said, stroking his head, as much to comfort herself as the animal.

She had been facing away from the room's entrance, when an explosive crash caused her to jump. The door flung inward and smashed against the wall, then bounced closed as though possessed. Alan entered the room, but this time she was ready. She didn't scream or turn her full attention to the box. Her friend was inside and Alan wasn't getting anywhere near the defenseless thing. If he beat Nem without a care, what might he do to Patch?

She threw a blanket over the carton and swung toward Alan, the scissors held out before her. He looked more a monster than a man, hair wild and his face red and flushed. His eyes, black pools of fury. Fury aimed at her, making her tremble.

Shattered wood hung at crazy angles around the lock. He must have strong legs and feet. Those feet and fists weren't getting anywhere near her. Or near Patch. If they did that to a door ...

Nem's mom appeared from nowhere behind him, her voice high and thin with emotion. "Please Alan. Please stop. Leave her alone. Calm down."

As though she hadn't spoken, he continued toward Nem.

She sized up her escape, or lack of it, in an instant. Even if she rushed past him, she couldn't desert her new friend. She also calculated she had no time to grab her kitten before he reached her. So she brandished her scissors and, without thinking her plan through, ran at Alan as fast as she could, waving her silly weapon. Maybe surprise might be on her side.

But this was the wrong move. With one swipe he grabbed her wrist and lifted her off the floor. Her eyes were at the same height as his and she looked into them, but there wasn't a man there anymore; she saw a nightmare. Something from hell.

Her mother screamed, "Nooo!"

Nem couldn't see her. Tunnel vision had set in, and Alan's anger solely aimed at her was all she could see. Now she worried for her mom. She must stop him. Use the scissors. Kill him and save everyone.

"You little brat," he said, through clenched teeth, "You're gonna learn who's boss. You and your whiny bitch mother need to understand a few things."

She wanted none of his lessons. Only feet away, Nem's mother cried and called his name. Nem's torso twisted and turned in his grip as she tried in desperation to release her arm. Her free fist beat at him as she kicked out to throw him off balance. A sharp pain in her wrist and shoulder seized her. But she couldn't fight him; with little effort he held her away from his body. With his other hand he yanked her useless, blunt weapon from her. Now she was defenseless.

"Didn't your mom tell you, you dumb kid, don't play with scissors?"

Alan waved them before her face, taunting her. She thought if she didn't escape soon he'd kill her, so she clawed at him like a cat.

He dropped the scissors to grab her other hand. His grip threatened to break her wrist. Jagged pain shot up her arm as she felt the tension build in her bones. Any moment she expected to hear a snap, her limb nothing more than a small twig.

An animal sound came from behind him. A frightening wail that stopped her heart.

"No-o-ooo!"

Alan yelled. "What the fuck?" It came out like a roar, an angry, monster scowl transformed his face.

"Mooommm," she screamed, as Alan dropped her. In an instant, she scooted backward on her butt to rest beside her bed, her gaze never leaving the pair. Her heart smashing against her ribs.

He turned from Nem to face her mother, who now beat at his chest as if breaking down a wall. In his back, embedded to the hilt was a knife; the one her mom used to peel potatoes.

She remembered a story of mothers becoming superhuman when their kids were in danger. They lifted cars off trapped children, swam rivers when they couldn't swim and fought off wild dogs. Nem's mom would help them escape. She'd grow her super-strength and become a heroine. Everything would work out and years later they'd talk of how amazing she'd been when she saved them. How strong and courageous.

That wasn't what happened though. Sometimes people don't become heroes, no matter how afraid or brave or hopeful.

Alan reached behind him and with a tug and a jiggle pulled the knife from his back. Blood streamed down his shirt and a growing, dark-brown stain seeped toward the floor. With his free hand, he took hold of one of her mom's wrists and held her arm above her head, just as he'd done with Nem. Her brave mother flailed and hit out at him with her other arm.

He was much taller, and the image that forever stayed in her mind was her mom battling a giant who felt no pain. For a moment, she even imagined she would win, like in the stories she loved to read, where the hero kicks the bad guy's butt. But Alan was much bigger and he had the monster fury on his side.

He now had the knife that should have stopped him but instead somehow gave him the super-strength.

She didn't see him stab her mom because Alan's broad back blocked her view. The crimson spatters on the walls and the floor were the first sign of things gone wrong, followed by her mom's screams.

She'd only ever seen blood trickling from cuts and grazes, so she found the spurting red arc difficult to understand. How could it do that?

So. Much. Blood. And so red, like thick velvet.

Alan kept hitting with the knife and her mom stopped screaming. Now she only gurgled and her body wriggled as if she was a worm with its head cut from its body.

Nem didn't know what to do. Her instinct urged her to leap to her mother's defense. And that's what she did. She jumped to her feet so she could fight him off and save her mother. But as she did words flooded her mind.

Her mom had told her many times, "If you feel danger from a stranger, run Nem. Escape any way you can. Find an adult. Get help."

Alan was that stranger.

But Patch?

She dived for the box beneath her bed and pulled the kitten from inside, wrapping her jacket over him. When she looked back, her mother was on the floor with Alan crouched over her, a hulk yelling and swearing. He'd stopped hitting her but had seized her arm, as if it was a baseball bat and shook the limb.

"You stupid, fucking bitch."

Her mom moaned as bubbles of red puffed from her mouth.

Then she heard her name. The words sounded as if spoken from behind a closed door or through the wind of a storm. "Nem, I'm sorry. Go, gooo..."

And Nem did go.

With Patch held to her chest, she took off for the exit.

As she flew past the two adults, she slowed for a moment. She wanted her mom to see she was okay, that she was a brave girl, doing as she'd been taught.

Their eyes connected.

Why was her mom's face so white? Her skin like crisp, clean paper pulled over her bones. Then she realized her face was the only pale part. Her t-shirt, jeans, arms and legs, everything else, was red. Rich, terrible red.

Her mom mouthed, "I'm sorry," and "B... B. Look."

She wondered for years why the last word her mom ever spoke to her was "look."

Look at what?

Look for something?

Look and remember. Don't make this mistake?

Yes, she'd relive this day forever.

Nothing would be the same again. Ever.

But her mother had not said look. By the time Nem discovered what she'd meant, she was old enough to understand the person she loved and trusted had been hiding a secret.

---

4

5 out of 5 stars
Amazing! Review by JANE on October 1
Back to that Day *by Orelia Mason*
Format: Kindle Edition Verified Purchase
If I could give Back to that Day a higher rating I would but since a 5 star is the highest, then it's what I have to give... One of the best I've read in a long time. I will read this more than once and I never read books more than once.

---

*W*illiam's addiction to checking the Amazon reviews Orelia Mason received on her books had become a bad habit.

Habit was too mild a word because if William was brutally honest with himself, laying every card on the table, then this habit had become an addiction.

The habit-addiction began in an innocent way.

In fact, the act was joyful and uplifting at the start. He figured most addicts declared similar sentiments. *Uplifting and joyful.* No harm done. Just something to pass the difficult days. An activity that let you feel good about life until the wicked thing wrapped barbed tentacles around you and took over everything.

The first time William checked Orelia Mason's Amazon page over two years ago he'd been thrilled. Way back then all he felt was pure delight at the quantity of positive reviews garnered by her debut *Back to that Day*.

Even though they no longer spoke because of that stupid argument, he still felt pride. Her success proved how valuable his assistance had been with her manuscript. She had nothing when she first came to him. Raw talent, and that was it.

This, of course, was when he still imagined the beginnings of poor sales of his own books came down to a simple life glitch. After all, *Suffer Them to Come to Light* had also ranked high in its categories and remained in the top twenty US charts overall for six months.

More than once, since helping her, he imagined he possessed *magic success dust*. By his mere sprinkle, he'd created this remarkable sequence of events, which had brought her soaring above other wannabe writers. This had satisfied him to no end, and more than once as he stared in the mirror, smiling, he'd thought, *William you're a great and wise mentor*.

This was because he'd expected she'd contact him soon enough, forget the argument and offer to help him, now that he had hit a bad patch.

They'd tour together or co-write a novel, or she might even mention his book on a talk show. She appeared on so many shows, including that idiot who made them mime to hit songs and take part in stupid games. What people did to sell a book, play or film was humiliating.

A decent, grateful person would contact their mentor, no matter how egregious the disagreement. Surely she viewed her past now through rose-colored glasses perched on that perfect nose. Did she not have a forgiving bone somewhere?

She didn't call though, and after months he couldn't look in the mirror anymore. Whenever he dared, the man who stared back was not a heartening sight. Unless baggy under-eyes, sallow, jaundiced complexion and hair that defied taming, was a good look. He recognized only a complete and utter fool; someone used for another's gain.

So once again he clicked on the Amazon link and waited the tortuous seconds for Orelia's author page to open. For convenience sake, he'd saved the address as a favorite in his browser bar. Each time it loaded, he held his breath and wished and wished, and hoped and wished. Could this be the instance her *number one* author ranking in the *Mystery and Thriller* genre slid downward?

Every visit to her book's page was a gut-wrenching experience, the smile on her author's photo taunting him.

Hadn't anyone ever told her that thriller authors should carry a serious and moody demeanor?

Her photo, complete with a big-toothed smile and oh-so-fashionable pixy hair, reminded him of a young Audrey Hepburn, and that didn't fit. She stood out among the day's transient best sellers, an apple among plums. Legends such as King, Patterson, Lee Child and the one hit wonder Paula Hawkins (*Cliché on the Train,* as he'd renamed her big one) didn't smile. They glared.

Why couldn't she be transient?

Where he'd once thought, *Good for you Orelia, be your own person,* he now believed her smile reeked of self-satisfaction, self-involvement and, to be honest, fakery. He imagined anyone would grin like that, knowing they hadn't put in the hard yards.

She expressed with that smile something dark and twisted and mocking.

"*Ha ha William. Here I am and there you are. Bite me.*"

Possibly not "*bite me.*"

Her message was more likely *"I'm exactly where I intended, and don't you forget it William Barnes."*

As he glared at the picture before scrolling through her reviews—for one and two-star ratings—he thought maybe she wasn't saying that at all.

Far worse, she might not even think about him anymore. Her life, filled with interviews, signings and keeping up with her fans on Facebook, Twitter and Instagram, might be so full there was no room for thoughts of him.

Those God-awful posts on social media, how he hated them. Every announcement from her ended with *May luck shine on you* or *Shine, shine, shine,* as if she was a goddamn angel or something heavenly.

Once they'd been friends. Well, mentor-mentee buddy-buddies. That was impossible now. He could never look at her again, breathe the same air, or listen to her voice recounting the joys of living her dream, without rage building inside.

She hadn't said she was living the dream when he'd seen her last. That meeting ended closer to a nightmare. No massive amount of shine, shine, shining going on back then.

Her final contact with him was the absolute kicker, considering *she'd* walked away from him. A text message had appeared on his computer screen a year ago and appeared innocent enough. He'd clicked on it expectantly. Her enthusiasm and cheeriness had once warmed his heart, but that was when he could afford generous goodwill.

First thing that bothered him: No mention of an apology. Later, when he studied her words, he felt their derision. She was giving him the finger. That's what she was doing.

Thought of u. Things amazing. (thumbs-up icon) Living the dream. (Pina Colada drink icon) #1 on all major charts UK/US 4 3rd week. Hope all gr8 w/u. TK 4 yr early help. U changed my life. xox (kiss icon) (wink icon) Orelia

William had leaned back in his chair and stared at the words and the stupid, little icons. Orelia had always peppered her messages with them as if she was thirteen.

She must know what had befallen him? His agent Morris was now hers too—the dysentery/stomach bug-afflicted man. Not only did they share him, but they shared the same publishing house.

Although the Mystery Romance imprint published Orelia's books, they still had the same main publisher.

In fact, after rereading her message, and copying out the words long hand to better decipher their true intent, he became certain she'd heard of his career stumble. The text was to taunt him, to rub salt in his wounds. Otherwise, why was there no offer of help? Of payback?

Why didn't she say:

Sorry heard about your bad run on the charts. What the? Let's catch up. I can help. (wink icon) (kiss icon) Orelia

This was her gloating; plain and simple in emoticons and tedious abbreviations. He understood a winking face icon. Her message shared only *her* good fortune, and no mention of his luck's downhill plummet.

Downhill was inaccurate. That word implied a gradient to his fall, whereas his misfortune was akin to the Challenger shuttle explosion with no survivors. His career had gone up in a puff of smoke entitled *Flying Toward the Sun.*

Orelia's though, had traveled upward and onward like Voyager entering interstellar space and traveling farther than any earthly object, ever.

He'd read in the paper that her book *Back to that Day* was a nominee for the National Book Award. This was the book's fourth nomination for a prestigious prize (he kept check). She'd already won the previous three. The article, ironically in the same section as his novel's review by asshole critic the Great Shitley, was a sign fate hated him.

Every night since, William had said a pretend prayer asking that she not win. If Orelia won another honor, he didn't know what he might do next.

Go mad, he'd told himself more than once, when he dared imagine her taking to a ballroom stage to thank everyone in her fake gracious manner. He saw the scene in his mind's eye; her pixie hair now with blonde streaks because that was the fashion. She thanked her publisher, agent, editor, her cat, the mailman, Voyager—traveling to galaxies beyond, heralding her success—(insert thumbs-up icon or star icon). She thanked every other nobody who'd ever crossed her path.

Everyone except him!

Why *would* Orelia Mason want her name linked to this has-been? Even if that has-been had assisted, mentored and introduced her to the business as he had done. Let them believe she'd found her own way. That's what she wanted.

He'd won his share of awards too with *Suffer Them to Come to Light*. The truth was though, his success was completely his own. No best selling author on his shoulder nurturing his talent with gentle care. His thanks had been to his publishers and Morris the agent because that's what you do. You don't bite the hand that feeds you even if they didn't do much. Even if they'd floated along for the ride. They were the lucky ones to have found him.

Miss Audrey Hepburn look-alike hadn't climbed the heights on her own merit. So she needed to show gratitude, most of all to the very person without whom she'd have nothing.

He realized though, she'd never thank him because that action revealed her relationship with William Barnes. Right now, everybody in publishing circles pretended he never existed.

If she was a good and gracious human being and, if she was to receive the National Book Award prize, he knew what she should do. Miss I'm-so-Worthy should stand at the lectern and, in a humble and earnest voice say, "Foremost, I must thank the extraordinarily talented and kind-hearted William Barnes. If not for him, I'd still be working in a boring job wishing on a star. Writing would have remained a dream.

"I'm sure most people think this success is due to talent and Lady Luck. My Mr. Luck is this great man and author. William, please join me on stage. This award is yours as much as mine."

Yeah, right! He wouldn't be there of course because she'd never invite him. She lived the dream. He lived the nightmare.

No, she'd deliver a different speech. She'd stand up there, smiling her demented Cheshire cat grin, the spotlight catching the tinsel-blonde streaks in her hair, as her gaze panned the room. The confident smile would remain on her face as she spoke.

There'd come no mention of his name.

And because William possessed a vivid imagination, despite what reviewers claimed, he listened to Orelia Mason's imaginary speech, after she won her imaginary award.

While he listens, he feels the gun in his hand, the coolness of steel against his hot sweating palm. His heart thumps in his chest as his right arm extends, and he takes aim.

He hears the buzz from the audience followed by a momentary hush as one-by-one the literary snobs notice him. And his wonderful weapon.

Orelia's wide smile drops as she understands what a mistake she's made in ignoring him.

He squeezes the trigger and in that loud, sharp split-second everything wrong with his world is righted. So perfectly righted as if coming to the satisfying end of a fantastic book.

Orelia Mason had somehow stolen his mojo. He knew this as a certainty, as if he'd read it in the Bible. Not that he'd read the Bible. That book was for those without belief in themselves. With his luck, she'd win this award and the next one too, because there was something freaky happening in this screwed-up scenario.

What she hadn't factored was a small detail. If he giveth good fortune, he now made a promise to do everything within his power to take that luck away.

5

*N*em couldn't recall when the thoughts of fairness wound their way into her imagination like tendrils of thick ivy. First, her view of the world altered as though someone changed the color of her emotional lens. Then, who she was, or the person she might become, disappeared, to be replaced with a new Nem. A steelier, cautious girl.

After her mom died, she cried and whimpered for the longest time, while life around her swirled into a blend of dark colors.

On that terrible night, she escaped the room unhurt and made her way to a neighbor's apartment—Mrs. Klein, the lady with the dog. The police arrived soon after to see her. A nice lady from a department, the name of which she didn't remember, also arrived in the following hours.

A nice policeman talked to her in a low, calm voice while the department lady sat by her side and placed her arm around Nem. Patch sat on her lap purring. As she retold the events to the policeman, the department lady squeezed her shoulder every time she paused.

"Can I see my mom?" Nem asked, as the policeman made notes.

The two adults gave each other a strange look. Then the department lady hugged her so tight she struggled to breathe.

They told her an ambulance took her mom to a nearby hospital. This she would learn later was true. They just hadn't told her everything.

Later, the lady took her to another house, where a large woman with tangled hair, reminding her of a bird's nest sitting on her head, also gave her a hug.

"Welcome Nem. I'm Peg. They tell me you've been a brave girl."

The department woman placed a hand upon Nem's shoulder. "You'll stay here while we work out how to help you and your mom."

Peg squatted and patted the kitten. "Who is this?"

Nem stroked Patch's fur but didn't answer. Why hadn't they said anything about her mom?

So much blood.

She must have needed a doctor. That would be why her mom was busy at the hospital and hadn't come for her yet.

Nem allowed herself to be led to a pale pink bedroom, which seemed already prepared for a little girl. A Disney Princess cover and pillow dressed the bed. Dolls and toys sat carefully arranged on shelves, inviting her to play.

Peg, now standing behind her, gave Nem a nudge into the room.

"This is yours while you're with me. Dolls. Teddies. Not sure what size pajamas I have, but we'll find something for you."

Nem had no desire to play with any toys in the room and she didn't care about pajamas.

"Shall we take your little kitten first and give him some food? Bet you're hungry too?"

Nem surveyed the room. *How could she escape and find her mom?*

But Peg might be right. Patch would be hungry and, yes, her stomach had growled too.

She pulled Patch even tighter to her body but nodded her agreement.

The woman took her to the kitchen and gave Patch a bowl of milk with breakfast cereal.

"Sorry, I'm ill-prepared for a kitten but tomorrow I can buy pet food."

Peg made toast with peanut butter and Nem ate like she hadn't eaten in days. She refused to speak even though Peg kept talking to her and asking silly questions like how old she was and if she liked any TV shows. She continued to eat her food while staring at Patch eating. Her thoughts were that Peg would eventually tire of her and go away.

She did for a moment but returned with pajamas that were too big. But she did let Patch sleep in the bed. So she wasn't a terrible person and Nem thought maybe tomorrow she would answer her.

Just before turning out the light, Peg said, "If you need me, I'm in the next room. Just call out, won't you darling?"

Even though she seemed kind, Nem still didn't acknowledge her. Instead, she rolled over and stared at Patch, who had settled himself below her pillow. She heard the door close and continued to stroke his back. The softness of his fur and watching him fall asleep comforted her.

Why hadn't they mentioned her mom?

The thought of her mother, alone in the hospital, made her stomach churn. Although, if she had needed an operation, she might be sleeping now.

Tomorrow she'd ask to see her mom but right now she was so tired she could barely keep her eyes open. No sooner had she closed them than Nem drifted into a dream.

She was in a garden playing with Patch. The dolls, which had been perched on the shelves in the room, hung from the surrounding trees, connected by colorful strings. They looked beautiful, but she sensed them watching her as if they were alive.

Her father, who she'd never met but like in all dreams she just knew it was him, appeared beside her. From his pocket he pulled a slingshot and loaded the band with a small, round pebble. Then he smiled at his daughter, took aim at a sweet doll with blonde hair and curls, and let the projectile fly. The targeted doll fell and as the toy hit the ground, its head shattered into a million pieces.

She looked up at her dad and he smiled again and pointed at another doll. This time the head shattered, without being hit, merely by the pointing of his finger.

Nem opened her mouth to ask, "Why kill the dolls?" but he had disappeared. All that remained was the slingshot lying where he'd sat.

Without warning, every dolls' head burst, one-by-one. Little pieces of ceramic and plastic exploded into the air, and though she should have heard the cracks and the bangs, there was only silence. Nem felt separated from the scene as if a glass barrier had appeared. The aloneness stifled her as if a thick band had wound about her chest.

She began to cry but then came her father's voice echoing in her head.

"Be brave little one. This is for you."

The words repeated in her head, growing louder with each repetition.

She pushed her hands over her ears but still the volume grew and her head vibrated with the rhythm of the words. She screamed.

Nem clawed herself awake to stare at Patch, who'd climbed onto her pillow and wrapped himself around the side of her head. His purring body so close, he vibrated her pillow.

As she nudged Patch to the side, a thought entered her head. If she hadn't brought him home and argued with her mom, Alan wouldn't have become angry. Instead, right now, she'd be in her own bed.

When she saw her mom in the hospital, she'd be sure to apologize and promise to never argue again. She hoped her mom would let her keep Patch. They'd been through so much together.

Two days later, Nem felt as if she was one of the dolls, her own head shattering with the news delivered by the department lady.

Her mom was dead.

And she wasn't allowed to keep Patch.

Her father's dream voice came back to her as she fled to her bed to cry.

Be brave little one. This is for you.

And she wondered if *this was for her*, what she'd done to deserve her fate.

6
---

he sky was everything-is-just-terrific pastel-blue. Clouds floated fluffy and scornful in perfect symmetry, as if a masterful-hand positioned them just so for the viewing pleasure of the mortals below. On a day like today, with the weather warm and wonderful, William should be in an uplifted mood. His daily sabbatical stroll invigorating. Life should feel good.

But life wasn't good. It would take more than blue skies and happy clouds to improve his existence. With each passing hour his disposition grew worse. Today was the worst of the worst.

Everything had begun with that terrible television show *Good Morning Something-or-Other*. He'd been eating his breakfast, always cereal and one piece of toast with a thin spread of butter, when the program came on.

William was a creature of habit; writing demanded discipline. A writer must know where he'll be each working day so his mind is ready to perform. Unlike commuting to an office, his travel required visiting a deep dimension within himself.

"Self-hypnosis," Stephen King called the process.

The Master of Horror had entered his dreams occasionally, handing William an award and inviting him to join his rock band of household-name authors. Yes, he could see himself and Stevie becoming good buds, sharing writing war stories and interviewing each other at university library fundraisers. Once he was back on his feet, he'd contact the great man. Someone in publishing would know someone.

For now though, he had the TV for company (no man's an island). He wasn't watching when he heard the words that made him choke on his toast.

"I'm living the dream," the voice said.

His throat reflexed with a surprise cough causing a masticated lump of crust to fly from his mouth and land in his coffee. He considered the black liquid. *Disgusting.*

More disgusting was who spoke. He recognized her, would recognize the words, the tone, anywhere.

It was she.

Her.

Pixie-hair.

Evil creature of downfall and doom.

On *his* television.

On that program with the toothy host who reminded him of the sixties TV show talking horse *Ed or Ted.*

A horse is a horse, of course, of course, and no-one can talk to a talking horse. That is of course, unless the horse is the blonde-haired, smiling clone sitting with Orelia Mason, the Queen of the worst, of course, of course.

She looked radiant.

Admitting this made him cringe.

He had hoped if he ever saw her again she would have wasted away from the pressure of the success and demands on her time. Since the moment he'd seen the article on her nomination for the National Book Award, he tried to avoid anything related to her.

This was real progress for William. At first, after reading of her good fortune, he took to watching YouTube videos of her at author conferences and giving interviews on shows. He'd hoped to hear her mention him. When he realized that in the dozen videos he'd watched there wasn't a single reference to him, he had forced himself to steer away from the torture.

As if withdrawing from a drug, he fought the strong urge to scour iTunes and the Net for new additions. After a week or so he felt proud of himself that the addiction seemed to lessen each day.

William rose from his chair and walked toward the image of a relaxed-as-can-be, smiling Orelia sitting on the set-sofa. In his opinion, she was a trained puppet, wound up to be bright and breezy as she told the same funny anecdotes he'd seen on the YouTube videos.

She looked poised.

She looked happy.

She looked successful.

She talked and nodded and smiled.

Smiling. *Smiling.*

Smiling in that way, which made William want to put the glob of toast back in his mouth and spit the muck at the screen.

"New book."

"Rave reviews."

"Seven-figure deal for the next three novels."

"Film rights sold to Twentieth Century Fox."

Oh God, a movie deal, no.

The interviewer oohed and aahed as if Orelia had invented a cure for cancer

A horse is a horse, of course, of course, except if you're the betrayer Orelia Mason, the talking author.

"Luck."

She'd used the word *luck!*

"How lucky was she?" she said, keeping a straight face as if she actually believed the lie.

"Right place. Right time. Right book."

Oh, baby, you don't know the half of luck.

A thought occurred to him as he watched her. If he didn't switch off the thing, she might slip out from the idiot box and appear in the middle of his living room.

How wonderful to see you William. How lucky! How fabulously exciting. How ironic.

He marched to the rear of the TV, bent and swung his arm so quickly that he cracked his knuckle on the cabinet. He had meant to tear out the power plug, not injure himself. As he grabbed his hand, he cursed that female hack for sending him more distress.

So he left his uneaten breakfast and escaped from the house. He paced around the block three times, as far a cry from his usual prepare-yourself-to-write stroll as he could imagine.

The lump of muscle inside his chest hurt; the ache so strong he wondered if this was a heart attack. He was too young, surely? Thirty-four's only a smidge outside youth, right?

When the tightness grew no worse, he realized this was simply the pain of Kismet smacking across his life. There was no comfort anywhere, anymore.

Over the past few months, each time he arrived at the path which led to his apartment block, he paused. He wanted to go inside. Knew he should get back to work. Write that next book. That's what they said, the author-sages. Move on from the failure, produce and find solace in the craft.

Except, he couldn't bring himself to face the blank screen, the television set, the radio or even the newspaper, which still sat provocatively on his kitchen table. He'd burn it later, just for good measure. Because there was no telling where Orelia Mason would appear with her *living the dream* taunt.

He understood her game plan. Ingenious. For she wasn't stupid. Oh no, from the beginning he knew exactly what was what. She'd played him like a foolish fiddle.

William looked down the street, then back at the apartment front door. No, he couldn't go in yet, so he continued walking, purposeless but with purposeful strides. Before he realized his actions, he'd climbed aboard a bus (he didn't even remember waiting at the stop). A cheery, redheaded driver with the audacity to brush his arm as he bought a ticket. "Today will be a great day," the dope assured him. How annoying.

He felt a touch better for a moment; in an odd way, unweighted. Then the emotional clarity left as he fought off the calm infusing his body. He looked at the man behind the wheel and thought, no way would his day be *great* or the rest of his life for that matter.

By the time he descended back into the world via the center doors (he wasn't going near the grinning, moron bus driver again), his mood had reverted to miserable. Darkness and despair returned like an incoming tide. He much preferred this feeling to that lightness. He couldn't be happy while she lived the life that should have been his.

When he realized where his body had brought him, he understood that this was a message just for him. By coincidence—although there are no coincidences in dark fairy tales—he stood outside the very bookstore where he had met Orelia.

Bountiful Books had, until his career had left for the South Pole, held only good memories for William. The manager, Diane-something (he wasn't great with names), had been effusive every time he visited. During the promotional weeks of *Suffer Them to Come to Light,* he'd given his first talk and signing here.

Diane had sprung for wine and cheese platters for the guests and some wonderful pastries filled with a delightful custard cream. Even in those early days, the buzz around books had seen the room full, with many forced to stand against the walls.

William had found that tour and talking to a crowd a heady experience. He recalled his hand shaking as he turned the pages of his own novel to read aloud to the reverent audience. The vibrato in his voice calmed minutes in, thank God. So many hands shot up at the end, Diane had said they'd be there until the next release if she didn't limit the questions.

William had launched his first two books here, but his last, *Flying Toward the Sun,* was barely a fizzle launch. He turned up when nobody else did. Cookies replaced the hors d'oeuvre and water instead of wine. The eight people sitting among the empty chairs offered no questions for him, though he'd be happy to answer them.

A woman with a novel clutched to her chest approached him, and his fragile ego lifted. He recalled her name as Anne because how could you forget the person who shattered your heart in one sentence.

"I'm Anne and I'm sooo excited. You cannot believe what this means to me."

He held out his hand to take her book with the biggest smile he owned planted on his face. That's when she said it, even before he saw the cover and title.

"We're the greatest fans ever of your friend Orelia Mason. I'd heard you knew her. Is there any way you might get her to sign this for me? We're all in a book club and we've brought our copies with us."

He couldn't help himself. His whole body recoiled, and his fist clenched as he yanked the extended arm tight to his body. She laid the offensive mass before him. On the table. Next to his hand, which now gripped his pen as if he held a knife. The only thing stopping him from using it like a blade was that you can't kill people with pens.

Orelia Mason's *Back to the Start* hardback stared up at him as if saying *You're not even safe here, my friend. Oh, and Orelia sends her regards.*

His face flushed red; a furnace had been lit deep in his core and his skin felt on fire. William recalled maintaining enough control to mutter, "I don't see her much anymore. We're both so busy."

As they walked away, he overheard the woman's comments about him "seeming odd. Peculiar." And he wished he had that knife so he could show them his version of *peculiar*.

He swooped up his glass and threw the water down his throat. Even that was a fail as the liquid traveled down the wrong pipe and resulted in a coughing fit, which left him gasping for breath.

Nobody came to his rescue because no-one was within earshot. Or coughing shot.

A straggly haired teenage girl standing at the door chewing gum called out to him.

"You done then? I got to put away the table and chairs."

He looked over to say, "Very done," but she was already on her phone. Even Diane had disappeared, perhaps elsewhere in the store shelving books which actually sold copies. Unlike his books.

Pretty crummy. So disloyal, considering William had made a point of continuing to frequent Bountiful Books, despite his success. Sometimes he'd buy a book or two of a read he'd heard was good and sign any of his they had in stock. Though the last few times Diane asked that he not autograph the three he'd found on a bottom shelf.

"Publishers won't accept them for return-and-refund if they're marked," she'd said.

Indeed! Once, not so long ago, his signature would have made them more valuable.

Now here he stood before ground zero, the place where his and Orelia Mason's worlds had collided. He, the moon, left in a shattered chunk of unlivable rock, while she, a fresh new planet, spun off in a magnificent orbit.

Why his subconscious brought him here, he wasn't sure. Maybe it was to give him strength to fight her and remind him his failure was not his doing. This might be a nudge from fate to say he couldn't let her get away with what she'd done?

No, he told himself, with a tentative step toward the front door, uncertain if he could bring himself to enter. The memories still raw and fresh, despite being over two years old, stung him. *Good must triumph over evil,* repeated in his head. And even though nobody would believe him, he knew evil when it visited to take his life and slam his world to hell.

7

*A*lan West never thought of himself as a lucky man. After all, look where he'd ended up-doing time in this god-forsaken hole of a prison. Later though he would call his incarceration the best goddamn intervention in the freaking universe.

In the beginning though he was angry. Some blame for what happened that night in the apartment was his. But really, the moment of his demise-when he'd officially become a murderer-happened because his temper got away from him.

That kid was the one who should be locked away. She'd pushed his buttons bringing home that mangy cat and argued. Her voice just irritated the shit out of him. And yes, he would admit, things shoulda coulda gone a different way. But from start to finish, the entire twenty-four hours were a dirty, rotten, why-hadn't-he-stayed-in-bed day.

A killer headache hit him on waking. Excuse the pun! The pain, no doubt delivered by the other bitch. The kid's mother always whining for him to come home earlier. He would have come home earlier if she made it worth his while. She was the headache.

Work was shit! That was his total comment on that place.

Need to let you go, the boss had told him that morning.

No apologies. No payout.

"Al, you're a casual laborer. You know how this works. Last in, first out."

That's how bullshit worked. Others had worked there less time than him. So triple bullshit.

By the time he got back to the two-bed hole, a furnace was alight in his gut. He'd tried extinguishing the anger with a few drinks on the way but the alcohol was like kerosene to his emotional flame.

Gonna kill someone.

Before all this, the idea occasionally shuffled around inside his head. His hands circling the neck of an imaginary enemy and stopping their heart. These thoughts popped in with his everyday musings as if a coin was inserted through a slot in his head.

Play that killer song one more time Al.

Murder wasn't front and center on his bucket list. No way.

Hurt the heck out of someone? Yes, but kill?

Murder landed you in jail and that didn't fit his plans. He enjoyed hanging out with his buds after work at Ted's and he loved his food. And women? He liked them too. Doing time because someone annoyed you wasn't worth it.

Shoulda coulda thought of that, he told himself as he stared out from the bars of his cell.

Damn, he'd love a burger and fries. Pizza. Even if it wasn't the super supreme kind with everything thrown on. None of this eye-tie-Italian, wilted-lettuce and scraps of sausage, party-princess crap for him.

How things change. With the inedible slop they fed them here, party-princess crap would do fine, and he'd enjoy the shit out of it too.

Fourteen years they gave him. Quadruple bullshit!

Fourteen years dreaming of a decent pizza and ugly women. He wouldn't allow his mind to drift past ugly or he'd slit his throat from frustration. Little wonder inmates turned violent.

He did want to inflict violence on his attorney though. That should be considered fair and legal. Man, give him the idiot, a knife and a quiet room, and he'd do the world a favor.

The stupid, weasel-faced moron suggested he apologize to the brat. Supposedly, showing remorse might lessen his sentence. Alan didn't have to think too hard on agreeing. No way he wanted to die in this joint. Period. No question marks.

What to expect from the brat bitch, he didn't know. Weasel Face would be there to ensure he said everything just as they'd rehearsed.

Yeah, he was sorry.

Yeah, given the time over, he'd never have hurt her lovely mother. He loved her, didn't he?

Something came over him. What, he didn't know.

He hoped she'd forgive him. He'd slash his own wrists if that helped.

Yada, yada, yada! Bullshit, fucking bullshit.

Still, if reciting this crap cut even a year off his sentence, good job.

The visit did not go to plan.

The kid was a psycho weirdo, and that was being damn polite.

No matter what he said, all the lines Weasel Face had fed him, she just stared. Stared, as though she saw into his insides or something; examining his pancreas, sizing up his heart and lungs.

Now he knew what they meant when they said giving the evil eye. She was giving it with both eyeballs. That wasn't right because he couldn't give it back.

No matter what, control yourself, Weasel Face had lectured him.

Look sorry. All I can say is sorry. Forgive me, please.

Sweat dampened Alan's armpits and he reached up to wipe beads of moisture from his forehead. He didn't want the little witch to know how much she unnerved him.

She'd changed.

She wasn't a little kid anymore. She'd become a hundred years old in the two years since he'd seen her in that room, running away after starting the whole thing.

Finally, Weasel Face spoke, interrupting the staring match, which he was losing, and badly. Alan could breathe again as if a window had been opened to allow fresh air inside.

"Miss Stratton, what Mr. West wants you to understand is his deep remorse for the events which took your mother's life. We believe he was depressed. This, brought on by losing his job, combined with too much alcohol and a possible chemical imbalance, made him mentally unstable."

Alan winced at the words mentally unstable, but held his tongue. The crapola meditation exercises they taught in this joint helped minutely with his supposed anger problem. He needed classes on increasing tolerance for stupid. Or make it easier for the world, how about classes on making the stupid less stupid?

While his attorney talked, Alan decided his best move would be to nod along and smile. He kept his gaze on the Weasel Face and avoided looking directly at the girl.

Those eyes of hers gave him the real heebie-jeebies. If he had the chance he'd reach across this table and in thirty seconds snap that neck of hers. Turn off those eyes.

He'd never noticed when they lived together what a truly creepy kid she was. Shame, because he might have hightailed it outta there sooner.

"Mr. West has asked me to emphasize how truly sorry he is and how much he hopes that one day you will forgive him. He knows this won't bring your mom back but since his incarceration he's found God. Going forward he wants to help with anything you need. He prays for you and your mother every night."

Alan looked at his lap. He wanted to puke.

Him find God? Now that embarrassed the heck out of him. What a crock of shit!

Weasel Face's earlier words repeated in his head.

"You've got to make her trust that you're truly sorry. We need her on our side. You hear me?"

Alan forced himself to glance over and see if she was buying this little play of theirs. He kept his head down so she wouldn't know.

He began to say, "Nem, honey, if I could trade places with your, with your..."

He stopped.

Because ... *What the fuck?*

He was baring his heart and she'd begun to read and write in a book, as though taking notes in class. Weird. He wanted to ask her what she was writing. Why she was writing?

But when she looked up to lock her gaze on him, the pen poised in her hand, she wasn't a child anymore. He was prey sized up by a predator. Her eyes held the faintest of glimmers; a flickering lamp in a window. The glow grew, and in unison heat rose in him, real heat on his face and inside his skin.

With every fiber of his willpower he tried to avert his eyes. But as though she possessed a magnetic power, he couldn't look away. The words he'd only just uttered coiled in his head like smoke.

If I could trade places with your, with your¬-

He couldn't focus; his brain afire, and he needed to get away, return to his cell, close his eyes and not see her anymore.

Suddenly she reached out to grasp his hand, still with that weird I'm-gonna-eat-you smile on her face. His stomach curdled at her touch. He expected her skin to feel hot or freezing, or like a static electric shock. He expected pain.

Nothing.

Just her hand touching his.

Something though, something he didn't understand happened.

He snatched his hand back, whipped it away from her and heard Weasel Face's voice.

"Hey, hey, what are you doing?"

Alan didn't care. Forget their stupid plan.

He shoved backward with all his strength, almost toppling over. The sound of the metal chair's legs loud and achingly high-pitched in the small room.

As he stared at his hand he entered a faraway world, where nobody else existed, except his own thoughts.

Ten fingers.

No red marks.

Nothing broken.

Yet, something.

Something.

He felt the pressure of his attorney's grasp on his arm.

"What's up Alan? You okay?"

He pulled back to stare at the man and for one second his name disappeared from Alan's memory. Then as though smoke had cleared in his head, he pulled himself together, just enough to reply.

"Man, I'm sorry, I, um, no, not okay. Sorry."

He remembered what he was meant to do then.

Say sorry. Yes, keep saying sorry. Get the kid on his side.

Unable to look at the girl directly, he half-turned his head, so his jaw jutted forward instead.

"Sorry. Just sorry. I gotta go."

He knew if he stayed in that room any longer he would be sick. He was already trying to stand when she spoke.

Her voice sounded happy though, and that confused him. Happy wasn't what you'd expect. And that near-joyful tone was what he remembered later when he began to understand what must have happened.

"That's okay," she said. "Everything will work out fine. In the end, I'm sure you'll be very sorry."

8

William's hand touched the ornate, gray-iron doorknob of the entrance to the bookshop. Why did independent stores inhabit ground floors of decrepit buildings? This store spread itself over two levels, separated by a worn wooden stairwell.

As he pushed open the door, a tinkling, happy, little bell announced his entry. He moved inside, embarrassed to be here, hoping nobody recognized him. If they did, he'd pretend to be someone else. They didn't deserve the honor of talking to him because they were part of the problem. They could have recommended his novels to their customers and ignored the reviews. Stores like this could have saved him.

"Can I help you?" a long-haired kid with glasses too large for his skinny face called from behind the counter. If William was casting a horror film, he'd have this one killed off first.

He declined assistance and walked toward the aisle where his books should be shelved. Sure enough, none were there among the hundreds of other hopeful novels filed spines facing out. Unless they were bestsellers, sat on the shelves prominently, or on a table at the store entrance, they had six weeks, at the most. After this, they'd be returned to the publisher.

How do you overcome that little obstacle? Books displayed in prominent positions sold. Cover out, you win. Spine out, loser. This small detail made a big difference to a book's sales and shelf life.

"Looking for a particular author?"

An ironic question indeed. *Yes, William Barnes! Me!*

He turned toward Diane, the store manager. He recognized her, but she didn't recognize him. Had he changed that much? It had only been what? Two years?

"I'm good." He backed away and headed toward the stairs.

"Call me if you need anything," she called after him.

"Yes, I'll, ah, call." William would prefer to give her a slap across the ears.

His hand wrapped around the shiny cherry-wood banister running along the stairwell, worn smooth by thousands of hands sliding over it, decade upon decade.

He descended to the basement, small pieces of his heart shriveling black with each step. He remembered the electric sensation when he'd been led down here in another life when he was somebody. In those days, his agent, and sometimes a publicist, accompanied him.

The memories of his first meeting with Orelia flooded back. He saw Diane walking in front of him, turning to say how excited everyone was to hear him speak, that there was standing room only. Somewhere in the crowd she had been there waiting and watching, smiling no doubt, knowing what she had in mind. Him unaware that he was traveling toward disaster.

Come into the parlor, said the spider to the fly. Enter my web and I'll suck your life dry.

This basement floor was the non-fiction section. Above the entrance hung a country art sign covered in painted flowers and butterflies. Scrawled across were the words *The Reading Nook*. The bookcases were on casters for easy wheeling back for the book launches and author reading nights, one of which must have been last night. Rows of chairs faced the front of the room, sentinels poised as if waiting. A small stage with a lectern and a microphone held their imaginary focus.

To the left was a folding table, across which lay a white cloth, partially askew. A half-empty glass of water sat perched near the edge, along with several abandoned and lonely-looking pens.

The podium drew William's attention, even though every fiber of his being told him this was a mistake. He was stepping right into reliving one of those nightmares you sometimes were happy to endure to discover the conclusion. Did he really want to go there?

The rostrum with its microphone, silent and waiting, called him. He climbed behind it and stood there, his eyes scanning the imaginary audience. A tingle of excitement traveled through his body as he remembered that once people had come here for him. His fans, his diehard readers who loved everything he wrote, until they didn't, sat here in this dream. He wondered what big-hit author they came to listen to last night? And how they could have forgotten him, as though he was just a character in a book, dismissed once the covers closed?

But way back then, when unknown to him his nightmare began, he hadn't seen Orelia Mason during the reading and his talk. She'd stood against the wall at the back, she'd told him later.

Between the manager Diane and his agent Morris nudging him around the store, the crowd and individual faces became a blur. He recalled clearly how the audience watched him in rapt silence, their eyes bright and expectant.

Yes, it was he, in the flesh, the ringmaster of his literary domain.

William had signed hundreds of books—handed to him with reverence as if they were ancient, precious parchments. Before finishing with everyone in the line, Morris had insisted they needed to leave. He had an early flight to somewhere he'd forgotten, for another round of interviews and appearances. His agent was a stickler for punctuality.

She'd caught them at the door, as they were thanking Diane. Since then, that conversation had run through his mind so many times, he could recite every word. The store manager had introduced them, and he remembered being charmed by the woman's enthusiasm.

She'd opened with, "Oh my gosh, I'm so excited to meet you. I'm pinching myself. I loved *Suffer Them to Come to Light*. Extraordinary. Inspirational."

He'd smiled, his fingers brushing his mouth in case there were crumbs from a canapé gobbled on the way out. She was engaging, better looking than most of the bookish types who frequented these events. He guessed she was around thirty but something about her eyes caused him to shiver. Just a little.

He put it down to their proximity to the door and possibly a cool breeze. Then it was gone, and her smile and excitement washed over him, and even exhilaration at being labeled inspirational.

She pushed at strands of hair, which hadn't quite made it into the ponytail hung over her shoulder. The action reminded him of a teenager on her first date.

He'd given her his stock standard line: "Thank you. You certainly have great taste. Really, you are too kind."

Her face had lit up as if an overhead spotlight had switched her on. The effect, so sudden and stunning, William had even glanced above to check if there was a light. There wasn't. It was her, dare he say, basking in the glow of him, he imagined.

"No, you don't understand Mr. Barnes, your novel is wonderful. The words, the rhythm of the sentences. I heard it in my head as a melody. The echoes are still with me, like a beautiful sonata. You're the Beethoven of literature. That book has changed my life. Absolutely and utterly transformed my view of writing."

William had blushed, heat rising in him as though *he* was now under a spotlight on a stage.

"Wow! That's, ah, probably the nicest thing anyone's ever said to me about my work." He had been genuinely thrilled.

"I felt compelled to talk to you," she'd added. "A voice in my head. Like this was fate, and I needed to do this."

Around then, Morris began to move him away, explaining they had somewhere they needed to be—only dinner at a nearby hotel but he made it sound important. They were enjoyable dinners in those days when they'd discuss the foibles of the publishing industry and his exciting professional future.

He imagined she had thought her praise might take them further. Although this had low prospects, if that's what she hoped. William didn't have a romantic bone in his body. He'd pretty much have to fall over a woman's bed for anything to travel past pleasantries.

For many years he'd remained alone. "Too dedicated to my work," he'd say if anyone asked why there wasn't a Mrs. Barnes. Truth was, he felt uncomfortable sharing himself. His inner thoughts and ruminations were his to wrangle and reshape into stories. He lived so much inside his head that at times he found it difficult to differentiate between fiction and fact.

"Your name again? Sorry," he'd said. She'd stopped touching her hair and wrapped her arms around her body as she gently swayed as though listening to music.

"My name? Orelia Mason. Well, not really. That's my writer's name. I think. I'm not set on it, but I thought if I use it in my real life for a few weeks, I could see if it worked."

He'd nodded thinking Orelia Mason sounded a touch pretentious. Then he decided, *who cares? I don't know her, so whatever.*

That was the beginning of the end.

No announcements.

No embedded clues alluding to the plot twist which came less than three years later. When she'd steal his mojo. Take what didn't belong to her.

A thief in fan's clothing.

My name is Orelia Mason. I'm coy and sweet but I'm coming for you.

---

9

*E*very time Alan West thought about his meeting with the creepy little witch, a shiver ran up his spine. She'd done something that day during the visit with him and his attorney. Put a hex over him or something. The evil little bitch. This could be the only explanation for his fate.

Although he enjoyed the last laugh. *Ha ha!* There was a god and he protected against unnatural creatures like her. Prior to his *apologize-and-everything-will-be-just-peachy* meeting, he was a healthy and kinda happy man. Of course, not totally happy. Who was happy thrown in prison for an act, which was *understandable given his circumstances* on that day? Anyway, that's what his attorney had said in his summation and it sounded about right to him.

Seven days after the little witch gave him her evil stare, he noticed a lump on the side of his neck. At first he thought the raised skin was an insect bite. This place could be infested with God knows what: spiders, mosquitos, wasps, fleas even.

The lump didn't go down though, and a few days later another appeared. This time in his groin, and this one hurt as if someone had shoved a plum-sized ball infested with stinging ants up his privates.

Two nights in a row he'd awoken drenched head-to-toe with

sweat. His bedclothes were soaked through like they'd been dunked in a bucket of salty water.

By the third day he struggled to get out of his cot at wake-up call. His legs felt as if the bones had been replaced with brittle sticks and his head ached like he'd gone ten rounds in a boxing bout.

Even though he didn't want anybody checking down there, he couldn't take the pain. Something was wrong. Outside, he'd ride it out; in here he had little choice.

Good medical treatment in prison was a joke. However, some do-gooders sure did *good* here. A 60 Minutes' segment, *Executing Prisoners,* aired after two old timers died unattended in their beds, shone a brief spotlight. Preventable deaths they'd said. So the prison had been forced to lift their game when it came to health support.

The place would revert to the same old dump soon enough. But just being here had begun his streak of luck. Right time to get sick. Right prison to be locked away in.

Multiple tests later, tests he wouldn't have received before 60 Minutes visited, he sat in the burning-bright prison medical center hearing the news he struggled to understand. The doctor's voice was matter-of-fact, as if describing the flu.

"Do you want me to explain anything in more detail?"

After pausing to be certain he wasn't dreaming, Alan replied, "Yes. All of it."

He wanted to say, "Are you fuckin' kidding me?" but he wasn't a complete moron. He needed this doctor's help, so he bit his tongue— an important skill he'd learned in here. Alan listened more carefully the second time and began to comprehend what lay ahead.

Stage Four.

That wasn't a good number. Both his parents had died of cancer.

Aggressive non-Hodgkin's lymphoma. NHL for short.

Short, as what his life would be now.

Diffuse large B-cell lymphoma.

He imagined thousands of big, black horrible cells gobbling up his body, eating their way through his organs and brain. Fucking monsters in his blood.

The doctor smiled and leaned back in his chair when he was done. Man, he wanted to punch him. You don't give that kind of news and smile.

"You're in luck Mr. West."

"Sounds like I'm outta luck, doc." He emphasized 'doc,' so the smug asshole didn't think he'd scared him.

"Lucky for you, I've been given authority to enrol you in a trial for a new treatment. There's no guarantee of success but initial early results are looking good."

Alan guffawed. "I'm not a guinea pig."

"No need to worry. This is not an experiment. They've already been in trial for eighteen months. It's worth a shot. I can request permission from the prison warden for your inclusion. He can't refuse treatment for serious medical needs because that now constitutes 'cruel and unusual punishment' under the Eighth Amendment. You can thank a few court cases and the recent media. They may have just saved your life."

Alan felt himself breathe again. He hoped to keep breathing for years to come. Even if it meant rotting away in here; he'd take rotting above ground any day.

"So you're saying I might get better? Get rid of these big B cancer cell things?"

The doctor leaned his elbows on the desk and steepled his fingers together.

"I'm saying there's a reasonable chance. This will not be easy. We'll be giving you mega-doses of a new form of chemotherapy drug and you'll require a stem-cell transplant. You'll be very sick and probably wish you *had* died. But you might just survive. If you do nothing, certainly you'll be dead within three months."

Hearing those words *dead in three months*, had Alan nodding his head as he said, "Where do I sign up doc? Feed me the drugs. Kill the cells and save me."

Two guards, who seemed oblivious to Alan's plight, led him back to his cell. He could tell by the way they unceremoniously kept shoving him along that they didn't care he was a sick man. He thought of the meeting with the little witch girl and the way she'd looked when she'd hexed him.

In the end, I'm sure you'll be very sorry.

He wasn't sorry, and he wished he could see her face when she realized her little game wouldn't play out. Medical science will triumph against any mumbo-jumbo she sent his way. The doctor had said it: he was lucky. He'd get this treatment, kill this NHL crap and get out of here one day to return to normal life.

And her mother would still be dead and he would be alive.

"Take that bitch," he said under his breath as he shuffled along. "I'm not that easy to kill."

10

W illiam had grown accustomed to people approaching him at events and sharing, what they believed to be, their exciting news. *They wanted to be a writer!*

Ooh, yay for them.

For some reason they thought he'd find this information fascinating. His standard reply to end the conversation was, "Really, have I read anything of yours?"

He recalled his thoughts about Orelia at their first meeting at Bountiful Books. In hindsight, ironic was the best word for that meeting and his unpreparedness for her future success. And his failure (that hadn't entered his mind of course). He'd found it amusing that an unpublished author even had a pen name.

Though Orelia Mason, as an author's name, did have a ring to it, he now thought. Something to do with the syllables, like James Patterson or J.K. Rowling, it ran off the tongue. He didn't think William Barnes sounded as lyrical, but back then his sales certainly hummed a merry tune.

Bountiful Books was in his home city and had sold thousands of his novels, his publisher had informed him. So he felt duty-bound to indulge this wannabe author. Show her his gracious side.

He used his usual line, *Have I read anything of yours?* knowing the chances of her replying with a title in print were slimmer than a book on the wit of engineers. *Apologies to engineers.*

Orelia wrapped her arms around her body and hunched her shoulders.

"Oh no, nothing published. What I mean is, this has become a dream. I read somewhere that if you write, then you should call yourself a writer. I've written a book, so that makes me one, right?"

Without pausing for an answer, she continued as though afraid they had limited time. *Which they did.*

"Mr. Barnes, only yesterday I finished writing my first manuscript. Now I'm completely inspired. You're wonderful. Not that I could ever create work as amazing as *Suffer Them.*"

He didn't love the way she'd shortened the title, but he thought best not to correct her. The sooner he could extricate himself the better.

"You've made me look at my work through different eyes," she said.

"That's flattering. And scary," he replied working to maintain his smile. After these long signing events, he sometimes lost touch with his facial muscles and couldn't be sure if he was smiling or how sincere he appeared.

He decided to give her a few quick words of encouragement, then he and Morris could go.

"Well, my writing secret is... just do it. Keep going. Write. Then repeat."

"Oh, I am. I spend every spare moment on my manuscript. Weekends, evenings, even while on the bus. I wrote this book in three weeks but I'm not sure it's any good."

Orelia unwrapped her arms and reached over to grasp his hand, as if he was the Pope and she wanted to kiss the papal ring.

"Mr. Barnes—"

Whether from excitement or nerves, the woman had a strong grip. The contact was over-personal and uncomfortable. In an attempt to make her aware of this, he tapped the top of one hand and said, "Please call me William."

The move didn't work and her hands continued to hold his.

"Thank you, yes. William. Can I ask a favor? I'm being forward, so say *no*. I'll understand. But fate favors risk-takers, right?"

"Should I be nervous?" William made a point of glancing down at her pincer-hands. He looked to Morris, but his agent was checking his phone, his usual go-to whenever a fan stopped William.

Her gaze followed his and she withdrew her touch with a giggle.

"Oh, sorry. Nerves. This is a dream here. That's why I'm going to take a chance and speak. And hope for the best."

She took a deep breath, like a swimmer ready to dive into a deep pool.

"Will you read my manuscript please? If you have time. Say no of course, if you can't... it's just that I read to get a publishing contract, you need an agent. But that only happens if you're recommended to one. What do you think?"

Tears formed in her eyes, glistening in the corners, fighting to be free.

William, surprised by her sincerity, hesitated to answer. Many before her had asked the same. The tears pulled at him though. Most people imagined because they could hold a pen or tap keyboard keys, writing a novel was the natural next step. He always declined. He wasn't a free copy-editing service for wannabe authors.

Orelia Mason's vulnerability touched him, and he found himself struggling against the feeling. He should say no. He wanted to say no. But that damn look on her face; what was he supposed to do?

When he replied he almost guffawed at his stupidity. He was about to make an excuse. *Too busy with the next book* usually worked. Instead, he heard himself say.

"Yes, okay, I'll help. Why not?"

He could answer that question even before reading her book.

The writing would be hackneyed, the story a yawn festival and the ending obvious from page ten. But he'd committed now, so he'd read a few pages and then politely extricate himself. The manager, Diane, was a witness and keeping on her good side helped sell books.

He caught Morris' quizzical look and secretly winked at him. To Orelia and Diane he smiled as though grateful for the opportunity.

And surprise surprise, the manuscript was ready to go. She pulled a thumb drive from her pocket, no less. Probably a way to keep it handy, so she could harass visiting authors. He discovered later she'd handwritten the whole thing and the pages on the drive had been scanned. He could already give her a piece of free advice right there. *Type your novel. We're not in the fifties anymore.*

Orelia pushed a business card into his hand and William couldn't hold back a chuckle.

He stared at the words.

Orelia Mason

Writer

Oreliamasonwriter@gmail.com

Twitter: Orelia_mason_writer

"Well, that's a confident move. A business card with your pen name already."

"The power of positive thinking. Live your dream to create the reality," she replied.

The line, though clichéd, sounded genuine. Almost inspiring. When he looked at her again, the tear had disappeared.

"See where being positive landed me? I didn't think I'd have the courage to speak to you. But as I read your wonderful book I kept telling myself, *This is your chance to change your life. And William Barnes seems such a nice man.*"

"Well, I can't promise anything," he said. Thinking nice didn't make you successful in the cut-throat business of publishing. Talent trumped nice.

"Of course, I expect nothing. You'll probably tell me, 'Orelia, this is terrible. Forget it.' At least I'll know then. Maybe you can give me a few tips? Or your talent and luck will rub off on me, do you think?"

"Who knows?" he said, thinking, *you'll need more than my luck to succeed.*

Much later, William would remember the glow of her face as he said this, and in hindsight he wondered at his naivety and prophetic talent.

11

The chemotherapy was son-of-a-bitch-bad.

Alan West had no idea you could puke that much and survive. But that was nothing compared to the stem-cell transplant, which was a peculiar torture. The crap those doctors put him through had him sobbing like a baby many nights and even days.

If anyone had caught him crying, he'd threaten them with extinction. Right now though, he didn't have the energy to raise his middle finger to a soul.

The transplant was bullshit.

This he chanted under his breath for near on three weeks. He also shared this opinion with the nurses and doctors who would listen in silence. Their lack of response told him they didn't care. Maybe they enjoyed his pain. They sure seemed to be entertained as they walked around him, pushing and prodding, as though he was a wax dummy.

When the doc said he'd lose his appetite that was a lie.

You didn't lose your hunger. You simply forced yourself not to eat because you knew everything placed in your mouth would come straight back as a hundred miles an hour projectile vomit.

Ten days in the ulcers bloomed, like mushrooms after rain. You can't eat when every bite is a bee sting on your tongue or your gums or even your fucking throat.

Then came the itch.

Oh my God! The itch of shingles all over his body. Everywhere on his skin these nightmare blisters appeared, as if the queen of mosquitoes and her tribe had descended on him for lunch.

Then the fever would hit, and he'd shake and shiver and wish for a quick death. This sometimes heralded the *psycho trip*, where he imagined himself floating down a river surrounded by exotic tropical trees. The cool of the air and the boat gently rocking gave him relief and a wonderful sense of freedom. Until without warning a swarm of wasps appeared from nowhere and stung the hell out of him.

He fought them off, arms flailing in the air, which only attracted more of the little terror-shits. With each sting his skin swelled, until his limbs were two overstuffed sausages. He stared at the swollen biceps—which he'd spent a fortune tattooing—and thought *I'll have to get those inked again.* Each time he got to that part of his nightmare, the skin on his arms would burst in a shower of blood, skin and thick, yellow, sticky gore.

Thank God he awoke, screaming but at least awake, to discover his arms were still whole but red and swollen, as was most of his body. The image of his skin bursting cemented in his mind and flashed at him whenever the itch started up. If he ever recovered, he'd remove those tattoos to wipe that fucking memory for good.

But as the doc promised, his body and system finally settled.

Six months later the doctor informed him—in the same office he'd been told he'd die—that the stem cells had done their job. His blood cell count had returned to nearly normal.

He was required to down a shitload of tablets and they also had to re-immunize him with all his childhood shots because technically his blood was brand new.

Out with the old and in with the baby-fresh white cells.

Even his blood type changed.

He was *A+* before. Now he was *A-*.

A handy thing should he wish to commit another crime. They wouldn't find him looking for his blood type on record. If he ever left this hole this was certainly worth consideration.

Nine months to the day he'd received the transplant, Alan was feeling pretty damn good. He'd cheated death, cheated the little witch's evil stare, and he was optimistic that in conquering this shit, there was nothing that couldn't be beaten.

Entering the exercise yard, for the first time since his ordeal, he felt lucky. His mood was so high he felt he could take on anyone or anything. He was the King of Good Fortune.

The sun shone in a cloudless sky like the world agreed with his conclusion. In the distance he thought he heard birds singing.

What a day to be alive.

He'd spoken to his attorney earlier in the week. Weasel Face sounded optimistic they'd secure a hearing on his sentence. Supposedly his trial judge "erred" in not giving due consideration to Alan's mental health and his *cancer.*

"Mitigating circumstances," Weasel-Face said.

The theory he'd floated to the courts was that his undiagnosed-at-the-time cancer provided a contributing factor to his mood and loss of control.

Just what Alan had always said.

He wasn't to blame. Those bitches caused all the trouble, especially the weirdo kid with the creepy-evil eye and her little green book of whatever. When he apologized to her, he'd made a mistake.

She should have apologized to him.

As he walked toward a group of what he loosely called his friends, he noted a workman on the roof just above the yard. You couldn't miss him. Two guards trained their beady eyes on the guy as if he was about to plant a bomb or break one of the guys out. He looked to be working on one of the exhaust fans that peppered the sloping roof of the rectangular block.

Alan was so chipper he tipped his hand to his forehead in the guy's direction in a signal of admiration. Man, you couldn't get him up to that height. Guys like that one must have steel balls.

Or floating ones.

He chuckled at that thought as he hi-fived around the group, even repeating the line to them.

"Check the floating balls on that guy."

"Safety cable looks too thin even with floating balls," someone added. They'd all speculated on the amount of danger money you got paid to do that stuff and whether using the same skill for a break-and-enter might prove more profitable.

Forty-five minutes later after enjoying himself just shooting the breeze, his stomach lurched. Not your normal after-meal growl but a you'd-better-get-to-the-can-quick, thick gurgle.

The lucky break for Alan was that his stomach gave him enough warning. He was within yards of the exit, but he didn't have long. He took off at a trot, wincing at the growing pain.

Three more steps and he would have made it too, and his blue-sky future life with new blood, no cancer would have been his to enjoy.

Timing's a bitch though. A second here, an inch there, and your destiny is really just bullshit sliding-door moments.

He heard a shout, but he wasn't sure of the words or their meaning and even if they were directed at him.

"Hey" or "Waay" or "Waa." Something like that.

Not a great warning if that's what Floating Balls intended. Even if the word was clear and he had time to decipher its meaning as *move out of the way*, he wasn't Usain Bolt.

Angles were the issue in this case. Throw a screwdriver at someone and unless you hit their eye, the damage is at most a scratch or a bruise. Drop a screwdriver from four levels and it lands point side into someone, well that's a different result altogether.

Said screwdriver becomes a missile. Even then you'd be fine if the missile hit any part of your body except your head. Or in Alan's case his chest.

The little tool pierced his heart, and he was dead before you could say *bullshit*. Although Alan managed to get the "bull" part out, the rest of the word remained lost forever on his lips.

As he descended into the darkness of the nether world between life and death, he managed one last thought.

What happened to my luck?

12

One week later after William read the last page of Orelia's book, he sat back and shook his head. Prior to this, he imagined he'd call her with an excuse of why he couldn't help her with the manuscript. He thought that like most writers, her first project would need a lot of work.

When he called her though it wasn't to say those words but instead to heap her with praise.

Effusive praise.

Her book, while raw, was original and engrossing, and he'd finished reading the whole thing in two sittings. With a little polishing, the book was certainly publishable. And with the right marketing who knows, she might have a best seller on her hands. Mind you, luck played a huge part, so she'd need to pray to the publishing gods.

Though he'd never been one to share, it occurred to him having a protégée might be fun. A wife wasn't on his dream list as yet. Never had been and probably never would be. What he desired was someone to share the trials and tribulations of sitting alone for too long staring at a blank page. Someone who understood that peculiar terror.

They could compare notes, understand each other's fluctuating moods, commiserate when the muse didn't visit and become encouraging allies. In short, helping Orelia suited his purpose. He'd wave a magic wand via his connections and make her dreams come true.

Well, he'd give it his best shot.

So Orelia Mason became a habit.

Twice weekly they met at a local coffee shop, and he would talk her through where in the work he believed she needed improvement. William grew accustomed to basking in Orelia's admiration and looked forward to their meetings. She always sat statue-like and wide-eyed, absorbing his every utterance. The more she listened, the more his stature grew in his own mind.

Not only did he share his thoughts on her work but he would also talk endlessly on the sparing use of similes, lack of character development in current best sellers, publishing industry foibles and readers' lack of loyalty.

Readers' lack of loyalty! In hindsight, how prophetic of him. He now could give a three-day conference on that one.

The way her big, brown eyes followed his every movement swelled his heart. By the third meeting he grew more impressed by her story's improvements and her keen implementation of his advice. That's when he decided he'd move heaven and a truckload of pulped paper to help get her book published.

Though they wrote in different genres, hers romance mystery and his literary drama, he wondered if in the future their books might lay together on a best seller table. Might they speak together on a literary festival panel as a double act? They'd sit in opposite chairs up on a stage and Orelia's tinkling laughter, along with his measured exposition on literary subjects, would be entertaining to the crowd. She, of course, would defer to his opinion. As part of the entertainment they'd joke at the mismatch of their friendship. The Punch and Judy of the literary world.

"William knows better than I do. What he doesn't know about writing doesn't bear knowing. He discovered me you know," she'd say.

He'd reply with a cool smirk. "Orelia you're too kind. Anyone would see your talent—a *rough* diamond awaiting a polish."

He'd emphasize *rough* too. The audience needed assurance that her talent wasn't obvious, and that he possessed greater insight into the craft than the average author.

For three months they met together for lunch, until one day he announced that her reworked book, thanks to his guidance, was ready. He'd give the manuscript to his agent, and he was sure Morris would seriously consider representing her.

"Don't get your hopes up too high. Morris must shop this to publishers. What they think at any given time is anyone's guess"

She had tears; transparent lines of emotion traveling down her cheeks.

"One step at a time okay? Lots of hurdles still," he said.

He didn't want her disillusioned or hurt. He needed her to keep writing because by peculiar osmosis, Orelia's success had become intertwined with his own self-worth. If she failed, this might declare something he didn't want to consider about himself. If he couldn't judge *great* from *mediocre,* then how was he to ascertain the value of his own work?

Her success may well be his own validation.

"Yes, I understand," she said.

Her next words exploded his heart. "William, you're a dream-maker. Before this my life was empty, which I hadn't realized. Terrible things have happened to me. I was meant for something else and I got waylaid. You're an angel of destiny."

At this, William's back straightened, and a wisp of a smile found its way to his lips. He shook his head in what he felt portrayed casual, dignified modesty. *Angel of Destiny* had a nice ring. Maybe he was a sage, a fulfiller of the dreams.

This gave him the idea to look into creating one of those online courses advertised on Facebook. James Patterson had one. Imagine having thousands of authors claim you taught them everything they needed to know. And earning a pretty penny!

His mind raced with the idea of the extra income. The money

from his books took forever to arrive and he wasn't earning as much as he'd expected. The publishers' contracts certainly weren't created by angels. They kept a big chunk of change in case of returns. Unbelievable, but being a best seller didn't mean you were automatically rich.

"Nonsense," he replied, "You've done this yourself. I'm excited to have helped."

Orelia's face grew serious.

"I want you to understand how much this means to me. I will never ever, ever forget what you've done."

"Well then," he said, his words dripping with humility, while he thought, *you had better damn well not or I'll come after you.* "You can autograph a copy of a first edition for me."

"I will do better than that, I'll dedicate it to you."

Looking back now on that conversation, William mused on how obscenely fast she did forget. The greatest disgrace: her book, the one he helped shape, had been dedicated to her cat. *Her cat!*

13

Nem wasn't sorry for what she'd done.

She still didn't fully understand how she'd killed the man who'd murdered her mom. That he deserved his fate, and this was her doing, gave her a sense of pride. Guilt didn't worry her at all.

Things were set in place the day she received Alan West's attorney's letter. The man had written, pleading with her to visit the prison, saying how sorry Alan felt for what happened. She didn't believe his apology, and she didn't care anyway. Sorry wouldn't bring back her mother.

More than two years had passed since that night. In random moments, Nem's mind still flashed to the terrible events, her memory set to automatic replay of the day she was orphaned.

Peg suggested she not go to the prison, but her arguments fell on deaf ears. Nem wanted to look in Alan's eyes and tell him how much she hated him and wished him dead.

She also wanted to try the *luck word thing.*

She'd been playing with the strange power, ability, *spooky thing—* well, she didn't really know what to call it. All she knew was it worked like a weird charm. Her mom always told her there was *magic in words,* but she had no idea how true this was until she found the diary.

Since discovering the book, she often wondered if her mom knew about the power. She'd found the treasure in the box of her mom's possessions a year after she'd gone to live with Peg and her husband Ray. The carton, delivered a month later, sat on a shelf inside the built-in wardrobe in her room for weeks before she had the courage to look inside. She knew inside would be her mom's things, which would make her cry.

Her world still trembled with uncertainty. Peg and the social services woman, who visited every few months, hinted she may not be able to stay with them forever. They were foster parents and not relatives.

In fact, they couldn't locate any relatives. Nem never gave much thought to the absence in her life of aunts, uncles, cousins and grand-parents. All she'd been told was her father died when she was a baby. And that was that.

She eventually forgot about the carton until one rainy day when she hunted for puzzles she'd seen stored in her closet. The box seemed to call to her, even though she tried her hardest to avoid looking at that shelf.

Open me Nem. You'll be okay.

Since today was a good, happy day, on impulse, she pulled the carton down to finally face the memories connected to whatever lay within.

Dislodging it from the shelf, she placed it on the bedroom floor and folded back the cardboard flaps. Her fear stifled the breath in her chest until she peered inside and squealed. Nestled among scarves, clothes items, books and a jewelry box lay the book she'd been desperate to read. Her mom had always promised this was hers to read if she did well in her English lessons. She thought she'd never see it again.

Nem gently lifted the gorgeous, rich-green, leather-bound book and walked across the room to her desk. Finally, it belonged to her. Her mom surely would agree this was the *right time* now. She was older and her reading had improved so that she understood most books given her.

As she ran her fingers across the embossed ornate, gold engravings on the cover, she felt her mother near. Memories of her looking through the book some nights but closing it as soon as Nem drew near, flitted through her mind. She'd always wondered about the mystery contained within. Like any secret, she'd been desperate to know, but despite her pleading, her mom never gave in. Nem never imagined she'd see the book again.

As she opened the cover, it came as a surprise that the pages weren't filled with a story. This was a diary, of sorts. A shaky, handwritten scrawl filled each sheet from top to bottom. She flipped them over in rapid succession and grew more puzzled. The notes made no sense at all.

What was this book? What was the big secret? It looked dull if she was honest with herself.

She ran a finger over the short sentences but saw no connection to each one. They were random. So possibly not a diary. Names were interspersed with the words but she recognized none.

"Hmm, you are a boring book," she said, placing the diary, journal, whatever it was, in her bedside drawer. She thought about throwing it away but then remembered how much it seemed to mean to her mother.

The strange little diary remained in her bedside drawer for another week until one night, as Nem lay in bed, a *memory attack* pounced. Tonight was bad; her mind filled with hate for Alan and sorrow for what he'd done. She saw herself taking the scissors and stabbing him and saving her mom. Many times she had imagined this, she sometimes wondered which was life and which was a dream.

An idea popped into her head.

Perhaps the diary notes were taken down from dreams.

Curious, she sat up in bed, turned on her bedside lamp and pulled the book from the drawer. As her hand touched the cover, she felt a tingle, like a gentle caress of her fingertips. Instinctively, she pulled back and stared down at her palm.

Hmm, what a weird thing.

Static electricity?

They'd been learning about forms of electric currents at school and how static was harmless.

Still, she was careful as she reached for the cover again. This time there was no effect. She opened the book and began reading. Inside though, were only short sentences and names. The first pages seemed written in fountain pen ink from a hundred years ago, smudged with flowery curves.

The more pages she turned, the more her curiosity grew. The writing style and ink changed to pen and modern print as if many people had previously owned the book and the object journeyed through many hands.

What the entries were about though looked similar. People's names and other details she didn't quite understand. A plus or minus inside a circle had been inscribed next to the entries. These alternated for each person. If one entry was a plus, the next contained a minus.

What did that mean?

When she came to the last page, Nem gasped. There was her mom's name and beside it the plus symbol. *Possibly good*, she thought. Plus seemed good, right? The funny thing was the date. Nem's birthday.

Patricia Stratton. September 21, 1982 Gift

Then she noticed the name written before this and she stopped, puzzled.

Miller Stratton. August 14, 1982 Betrayal.

Next to this one was the minus in a circle. Sounded like that meant a bad thing based on the word *Betrayal* written next to his name. Betrayal was a bad thing to do, wasn't it?

Her dad's name was Miller and so far in her life she'd met nobody with that same name. He'd died before her birth and her mom never spoke about him, so she couldn't be sure if this was the same Miller.

Then an idea occurred to her. She walked to the desktop computer—which Peg organized for her the first week she'd come here—and typed the name into the search window. Countless entries appeared from all sorts of articles. One caught her attention because it was from their city. Nem clicked through and read.

Lovebirds Miller Stratton and Wendy Froude, tumbled fifty feet from a rooftop.

Miller Stratton's and girlfriend Wendy Froude's bodies were found in a side street by a passing cab driver. Both were naked and had died from severe trauma.

Police say, in investigating the area, they discovered their clothes in a pile on the rooftop of a building overlooking the street. No suspicious circumstances were declared; with investigators believing the couple died from an accidental fall while in the throes of passion.

Miller Stratton, married at the time but not to Miss Froude, left behind a nine-month pregnant wife Patricia Stratton, who reportedly remained unaware of the affair until police notified her of her husband's death. Is this justice one might say?

Oh no, this name was the same as her dad's and mom's!

She didn't completely understand everything in the article but she knew him being naked with another woman was not good. She'd look up the meaning of 'throes' later. Her poor mom.

Nem returned to the diary she'd left on her bed. As she opened it again a sharp tingle flickered across her finger tips. This time it didn't hurt but seemed more like the warm gentleness of water running across her skin.

She paged to her mom's entry and paused, cocking her head to the side, surprised by what she saw now written on the page. Another name, which she felt certain hadn't been there before she'd closed the book.

But how?

She ran a palm across the page to see if the ink was wet. The words didn't seem fresh. Then she noticed the name, with its little minus in a circle. This one had no date. *Weird. Weird. Double Weird.*

Maybe she'd missed this before, surprised at seeing her mom's name? No, no, this couldn't have been there when she'd first read it. She hadn't imagined this. Her mom's inscription had been the last entry in the book.

Her heart banged against her chest and her head spun. Could this be a dream?

She pinched herself but no, she was awake. The book somehow put the name there. Of course, this was impossible. She knew this, but that's what frightened her the most. Something impossible, inexplicable had just happened and her mom wasn't here to explain.

The inscription next to the name left no doubt the diary was connected to her mom. Maybe to her. She wondered if finding this was no accident and if she was meant to do something.

She ran her fingers across the page over the writing. The word *murderer* ran in bold black alongside the name. And the name could be no coincidence.

Alan West.

14

William stood at the lectern gripping the stand's side, staring into the empty room filled with an imaginary audience, remembering everything in crisp, clean detail.

One thing about Orelia, she was half true to her word. He did receive that first autographed book. The thing arrived, decorated with a plump pink ribbon, as though it was a wildly extravagant gift. Her book was published a whirlwind fourteen months, almost to the day, since he'd taken it to his agent.

Morris had loved the story eventually—took some persuading to get the man to read it—and he whipped up a bidding frenzy that saw five publishers desperate to own the book. Morris confided that he didn't do much. All the editors *adored* the manuscript with a passion.

Seems they loved her image too. Everyone loved Orelia Mason.

He didn't love Orelia Mason. *Author Envy* entered his mind for a matter of minutes. Well, maybe days if he was being honest. And maybe not entered, more like seeped inside his psyche, a gently rising tide lapping at the shore of his confidence.

They hadn't spoken since the unfortunate incident in the café, which he didn't want to think about at this moment. Just seemed so silly, pointless and annoying, considering if they were friends now that would be a big help to him.

Even though Orelia's manuscript received a much higher advance than his first, he wanted to be a bigger man. He wouldn't fall into the comparison game. That was a quick road to hell. The disparity in money was understandable, he'd rationalized. Their book genres, so vastly different, didn't bear comparison. Stick romance in a story and your market broadened by millions. His more craft-driven work in modern literature could be considered for literary awards. Hers, only popularity prizes. Popularity prizes meant money though, and he could do with some of that about now.

His true desire was to write the American masterpiece, to be taught for years to come in schools and universities. The *To Kill a Mockingbird* of his era. He was William Faulkner to her Nora Roberts.

Morris soon became besotted by her as if he'd been the one to discover his star client and mentor her through the first book. The history of Orelia Mason's success soon became manufactured without him. He didn't factor a mention.

"Embarrassingly large," Morris said, when William asked about the rights' sale. "Ten foreign language rights sold too. Woo-hoo. Right?"

William pretended to be happy for her, but a nugget of something solid and knotty formed in his chest. That same feeling came over him at this moment as he imagined her standing on this stage instead of him.

"She's planning a series," Morris informed him.

"Writing a series is for hacks. Haven't you always said that? What happened to handling true artists and not *one-night stands*?"

William remembered being puzzled at the man's enthusiasm.

"Netflix, my friend. Streaming content is the new King. Queen in her case. They're talking Blake Lively to play the lead."

William recalled the resolute stiffness in Orelia's smile when he'd tried to give her his opinion on fine-tuning her writing style.

"I know you know so much more about the industry than me, but..."

She'd said those words the instant before their conversation and relationship went south. That was because she knew nothing then, and he'd been trying to help and... well, it didn't matter anymore.

When Morris told him the publishers were rush-releasing her book for a Valentine's Day promotion, followed by her next six months later, William had been confused. His first novel took two years from acceptance to publication date.

When he'd queried that timing in comparison to his own, Morris replied, "Her editors want to strike while the iron's hot. Makes sense with the publicity from the sale. And the Netflix deal."

"Sky's the limit," Morris repeated enough times that William wondered if the man had one of those talking-toy pull rings in his back.

"But how can she write that quickly?"

"Really, I don't know, but I'm not complaining. She said she learned a great deal from you William. Says she has a lucky muse."

"Learned from me?"

Well, at least she acknowledged him in the beginning.

"She says you kept telling her to push through even when the muse doesn't alight. But she told me *that* never happens anymore. She just sits there at her desk and out flow the words, like she's watching a video."

"Well, that's ah, fantastic," said William, as he wondered if words spewed on a page could possibly be any good.

At the time, he even felt a twinge of something akin to envy. For he'd spend days pushing words onto the page as though they were pressed through a sieve. He calmed the uncomfortable twisting in his stomach by assuring himself whatever Orelia wrote in thirty days would most likely require an enormous amount of editing.

In the end, he decided to call her. Thank the hot new author of the summer for her gift.

All he got was her message.

He left hesitant congratulations—not heartfelt but cordial.

He'd decided the best move was to build a bridge. He might need her to write a blurb for *Flying Toward the Sun*, since early reviews had not been as enthusiastic as he hoped.

He'd seen how these juggernaut authors became overnight sensations. And maybe she would be one of them. He hoped so at the time because Morris also informed him her Facebook page already totaled more than fifty-thousand *likes*. He said it as if *likes* were the equivalent of winning an Olympic event.

To help William all she needed to do was mention his book on her social media and who knows what that might do. Bypass the Great Shitley's New York Times' creep critic's opinion possibly and show him his error.

Would have been nice to have her write a blurb for his latest book. Something like:

William Barnes is back with a stunner.

or

Hidden in the Shadows deserves the full light of day.

Just one line that didn't mention *clichéd* or *poorly constructed* or *disappointment*.

If he read *disappointment* in the same sentence as *Flying Toward the Sun* one more time, he might buy a gun. Then he'd find the reviewer and show him what happens to critics who can't differentiate between genius and garbage.

Orelia wrote commercial garbage and he wrote articulate and carefully groomed prose. His world had suddenly become transposed and William couldn't understand how, why or when this occurred. But she could have fixed that. Righted him by rubbing some of her new-found luck over his work.

When she didn't return his call, he had tried again. And again. The more he had thought about her endorsing his book, the more he believed a few simple sentences from her would partway help restore his career.

He tried texting and after several messages she did respond with a reply peppered with *busy living the dream*. *Busy* apparently was a reasonable excuse to ignore the very person who'd made *living her dream* possible.

A year had passed since he'd heard anything from Orelia, until the message three weeks ago. The *living-the-dream* text, as he'd named it.

He saw her in his imagination when he'd spoken here those few years ago. Imaginary Orelia stood at the back of the crowd, sizing him up. Her perfectly-styled, too-cute-for-words pixie look hiding her dark thieving intent. The anger rose in him to the point where swear words seemed the only choice to describe his feelings.

William detested curse words. Even thinking them recalled that little nugget: *swearing is for those with a limited vocabulary*. But when he imagined Orelia typing that message, he read between the lines and realized her true message.

"Fuck you, William Barnes!"

He saw his imagined tormentor pause to decide whether this line required a smiley face or a reversed single finger. The smiley face she'd choose because that's humorous irony. With a self-satisfied nod she'd hit send, then grin at the distress delivered to him.

William looked down at his phone, expecting the offensive message to appear, but of course it was all in his head. Orelia Mason wouldn't waste time sending him messages, vulgar or not. She was at home with her fabulous life, working on the next book, finished in fewer than thirty days.

"Wouldn't that be amazing, William, my books taking up the top three slots of the New York Times Best-Seller list?"

"Oh, yes, so amazing Orelia. I'm choking on my keyboard."

William breathed deeply. His heart took off at a gallop again. He felt suddenly hot and faint. Thirsty too, like he'd eaten a bagful of pretzels, which now stuck in his throat. And like that Seinfeld line, *these pretzels were making him thirsty.*

He managed to find his way to the signing table. The half empty glass of water beckoned like an oasis waterhole. He fell into the chair, reached for the glass and swallowed the stale contents in one swig. When he breathed out, all the tension within him released as if his body had been deflated.

As he sat in the present, looking out at the ghost audience of the past, he fought back the tears burning at the corner of his eyes. His limbs felt weak and his exhaustion so engulfing he could sleep for a thousand years—a clichéd line, yes, but oh so true. William rested his arms on the table, nestled his head in the pillow they made, and closed his eyes.

Orelia Mason stood behind him patting his back. "There there William, it will all be okay. Authors like me are soon forgotten. True art wins out."

William didn't want to wake up from the dream even as he felt himself tugged awake by a God-like hand shaking the stage floor, then his shirt and his head. He wanted to first thank Orelia for being such a good sport; for stepping down from the podium; for giving him back what belonged to him, what he'd earned and what she had stolen.

The store assistant—the one he'd kill off first in a horror film and would now make it messy as hell—awoke him with a rough push of his shoulders.

In his half-awake state, William exclaimed, "Thank you. You're too kind."

First-to-die's expression said it all. William must have looked and seemed crazy, drunk or drugged, sleeping here on a desk in the basement of a store.

He wanted to explain to the young man he was an author, and that he'd been sleeping badly because he'd endured a tough few weeks. If there was anywhere a sleeping author should be welcome, surely it was a bookstore.

But the derision in the man's voice when he said, "Buddy, you need to sleep this off somewhere else," stopped him.

He shot up without addressing him, hastened to the stairs, took them two at a time, and bolted out the store's door at a sprint. Someone looking at him that way after everything he'd achieved was the final humiliation. In his head, he heard Orelia laughing at him and saying, "Just what that man deserves. The hack."

How dare she? How *dare* she?

He didn't deserve this. Any of this. All he did was help another human being, support a fellow author, and somehow this offloaded his luck. This failure of everything important in his life was what he received in return for his trouble.

It took him nearly two hours to walk home, but he relished the time because as he walked he thought hard on what he might do. With each step, the kernel of a plan took form, ideas swimming in and out of his imagination. By the time he'd arrived at the front door he stopped, holding the handle, breathing out the anguish and humiliation.

His mind now danced with lightness; his spirit uplifted. He had a plan. Not complete but some interesting ideas of what he could do to turn this whole thing around. He thanked his creative mind for remaining sharp when he had faltered. Where only hours ago there had been tears on his face, now rested a confident smile.

No longer would he be the one crying. No longer.

15

*D*octor Shepherd leaned over his desk and took more notes. This patient equally fascinated and unsettled him. He studied his recorder for a moment, as though the electronic device held a puzzling secret. In her case, perhaps it did.

His thoughts now noted on paper, he pressed the play button and continued listening. Patient MENO3's voice filled the room. He never included a patient's full name in his reports. He worried if something went wrong, his notes might be used against a client, or him for that matter.

A few years ago the police had been relentless in their harassment of a colleague. They accused him of withholding evidence in his files of a suspected ringleader of a pedophilia ring. So Dr. Shepherd created a system for his files. He used the last two letters of the first and last name, along with the day of the month of the client's first appointment. Any good detective would probably break his code, but it gave him some deniability.

This was his third play through of this recording and he grew more troubled with each listen. Her voice filled his office; it infiltrated every corner, even more so than the light thrown from his solitary desk lamp.

"He wanted to apologize to me, but I didn't need his apology. I already knew he'd be sorry," she said.

"Oh, how would you know that for sure... him being sorry?" he heard himself ask.

"Because they're always sorry once they realize."

"Realize what?"

"Fate's no longer in their hands. Fate is not a right."

Doctor Shepherd stopped the recorder, rewound and replayed the last sentence.

Fate is not a right seemed a peculiar phrase to spring from a child's mouth. Then again, nothing about patient *MENO3* felt right for her age or circumstance.

This girl was young, just entering her teens, yet she behaved as if she'd already lived many lives. An old soul in layman's terms. He called children like this emotionally age-advanced. He would admit she frightened him on occasion, with the way she studied his face when he asked certain questions.

Once or twice during their few sessions, he sensed something strange in the air, like a swirl of, of... aghh, he struggled to find the right word. An imbalance around him. The world at a tilt.

Pretty silly, really. His job was to help people find balance, not have patients unbalance him. Especially a young girl.

That's why he used the recorder with Nem. He didn't always tape patient sessions, preferring to take notes. But, after the first session, he realized he needed a backup. At first, he'd forgotten what she'd said and been left staring at a blank page, only recalling her answers in a vague way as if they were hidden in a mist.

Upon returning to listening to the next visit, it felt as if he experienced hearing what she said for the first time, though it was his voice on the recording. Mind blowing peculiar, he'd say, if he wasn't an educated man who should possess better words to describe the experience.

Pen poised, he pressed the play button again.

"Fate is not a right."

"Hmm. That's an interesting idea." He heard a faint smile in his tone. "Isn't fate just a theory? If life is random, then wouldn't that make your statement true *and* false? Or you can have faith in God and destiny. From that we might surmise all existence has meaning. You've never mentioned your religious beliefs in this."

"I don't believe in any God. That's not the right word for luck."

The girl argued philosophy well, and this impressed him initially. If she weren't a patient, and he met her at a dinner party as a grown woman, he could imagine a lively, enjoyable debate.

"So tell me, how does living work? One may argue life works in different ways for each individual. Some say you're born lucky. Or unlucky. I imagine there's simply wise and unwise people. The rational, balanced view on existence is to understand that we make choices. Our fate is a result of those choices. Good or bad."

"Are you convinced of that Dr. Shepherd?"

"I am. How does life work for you?"

He recalled the way she'd looked when answering this question. Though he was unable to initially remember details of any session, listening to each recording the details came back, as if his mind had been pricked and the memories dribbled out.

He listened to her answer, paused and played it again.

Then again.

He scribbled two paragraphs on that one comment, underlining the last sentence several times without thinking. After reviewing the words, he decided to cross out the line. His hand moved furiously, drawing line after line on the page. He was unable to say why erasing all record of this thought seemed so important. After all, she couldn't know what he'd written.

He rewound the recording again and listened, telling himself the way she'd looked at him was only in his imagination. His nerves had been on edge and his judgment must be flawed. Her demeanor was arguably normal given the circumstances of her referral to him, and her history.

Tragic was too light a word for her case, and at the start, he was determined, almost obsessed, to help. Now he'd begun to reason he wasn't the right person to assist her. Yes, yes, his specialty was childhood trauma. Despite his twenty-three years of experience, with her though, he felt out of his depth.

He stared again at the page. Maybe he should have kept the words, just in case.

Just in case! Was he crazy?

He pulled out his cell and dialed his colleague, Dr. Sanders. Psychologists were privy to disturbing stories, so it was necessary to have a consigliere, of sorts—a title he'd jokingly given to Sanders.

He wasn't available, but Shepherd made an appointment with the doctor's receptionist, before returning to his notes. What *had* she meant by those words? He worried that in scrubbing away their existence, his action might be a sign of disrespect. Or craziness on his part.

He decided that her response could be interpreted many ways. None of them as threatening as this made him now feel. Jesus Christ, she was only twelve.

"How does life work for you?" he'd said.

The first part of her answer was reasonable, displaying the emotional intelligence he'd come to expect.

"Life and fate are neither good nor bad. They distribute luck in proportion to what is deserved. It took my mother's death to show me that."

"That's exceptional and profound Nem, but I don't accept you or your mother *deserved* what happened. And you haven't answered the question. How does everything you've experienced work with that idea of luck?"

"Look at what happened to Alan. He got my reply to his fake apology. I miss my mom. But what if she did the wrong thing lying to me?"

"Okay, let's first discuss Alan. You could have no control over his fate, whatever that was. And secondly, I'm sure your mother did what was, in her mind, best for you."

To his dismay, on playback, he noted the disbelief in his tone. He should have kept that subdued to avoid alienating her. That could have explained her reply.

"Really?" she'd said. "All these visits and you don't believe me?"

He had cleared his throat on the recording and now wished he hadn't done that. She may have realized his discomfort, perhaps read his body language. In letting down his guard, somehow this young patient had taken the power in this interaction.

"Then you'll see, Dr. Shepherd. I'm not here by chance."

"Okay Nem. You believe... what you want if that... helps you."

A faltering in his voice made him sound as though he was the patient. When she'd said *not here by chance*, she couldn't be referring to his *issue*? How could she have any knowledge of that? Impossible. Nobody knew. *Nobody.*

"And what does that mean Nem? Should I be afraid?"

He'd punctuated this question with what he'd imagined was a friendly chuckle, as if they were both in on a joke. His training made him skilled at keeping his impression of patients' statements to himself. But something about her was so unsettling, his emotions were not within his control.

A long pause followed. In those seconds he heard his breath; slow and deep.

"Nem? I'll ask again. What do you mean by *then you'll see?*"

"I'm sorry," came her reply, in a voice far calmer than his. "You'll receive your due in correct proportions. That's my meaning. I think you understand perfectly. You can't take back what you've done, just as Alan's apology changed nothing. What did you say about luck? Not luck. Poor choices."

His tone had risen an octave. "But I didn't... haven't killed anyone?"

"Haven't you?" came the reply. "You must suspect that's not true."

Dr. Shepherd switched off the transcriber and stared at the device for long seconds, before pressing delete as if it contained an abomination. He rewrote the redacted sentence on his notepad, gazing down at the words as guilt flooded his mind.

Then he began to shake.

He wanted to tear up the paper or even burn it, but he felt as though the action might anger fictitious gods, who would wreak vengeance upon him. His control had been maintained for many years but the need to share his dark secret never relented.

Written across the page in shaky lettering were the words:

What have I done?

Now his body shook out of control and his teeth began to chatter as if he was outside in a snowstorm without a jacket. He suddenly understood that she knew, and she was sending something to find him. And the thing would be terrible and painful, and he wouldn't see the approach or know what came for him until it pounced.

One thought kept swinging through his mind as if a perpetual pendulum hung above. Whatever his fate, no matter how dreadful, he deserved everything he had coming.

16

The first day of William's *Orelia Mason Campaign* was a huge success. His plan, created as he walked home from that devastating day at the bookstore, was brilliant.

For over three months, work on his latest novel had stalled. Nothing felt good enough to him. He found no rhythm on the pages; his sentences were awkward and convoluted; and he spent more time hitting delete than the return key.

Not so with his revenge campaign.

The first negative review he wrote was poetic. Where finding words for fiction was a challenge, scripting caustic comments proved a breeze.

1 out of 5 stars
I will never buy one of Kindle's recommendations again By H.E.
Dash Ed
Format: Kindle Edition |Verified Purchase
This was the most tedious and boring book I can remember reading.
The most interesting parts were the grammatical errors.

William leaned back in his chair and admired his handiwork.

H.E. Dash Ed as a name was a stroke of genius. That's what he planned to do. Run in to her life, create havoc and dash away.

Mind you, Orelia's latest book *The Mysterious Heart,* enjoyed 423 reviews, mostly four and five stars. This was despite only being released two weeks ago. So if he was to lower the book's rating of four-point-two-five out of five stars, he'd need to write at least one hundred negative reviews.

Two hours later, he'd added another fourteen. Each time he had to open another account with a new name because book sites only allowed one review per book. Around number eleven he'd run out of ideas for fanciful names. His wit had performed long enough and then left the building. Now they appeared as simply *Anonymous.*

He'd added three stars as well because he didn't want to appear obvious. He figured a run of negative reviews might appear suspicious. Even the three stars, he'd peppered with negative comments.

An okay read.

Have read worse but not by much.

Just seemed like this story bounced around dragging its feet.

When he'd had enough, he took time off to shower and eat his lunch. Upon his return he gasped. Other reader-reviewers had piled more four and five-star reviews on top of his, thus diluting the impact of his work.

This job was too big. Not to mention he'd hit a snag with Amazon's policy of requiring reviewers to spend a certain amount before they could leave a comment. He'd already spent hundreds to open separate accounts, and buy things he didn't need, to enable his review privileges.

In a flash of genius, he visited a website which he'd heard about in the news.

Fiverr.

Any creative service was available for five dollars.

He typed the search term *book reviews.*

Hundreds of proffered services showed; all offered the same with a choice of video or written.

$5 will get you a video

- A 50 words script (provided by you)
- My choice of background **(choose background for extra gig)**
- Professional lighting, sound and video quality
- My choice of wardrobe **(choose wardrobe for extra gig)**

Took William a while to work out *gig* just meant job. Why confuse things? Just say *job*. If he couldn't get his career back, he could put an ad on here for a *gig*. Maybe copy-editing errors in these ads.

He searched through dozens of providers offering written reviews and settled on *Cathy123: Money Back Guaranteed.* He loved the typos.

Book Review or feedback about anything any-place

Will post helpful, natural, unique and positive produc revuw, service testemenials from different IP and different User Any website you want!
Provide me gift card for verifyed review. so that I can purchase book free, inbox me eny question.
I WILL REFUND IF U ARE NOT 100% SATISFIED.

William's hope was that, as in her ad, spelling and grammatical errors would riddle her reviews. This might imply that Orelia's readers were an illiterate, uneducated slice of humanity.

Twelve of the Fiverr accounts replied within a few hours, agreeing to review any book he wanted. He paid them and even paid extra to the girl who video-reviewed, asking her to wear something which looked *old and tired.*

When the reviews appeared several hours later, William experienced a thrill as if someone had not just danced on his grave but also brought a bunch of their friends. They were fantastic. Derisive and hilarious to read and he patted himself on the back for his sheer ingenuity.

1 out of 5 stars
Quit when about 70% read
By Rebecca
Format: Kindle Edition
I got to the point that I had to stop reading because it became way too boring. I read to be inspired and for pleasure and am old enough to choose to avoid that which is horrid and I do not need to handle or see.

1.0 out of 5 stars No Stephen King
1 out of 5 stars
By JET
Format: Kindle Edition
This story is really slow and boring. Go back to doing whatever you did before you attempted to call yourself a writer.

Every addition was so fabulous, William's spirits lifted as each new one appeared. He continued to open new accounts using different email addresses and wrote his own reviews too. No amount of negative reviews was enough for his Orelia campaign.

By around ten that night the total of added reviews was over two hundred. Orelia's star rating had been lowered to 3.30 out of 5. The two-star ranking was so close he could taste success. His eyes felt as though he had minute paper cuts sliced across his corneas. He needed sleep.

When he put his head down, he slipped off to the twilight zone of nothingness within seconds. He slumbered as a man who'd already won his battle.

The next morning, he noticed a few four and five-star reviews populated among his scathing comments, moving the book's rating up to three-point-seven-five. Several even commented on the low reviews, condemning them as written by trolls and accusing the reviewers of never having read the book.

"Well, you're right," William said to the screen. Another habit he'd developed. Talking to inanimate objects. This had better work before he went crazy beyond repair.

Today he'd contract other Fiverr people to write extra reviews. If he set a daily budget and spread them over time, he wouldn't burn out, or his actions appear suspicious.

So far, he'd spent two hundred and twenty-four dollars on the campaign. He'd limit his budget to five hundred for the week. He got smart and hired one of the Fiverr contractors to book other Fiverr reviewers, which freed him up to work on the next part of his plan.

He needed time to think too. Reviews popping up on Orelia's book's page were satisfying, but his efforts hadn't affected her sales one bit. *The Mysterious Heart* still ranked in the top fifty books on Amazon, Apple iTunes, Kobo and everywhere else. Her stupid romance would probably appear on the *New York Times Best-seller* list for the fourth week, no matter what he did.

Didn't people read reviews anymore?

William had checked Orelia's website and Facebook page. In fact, he'd stalked her blog these past few weeks. He now spent the morning writing nasty comments on her most recent blog posts (those fake email accounts had come in handy).

In the last half dozen posts she'd made, she'd gone on and on raving about the *fantastic sales results* of *The Mysterious Heart.*

Ugh, how many times can you thank readers and express surprise at your success? Of course her book sold well. The publisher clearly invested a bucket-load of money on promotion. It was impossible to miss the subway signs, the posters in bookstores, full page ads in women's magazines and ads in *his* Facebook feed. For heaven's sake, did Facebook think he was a brainless person who read Orelia Mason's books?

If you weren't aware a new Orelia Mason book had been recently released, you were living under a rock. He thought he'd even seen her name on the cover of Vanity Fair when he was at the newsstand. Of this he was uncertain because he'd averted his eyes. If that was her on the cover, he couldn't bear it. He told himself he'd made a mistake and refused to pick up the publication.

On her website, he checked under the tab for *Personal Appearances*. Orelia was to appear on two local radio stations, a breakfast TV show, and visit a dozen bookstores in this and neighboring states.

Two appearances were in the city this week.

Hmm, interesting. He had an idea. What a stroke of luck. Maybe fortune had turned in his favor.

Immediately he began making notes. He wanted to create a script of sorts to convey authority and conviction. He put himself in the mindset of the character he'd play, and he imagined the delight if he succeeded with even half the phone calls.

This new plan, added to the accumulating Fiverr reviews, raised his mood to the euphoria he'd experienced during publication of his second book. That was back when his luck began to fade or, more accurately, had been drained by Orelia Mason.

Impossible that her good fortune and his decline were coincidence. Crazy as this sounded, he knew he was right. For he understood luck now. Luck wasn't unlimited. Luck wasn't something shared fairly among hard workers and dedicated souls. The idea a rising tide lifts all ships was garbage, honest-to-goodness-do-gooder trash. Success in the publishing world meant readers chose one author over another.

Despite popular belief, there were limited numbers of readers. Numbers weren't growing either. They'd drifted away to other pursuits. Playing apps on their phones. Binge watching *Game of Thrones* or *Darker Things*—or *Black Things* or *Stranger Things,* whatever the latest big show was called. Posting pictures of themselves, their pets, their food on Instagram or Snapchat or whatever was the latest social media thing.

In helping Orelia embark on a publishing career, he'd given away his mojo and his readers. They weren't reading his books because they'd devolved and become Orelia Mason mindless, idiot fans.

Orelia Mason, *everybody's new favorite author.* That was the one phrase repeated in so many reviews. *Count on Orelia Mason to deliver a good story.*

Well, that would change.

He read over his script, polishing here and there, and then read it aloud several times. *Perfect.* Names, addresses and phone numbers were listed on an A4 sheet next to the notepad.

William Barnes picked up his cell and dialed.

His heart beat was a banging drum and as the phone buzzed on the other end he drew in three deep, calming breaths. Despite the gnawing in his stomach, he noticed one thing he hadn't anticipated. He felt damn good, like a powerful drug suddenly fueled his mind.

But when the voice answered in a split second, his nerves disappeared. The performance was flawless, his voice conveying the exact tone he'd practiced. Yes, yes, this would work!

He was getting good at messing with her.

Now he understood the term addiction. The feeling was of *ruling the world*. He smiled. Correction, not the whole world, just Orelia Mason's world.

17

After the last session with Nem, Ken Shepherd referred her to a colleague. The earlier recording he'd made of her visit unsettled him. His desire was to help anyone, but he wasn't convinced he could help her or if she was, in fact, in need of his assistance.

His knowledge of her earlier circumstances was vague, most of it he learned from a case worker's notes from her foster placement. As a professional he could access those records. There wasn't a great deal of information included on the mother's murder or of Alan West. He'd decided, after sensing a threat so subtle he continued to second guess himself, that he needed the straight facts.

Patricia Stratton's death was clearly a domestic homicide. In most cases the warning signs were there. With this though, there had been nothing on record. No visits by police to deal with violent arguments. No assistance requested in fact from any government body.

Shepherd contacted a cousin in the police department, who helped with accessing records. He attempted to gain as much corroborative detail as he could with a patient's history. While he treated Nem, he sensed she thought of him as an enemy and so this was his way of protecting himself.

He stopped.

Doctor, are you seriously thinking that a fourteen-year-old represented a threat? Really? You need to settle down.

Okay, he decided, after this he'd take a break, schedule vacation time. Get his head straight. The last few days, he'd felt unwell. Off. A virus perhaps? A rest was what the doctor ordered. After completion of this research, he'd put young, troubled Nem behind him, just another file with a coded number.

The details of the case were interesting and sad. Human beings' potential for violence, while fascinating, always left a bad taste in his mouth. Sadly though, it came with this job, so he'd seen and heard more than his share of terrible, heart-wrenching testimonies of man's inability to control his darker emotions.

Four years ago, Patricia Stratton, thirty-seven, died at the hands of Alan West, thirty-eight. The man had a violent history, with a long list of misdemeanors. Bar fights, drunk and disorderly conduct, speeding, assault, and a DUI charge.

West must have attempted to get his life back on the right path with no convictions or charges recorded against him for the year before the murder. Not unusual in these cases. Self-medication with alcohol or drugs was the go-to choice for most when dealing with anger issues. Below the surface though, they'd slow simmer until a random event caused them to boil over into a catastrophe. In West's case, explode, leaving a devastating mess.

Whatever set West off that night wasn't noted. His statement was that he didn't understand what came over him. That he'd had something akin to an out-of-body experience.

"Suspect overwhelmed by a thought, but he doesn't remember what," the interviewing detective noted.

Again, not unusual. Domestic murders did not result from logical reasoning. *Swept away by their emotions* was a common excuse. After pleading guilty, incarceration followed for West, with an eighteen-year sentence.

The irony, considering his own interview with Nem, was West never served the full sentence. This information was new to him.

He'd presumed it was an open and shut case. To a degree it was closed, only not in the way you'd imagine.

While imprisoned he'd developed Non-Hodgkin's lymphoma. In the preceding year, this prison had *enjoyed* poor publicity from a decided lack in patient care. Several inmates had died from *absent care* and downright sloppy procedures—meaning nobody paid any attention to sick men. The warden was in the firing line of an inquiry and a law suit. To cool the media heat, suddenly ill prisoners received health support second to none.

West, who was just about as lucky as anyone could get, received a stem cell transplant. After doctors gave him high doses of chemotherapy, the new donor bone marrow replaced his destroyed cells and he recovered. Ken wondered if the generous benefactor might be so agreeable if he'd known his lifeline donation afforded a killer a fresh chance at life.

Until one year to the day after doctors gave the *all clear,* when his luck dissolved, that luck like ice melting away, never to be whole again. This information wasn't in any files, and Shepherd only discovered this after a visit to the library and a search through microfiche newspaper records.

There was a new thing called the Internet, which might make research and accessing medical information easier. What he needed wasn't available yet though. Roll on technology.

As he read the copied pages, he pondered if this wasn't a case of the worst bad luck bestowed upon anyone. What else could it be? The man was in the wrong place at the wrong time. Still, a strange thought whispered inside his mind; as much as he pushed it away, and as much as he told himself even thinking this was unprofessional, it kept coming back. He'd never tell a soul, nor would he even commit this silly idea to paper. For some reason all he could think was that Alan West had entered the *Twilight Zone.*

Sleep did not find Dr. Shepherd later that night. Coincidences appeared inbuilt into the fabric of life, but this was nine-tenths weird. Not a proficient summation, but how do you explain such a thing?

Misfortune? Providence? Irony? *Irony certainly.*

These thoughts floated in his mind as he attempted to doze. He even tried thrusting the words over a fence, instead of sheep. The concept being, they'd disappear on the other side and let him alone.

Nem's words returned to him as if someone waiting beyond the barrier had thrown them back. He imagined the enemy on the other side, laughing as they said, "Here, take these and choke on them."

Fate is not a right.

He heard her child's voice and thought, *what an odd girl.*

If she weren't so young and the circumstances of the man's death not so bizarre, he'd swear on her involvement. Though, that would make her a witch or God knows what, and he didn't believe in fairy tales. He believed in provable facts and science.

Christ, you hearing yourself Shepherd? That's hardly professional thinking.

He underlined and made bold the word **vacation** in his mind and catapulted the image over the fence.

"Ridiculous," he said to the empty room, then "Damn it," because he wasn't any closer to sleep.

Pushing aside the covers, he threw on a robe and padded to the dining room where he poured a brandy. He shook his head at the crazy thoughts keeping him awake, then stopped to toss back the drink. His throat burned, but as the alcohol hit his bloodstream, he felt calm descend on his manic mood.

The intensity of her stare flickered through his mind. After her tragic experiences, he'd expect confused and timid behavior, or defiant and belligerent. Nem displayed neither. She had a fight and strength he didn't see often in adult patients, let alone a child. She'd looked at him in a way that even now made him sweat. Even recalling those moments, sent a mild tremor through his body.

He took another swig to calm his rising heartbeat. Yes, this drink helped. Sleep would wash away these nonsense thoughts too. He was overwrought and tired. Simple as that.

Vacation pinged in his mind again.

At first, he'd thought the flare in her dark eyes was her recalling a tragic past but that didn't fit when he examined the session in hindsight. When she talked history, she spoke as if she felt unaffected, with everything tied up in a neat conclusion. Therefore, it must be him who'd angered her. Fair enough, not uncommon in patients.

"You'll receive what you are due in correct proportions."

She said this staring at him as if she saw everything. His past, present and... his future. *Really, calm down, man.*

But she did hint at what he'd done. Or was that his guilt coloring her words? *How would she know?* Did she suspect something or was this a guess?

He'd been careful.

He'd tried to stop.

If this was her way of seeking justice, surely his efforts to curtail his behavior mitigated a small forgiveness? In fact, becoming a psychologist was his attempt to understand compulsions. His story wasn't one of an abusive childhood. His *leanings* were inbuilt from birth. Genetic he'd often thought, and if God made him this way, then whose fault was that?

Research suggested addiction was genetic; he'd even written a paper on this subject. That's why child psychology was his chosen specialty. Unlike many others afflicted—and that is how he viewed this condition—he knew what he did was wrong. He took the occasional risk hoping for discovery. Never with patients though, because his oath, to never do harm while practicing, he held sacred.

For almost a year he'd curbed his urge with photographs and videos, and diligent focus. The damn itch still built over time, demanding he scratch. He'd fight it but always the whispers came back.

But she could not know all this.

She. Could. Not. Know.

In his mind, he hurled those words over the barrier too.

Be gone, demon thought.

He hauled himself back to bed, thanks to the alcohol, a nice buzz humming in his head. Tiredness seeped into his body as he pulled back the covers. They felt heavy, as if lead had been stitched into his blankets. Now he felt hopeful he might escape into the pitch-black nothingness of sleep.

Minutes or hours later—he couldn't tell anymore—he did doze. Oh, it felt good, but as he rolled over to snuggle deeper beneath those weighted coverings, he experienced a trapped, claustrophobic sensation. *Not so good.* Then a moment after, a sharp, burning pain just above his tailbone nagged at him.

The brandy deadened his nerves and mind somewhat, so the aching didn't fully rouse him. Half-asleep, he told himself to get up more often from his desk. A good idea too because walking calmed him and might help with the desires.

He awoke a few hours later with an orchestra of agony shooting up and down his right leg. The alcohol-dulling effect had now dissipated, so he bore the full brunt of what he could only describe as a nest of fire ants crawling under his skin. Panic erupted in his confused mind.

Thankfully, his training kicked in and he managed to calm his thoughts by assuring himself the likely diagnosis was a pinched nerve. Damn though, it burned deep. He grabbed at his hamstring and massaged the ache but found the contorted position only inflamed the throbbing.

Shepherd climbed from his bed, limped to the medicine cabinet and pulled out a bottle of painkillers. He shoved more than he should into his mouth and washed them down with water drunk direct from the tap. He was uncertain of making it to the kitchen for a glass.

Now that he'd stood, he noted a soreness around his groin also. When he reached below to massage the muscle, he detected a small lump below the skin. *That was new! And disturbing!*

Something felt wrong, and he sensed an unknown thing had invaded his body. The scene from the seventies *Alien* film flashed in his mind; a hellish creature exploding from a crew member entered his imagination, except this time it was him. The thing bursting, not from his chest but from his nether regions. This image so horrific he felt his legs go weak.

He managed to limp back to bed and climb in, still writhing in pain despite the medication. He debated calling an ambulance, but after a few more minutes, the painkillers kicked in and helped a little. First thing tomorrow though he'd be seeing a doctor, though he sensed what the answer might be.

He'd studied enough in med school to recognize possible prostate cancer symptoms. Twinges of something down there had bothered him leading up to tonight but nothing as painful as this. This was a worrying development, but one good thing, it had wiped away his mind's focus on Nem. Now he had something new about which to worry. At that thought, she was back in his head again.

God, he just needed to sleep and tomorrow everything would seem a whole lot better.

Finally, the world slid away, and Shepherd jumped over the imaginary fence, following all the words he'd sent that way earlier in the night. As he turned his dream head to marvel at his agility to leap so high, the girl's words flew by him, jiggling and jangling as if they laughed at him.

"You will receive what you are due in correct proportions."

When they landed on the other side, they both stopped. A snake noticing its prey. Within a moment the sentence wrapped around his body, stifling him from his feet to his head. The only part free was his mouth, which had opened and begun to scream. A terrible, high-pitched scream sprung forth, of desperation and pain; not pain now, but what was to come.

The dream snake-sentence squeezed tighter and tighter, and he gasped for breath, his ribcage crushed by the pressure. Just as sleep claimed him, one final thought seeped into his darkening mind. Was there anywhere in the *Twilight Zone* where he might plead his case?

18

William made the phone calls, but he wouldn't know for days, possibly weeks, how well his plan had worked. He figured, the first few would return brilliant results but eventually one of the publisher's publicists would call around to check what had gone wrong. Then they'd work it out, but the idea of wreaking havoc even for a few days tasted delicious.

The first contact he made was perfect. They'd bought the story, hook, line and sinker. He'd followed up with an email from a fake account which added validity. Those fake accounts were beyond easy to create. To make the emails appear authentic, he only needed to buy a web address of a similar name to a legitimate business. Nobody checked email addresses exactly, if at all.

The publisher had already registered *darkdoors.com* and *darkdoors.net*. *Darkdoor.net*—minus the *s*—remained available. He bought that and the dot com version.

William then copied the publisher's logo so, at a glance, his emails would appear official and unquestionable.

He also used fake identification to set up a PayPal account to pay for the websites and the Fiverr business. That was easy too. Everything you needed in the world could be found online. William was good at research and this subterfuge. He jovially considered focusing on writing crime novels. Once this was over he might give it a swing under a pen name. J.K. Rowling had done well with that.

The other unexpected benefit was that this whole exercise proved tremendously cathartic. Each day he awoke with renewed energy and an emotion close to when *Suffer Them to Come to Light* rode high in the sales' charts. For a few small moments, life felt good and he believed he might actually win over Orelia Mason.

He'd done the hard part, now the first stop in confirming whether his plan had worked was the downtown Barnes and Noble, the biggest bookstore in the city. Her current promotional tour was scheduled to begin there with a seven pm presentation. William arrived at six, positioning himself in the coffee shop, inside but situated in a separate area to the selling floor.

Weaving his magic had encouraged his appetite, another thing which had disappeared along with his career over the past year. Tonight though, he wolfed down a sub and large piece of cheesecake like he hadn't had a meal in months. Two cups of coffee later, he bounced on a euphoric high as he sat close to the window waiting with excitement. From here he could see who came and went into the building.

Several fans entered the store, easily recognizable as they carried one or more of Orelia's books. Others he recognized simply by their age, gender and appearance. Forty-plus, female, and looking as though they'd walked out of a life insurance ad for over fifties, even if they were much younger. He knew the type. They would describe their addiction to romance-trash as a 'way to escape the realities of life.' What about enhancing their minds with thought-provoking literature? How 'bout that for a neat trick?

What pleased William was that there weren't many, only twenty or so; small compared to a usual turnout for an author enjoying her massive sales and public awareness. He knew this first-hand from his own experience. When he gave speeches after his books had skyrocketed in sales, he'd enjoyed standing-room-only crowds.

He'd followed Orelia's Facebook and Twitter feed all day. She shared her thoughts constantly with her minions—he thought of them as *Despicable Me* yellow slaves, stupid and evil.

Please come say hello at the reading today. It'll be fun!

She'd pronounced this all day on her social media feed. Some of those would still turn up he imagined. Right from the start, she'd been the queen of social media. Filling her *feed* with pictures of her and her fans together. Romantic spots in the cities she visited was another nausea-inducing share of hers. If pictures of hearts were worth a dollar, she'd be a millionaire just from them.

He couldn't do Facebook or Instagram. Real authors didn't indulge in such frivolity no matter how well it paid. What would he share in pictures? Mental asylums? Pictures of sliced wrists? Tombstones? He wrote about life's angsts and the big questions, which didn't translate into memes.

This wasn't the first time William had attended a reading by Orelia. A year into her success, he'd thought what would it hurt to go along and approach her? That's back when he still hoped if he rekindled a relationship with her, it might help his sales. A best-selling author as a friend certainly could increase your social value.

He'd stood at the back of the room slightly embarrassed he'd even considered the idea of leveraging her fans. Nobody who read Orelia's romantic romps would read his carefully-crafted work. Her fans fawned over her like she was a movie star and he'd spent the entire time fighting nausea.

At the time, he'd imagined the satisfaction he'd enjoy in two months when his third book would be released. He wouldn't need the great Orelia Mason to help sell his books. Back then, he'd thought that book would return his career to success. When he was on top again, his hope was that she'd realize she had made the mistake in walking away from their relationship.

He was the one who deserved a long, successful career because *he* wrote quality. She wrote pulp for desperate housewives who read to escape the drudgery of their lives.

Months later, while speaking at one of the few appearances his publisher managed to secure for his third book, William recalled the Orelia reading and the way she engaged with her fans. As he stood there before the meagre audience, he decided he'd try her tactic with the desperate housewives. Without thinking it through, he'd clumsily flirted with them, which only ended up an embarrassing mess, when half walked out before he'd finished. Some even complained to the bookstore owner that he'd been offensive and inappropriate.

Now though Orelia Mason, Miss Best Seller, would see how it felt to be greeted by an empty room. Despite his plan seeming to have worked, disappointment tapped at William that even with his inter-ference, she still enjoyed more than three fans waiting for her.

William was on to his third coffee, when he recognized Morris' car pull up and attempt to park right outside in a no parking zone. *Typical arrogance.* He hoped the traitor would receive a parking fine and wondered if there was a way to report his crime.

The man appeared to have recovered from the various ailments, which had caused him to be unavailable every time William called. It had been three weeks since he'd given up on Morris ever returning his calls after he'd begged off with *diarrhea*.

What a bonus to see him here. Two birds killed with one stone.

Orelia climbed from the front passenger seat, princess-like in her knee-length, long plum coat. He would admit the black-collared shirt and tight, white cream pants—designer, no doubt—did look good on her. A black necklace of oversized beads completed the fashionista effect. *How modern. How funky.*

His two nemeses stood next to the car talking and William wished he was a fly on the car door. In fact, he wished he could personally witness the proceedings to follow. The risk of being seen if he left the secluded window table to enter the main bookshop area though was too high. Should Orelia or Morris see him they might put two and two together and realize he was the culprit behind the poor attendance.

Then again, this was a large store. If he kept his head down and covered his face with a magazine if they looked his way, he might get away with it. And he really did want to see the despair written across her face. The sweetness of witnessing that was so tempting.

Beside him a rack of courtesy newspapers hung on the wall. As he noted them, an idea came to mind.

Oh, well, I've come this far, he thought.

He rose, left a tip and retrieved one of the selections, folding it in half. Yes, if he held this up in front of his face, it might just work.

19

Two days after Dr. Ken Shepherd's oncology visit—after the night of agonizing pain—he sat in his car in the garage below his building feeling lost. The gray shadows, cast from aging overhead lights, shimmered down on the surrounding concrete pylons, creating an oppressive gloom.

Until now, he'd always believed luck to be his friend. How else could his obsession slide under the radar in his personal and professional life?

Only during his university days had his secret almost been uncovered. Alone in his dorm, he'd left photographs by his bedside while visiting the bathroom. The type of which would reveal his predilection in taste within one glance; a secret he'd kept since his mid-teens.

Usually meticulous in covering his tracks, the shock of returning to discover his roommate laying on his own bed was a jolt to his system.

"Blinding headache," the fellow said, an over jovial personality to which Shepherd had learned to adapt. A joke here and there and he'd created an insincere bond with him.

"Migraine. Barely managed to get through ... door."

"So I see."

Ken walked over to his bed, casually, despite his heart galloping. He touched his forehead in a gesture of concern, as he picked up the photos and slipped them into his pocket with the other hand.

"You're in my bed but don't worry, you stay there. Need anything?"

"No, I've tak-en my medicashoon. Kickin' 'n. Gotta shleep."

Ken left the room, a lump lodged in his chest. As he closed the door behind, he released a gasp.

You need to be far more careful, he warned himself.

As he walked up the hall, he shook his head and whispered under his breath, "You were lucky this time. So lucky."

Good timing saved him too. The police raided a group he'd planned to join on the very morning of the day he was to meet with them. So close and so stupid of him to even consider meeting anyone in person. If he'd been caught that would have been a fitting punishing for his carelessness.

Over the following weeks, his stomach somersaulted every time he heard an unexpected knock at his apartment door. He wasn't certain if anyone he'd contacted in the group had kept his number and name. He'd been careful not to use his real name, but he'd heard the police had become good at finding people like him. An article in the newspaper revealed the FBI had become involved in the hunt for his mutual hobbyists. No, he shouldn't think like that because he knew it was somehow wrong, but he couldn't get his brain to switch off. He told himself if he was caught, then that might be a good thing because he would never stop on his own.

They never came, and he survived the scare although that's when his hair started graying. These early close shaves made him extra cautious though and since then he had never had another scare. Of course, complete safety would only be certain if he stopped. He had tried so hard too, even practicing psychology in the hope of discovering an answer to curbing the obsession.

Death wasn't upon him yet, but his life still flashed before his eyes. The embarrassing, disgusting collection of images he saw shamed him. He recognized his luck had expired. Not just expired, but nuked. Completely.

Prostate cancer delivered to him in ironic black humor. Fourth stage. Aggressive. Incurable. Metastasized into his back and leg bones.

How he hadn't noticed the changes in his body surprised him.

His options, explained to him in gentle, supportive words that he didn't deserve, was chemotherapy, radiation and hormone treatment. Most likely none could save him, but they might extend his pitiful life. He took it well, nodding, agreeing to *stay positive*, and thanked the specialist.

After the initial shock, he decided to do nothing. This ending fitted his crime. Cancer was truly the cure for which he'd prayed, and he accepted this fate.

His work would continue, with priority on the article he'd been meaning to write, *From the Inside: The Life of a Reluctant Pedophile.* Of course, this he would publish post-mortem, which without treatment awaited him in only a few months. Perhaps thanks to his training, he'd find no challenge in pushing his fate from his mind.

What proved more difficult to forget was Patient Nem's words—and the way she'd looked into his eyes as she said them. Something was wrong with that girl. Something completely wrong and frightening.

"You'll receive your due in correct proportions. That's how this works."

Prophetic words? Or a lucky guess?

He turned the key in the ignition and checked his side mirror as he reversed. So many thoughts traveled through his mind. This moment began the rest of his existence. A new life to be lived as best he could. His time remaining may be short but he'd attempt to right his wrongs. While his health was good, he'd use any spare time in pursuit of this endeavor. He'd find the kids he'd harmed, every one of them, and apologize.

Maybe if he made good, like in those fantasy films, the disease might disappear as suddenly as it appeared. He felt uplifted at the thought and a silly idea entered his head.

Would patient Nem forgive him?

She was the person he needed to appease most, despite never

having touched her. Even as his scientific mind rebelled against the concept of another human being controlling life and death, he knew the truth. He recalled her smile as she discussed Alan West's fate. *A Mona Lisa smile*, he'd thought at the time, revealing little.

Dr. Ken Shepherd's answer to his question of forgiveness became crystal clear.

Patient Nem, whoever or whatever she was, most definitely wasn't in the business of forgiveness.

20

William moved into the bookstore area holding the newspaper halfway over his face as he kept a constant check on the door for Morris' or Orelia's entry. They'd never believe him being in this store at the exact time of her appearance as a coincidence.

He found himself in a book aisle before he'd stopped to consider whether entering here was the wisest of moves. As he maneuvered behind a bookshelf, the pair entered the store.

William ducked down to sit on his haunches and pretended to examine the back cover of a book he'd pulled from the bottom shelf. This seemed a good strategy. He continued to stoop and weave until he'd moved to be behind the shelf nearest the large square counter. Here he waited and anticipated the joy of seeing, or at least hearing, the results of his little scheme.

Even though he couldn't risk looking up and over, it wasn't necessary. For within five minutes he heard Morris' voice, loud and clear. The agent did not sound happy.

"I keep telling you but you're not listening. Nobody canceled the reading. When did I supposedly call?"

A young female voice replied. "I'm sorry Mr. Usher but I didn't take the call, so I don't know."

Now a mature, female voice interjected. "I think Bethany was the one. Do you want me to ask her?"

"Of course, I want you to ask her. This is ridiculous. A real screw-up on your part. Not mine. Orelia Mason has arrived to give a reading and you've nothing organized. Plus, there's barely anyone here. Do you know how lucky you are to have her visit your store? She's wanted for appearances everywhere."

The mature female replied, "I understand, but if we knew she was still coming, we would have done everything to promote her being here. When you called... sorry, when somebody called saying you'd canceled, we notified everyone who'd booked. The few who've arrived must have missed the email."

William stifled a giggle with his palm. He couldn't get the smile off his face. *Missed the email* just sounded hilarious for some reason. Like *missed the boat*. Like how his own boat had sailed without him thanks to her. See how *missing* feels Orelia?

Then another voice joined the conversation, younger and anxious. "You wanted me Grace?"

"Yes, it was you who took the phone call from Morris Usher yesterday?"

"Um, I'm not sure. What was it about?"

"This is Mr. Usher, Orelia Mason's agent. You said he called and canceled her reading."

"Oh yeah. That *was* me. Yes, he did cancel."

"I've never spoken to this person," said Morris.

"You said Orelia Mason was ill. She was very sorry and we could reschedule. You also said you'd send a carton of free books to apologize for the disappointment. I remember the call because I thought, *wow, we had sold out her talk weeks in advance. Going to be a lot of disappointed fans.* Besides, I love Orelia Mason books and I'd been looking forward to the event myself."

William pointed his finger at his mouth and motioned as if to gag. He mouthed "I love Orelia Mason books."

Hmph. If this is the type of person working in bookstores these days, no wonder publishing is heading downhill.

"Something's wrong here," said Morris. "I didn't call and Orelia has never missed an engagement. She's a professional. This is not good enough. You should have a system in place to check on these things."

Again William mouthed without speaking, "She's a professional."

Then Orelia's voice intervened, calm and dripping with sweetness. "It's okay Morris. There's been a mix-up, that's all."

Another voice interrupted, older, and high-pitched with enthusiasm. "Miss Mason, I'm so thrilled. I love your books. My daughter loves you. My mother loves you. I'm pinching myself. My friend Annie and I have waited all week to come to this. Then when we arrived they told us you'd canceled. We were two Mrs. Long-Faces. But you're here! Wow! Will you do the reading still?"

A long, silent pause, then Orelia's voice, "Hmm, Morris I still can, can't I? That's if ... it's okay with you Grace."

"I guess," said Grace. "Yes, we could set up the chairs. There's no refreshments though. For evening presentations we have wine, cheese and crackers. I'm not sure how many of your books we have for signing. We stock a good quantity because they sell so well, but when an author of your caliber visits, well, we bring in more."

"Oh that doesn't matter," said Orelia. "Selling books isn't the main thing. Connecting with my readers is what's important."

William shook his head. If he was stuck here listening to Orelia's faux humility much longer, he'd be sick all over the science fiction tomes surrounding him. *How did these nerd sci-fi authors sell these thousand-page door-stoppers?*

"Are you sure Orelia?" said Morris.

"Ye-es, Morris, even if there's only two fans here, I'd do this. There's at least ten, fifteen, who've come, that I can see. We can't let them down."

"That's wonderful of you," said Grace. "Quick Bethany, go grab Josh and Helen and tell them to get out the chairs and set up a table.

Grab the hot-water urn too, and all the Orelia Mason books we have.
I'm sure others in the store will stay for the talk."

Morris gave an exaggerated sigh.

"Alright then, but I hope you've learned a lesson. Next time—
check," added Morris, sounding appeased and calmer.

Seconds later the woman, fan-idiot who'd fawned all over Orelia,
squealed like she'd been stabbed. He sure wished he could have
stabbed her for being so dumb. And loud. *Who screams in a bookstore?*

Orelia said, "You're welcome. How awesome you came tonight.
We'll just be fifteen minutes getting organized. Text your friends and
tell them to come down."

William felt a sudden quiver in his legs. He wasn't accustomed to
squatting and he lost his balance, fell off his haunches, dropped the
book in his hand and ended up sprawled in the aisle. Even as he
landed, his head swiped from side to side to check for witnesses. Just
like his last bookstore appearance, nobody was there. He sat on the
floor, head in his hands, contemplating another failure.

Nobody came into the aisle or even noticed him, so he heaved
himself back to a squat and waited, contemplating his next move.
Best thing would be to wait until her presentation began and sneak
out then, unseen. This had been a failure. All he'd managed was to
annoy Morris for a few minutes and that was hardly worth all the
effort and anticipation.

His initial euphoria faded in that instant and a sudden headache
threatened to explode his head. Too much sugar. Too much coffee.
Too much of nothing going his way. No doubt they were on to his
plan now and would check before her other store visits. *Darn, damn
and his life was a disappointment, yet again.*

The poor turnout tonight wasn't even a blip on Orelia's radar.
Morris' fury was minimal and, anyway, he didn't care how Morris felt
about anything. He wanted to devastate Orelia the way she'd devastated him. He wanted to whip the rug out from beneath her feet and
laugh as she fell.

But she wielded an impenetrable good luck shield. Even his negative reviews and trolling of her social media accounts didn't amount

to anything. Plus he'd wasted a lot of money that he didn't have to waste.

He'd paid several Fiverr contractors to visit her social media accounts and stir up trouble. They left posts calling her books what they were: over-fantasized, outlandish stories. One was particular in its wit and cutting tone, citing her books as unworthy of the paper on which they were printed or the bytes used by the eBook versions.

What he hadn't expected was Orelia's fans, who were savage chumps. Their retaliation reminded him of a video he'd seen, where white blood cells chased down bacterium, engulfing the invaders. Her diehard fans destroyed the impact of his reviews and troll remarks, so his commentaries looked bad, instead of her.

William's excitement had drained, replaced by a flat and empty gnaw inside, as he heard the bustle of staff preparing for Orelia's event. This wasn't fair. Orelia made a mockery of literature, enjoying such success with her banal romances. But worse, she'd stolen his fans (maybe not his fans but readers who might have bought his books), stolen his luck and now she'd stolen his muse.

For William hadn't written a fictional word in over four months. A word drought like that had never happened to him until she came along. The irony of squatting in the aisle of a bookstore contemplating his lack of production wasn't lost on him. Damn her and whatever voodoo she practiced. Why did she have to choose him? All the authors in this world, and he became the unlucky duck.

His legs burned, forcing him to stand. Now he pretended to look at books on the third shelf, so he could bend below the top rack. If he stood any higher his head would be within sight of the counter. Half standing though did not release the pain. In fact, the throbbing ache had traveled through his loins and into his stomach. His intestines were on fire like he'd eaten something bad. The gnawing ache though wasn't from food or physical exertion.

Damn, damn, damn. This agony was Orelia Mason. What she'd done to his life was eating him inside. The emotions she stirred, pulled and pushed at him until everything was a boiling mess of hatred.

A tiny voice had whispered to him every time he sat before his computer. *Give this up and return to work and write something*, it said. He couldn't listen. Wouldn't listen because this vendetta seemed too important as if he had been chosen to save not just his own life from her evil, but the world.

William had begun to imagine Orelia Mason had cast a spell on him, something like Oscar Wilde's *Picture of Dorian Gray*. The more successful and beautiful she became, the more his career would wither and grow ugly. He was the painting in the attic reflecting all the corruptness she hid so well.

Deep in his thoughts, William jumped at a tap on his shoulder. He stood upright and turned, ready to explain to Morris or Orelia how he accidentally happened to be here. Already on his tongue was "Imagine seeing you here."

In a chipper tone, she said, "If you don't have anywhere to be, we're about to have an author talk. Orelia Mason. She's a New York Times and USA Today best seller. They say she'll sell more than *Fifty Shades of Grey* this year."

He recognized the person by their voice even before he faced them. Grace smiled at him, looking nothing like he imagined (cherry-red bob with a fringe and deep mulberry lipstick).

William's hesitation must have given the impression he wasn't interested—which was true—because Grace then continued.

"Oh, you're probably not the demographic, but even so she has an interesting story. Motivational. You know she worked in a bookstore just like me. Nothing wrong with that of course. Then her agent finds her manuscript sitting in his pile of to-be-reads. Someone left it there by mistake. He's eating his lunch and thinks he'll just read until he's finished his food. Well, he sat at his desk for the rest of the day not stopping until he'd read it all. Isn't that just the best story? Dreams really do come true. Orelia Mason is proof."

William took several deep breaths to calm his anger, which had fired inside at the mention of Orelia's taunting quip *Dreams really do come true*. The lie that Morris discovered her was outrageous. He'd read that somewhere but hadn't realized how much it had become part of her legend. He wished he could set Grace straight with the truth, and share that plum was not her color.

More pressing though was his need to escape the store before Orelia or Morris spotted him. Grace didn't seem in a hurry as she continued to linger as if waiting for a reply. All he could think to do under pressure was pretend he was having some sort of attack, so he coughed. Then coughed more.

"Aheh—uheh. Uh-ah."

He put his hand to his mouth and hacked. The cough wasn't too much of a stretch as now he did feel sick. First thing he'd love to do was to vomit all over this one's pristine blue uniform. That would show her what he thought of her version of Orelia Mason's story.

"Aheh-ehh-ahh. I've ... aheh ... got a bad cold. Aheh. Can't stay."

"Sure. Shame, as Orelia Mason is something special," she said, as he pushed past her with his gaze lowered.

All the forced coughing had made his head spin. Now with his throat raw and aggravated, he began to cough for real, until his breath stole from his lungs.

Around him, books and shelves melted into a vortex of color and words. Even the floor seemed to shake as though he'd stepped on a twirling roundabout.

Panic rose inside his head and he wondered if he would pass out. Or something worse. Maybe the ultimate irony was he would meet his death, right here in this bookstore with Orelia nearby.

By the time he'd staggered to the door and flung it open to escape to the night outside, he'd forgotten why he was even inside the store.

The only thoughts in his mind: *something's terribly wrong. William, get far away from here.*

Something inside that store had made him sick. With all the stress he'd been under, with his Orelia campaign and what she'd done to him, this might really be a heart attack.

William made it to the end of the street and turned the corner before exhaustion and coughing overcame him and he fell against a brick wall. He leaned there for a few seconds before, without warning he collapsed, without a modicum of grace, onto the pavement.

After his head hit the ground, he had one terrifying vision, as real as anything he'd ever lived. Books, thin, wide, large and small, books and more books flying at him as if thrown by a tornado, each one hitting him with increasing force. As they landed on him, the weight built in seconds until he couldn't breathe and couldn't see.

Just before the lights went out in his world, everything became clear to him, clearer than since this whole Orelia thing had begun. Literature came to kill him because he'd been foolish. Oh so arrogant and foolish. In opening the door to Orelia Mason, he had destroyed all things precious to him and his world. His work and his dignity.

The travesty of his death here, now, was that the last words ever spoken to him were said with such enthusiasm by that girl in the bookstore.

Orelia Mason is something special.

What killed him, more than this heart attack, was dying with the knowledge he'd never get the chance to prove that statement wrong.

21

The book held a power Nem didn't understand. That ignorance, she'd told herself, was why she couldn't be completely at blame for what happened to Lacy Carmichael.

She was sorry, for sure, and guilt played around the perimeters of her conscience for years. When she grew older though and examined the results of the luck thing, she reminded herself she'd done more good than bad. Alan West and Dr. Shepherd, for example.

Sometimes bad things happened to good people. She'd heard Peg say it enough times, tutting as she did. Others believed in that truism, so why shouldn't she?

When the luck thing struck those men, she'd guessed the power came from her anger. This book and what it could do was a weapon to punish bad people. After using the diary several times again, she'd learned to control what happened, to a degree. Though sometimes she thought of the results as clumsy and unreliable.

The bonus of the way it worked was that for every minus entry which occurred, there was a positive, as though the book balanced good and bad fortune in equal measures. Sometimes she recognized the people's names and sometimes not.

The woman who'd lived in the next apartment to her. She'd sheltered her the night her mom died. She was in there. A nice lady who deserved her plus.

Lacy was a mistake, and what happened with that error wasn't revealed until much later. By then, the book had created many minus and plus entries. She grew to understand she contributed to these, made the diary aware of these bad people, somehow. That's how she'd been able to use it against Alan and the creepy therapist. But before then, before she'd learned how to control the power, there'd been mistakes. Lacy being one of them.

They had shared the same class at the school she had attended after coming to live with Peg and Ray. Nem wondered why someone so pretty, with such a sparkling personality, would befriend her.

Lacy had pounced on her as if she was a little mouse with which to play. Even though sometimes Nem sensed she was nothing more than an amusement to her friend, she reminded herself that without Lacy she'd have nobody. Already parentless, friendless certainly wouldn't help her fit in. Besides this, Peg would ask her constantly how she was doing and if she had friends. She'd grown to appreciate her foster-mother's kindness and she didn't want to disappoint her.

On the stupid day it happened, the two of them had sat eating lunch on a bench beneath a gnarled, shady oak tree which provided cool respite from the summer heat. Her friend had spent the ten minutes so far boasting of her upcoming European family vacation.

Nem had the distinct feeling the intention of this conversation was to rub her nose in a lifestyle she didn't live and probably never would. The best tactic she had found was to play along in the hope that her friend would grow tired of the game.

"That sounds awesome," said Nem, thinking it really did.

"Oh, I'm not so excited. We go somewhere *exciting* every summer and it means I've got to do whatever my family wants to do. Dullsville. We only travel overseas because my dad runs a big company, and he saves money on tax or something. I don't really understand. He always hugs me when he talks about it and says, 'Making memories with my princess is worth every cent.' Where are *you* going?"

Nem might have been only fourteen but when someone spoke down to her, she totally got the message. She understood people, more than anyone suspected. One thing she did attempt to believe in was kindness and fairness. "Be kind and you'll receive everything you deserve," her mom had told her countless times.

Lacy wasn't being kind. In fact, the way she spoke made her seem arrogant and she didn't like how she smiled when she asked Nem about her plans for summer. She must know Nem had no plans and her life with Peg and Ray was uncertain. Every time the social services woman came, she felt a quickening in her chest and a thick knot in her stomach. She had grown to love them. And she'd even shared this with her friend.

"I'm not going anywhere. Why do you ask things you already know?"

"Gee. Touchy-wuchy. Just saying. Sometimes you're so weird Nem. Must be from what happened to you with your mom. *So sad.* That's why I forgive you for acting the way you do." She said so sad in a patronizing tone as if she didn't really think it was sad.

Lacy's lips briefly curled up at the side in an unconvincing smile.

That's when Nem's temper began to burn a slow fuse. *Some friend. In fact, no friend.*

"I think this is you trying to be mean. You want me to be jealous of you. Well, I'm not. Everything works out in the end. My mom said, *life swings in ups and downs.* Mine will swing back. Peg's really nice and she might keep me. I could be her daughter one day. I don't need a fancy vacation. I'm sure my upswing will happen if I remember to always be kind."

"Oh really! What are you pretending? You sound like *Cinderella.* Be kind and be brave, blah blah. That's what that ridiculous girl kept saying in the film, right?"

"Not lame at all. Or from the movie. I haven't seen *Cinderella.* I don't go to the movies. Anyway, she wins in the end and the ugly sisters get their just deserts. Isn't that how it goes? So I'm right."

"Huh, well I bet the prince ends up being a horrible snorer and they don't live happily ever after. You and your, *my mom said this, and my mom said that.* So boring. You got to grow up. You're lucky I'm your friend. Really, you should be grateful I even put up with you. Go on, thank me. Or we won't be friends anymore."

Perhaps because Lacy mocked her mother, or she finally understood this girl was not her friend, Nem didn't push back at the anger. She had developed a way of curling her mind around the twine of powerful emotions like anger to send the luck thing outward. Right now, words should be appearing in the diary, on their own. Beside the name the little minus sign would be written. Later she could add her own phrases and comments next to the entry. She'd learned this was how she could have some control.

Lacy stared at her, blue eyes wide and demanding. She expected her apology but Nem had no intention. Miss smarty pants needed to learn a lesson. Or two. She met her friend's gaze.

"I think you're the one who'll be sorry. I don't care if we're not friends anymore. You're not a very good friend."

Lacy glowered at her and a little muscle pulsed at the side of her neck. She shook her head slowly while maintaining a sweet smile stretched across her face. When she spoke, her voice was cold.

"Well Nem Stratton, you've got your wish. You're officially no longer my friend. You won't have anyone because I'll tell everyone you're nothing but trouble. They all told me to stay away from the *weirdo.* Now I will. Hope you have a bad life. Seems as though you have exactly what you deserve. Bet your mother's glad she's dead, so she doesn't have to..."

Nem slapped the girl's cheek. She couldn't help herself and she wasn't sorry. She was livid.

Lacy raised her palm to the red mark which had already begun to appear. Without another word, she rose and marched off across the playground toward a large group of girls. When she reached them, within seconds they all looked back in her direction and laughed. Several called out taunts.

Cind-ugly-ella. Little Orphan Nemmie. Twinkle, twinkle little bitch.

Nem felt her cheeks burn and she didn't know what to do. The anger still whirled within but now embarrassment and shame had been thrown. Like kerosene to a flame, her emotions exploded but she didn't know how to handle the feelings. All she could think was to get away.

She stood, but kept her head down to avoid their eyes as she hurried to the bathroom. Anywhere to hide from their mocking laughter. So much for kindness bringing you everything you deserve. Being brave and standing up for yourself got you even less. She hoped the diary didn't see her hit Lacy. She'd been provoked, but she wasn't certain how the luck thing judged. These feelings though were what worried her. Anger like this was never good. When she lost her temper, bad things happened.

Upon arriving home after school, she rushed to her room to check the diary. Sure enough Lacy's entry, with a little minus, was there, written in the neat child's print style the book had been using since she'd first discovered it. The word *Cruelty* had appeared beside the words.

Still smarting and filled with angst and pain from what had happened earlier, Nem picked up a pencil and wrote by the name:

Mean Lacy deserves to get sick and die.

Then she paused, staring at the page as her lips twitched from side to side. Then she thought better of it and crossed out ~~and die.~~

School wasn't much fun after that, but if she was one thing, she was adaptable. So what if she had no friends? Then she would be safe. Friends were dangerous.

The girl was just a mean, stupid show-off, not a criminal. The anger had faded and ever since the argument she had ignored Nem. She must have imagined that turning her into a non-person would hurt more than teasing.

For a week or so, Nem even worried how ill Lacy might become from the diary entry. She kept seeing those words on the page crossed out but prayed that in erasing them, all would be okay. Writing in the book had been a silly reaction and she told herself to never do that again, to just be normal and walk away.

Every day she searched for her ex-friend as she entered the classroom, then exhaled in relief when she found her at her desk. Lacy looked as healthy and happy as ever and was still her loud-look-at-me persona, as always.

Of course, she'd be happy. School broke soon for two months over summer, and who wouldn't enjoy a European vacation. She was a loved princess and Nem was a nobody, not even worthy of teasing.

She didn't examine the book again for a while for fear of discovering terrible things. For she'd regretted writing her own comments against Lacy's name. The luck thing worked on emotions and that made her additional notes dangerous. Very dangerous. From that day Nem learned something, thanks to Lacy.

Once a name appeared in the diary, it was impossible to remove. Like a death sentence. Literally.

Poor Lacy. Poor, poor Lacy.

22

When William opened his eyes, he surmised instantly he hadn't died.

A lamp he didn't recognize glowed gently by his bedside. That didn't bother him nearly as much as the sense somebody else was in the room. In the dim light, he realized a person sat in a corner chair hidden by the shadows. He thought he recognized the intruder, but decided his imagination had gone to hell and come back to terrorize him.

He closed his lids to calm the whopping agony of jagged rocks inside his skull. Through the pain one question sprang to mind. Why of all the hallucinations, had that woman's doppelgänger visited him? What the hell was she doing in that chair?

The prior events rushed into his mind in a gut-churning flash. The bookstore. Orelia Mason. Morris. Hiding behind the bookshelf. Her fawning fans. Falling. His heart attack.

Of course Orelia appeared to him now; she was all he thought about these days. How clever the way mirages could trick your mind. He could swear she was there, breathing, sitting in this room—wherever this room might be—as if she had every right to be there haunting him.

The vision's stare made his skin prickle. Wow! Such a vivid illusion. He embraced the swarming feelings of fear and confusion because even a negative experience might prove useful for a story later.

The not-dying was a relief. The bring-his-enemy-down mission could continue because now he survived that encounter, he felt as if he could go another round.

He decided the Orelia Mason mirage was a positive message. *Keep going, even while facing death. Go ahead and ruin her day. Live and fight.*

Without processing them yet, events at the bookstore must have deeply wounded his psyche and confidence. This image had been constructed by his mind to remind him of his goals. He couldn't chase Orelia around bookstores or the internet forever. He needed to change things up and soon.

"Okay, okay, I get the message," he whispered, his eyes still squeezed shut. *I'll be fine. When I look again she'll be gone*, he silently promised himself.

He lifted his lids gently, carefully. The room glowed as if a setting sun had slid behind the chair making the figure's face darken and distort.

William repeated the thought *I'm okay. Be gone,* as he blinked, squeezing his eyes closed for just a second.

When he looked over again, the figure remained. Still as a statue.

What the f...? Could this thing be real? How did that work?

No, not possible.

He wanted to pull up the sheets, cover his head and hide, but that wouldn't help when the uninvited visitor was in his mind. He must be going mad. What would be worse? Her being there for real or losing his mind? Both made him feel a little dizzy.

When the apparition leaned forward he gasped. He gave his mind one more chance to lose the illusion as he blinked like the blonde girl in *I Dream of Jeannie.*

Blink the damn creature away, that's what he'd do. If he couldn't fight her in real life, he could darn well whip her ass in his mind.

"William, how do you feel? It's me, Orelia."

Blink. Blink. Blink.

"Can you talk?"

Blink. Blink. Blink.

Gah! The blinking didn't work.

"Water? You want water?"

Oh God. Oh God. Oh, God-awful. Nightmare city was real!

Blink. Blink.

Another desperate Blink.

"William?"

The imposter rose, walked toward him and reached out to ...

kill him?

No, that was him being real crazy now.

Yes, the apparition was of Orelia Mason, but he had begun to almost believe she wasn't an illusion. She sure looked real and she had the audacity to wear a smile. Not your garden variety smile either. This was a bold, *great to see you* grin, as if she had every right to be sitting in this room.

And by the way, where was he?

He raised his head off the pillow and twisted his neck left to right. Big mistake; that movement hurt. He took in a few alarming facts. A tube protruded from the back of his hand running to a liquid bag hung beside his bed. Not good. His head felt as if someone had hit him against a wall. Also not good.

As he was incredibly intuitive—thought with a sarcastic tone—he surmised this must be a hospital room, which wasn't great either. Still, a whole lot better than awakening on a trolley in a morgue.

The last thing he remembered was Orelia at the bookstore. Wait though, if he didn't know where he was until this second, how could she?

"Or—el—ia?" His voice sounded piped through cotton wool, distant and unclear.

"Oh! You're awake. You scared us. And, well I very nearly broke down when I saw you. I'm just devastated we lost touch. I sat here for hours waiting for you to wake. You know, years ago this happened to me too. I ended up in a hospital bed too. I won't bore you with the details because that was another lifetime ago. I bet your first thought was that you'd died. Same here when it happened to me."

William tried to say, *how did you even know I was here?* But only managed, "Ho-ow?"

Orelia must have misunderstood because she leaned forward and, in a conspiratorial whisper said, "The nurse on duty is a fan and let me in."

Then she patted the blanket over his chest and said, "Now you, mister, need to take better care. Not to be negative but, William Barnes, you look awful. You've lost weight. Are you eating? Seems you have low blood sugar. I told Morris you're probably working too hard on another book. Not taking time for yourself."

William replied, "Hm-hmm," wondering what the hell she was saying and what she actually meant. He hadn't *lost weight*. Lately maybe his clothes were a little looser. But he *had* eaten. Least he thought so. Didn't he eat before entering the bookstore? Did he even pick up his fork?

No, he was fine. This was her, his enemy playing mind games to divert his attention from what he must do.

And what is that right now William?

Well, for a start to get the hellish woman out of his room. Or escape himself.

He glanced at the tube on the back of his wrist and there was his answer; leaving would be difficult and she would know that. The fact she appeared here, when he was at his most vulnerable and unable to fight back, was her sending her own message. She intended to force him into actions he'd regret, like she did that night at Bountiful Books when she'd cast her spell and convinced him to help her.

The meeting, working with her, and everything that followed, seemed innocent until in hindsight it revealed her manipulative intent. This visit meant one of two things. She wanted something from him or she wanted to send a message.

He needed to proceed with caution, so he gathered every ounce of strength to attempt to outwit her and discover her plan. See, he had one up on her. She didn't know he knew what she'd done to him.

"Orelia, I, I … am, shocked…"

No, no, shocked was too strong a word. She'd think she had all the power. "Sur … surprised to see you."

A smile spread across her face and she touched a hand to her hair.

"Yes, this was a turn of fate. I had an engagement at a bookstore nearby and I was just getting ready to give a talk when a woman came running in saying a man had collapsed outside. I worried it might be one of my fans, so I ran out there. When I saw you lying there, I instantly knew why."

Oh, my, no, how could she know? She must have seen him as he left the store. A tremor ran through his veins and settled in his stomach, then exploded into butterflies trying to escape.

What did she know?

If she knew of his stalking, he could be in trouble. *Did they jail you for hiring trolls on Fiverr?* Surely misdemeanors, if they were criminal at all. The embarrassment would be terrible, and the knowledge she'd destroyed his career and won even more devastating.

"Knew," he said, feigning a weakness he no longer felt. Now with the adrenaline he could probably run a mile on a single breath.

She watched him with a gentle, concerned look which surprised him. She hadn't cared about him for two years, so what was this? He began to think of excuses in his head for what he'd done.

He'd made a mistake. Jealousy got the better of him, but he was sorry. Could she forgive him?

"Of course I knew why you'd come. Bad William."

He held his breath. Here it came. Nausea rose, and he wondered if at the very least he might projectile vomit toward her.

As though nothing was wrong and she'd already forgiven him, she smiled and pressed his arm. William shook his head to dissipate the creepy feeling of her touching him.

I'm sorry. I'm sorry. I'm sorry. Please forgive, he practiced in his mind. But he needn't have bothered.

"I feel *soo* guilty," she said. "This is my fault. You'd come to see me talk, hadn't you? A surprise. We had a silly argument and you were being the bigger man."

William exhaled, releasing the tension he hadn't known had built inside. He tried to open his mouth to agree, to continue his ruse but he laughed silently in his head. He felt saved, freed to continue his vendetta because no matter how sweetly she smiled, he would never forgive her for what she'd done.

"Now don't speak. You save your energy. I've been *soo* naughty."

William wished she'd stop saying *soo*. Didn't her editor explain the annoyance of superfluous words? The way she phrased language insulted language.

"My schedule's been crazy. Blame Morris. He's got me everywhere for this release. Sometimes I wish success hadn't happened with my first book and my days were still just writing. Then, I remind myself that would be *soo* ungrateful. Luck can go either way."

Didn't he know it.

"William, since you're so kind to forgive me I've brought a special treat. If Mohammed can't come to the mountain, then the mountain must come to Mohammed. Ready?"

She appeared positively gleeful as if this was Christmas morning and he was a child awaiting his surprise. A sudden dark thought hit him. Was she a woman who might take a pillow, push it into his face and stifle the breath from his body? For one moment, he considered owning up to everything and begging her forgiveness.

But she didn't reach for a pillow, instead Orelia walked back to the chair and pulled an object from a bag on the floor. That's how she'd do it, he realized. In that bag was a syringe and she would kill him by injecting air into his IV; untraceable and quick. He'd seen that on crime TV shows a number of times.

He closed his eyes so she wouldn't enjoy the satisfaction of his fear as she ended his life. A roar in his head drowned the wild thumping of his heart. *Thump-whump. Thump-whump.* Maybe a heart attack would take him after all. *Thump-whump. Thump-whump.*

When he heard her words, he felt a moment of relief that he wasn't about to die. Now he understood her game; and she was evil.

She had no intention of killing him because she planned something worse. Jealousy could eat you alive, and this was his punishment for allowing himself to be eaten.

She returned to his bedside, dragging the chair with her to place it by his bedside. Then she settled herself into the seat and said, "Don't you fret at what's happened. This might seem overwhelming but when I ended up where you are it changed my life. You've been *so* forgiving, here's your reward. I'm sharing a treat... an excerpt from my new book."

The bed seemed to engulf William, sucking him alive into the lumpy folds. White, crisp sheets wrapped about him in such a stranglehold his consciousness began to dissolve into knots of panic. He closed his eyes willing her to become just a mirage, to make the nightmare disappear.

"That's right, close your eyes. If you doze off, don't worry. Knowing you're okay is my reward. I'll just slip out and leave you to rest. Morris will be *so* pleased to hear you're doing well."

He wanted to say, "Hardly!" His ex-agent would *hardly* care, but no words came. A thought crystallized in his mind though. Crazy or not, he saw her plan in all its glory. Destroy his lifestyle, his work, and then torture him until he took the coward's way out. He would always be on his own because nobody would understand what she was doing. Only him, William Barnes *the has-been best seller.*

Orelia began to read. Each word pierced his heart as if the syllables were minute acerbic arrows. This assault was the final straw and as weak as he was now something had begun to grow inside. A determination to find a way to beat her.

Fiverr and internet trolls were amateur hour. Messing with her schedule was small time. To rid himself of this malicious pain in his life, he must do more. If he was to return to writing works of meaning, Orelia needed to be gone.

He kept his eyes closed and imagined all the things he might do to her including running a knife across her throat. He hated blood, but in her case, he'd make an exception. Even though he was determined to stay awake, her voice became a murmur away in the distance, beyond an ocean of gently undulating waves of words. As he fell back onto a giant book that morphed into an island an answer to all his troubles swooped down from the sky. He reached up and pulled the idea in to his heart.

This half-asleep moment was his line in the sand. The bookmark on the page of this battle for his future, his life, maybe even his soul. When next they'd meet, one thing he would do his darnedest to ensure. Orelia would not be *soo* happy. In fact, the only thing she'd be was gone. He'd played before with small tokens of revenge. Now things were about to get real.

23

---

*N*ear the end of summer vacation, Peg called Nem into the kitchen. Ray sat at the table, while her foster-mom stood at the counter pouring iced tea into two glasses.

Handing the glass to Nem, she motioned for her to sit down and said, "Would you like a slice of sponge cake, sweetheart?"

Nem nodded but was instantly concerned by Peg's seemingly forced smile. Oh no, was this the day she would be told she must leave? That they could no longer take care of her?

Her mouth felt instantly dry and she took a large slurp of the drink. How could she eat anything when her life was about to change again? She shook her head as a *no*.

"We've got some news, honey."

Peg smiled at Ray and then back at Nem, her smile was nearly as wide as her cheeks. Ray's smile was less generous, but his eyes sparkled as a piece of cake was deposited before him.

Maybe this wasn't going to be bad news. But Peg kept rubbing her hands back and forth on her arms and she only did that when she was upset or nervous. These mixed messages puzzled her; she couldn't imagine what would make her foster-mother nervous and happy at the same time.

Peg sat beside Nem and reached for her hands, squeezing them tight as if afraid Nem would run away. She may have sensed Nem's reticence because she added, "Don't be afraid."

Nem still expected heartbreaking news and her body tensed for the worst as she pushed back unexpected brimming tears. So when she heard the first words, seconds passed before she began to understand.

"We applied to adopt you a few months ago. I'm sorry we didn't share this, but Ray didn't want to tell you in case we weren't successful. We love you honey pie. The agency said our prospects were good, but nothing's ever certain with these things. But we're just so thrilled to share our news."

Now Peg's eyes brimmed with tears as she said, "We've been approved! All that's left to make it official is a hearing date in court to formalize the adoption."

She took Nem's hands between hers and Nem's focus became a single tear traveling down Peg's face to rest on her top lip.

"But it's up to you. If you want to stay here. With us. We'll be a real family." She paused and added sheepishly, "You do, don't you? Want us as parents, I mean?"

Nem's brain finally processed the information. This was amazing news and her heart felt suddenly filled with emotion. She had come to love the kind couple, especially Peg, with her big, loud laugh. But this was confusing too. Peg had only told her a few months ago that they needed the government's foster-care money. Without this, they couldn't afford to have a child.

"But I thought you said that you couldn't..."

"I know ... afford to adopt or have a child. But something wonderful's happened. We have more to share. Extraordinary news!"

Her foster-mom looked ready to burst from happiness. The grip on Nem's hands tightened.

"Two months ago, on the way home from an errand, I stopped to buy a lottery ticket. Not sure why, because I don't believe in gambling. I know someone's got to win but the chances are nil, I would have thought for someone like me, us, Ray and me."

A huge grin lit Peg's face.

"Not this time. You, my girl, have brought us good luck. Because, because ... we won! And the first thing I did was check with Ray and then the adoption agency, and yes, that money sure did help our case. Big time. I can't believe how quickly it all happened. The approval. We couldn't tell you about the money because then we might have let it slip about the adoption. And please forgive us for not being honest but we had good reason."

Nem's answer was to fling herself into Peg's arms. Unchecked tears rolled down her cheeks, tickling her face and her lips. Even through her clothes she felt Peg's warmth against her skin. These were good people and if you were kind and brave, good things came to you. This was about the best thing that could ever happen: for her to have a real family again.

She felt Ray beside her, patting her head and stroking her hair.

Peg pulled back from Nem to stare in her eyes but still held her arm. "Are you crying, little sweetie?"

"Give her a moment to take it all in," said Ray, returning to his chair.

"Happy tears Peg," Nem said, "or ... Mom? Is it okay to call you —Mom?"

"Oh sweetheart, yes, call me mom. But you don't have to. I don't ever want to replace your mother. She must've been one special woman to raise a beautiful daughter like you. Everything's so perfect. We feel like the luckiest people in the world."

A sudden thought entered Nem's mind.

"Peg? I mean Mom ...?" She paused, uncertain whether to ask the question on her lips.

"You ask what you like about the adoption, honey, or anything. I don't want you worrying your lovely head."

"Nothing like that. I'm happy too. Thank you so much." She paused, uncertain if she should ask what she was thinking, but she had to know.

"The ticket. When did you buy it?"

"Like I said, two months ago? Just before your summer vacation started. Maybe the week before, I think. What difference does that make? Please don't be mad at us for keeping it from you for so long."

"And the time."

"Ooh, oh, okay. Let's see."

Peg removed her hands from Nem's arms and rubbed at her chin, clearly casting her mind back.

"I can pretty much remember everything on that day. Don't think I'll ever forget it because I'll be telling this story for the rest of my life."

She chuckled, and Ray joined in.

"You sure will, lucky woman, and I'll never tire of hearing it," he said.

"Right, so, I'd just finished the groceries and was walking to the car. Suddenly this, this, compulsion came over me. An alarm went off in my head. *Ping, ping, ping. Get back inside and buy a lottery ticket Peg Walters.* So back I went as if an invisible hand pushed me along. Such a strange feeling that..." She paused. "You know what? I do know the time because they give you a copy of the ticket, and I'm sure there's a date and time stamp on there."

Peg rose, went to the counter and opened a drawer. She rifled inside for a moment before drawing out an envelope and from that taking out a slip of paper.

"I put it here so it'd be handy because I knew you'd want to see it."

She walked back, sat down next to Nem and stared at the copy of the ticket.

"Let me check. Ah, here it is. Time stamp is 1:23 pm, the fourteenth. A Wednesday. That I knew for sure. And look at this." She shook her head. "I'm a fortune teller too. I wrote, *Here's the winning ticket* down the side. I thought I was being funny. Can you believe that?"

"No," said Nem, although she could.

Peg continued, obviously thrilled to finally be able to share her wonderful news. "It's just like Lady Luck took my hand. When luck smiles on you, boy, nothing can go wrong."

A smile crept across Nem's face, not because she was happy,

although she was thrilled. Or because Peg looked so gleeful at discovering the exact time she'd bought the winning ticket. No, Nem smiled because everything now made perfect sense. She'd already presumed the time was the exact same moment Lacy and she argued, and she had been correct.

She might have known about this sooner but she'd had no reason to check in the diary over the last few months. In fact, when nothing extraordinary happened in her life, she could very nearly forget it existed. She'd also been a little afraid to see if anything else had appeared against Lacy's name.

She knew now if she looked in the diary, she'd find an entry for Peg with a little plus sign. Lady Luck had nothing to do with this win or Nem's adoption, and she wondered what kind of bad luck Lacy would receive for this gift. For whatever luck was coming for her ex-best friend, the one thing she could predict with her own fortune-telling skills was that it wasn't going to be good.

stress incident is what the doctor called William's *heart attack.* Orelia had been right. Low blood sugars and the lost weight (he hadn't noticed) were contributing factors. Typical, she would learn about this before him.

"Follow up with your regular doctor," said the young female physician who looked barely old enough to hold a thermometer.

William wouldn't see anyone because he knew what would fix his health problems and alleviate his stress. The cure was not rest, eating better and anti-depressants, as they'd suggested.

He'd seen that writer on 60 Minutes who'd been involved in those mass killings talking about the link between SSRIs and violence. She called herself a messenger or something equally profound.

Well, he had a message for Orelia Mason. *Get out of his life* because he didn't need chemicals to contemplate violence.

Seeing the witch in person, while a very painful thing, infused him with a passion to finally end this tussle and change his destiny. She meant him harm. All the success she'd achieved with her pathetic romance stories, had been stolen from him and drained away to fill her coffers. Her indifference to his pain from the loss filled him with only one emotion: hate.

While for months he hadn't been able to face writing anything fictional, it surprised him, as he scribbled on his notepad, how easily he created a plan. After four rewrites, the results pleased and encouraged him. In fact, he felt tingles of excitement; if nothing else he could be proud of his resilience. Most would have given up and admitted defeat by now.

He read through the pages several times and even though he wasn't a thriller writer, he certainly had the mind for crime. The only fear was that when the time came, he would not be able to bring himself to go through with it.

When questions crept into his thoughts, he only needed to think of her book ranking high in the Amazon charts and the New York Times Best Seller list. Throw in her chipper voice reciting "I'm living the dream" and he knew he'd do anything it took to stop her.

Just this morning, fate had sent him a message via the newspaper. In an article in the literary section, there was good old Morris the-betrayer-agent, suave in his double-breasted suit and smarmy smile. Some stupid journalist had written a piece on him.

The Groomer of Best Sellers

William scoffed at reading the headline, "And dropper of them when they're no longer producing,"

He couldn't even finish the article because he'd begun to feel sick again. As he rifled through his cupboards looking for a cookie to help his blood sugars—God, there was another thing to worry about now too—it occurred to him that Morris and Orelia were in this together.

Had this all been some massive plot from the start? Did Morris already know Orelia and had set her upon him at the Bountiful Books event? Maybe Morris had decided he wanted to be rid of his loser client and engineered his downfall, while feigning disinterest in Orelia's manuscript. Was that user of a man, in fact, behind this?

No, no, that didn't make sense, he decided, as he ate the stale, sweet cookies he'd found at the back of what he now noted was an empty fridge.

He remembered the hospital visit and the way Orelia smiled as she gleefully shared her insipid book. *No, those two simply attracted each other because evil, bad energy attracts its own kind.*

He couldn't help himself though and picked up the article again. He wished he hadn't. The more he read, the more bile rose in his throat as the insult traveled through his body like toxin. William had been mentioned in the article.

How dare Morris talk about him in such a disparaging manner? How dare he take credit for discovering Orelia? How insulting!

Morris Usher, agent to Orelia Mason, author of the best seller phenomenon "Back to the Start", admits, "When you read talent, it hits you in the heart. Orelia has that special gift in so much abundance, her work glows on the page."

Under Usher's management, there'd be few bookstores or supermarkets, which didn't feature Mason's novels prominently on the shelves. The modest agent, who literally plucked the unknown author from anonymity to a seven-figure book deal, says "sometimes you get lucky."

Usher met Mason through a mutual friend and their meeting "changed everything in his business." He had previously managed several authors, most notably William Barnes, who enjoyed best seller status for a short period.

Usher now spends his time "supporting Orelia because she's going to be around for years to come. Until her, I'd never realized romance can also be art. Compared to her, the rest of my clients were good, but she is a superstar."

The agent's face lights up as he remembers his initial read of his star client's book. "When Orelia's manuscript came across my desk, I was having a bad month. I even considered getting out of the business, thinking all the great books had been published and I had nothing to contribute. We'd begun to see a decline in authors' earnings and I decided I couldn't help anymore."

Usher is most likely referring to the poor sales at the time of his headline author William Barnes, whose second book "Hidden in the

Shadows" was a flop, selling way below expectations to unfavorable reviews. His third novel "Flying Toward the Sun" received an even more hostile response, selling only a few thousand.

When asked about Mason's simultaneous rise while another author in his stable faltered, Usher admits, "You can't help everyone. Some authors may only have the one great in them. The focus is now on Orelia. My job is to take care of her so she can concentrate on what she does best; creating worlds and characters readers love."

The wistful groomer of talent stares out the window of his tenth-floor office and muses, "This business has ups and downs, and some get burned. Ultimately, I tell myself, if I bring talent such as Orelia's to the reading public then I can sleep well at night."

Morris Usher will be speaking at the Walter Bridge Literary Festival this weekend on a panel How to make it in publishing the easy way.

Tickets are available at www.walterbridgeliteraryfestival.com

William stuffed a handful of cookies into his mouth because he felt faint. He presumed his blood sugar had plummeted because his head had begun to spin. Although he doubted the sick churning in his stomach was due to blood sugars.

He tore out the page from the paper, crumpled it into a ball and threw the disgusting article across the room. That didn't make him feel any better. Maybe he needed more cookies?

William looked down at his plan, picked up his pen and added three more lines to his things-to-do list. The choices Orelia forced upon him weren't good if he planned on entering heaven, but there seemed no other way.

Thanks to Mr. Wonderful Agent and the fawning article, his resolve had been strengthened. Low blood sugar or not, he'd find the energy to do what must be done. He laughed at that thought. What was he becoming now? Some kind of hero?

25

*N*em loved having a mom again. Peg and Ray Walters were people any kid would feel lucky to call parents. Although, when hugging her foster-mom with an "I love you," Nem's guilt at her feeling joy sometimes shrouded her like a descending veil.

She kept a picture of her real mother and her when she was six (taken during their one visit to a theme park). On nights when sleep did not come easily, she lay in bed wishing her own mom was still alive. They could then live happily together with Peg and Ray. The Walters were such giving, kind people she knew they'd welcome her with open arms.

What played on her mind was the idea that if she'd known about the diary before the night her mom died, maybe she might have lived. Maybe she could have used the diary to protect her. Why her mom hadn't used it herself to stop Alan, she still couldn't understand. All she did know was that a piercing ache squeezed her heart every time she tallied the *what ifs*.

Look what the diary did for the Walters. She discovered after checking that beneath Lacy's entry had appeared Peg and Ray's names along with the plus sign. Beside their name were the words:

all the money they need

In a funny kind of way, gaining a family was her reward for delivering justice. *Justice* may have been an exaggeration because Lacy and she only had an argument, but still her words had been mean, and she'd meant to hurt Nem.

Her life though had become busy. The Walters finalized the adoption and used their winnings to move to a bigger house in a very nice suburb. Remove the money barrier and of course you'll buy your dream home, a new car and take that vacation to Europe. They embarked on these fulfillment of wishes gradually as though dipping their toes in warm water to test for comfort.

Nem felt a wonderful glow inside every time Peg dragged out the vacation brochures. Such a change from their normal life. They'd gone from *where is the cheapest gas* to *where are we going on vacation*?

Nem continued her schooling. Her clothes were nicer, and the kids began to accept her after Lacy left.

That's what bothered her. Lacy.

She was the little catch behind their great fortune. Before this, she'd puzzled a lot on how the diary worked. She now thought of the book and its power as a game. Good for bad. Bad for good.

The person losing the luck suffered a misfortune, which transferred good luck to another, where things worked out just great. This trading wasn't always equal and the timing not immediate either. Lacy gave her clues to the rules.

The girl had apologized to her on the last day of school. So she'd worried through summer about what she would discover when school started, especially considering their good fortune. Would she learn her classmate or someone in her family had died, or their house had burned to the ground or another terrible fate?

First day back after school break, she discovered Lacy was absent. Something had happened; Nem knew it in her bones. The diary always had an effect. As much as she'd tried to erase Lacy's name, scribbling over the entry (it returned later the same), nothing worked. She couldn't even tear out the page because magically the words returned on the next. Once you were in the book, what was to come became inescapable.

How could she be so sure it was the book taking control of people's lives?

The ticktock feeling of cogs in her head as though she had connected to the diary's magic. Each time she sensed them move like a clicking, pieces slipping into place as she traveled along a guided path. A foggy impression of who was wrong and right invaded her mind. Doctor Shepherd, the therapist, was one chosen by the book to punish. Shaded, terrible images came to her when they'd first met, making her skin crawl. His name appearing in the book, written in bold, determined strokes was no surprise.

So she expected Lacy to be absent from school and felt terrible at the thought her classmate had been punished for a simple argument. Whatever the effect might be, she prepared herself, ashamed she'd sent the *luck thing* after her friend.

"Where's Lacy?" she said to Amy who was in one of the popular gangs.

"Sick. Bad." The girl shook her head as if the idea was crazy.

Waves of panic traveled through Nem.

"What happened?"

"Some weird brain stuff, I think. She could be a veggie. Kind of freaky, right?"

For two days Nem tried to put Lacy's fate out of her mind but she couldn't sleep. She awoke from nightmares, her body wet with sweat. When this happened she'd check the diary, hoping the sick girl's entry had changed. She even wrote her name again, with a plus sign and the words *Lacy recovers from illness.* But the sentence had disappeared by the next time.

Apparently, she wasn't in complete control of who was chosen and what happened to them. What would help was if the power came with a rule book or lessons from somebody with experience. Like that would ever happen. For all she knew she was the only person in the world to possess such a power.

Peg noticed her melancholy mood of the past few days and asked her what was wrong. When Nem confided her friend was very ill, she replied, "Well, let me contact her mom and find out. I'm sure she'll be okay."

Nem stood by her side, fighting tears, as Peg made the call.

Don't worry, Lacy will be fine, she kept telling herself, until the color faded from Peg's face. She kept repeating, "Oh no, so sorry," to whatever Lacy's mom was saying. That's when Nem knew, even before she put down the phone and turned to her. Tears glistened at the corners of her new mom's eyes.

"Sweetheart, I'm sorry, it's terrible news. At the beginning of summer break your friend couldn't stop vomiting. She had a headache for days, so they rushed her to the hospital. After lots of tests they found a tumor. Inoperable. So, so, so sad. That poor family. I told her if we can do anything, just call. They said if you want to visit at the hospital, you're welcome. Might help cheer her, although sometimes she has bad days and doesn't talk much."

Peg pushed a palm against her chest and caught her breath. The threatening tears spilled out and ran down her cheeks. She pulled Nem to her and held her in a warm embrace.

"This is a huge, terrible thing to experience at your age. Might be nice though if you go visit. Let her know you care. Every little bit helps."

A tightening in Nem's throat made it difficult for her to answer. She wondered if she was sick too. Her head felt heavy and filled with cotton balls; Peg's voice, muffled and distant, barely registered in her conscious mind.

She'd wanted Lacy punished, but not this. Her foolish hope had been Peg and Ray won the lottery by pure chance, that just this time the book didn't need to balance luck. In that moment, she hated the little pluses and minuses. They were out of control; the randomness the danger. Hideous, terrible, little marks that didn't care about anyone or about justice.

But that wasn't completely true. She, as well as the diary, had made Lacy sick. Her temper boiling over caused this, and now a girl who didn't deserve to die would suffer a shocking fate. Her family would keep the money and she must live with what had been set in motion by her lack of control.

―――――――――

Nem never did visit Lacy. Three days later Peg greeted her at the doorstep upon her arrival home from school. For this news, no iced tea, just a glass of water and a cookie.

"I'm sorry," she said with a hug. "Her mom called earlier. Lacy just closed her eyes and was gone. Thank God it was peaceful. Maybe for the best you didn't see your friend so sick. You can remember her how she was."

But Nem did see her.

Every night in her mind's eye, and in her nightmares. For a long time she saw Lacy's face contorted in pain and staring at her, angry and unforgiving. She wondered if the guilt would ever lift or would she spend the rest of her life feeling as though she wore a jacket made of lead.

She'd learned something important though that would change her behavior from now on. She realized that nothing was certain with the *luck thing,* that once freed, she no longer had complete control of what came next.

This meant she needed to keep her anger in check because otherwise she was to blame for the bad things that happened. Bad things that shouldn't have happened. Like Lacy dying.

From this grew a determination to stick to one rule she would now create. If she was ever to use the diary again, she needed to be certain of one fact. That the person deserved their fate.

*M*orris Usher shouldn't have died. His death wasn't part of the plan. Well, it was, but William had changed his mind. He'd admit, sometimes he had wished his ex-agent's demise. He realized too late, wishing someone dead and the person actually dying, felt very different.

Not to say, once the dust settled, he didn't derive satisfaction that the man who'd besmirched his work had received his due. But, as he did in life, Morris in death would cause him hell. Instead, if he had died in a far-flung exotic place like a brothel in Thailand or by shark attack in Australia, William might have enjoyed the irony. This close to home though, meant he found himself in the peculiar position of wishing Morris had survived.

In hindsight, he should have gone to the police. That idea entered his mind for twenty seconds, then panic kicked in and he ran.

Well, not ran exactly, because that would make him look suspicious. So he walked as fast as you'd walk if partaking in mild exercise and not walking away from a crime scene. Despite the slower pace he arrived back in his room breathless, as if he'd completed a marathon.

To kill somebody was tiring work.

The killing bit wasn't cut and dry. Maybe partial killing?

No, he was pretty sure his actions would be called *contributing factors*.

The terrible man had abandoned him in his moment of need in his career. Now in death, the nasty creep hitched himself forever to William, like a parasite embedded in his skin.

His first plan had been to approach his ex-agent, explain that Orelia was a witch sucking him dry and, if he was being perfectly honest, he might have thought to kill Morris. That's what he'd written in his note book. Yes, recording your murderous plans would seem foolish, but William was a writer. What he'd written could be just a simple plot outline. He had used alternate names for that very reason.

Morris was *Micky*, an unscrupulous insurance salesman, who preyed on innocent, elderly folk with no use for his services. Orelia, aka *Orange Blossom*, a surgeon, who is in hiding since killing a beloved hip-hop artist. His gang won't rest until she ends up the same way

The outline wasn't his best work, but his imagination spun a plot around the two, and with every second the idea grew more interesting. And do-able.

William never pinpointed the moment he changed his mind. Maybe because he hadn't really been serious. In one minute, murder floated through his mind, and in the next he'd become horrified to even think such a thing. For the entire day at the Walter Bridge Literary Festival, he'd sworn nothing would stop him. Deep down though he knew all the stars would need to align if anything was to happen.

He snuck in and secreted himself toward the back of the *How to make it in publishing the easy way* panel discussion. He didn't need to look at the panelists to know he wouldn't like them or care diddly about their advice on the industry. How ridiculous to say anything to do with this business was simple. He was living proof that despite talent, a fan base and success, you could still lose everything.

William knew why they titled the event as such. The festival organizers understood if they put easy and publishing in the same sentence, it guaranteed wannabe writers would arrive in droves.

For the panelists this meant money for nothing more than gossiping before an audience; an open bar at night; and complimentary luxury accommodations. If they had novels, then add the sales of those as a bonus.

He recognized Lorelai Smith up there. She was one of the acquisition editors from Harper Collins Publishing, the second largest publisher in the world.

Morris and he had enjoyed lunch with her once when Harper Collins had expressed an interest in a future book. Nothing came of the discussion and looking back William believed his ex-agent was to blame. His theory was that the traitor had instead pushed Orelia's genre trash. Even though she went with an alternative publisher, that's how bidding wars began.

Let the editors fall in love with the story, then the author and, when they're on the line, dangle the offer around elsewhere. Publishers would often bid high, not because they believed they'd make money from the deal, but so others couldn't secure the book or its author. A game of silly chess played with writers' careers.

William had feared someone from the industry might recognize him today. With one glance in the bathroom mirror this morning he knew there was no chance of that. He would have to agree with Orelia's observations of his weight loss. Unbeknown to him, he had let himself go a little.

His hair, going on four months' ungroomed, sprouted from his head, wild and kinked. Not in a good way, like Johnny Depp or Mark Wahlberg, or those photo-shopped images on the covers of the porno-romance novels. No, he looked as though someone had thrown a bucket of jelly over his head and the mess had dried in horrible clumps.

He was a writer, so he didn't check his appearance often. Only for publicity photo shoots, appearances and publishing parties would he make somewhat of an effort. All these had dissipated along with his sales, so looking in the mirror had become a thing of the past.

Something was wrong with his skin too. The color was

unripened-corn sallow and his cheeks protruded, like little plums had embedded beneath the surface.

He pushed his fingers through the mass of tangles and tried to neaten the mop. Then he stopped, because in a flash of genius he didn't see an unkempt man, but rather a perfect disguise. So he used his palm to smooth over the fringe and he rubbed so that the hair knotted even more and flattened to cover his eyes.

Faded jeans and a shapeless t-shirt completed the persona. Not because this increased his disheveled appearance but because he'd blend better. In the good old days when he would guest speak at these festivals, he'd found it amusing that the would-be-scribes attired themselves as they imagined authors dressed—in what he called comfortable clothes.

A correct assumption, but William had always thought you should earn the right to look like an author. Few attending how-to workshops would become the professional creatures to which they aspired.

Once he arrived he hurried to the workshop tent, comfortable he was just part of the throng. Inside, he dodged and side-slipped his way through the milling crowd of over two hundred, looking for a seat. He grew more confident of his invisibility, becoming as unseen as those around him were to the publishing world.

William found the perfect position where he could hide in plain sight, near the middle, twenty rows from the stage. He pulled out his notebook and pretended to be studying the contents, hoping his neighbors wouldn't bother to speak to him. The last thing he wanted to discuss was somebody's dream of becoming a best-selling author. *Get in the short line*, he'd be tempted to reply. Short, because it leads over a cliff where you'll dive to your death.

A wave of hush traveled through the tent as the host speaker bounced onto the stage. She was a blogger with enormous enthusiasm and a chest just as large, which her shirt did nothing to conceal. Easy to see how she got her *likes* on Facebook.

She wasn't a writer. Writers did not behave that way. They carried themselves with *solemn intelligence and artists' introspect.* Not bouncing around as though they were attending a block party.

The so-called popular influencer, Cassie-something, introduced a male author—rat nosed and balding—of whom he'd never heard. Whoever he was, he managed to drop the title of his book, *Bursting Balloons,* into his thirty-minute talk at least two dozen times. William counted to eighteen in twenty minutes, and then grew tired and gave up, his case proven. Rat nose, so filled with his own importance, was dull.

Two more bores droned about what fantastic and exciting opportunities existed in publishing until the man he'd been awaiting stepped on the stage. Morris Usher. His name on the program was the reason he had come.

The entire crowd hushed as if the Pope had walked across the stage to sit in the large lounge chair ready for his interview. Oh yes, agents were the shiny goal for all writer-lemming-hopefuls. Without an agent, you weren't getting that contract or the nice advance, and your book would not be gracing bookstore shelves. What they didn't understand was that these days you received only the one shot. Make low sales and you were on your own again. He was living proof of the three-strikes-and-you're-out rule.

Seeing Morris up there, preening and even flirting with Miss Social Media made him sick. He'd forgotten to bring his cookies, so he wasn't sure whether it was his low blood sugar again or just being in the same room as Morris. Even if the room was a tent.

As he listened to Morris talk ad nauseam about the *amazing* work of agents and how to write a good query letter, William dug his nails into his skin. When he recognized the pain, he opened his hands to discover in his palms little crescents marked with blood.

William should be up there on stage offering an alternative point of view. *The truth.* The conceited liar made everything sound hunky dory, so easy and exciting. But that wasn't the worst thing he did.

Then he mentioned Orelia.

Not just dropped her name in passing, no, he sprouted accolades and tall tales of how her book leaped from the slush pile. Talent like hers destined always for discovery. Same trash as that article.

What slush pile was he talking about?

William had handed her manuscript *Back to the Start* to Morris. That wasn't the original title, either. She'd called her novel *A New Hope,* until he'd pointed out that was the subtitle of one of the *Star Wars* films. Who didn't know that pop culture gem?

He leaned forward, barely breathing, wondering if Morris would mention him too, which would go part-way toward his ex-agent's redemption. If he was nice and respectful.

But he said nothing about William. For ten minutes his focus was Orelia's brilliance, her talent and, the real kicker, what a wonderful person and so humble too. What a package!

William couldn't help himself; a cough tickled its way up his throat. Once started, there was no stopping. His throat felt scrubbed with brush bristles and his breath stolen. Those nearby stared, and he realized being recognized could be a danger. So he bit down into his palm to stave off the convulsions. Through sheer will he calmed his heaving chest.

All eyes returned to the magnet of their owner's adoration: the person on stage who possessed the ability to make all their dreams come true.

What they didn't know was this agent wouldn't be available to read through any more slush piles or manage any of their careers. The man speaking to the rapt crowd now had only one destiny.

Death.

27

*A*fter Lacy died, Nem grew desperate to find a way to make amends. The guilt climbed on top of her; the weight heavy and suffocating. If Peg and Ray ever discovered what she'd done, she worried they'd no longer want her. How could anyone love someone who'd done what she did?

"The parents are devastated," Peg said, when she dared ask what would happen to the family. "Nothing eases the loss of a child. Another baby possibly? Still sadness will follow you until the day you die."

Another baby.

Nem's mind wrapped around that thought. Her spirits lifted, thinking that she may have hit upon a way to make amends. She excused herself and raced back to her room to pull out the diary. Her palm smoothed over the green cover and the tingle she always experienced when touching it, shivered through her hand.

She flipped to the recent page and tried not to look at Lacy's line. To change that event was impossible but she could make amends. Her dead friend's parents might be able to recover with the help of the power of the book.

Even before she'd made a single mark, Mr. and Mrs. Peter

Carmichael's names had appeared on the last page. The plus sign wasn't marked beside them yet. Each luck entry demanded an opposite to set the wheels spinning, like flashlights require two batteries.

That balancer would come once there was a matching minus entry. She'd have to work that one out, mindful of her new rule of not harming innocent people.

She paused, holding the pen over the paper, as she thought what to write. In her mind she saw herself handing the couple a baby. Her heart warmed at their smiles as Mrs. Carmichael took the swaddled infant and cuddled the little one to her chest. They gave Nem a nod of thanks before returning to the child, cooing and kissing her cheeks.

A smile touched her lips at the happiness she'd deliver; a pleasant rush traveled through her as she put pencil to the paper and wrote:

Mr. and Mrs. Carmichael get new baby.

She wasn't positive how well this might work. Though she was sure they'd receive a replacement baby. Of what she was less certain, was where she'd find the person who would receive the bad fortune. Nem needed to find a worthy recipient to cement the swap and deliver a baby to the Carmichaels and soothe her guilt. If she could do this, everything would be right in the world again.

This task was not so easy. It was one thing to hurt people who deserved what they got, but another to search for someone you didn't know who hadn't personally harmed you.

As if delivered to order, it took only two days before she found her *minus* person. When she came upon Vice Principal Pension berating a young boy in an empty corridor after school she was at first curious, then horrified.

The kids called her *Miss Detention,* not just because of the rhyme with her name, but because she handed out more detentions than any other teacher. Most times for seemingly nothing. Dropping a Kleenex ("Cleanliness is next to godliness."), walking too fast ("Walk or you'll be losing those legs."), untidy hair ("Have you no pride?"), along with many other minor infractions.

Ben was the kid's name. Everyone knew what happened to him. He sported a white cast on his arm, now turning ash-gray and lacking any scribbled well-wisher autographs. The kid was a bit of a 'loser' (Lacy's words not hers). His mom was a weirdo who wore too much lipstick and had creepy eyes. Her short, brown hair, even scarier, as if she'd pushed a finger into an electrical socket and then brushed the resulting mess. The effect: spiky, thick knots.

Ben had been shoved around by bullies a few weeks prior, and he'd come off the worst. She was sorry for the little boy. He had a lost, puppy dog look, and his response to Miss Detention's harsh words was an impression of a beaten animal. But her tight-lipped mouth and deep-lined frown remained unmoved.

Nem stepped back into a classroom's doorway so as not to be seen.

"... and if you were pushed, and I don't believe you for a moment, young man, you brought it upon yourself. You hear me? You can't go around calling other children flippery maggots."

Ben's head hung low, as though too heavy for his neck. The exposed skin on his chest had turned a blotchy red and his shoulders hunched so much he could be Gollum's twin.

"Well," she said, reaching out and shaking him by the shoulder, "what have you to say for yourself?"

"Yes, miss. Sorry miss."

"Miss what?"

He looked up, and the tears that rolled down his cheeks and dripped from his nose dissolved Nem's heart. The little guy didn't even bother to wipe them away. The droplets fell from his face to drip on the floor at his feet.

What a bully!

"Ye... es, Miss Pension."

"Much better. And why does your mother need to see me? I hope you told her the truth of how you broke your arm? More time wasting while I tell her exactly what happened. I'll be sharing my impression of you too and your foul mouth. You're the dangerous one. Now get out of my sight. And blow your nose, for god's sake. Call others beggars? Well that's how you look this minute. A pathetic beggar yourself."

Miss Detention turned, shaking her head, and stormed off along the hall, fortunately in the opposite direction. Last thing Nem needed was to bump into the furious woman.

Ben hadn't moved. His chin appeared glued to his chest and his arms hung limply as if drained of all energy.

"Hey," Nem said, as she walked toward him, bending to the side to catch his gaze. "You okay?"

The little boy looked up with saucer-wide eyes. For a second she imagined he might come at her and attack, like the bullies had attacked him.

Had Miss Detention been right about him being dangerous? Then he appeared to stop himself. Without saying a word to her, he wiped the back of his hand across his nose and turned away, disappearing at full run down the corridor, his arms pumping.

Whether he'd made the older boys angry or not, teachers were meant to help students and the Vice Principal obviously didn't like children. *She shouldn't be a teacher*, thought Nem. In fact, she shouldn't be allowed near a school ever again.

"Don't you worry," she said under her breath. "She won't hurt any more kids."

Miss Detention did receive her just deserts. Ben's mother, it seemed, had an anger problem too. The parent-teacher meeting the following day between the Vice Principal Pension and her did not go well. She'd brought a box-cutter and...

Michelle Reid (nice girl, but usually in trouble) discovered Miss Detention when she arrived for her own appointment with the Vice Principal. Her screams were heard in every corner and classroom of the school. *Louder than the bell*, everyone agreed later. There was blood in the meeting room. Lots, as if sprayed from a hose. Michelle was the celebrity for weeks, detailing what she'd found.

When Nem checked the book after, the line next to the teacher's name read: *non-survivor of mitigating circumstances.* She hadn't expected the bloody result delivered in her own school. When she'd hoped for a minus luck event, she hadn't seen this coming at all.

She shouldn't have felt guilty because the woman was a mean terrible person and an equally terrible teacher. But she did feel bad for a few days. Every time that little, emotional worm squirmed in her gut though, she need only think of Ben to settle it down. His tears and the curve of his slumped shoulders only strengthened her belief in the diary's fairness. It had dispensed justice as it saw fit and who was she to argue? A small pain for a greater gain; it had delivered the bad luck she'd hoped to find in order to grant her wish.

Twelve weeks later, she learned the Carmichaels were expecting a baby, and a thrilled Peg told her that they were "overjoyed." So was Nem. And once she filled up that diary page, she never gave Mrs. Pension, better known as Miss Detention, another thought.

28

The Walter Bridge Literary Festival had been held for the last fourteen years in a 20-acre manicured-to-its-last-blade-of-grass, tree-filled park, adjoining the prestigious Mary Cowan University. Like all these writing events, this one attracted more mom and pop writers than professionals.

William had earned a master's degree in literature believing this would leapfrog him ahead of the pack of hopefuls. Where did these wannabe novelists grow their belief that possessing a story idea meant a future as a writer? He'd paid his dues and groomed his patience until his best seller galloped onto the charts.

As a child, his parents taught him to bide his time and not imagine more than he deserved. Although he held no sentimentality toward them, he did heed the wisdom their actions imparted.

His father, a large man, who spent an unhappy forty hours a week behind an insurance clerk's desk, chided him often when he caught him reading. "You a fag, are you? Reading's for gay boys. You'd better think about work. How you'll contribute to the goddamn world. Get your nose out of that crap or I'll slam it down your neck so hard, you'll be shitting pages for days."

If he argued, there'd be a whack for his trouble. Once he'd even caught a punch to the head, which knocked him out. He'd been nine or ten.

Did he blame his mother for not defending him or spiriting them away? In retrospect, no. As a writer, you come to empathize with your fellow men and women because you spend your days walking in another's shoes. At the time though, he had designated more guilt to her than his father. Mothers, he'd learned from the books he read, should protect their children; encourage, love and sing them to sleep with lullabies at night.

She instead simply hid his books away. Hindsight revealed she endured far worse from the man and taking what her son loved the most was her way of protecting him.

Cancer took them both. In his mind, the disease was like the yellow Pac-Man, which ran through their veins gobbling up the anger, frustration and hatred in their bodies. Meanwhile, they ran from the ghosts. But outrunning ghosts always ends with them catching you in a corner.

That was years ago, and he was now able to read without hearing the Pac-Man munching tune. *Wha-ka, wha-ka, wha-ka.* He allowed those yellow munchers to eat his inhibitions and fears until he believed in his future as a novelist.

Funny enough, he imagined they'd be proud of him right now. Proud, not of his success as an author, but of his determination to fight his enemy and her invasion of his world. His father had never taken anything lying down and now neither would William.

After his bellyaching over Orelia and Morris the time had arrived to set the ghosts upon them. To walk the talk. The more Morris' voiced droned, the louder the squeaky Pac-man sounded in his head.

Wha-ka, wha-ka, wha-ka.

His words blended into each other.

Blady-blady-blah to win a publishing contract.

Blady-blah-blah how to write your submission letter.

Blady-blady-blady-bleh how agents earn their commission.

He wanted to stand up and shout: *Nothing. They do diddly squat for their commission. Mother-suckers!* But tumultuous applause engulfed the room.

Shimmering rage bubbled inside him, folding in on itself as if the twisting, dark monster came more alive with each passing second. The Pac-Man missed many of those glowing dots so his anger flamed unchecked. He felt a scream build in his throat and suspected if he didn't get out of there, he would lose all control. And he'd brought a gun.

Had he intended to use it?

Maybe. He sensed an invisible line embedded in his psyche which he struggled to cross. The violence he would perpetrate was only in his imagination. He felt a barrier, possibly built by his mother, which pushed back at him each time he took a step closer to the edge of no return.

At his angriest as a child, his mother would hold a forefinger to his lips, and say, "Shh, walk away."

He'd done just that; got out of his childhood and the house, alive and functioning, and enjoyed undreamed of success. Right now, if he walked away he could rebuild, couldn't he? Write another book. Find a new agent. Take pleasure in the process instead of bowing to the pressure of producing some mythical, magical manuscript which might win awards and critics' acclaim.

"You need luck too. And stamina," he heard Morris say from the stage. Spoken with such conviction, he'd convince almost anyone.

"Nobody can snap their fingers and make it happen." His ex-agent snapped his fingers for emphasis.

William had a *wow* moment with that click. A veil lifted, and the world changed color as if someone turned on a light. He saw clearly, as if the words had been painted on a board, he was as much at fault as anyone. How did he not see that from the start?

He had tortured himself to a near breaking point, and here he was sitting in a hot tent, surrounded by poor hopefuls, like himself; Morris, sprouting clichés for all he was worth; and Orelia probably not giving him or his reviews and little pranks a second thought.

He was the one who needed professional help. This vendetta had taken over his life. If he continued, he saw now he'd be forever chasing ghosts and end up like his father. Bitter and lost. If your answer to fate's twists was anger, violence and revenge, then you would disappear down a dangerous rabbit hole.

This morning, staring into the mirror at a stranger, then the crazy idea of attending this event (correction, stalking at this event) had brought him to this what-the-hell wake-up moment.

The tent had grown increasingly more stifling as if he sat in the center of a hot furnace which piped the air about him. On his forehead, drops of sweat beaded. Even his palms felt sticky and moist. William undid the top button of his shirt but that had nil effect. He looked to his left and right, but nobody else appeared to match his discomfort. They all continued to stare, mouths agape, at Morris like a pack of hypnotized zombies. Lights barely on and only the animals left at home.

"And that's why... should put... odds in your... favor."

Morris' voice crackled in and out as if his microphone was faulty. The fault wasn't in the mic, it lay in William's head. The wires in his brain had crossed and tangled. The backs of people's heads blurred in and out of focus, and his heart hit the super-pump button; next stop heart-attack.

He wiped his hand across his brow and stared at his palms. They were wet and pale. His hands looked sick. He felt sick. Tight bands of pressure wrapped about his chest and squeezed. The air thickened, at least he thought it had because he now struggled to catch his breath.

Get out.

The words smashed into his mind as if someone else had hopped inside his head. Not his muse or his mother or father or that distant subconscious voice who occasionally spoke sense. This voice was a giant, forceful nag who didn't seem to care that William was already in great distress. Shouting in his head was no help at all and he sensed he'd get nowhere arguing.

Get the hell out of here!

Okay, too bad if they recognized him. If he fainted again (which seemed his go-to response lately) that'd be worse. Maybe that was thanks to the voice; it might have control of his brain like an alien invader.

Should he faint, should he be discovered, he doubted he'd convince Morris or Orelia a mere coincidence had placed him at two events of theirs in one week. No, the game would be up. The sweet irony, that he'd already decided to stop, would be all he would enjoy.

Fate hated him and he needed to accept that.

Get out now! Leave.

Yes, I'm going, he silently screamed back as he half-rose, stopping at a crouch. He then proceeded along the aisle (why hadn't he sat on the end for a quick escape?), excusing himself as he side-maneuvered along the narrow gap. Nearly at the end, he almost lost his balance when he tripped over a woman's bag placed in a most inconvenient spot.

By the time he cleared the row and reached the aisle, his panic had him close to hyperventilating. When he burst from the tent into the afternoon sun, he had to stop and grasp the canvas wall to steady himself.

Deep breaths and calm, he told himself.

The human bustle of hundreds of bodies milling, walking and talking, surrounded him. Little bees, they were. Little, idiot bees seeking flowers which contained no pollen for them. Flowers controlled by the elite and only open to the anointed few.

The buzzing increased even as he managed to gain his breath and bring some calm to his mind. A migraine perhaps was on its way. Low blood sugar maybe around the corner. He probably needed to just get away, like the voice said. And sit. Just sit. And soon, because his skull felt as though it vibrated like a dentist was mining a cavity in there.

He wasn't getting back his life. He was giving more of it away to Orelia because of his obsession. Once he got these bees out of his head, he'd work out how he could live with that revelation. Right now, he needed to dunk his head in cool water and flush his mind.

Get away.

He didn't like the voice, but its insistence forced him to listen. It was right too, he needed to get away to somewhere quiet.

Off to his right he spied a path which wound down to a quiet section of a river which formed one boundary of the park. A wall of tall trees, dotted in between with weeping willows, hid the secluded spot. He'd discovered the place a few years ago at this same festival, when he had been one of the speakers (back when people would listen to him). A memory of once sitting beside the fast-flowing water, considering his marvelous future, dragged at his mind.

Come on, get moving!

Well, the voice wanted him to go and that seemed as good an idea as any other. He would go there, and in the quiet beauty decide his next move, decide how to live without the future he'd once imagined.

That thought made him sad, which led him to think about the plan he hadn't completed, which led him to hope that the demanding voice didn't know he still had the gun in his pocket.

29

*N*em had learned through the years to duck and cover, and bob and weave. She tried to stop using the diary, which was easier said than done. Sometimes she felt as though the book had its own agenda.

In her last year of school, she'd given up trying to fit in. Always a niggling worry would intercept any hope she harbored of friendships with other girls: the fear she might accidentally cause some innocent person's death crossed her mind. But really, that wasn't the whole truth, because on the odd occasion, she engaged in a little purposeful luck swapping.

Small-time stuff where nobody even got sick. They tripped over bags and random objects, fell asleep at inappropriate times (that was sometimes very funny), failed exams or lost things. Nothing really. Others who'd shown kindness, teachers and people deserving a break, well, they enjoyed unexpected good fortune in many ways.

She'd grown creative, even as she grew more careful to not overuse the diary. She pondered at times if there was a limit to the swaps. After all, the book had a finite number of pages, and she couldn't know what lay in the future.

Her adoptive-parents never wanted for anything, health or otherwise, and Lacy's mom and dad did receive a healthy, new baby. Sometimes she reminded herself of the good achieved when guilt crept into her heart in unexpected moments.

No, she probably didn't play the friendship game because the other girls just weren't of interest to her. They talked about the inanities of teenage life and Nem just didn't care. She'd seen too much, delivered already too many life lessons. She didn't even look like them, as if she was an alien creature placed on earth to observe the local fauna.

When Nem looked in the mirror, the supposedly beautiful teenager Peg assured her she was, did not look back at her. She saw a leaning-to-overweight girl, with dark, style-defying hair no matter how much product she fluffed through the strands. Her ears stuck out too far; and brown eyes are beautiful when they're big and round and not squinty like hers.

So what happened on the last Friday of October, ironically only days before Halloween, shouldn't have been a surprise. She always looked back on that day and thought of it as the day she learned her most valuable lesson about the diary. That she had about as much influence over the book's distribution of luck as she did in stopping the tides. She finally understood, this wasn't a matter of practice makes perfect, but if she wanted any control it was her feelings she needed to tame.

To her credit, she had developed a way of keeping her anger in check by imagining emotions as jelly held in containers. If the jars started to leak, she'd flick the switch and lock-in the emotional energy. What she couldn't have known was that holding in feelings was only delaying the inevitable.

Nem entered the English class and took her usual seat, back, far right, to stay out of anyone's sight. As she pulled out her book, she noticed Annabella. The girl reminded her of one of those preening models in game shows, who walked across the screen, their hand outstretched toward prizes. They seemed to be saying, "Aren't I gorgeous?"

Annabella leaned forward to Angie Capel (a smart-mouthed,

redhead) and whispered something and Nem heard her name just before both girls began to giggle.

Angie, and her nasty pals Annabella and Shayna, ruled the corridor between rooms 21B and 24B like security cops, and they were mean. She and the diary could put an end to their rule, and she'd considered it many times. Except, she wasn't sure if things might escalate as they did with Lacy.

Anger and the *luck thing* didn't mix well. They seemed to be a volatile recipe for disaster.

Nem should have ignored them in class, as she had done in the past. Maybe it was the wrong time of the month, or all those times she'd thought about sending a little misfortune their way had left remnants of punishing them in her mind. But it only took an instant reaction to start something she couldn't stop.

"What are you laughing at?" she said to the giggling Angie.

Angie's giggles faded to a smirk, then a frown and finally a sneer.

"Are you talking to me like we're buddy-buddies and I have to tell you what and why? Are you my mom now?"

A flicker of heat tickled at the back of Nem's neck. She shut the switch on that and calmed herself.

"Sorry, I thought you were looking at me. Forget it."

Angie glanced at her friend, tilted her head and shrugged her shoulders as if to say, "Shall I give it to her?"

She stood and crossed to Nem's desk and proceeded to tap her long fingers across the plastic desktop as if she was playing a piano.

"You know weirdie-woo, we're onto you. As much as I love a good laugh, it's kind of mean what's going on here."

The heat rose again, not just on the back of her neck but deep within. Her cheeks reddened, even as she desperately pushed at the off switch in her mind. She saw the small, jagged splinters appear in her jars; they weren't going to hold.

"Really, I'm sorry Angie. My mistake."

Nem turned back toward the front of the class and willed the teacher to appear.

"No, we're sorry for you. They shouldn't let you be here. It's not fair to you. Little weirdies should be stored far away from *normal* kids."

Annabella giggled and the others nearby twisted, leaned or shuffled to gain a view of this exciting diversion.

"We don't appreciate you sitting so near. Not good for our air."

Nem heard the cogs turn and push against the jar.

They crunched and whirred and slid and there was nothing she could do to stop them.

Ticktock. Ticktock.

A grind, then a click echoed in her head as an altered destiny fell into place.

Darn, darn, darn! This wasn't what she wanted. Not while anger had escaped into the mix. She saw the diary in her mind and the entry she imagined would appear.

Let it be something small, she willed.

A trip over a curb or a fall down the stairs. A broken arm or leg. Anything minor, anything from which you could recover. What about if the girl's hair fell out? She laughed to herself and that broke the spell and released the pressure.

So she begged because she'd never tried that before. She'd always just let the diary have its way. Yes, it might accept her written suggestions on occasion but most times it seemed to interpret them however it saw fit.

Okay, let's go with that please. Please, please let Angie Capel lose her hair.

The little wheels rolled—*tic-tic, ticktock*—and moved, as the magical power of the diary shifted and spun, until it found its slot. To her, it felt as if one piece moved, so another could align and serendipity could spin a different version of the person's life. A worse version they wouldn't enjoy.

When she turned her head to face her tormentor, her anger evaporated like a puff of steam. Angie didn't understand this round was lost and that she'd never stood a chance.

"Things won't end well if you don't leave me alone," Nem whispered. She instantly regretted the melodramatics because it only served to prove the taunts true: she did sound like a weirdo.

"Not end well for you maybe, weir-die-woo!" laughed Angie.

She thought to say something eloquent but there was nothing more to add that would make sense to anyone but her. Angie would soon eat humble pie if the diary accepted her wish. See how confident she felt when things didn't go her way.

In Nem's mind she saw the girl bald and crying in her bed and that gave her some satisfaction.

When the girl's hair did fall out in big clumps, revealing patches of white scalp, Nem wasn't sorry in the beginning. Later though, when she learned the cause of Angie's baldness, it did cross her mind, she'd made another mistake.

Hair falling out was a side-effect of chemo-therapy, and she hadn't considered this when she'd begged for the diary to deliver her wish. On the bright side, she had learned a valuable lesson. Never underestimate the power of anger or the diary.

30

When William first noticed the figure sitting on the bench beside the river, the intrusion into his plans annoyed him. He wanted to be alone to think. He wanted to take out the gun, hold it in his hand, and play with the idea that wouldn't let him alone: that the small weapon snuggled in his pocket was a way out of the disappointing mess of his life.

He'd wandered around the park for a half-hour, dodging casual strolling people by slipping into the trees and bushes by the pathway. If someone was stalking him, he must have looked ridiculous. Unsure what he intended to do, he wanted to remain unnoticed.

By the time he slipped from the tree line, shadows had begun to flow over the landscape and alter the peaceful atmosphere to one better suited to a late-night thriller.

He sat down on a wooden bench facing the river, took a deep breath, and surveyed his scenery. Lights from houses and buildings, way across on the other bank, twinkled on as dusk descended. The river, normally a murky green-brown, darkened to take on the color of swirling oil. The faux turn-of-the-century, green gaslights dotted along the path flickered to life, bathing the area in gentle, gold light.

Yes, this would do well as his last image of this earth. He could close his eyes and imagine slipping into the river, to be dragged under by currents and dissolving into the cool blackness.

Upon hearing that thought, he panicked. Was he really considering this? Was that the loud voice again or was this him? Truly him. His truth. Maybe it had come to this because without his career and without his Orelia obsession what did he have, but nothing.

The idea though had merit, and he told himself this might be the only way to rid himself of her and the pain in his chest every time he thought about the loss of his success.

It was only as he took a final glance around to check if he was alone before bringing out the gun, that he saw he had company. At first, he told himself he'd made a mistake, that his mind, so close to losing all threads of any sense had manufactured a mirage. He seemed so real though that he soon dismissed that idea and decided it really could be him.

If it was, that begged one question: Why was Morris sitting here by the river?

Then the bossy voice which he'd begun to hate, replied, "Why *wouldn't* Morris be here, in this exact spot, at the crappiest moment of your life?" Said moment being one tick past can't-take-this-shit-anymore.

He might be here to help William pull the trigger. Wouldn't that be fun and dandy? Despite the dark and somber moment, William laughed out loud at the idea of Morris explaining he'd like to handle everything for his clients, suicide notes included. *"Remember, William, you signed a contract. I get fifteen percent of everything. Forever. Even after you pull that trigger; that's a binding deal, buddy."*

Wait a minute. What if this is like that soppy Christmas movie, "It's a Wonderful Crap-Crap Life?" The one where an angel is assigned to save the life of the poor sap played by Jimmy Stewart. The bumbling fool convinces the Stewart character his life really is wonderful. *Yahoo, yippidie-doo, and they all lived happily ever after.*

Maybe fate has a twisted sense of humor and this was Morris' chance to redeem himself by proving to William *It's a Wonderful Career.*

Well, no he wouldn't buy into that. He wasn't here to save him. He probably wasn't here for William at all. That was just his own crazy imagination on fire from the stress of facing reality.

So if he wasn't here for William, then what was he doing sitting on that bench instead of sipping cocktails in the green room or taking manuscripts from wannabes after his scintillating presentation? Maybe it wasn't even him. But, it sure appeared to be him even from this distance. Well, he could spare a few minutes to see how this little twist eventuated. Why not? He had nowhere else to be.

He studied the Morris look-a-like and watched with increasing curiosity as the man drew something from his shirt pocket. Just that one movement told him he wasn't imagining anything. The way a person moved was as personal as a signature. This guy moved like the agent; he'd seen him pull his card out enough times to recognize the tilt of his head, the angled movement of his arm.

Well, wasn't that good and dandy? Here they were, together, staring into the same river. This couldn't be accidental.

A sign perhaps? Life telling him to *wait, you have a future.*

He saw the headline of an imaginary article reporting on the rise of his next book to the top of the charts.

Saved by Serendipity.
    An inspirational story of loss and perseverance.

People would read it and go buy his book just to support him, to say thank you for giving them a nugget of hope.

About to give up on life, William Barnes has a chance meeting with an old friend. Instead of taking his life on that fateful night, he writes his comeback best seller.

Didn't some celebrity like Oprah say fate slaps you on the side of the head if you didn't listen and keeps slapping until you do? Well, he was all ears now. Maybe now was the time to ask the question of Morris he didn't have the courage before to ask.

What did the almighty Orelia Mason have that he did not?

By the time he'd decided to stand and walk over to the shadow figure, the river had transformed into a rippling, black mass of water. They were still alone, which it occurred to him was unusual in a park this size. Fate, maybe setting the stage?

If he had maintained any thought of following through with his murderous plans, this had become a perfect spot. Morris was a sitting duck, *quack-quack*. He didn't even notice he had company.

But if God, Joseph or anyone else watching from above, had sent anyone down to save him from making a mistake, either with his life or Morris', they'd find they'd wasted a trip.

In fact, as he drew nearer to Morris, his melancholy, hopeless mood disappeared; he felt refreshed as if the gentle breeze whisking leaves along the riverbank pathway blew the pain from his soul. Now he burned with simple curiosity.

Morris sat with his head in his hands. The arrogance William associated with him, non-apparent. Puzzled, he paused, staring at the man and wondering what he should say. His ex-agent had made himself perfectly clear in their last conversation. Had he anything to gain by confronting him now? His *it's-a-wonderful-goddamn-fateful-intervention* bravado evaporated in the fifteen steps he'd just taken.

Morris sat back but continued to stare at the water, unaware, it seemed, that he was no longer alone. He shook his head and mumbled something to himself.

Less than forty minutes ago Morris had postured on stage as the confident agent representing one of the hottest authors on the planet. Now he looked more broken and lost than William. A ghostly, paler version of himself.

Morris stood and walked toward the river, so lost in his own thoughts he still hadn't seen William. He stopped a few paces back from the edge, hesitating as though surprised to find himself so near the river.

William held his hand against the outline of the gun. None of this felt right, as if he'd walked into a play and nobody had given him the script. He began to wonder if making his presence known to Morris was even a good idea. Should he turn around and head back along the path and leave him to whatever he was doing?

Morris' behavior made no sense. Now he moved from one Italian-shoe-clad foot to the other, rocking his weight left then right, forward and back. He looked like a sapling blown by a gale wind. He looked like a man contemplating something terrible, the same action William had just been considering.

Was Morris Usher about to kill himself?

William had arrived at the festival determined to kill this man and avenge himself. Here he was now thinking he should speak and interrupt whatever plans Morris might have made.

You'd better do something, the damn voice in his head insisted. For a minute he wondered if it was an angel from that film, but then he was doddery and sickly sweet, where this voice was demanding as hell.

Morris shuffled a little closer to the edge and William stretched an arm out toward his back. *Boy, he sure looked like a man ready to jump.* Maybe William should ignore the boss-voice in his head and let him.

He wondered though, if he did nothing would that make him just as much a killer as if he cocked the gun and pulled the trigger.

What if he's in the same boat as you?

If Orelia Mason caused his downfall, maybe she'd also turned on her agent. Now that might be of benefit to him because he wouldn't be alone anymore. They could join forces and fight her.

Are you hearing yourself? This man threw him into the wind like a used napkin. Whatever is his problem, he could find his own way out.

Wait a minute though, if two of them put their heads together, maybe they could find proof of Orelia's deeds. This might be his only chance to discover answers, and though watching Morris suffer might be a satisfying reward, that would be only William cutting off his nose to spite his face.

What he needed to do was talk to the man. So he reached out and slipped his hand over the man's shoulder and said, "Morris! Morris..."

He expected him to turn around, surprised to see his ex-client, but Morris didn't seem to hear. As if sleepwalking, he took another step closer to the edge.

Six feet below the man-made concrete wall bank, the river swirled, and William knew without a doubt he had only seconds to save the man. Somehow, without even trying, he'd become a second-class angel intervening in a life. As he pulled at Morris' jacket, he wondered if he succeeded in saving him, would he earn his wings. Right now though, he'd settle for getting some answers.

31

Nem blew out the glowing candles on the cake. Twenty-seven extinguished with one loud puff.

She looked up at Greg, beaming by her side, and smiled back.

"There! I've saved us from a fire hazard. Pay me later."

He swooped an arm around her waist and kissed her on the head.

"So noble, young Padawan."

"Yeah and I'll kick your nerdy butt if you reference *Star Wars* again on my birthday. You know that good force, bad force stuff is lame, right? It doesn't exist. Not to mention it's commercialism, big time."

"Okay, okay. Wisdom, this of, I will speak no more."

Nem rolled her eyes.

"Seriously! You're the only girl offended by Star Wars."

"That's because I'm smart."

"And I'm not? Nice."

Nem shook her head and sighed.

"Take it how you like Sir Nerd. Thought Jedi read minds?"

"If I was you, Princess-Lame-Humor, I'd be careful with the name-calling. This royal geek has a surprise."

Greg reached into his jacket pocket and pulled out a small box covered in gold paper and tied with a pink ribbon. Before Nem could say, *you know, I don't enjoy surprises*, Greg fell to one knee and looked up at her.

"Nem Stratton, I love you and your quirky, mysterious ways."

Then he paused, more uncertain than she'd ever seen him. He took a deep breath and continued. "Please do me the greatest honor of coming over from the dark side and living in the light, until the day we die? Which I pray is a long way off. Like a hundred million years."

Nem stared down at Greg; inside a dozen emotions swirled. Happiness, excitement, gratitude, hope, pride. For one glorious second, her joy was so pure, she wanted the moment to never end. Then in an instant, swarming blackness entered her heart and devoured those feelings. She wanted to cry, stamp her feet and shout at the gods, in which she didn't believe, by the way. Life was sometimes too unfair.

Tears stung at the corners of her eyes. She blinked several times, trying to hold them back but a drop still slipped down her cheek.

Oh darn. Now he'll think I'm crying for happiness and I'll accept his proposal.

Nem would have loved to have said, *yes.*

Greg was adorable and Nem might even love him, and that made this so achingly difficult she could scream. This relationship should always have been temporary, but she'd begun to enjoy herself. Fun had equated to foolish.

Her mind darted around, looking for a reply that sounded believable and contained minimal hurt as to why they shouldn't marry. Then over the following weeks and months, she'd dial down her enthusiasm and he'd leave, eventually.

Peter, her first love in her early twenties, deserted when her answer had been *no.*

This, despite her attempt to explain to him and share the truth. He laughed at her, making her angry, and she'd allowed herself that anger; never a great idea. When he left without a fight, she felt only gratitude knowing he'd be okay.

Greg would survive too but not if he stayed with her.

The ability to control her darker emotions had improved over the years, but there was no guarantee. If he knew her secret, he might not have labeled her a princess. She'd be closer to Darth Vader, the young version who tried to stay on the good side but his rage drew him away.

Of anyone, Greg the great dreamer, sweet *Star Wars* nut, had the best chance of being the one who understood. But Nem didn't dare take that path, which could fork at any moment into unknown, dangerous and terrifying destinations.

Marriage and children were a no-no because she'd learned the world didn't work the way everyone imagined. Her child could inherit the duty of the diary, as she sometimes called this, and that wasn't fair. After many years, she still worked hard at managing her feelings, guilt and sadness, surrounding the things she'd done.

In quiet moments, she wondered if she should do more. There'd been no rules given to her. She'd made everything up. She stumbled, even fell, losing her way in the enormity of the power she'd inherited through her mother's death.

In Greg's case, she'd run scenarios of *if she said this and he said that*, maybe this might work. Then she'd fast forward her future-life story to their imaginary child and Nem making the wrong choice, as did her mom. The story switched to the likeliest outcome: Nem standing beside a grave or attending a funeral, crying in the front row and hoping nobody put two and two together as to why those closest to her seemed to encounter such bad luck. Coincidences only explained misfortune for so long.

Greg still stared up at her, the big sap. More than ever, she wished she'd stuck to her three-date rule. Too late now. Shoot her for being human. Her curse, as she sometimes called it on bad days, or duty on good, had brought her to a crossroads.

Alan West's death was the good. Dr. Shepherd, another. The strange scrawling writing she'd grown accustomed to reading, delivered his name. After reading what he'd done and could continue to do, she was glad to send him his just deserts. She had meant to stop him, not kill him though. Killing hadn't entered her head.

Righting the wrong was a better description. But those were early days.

What gave her the mandate to decide another's fate? Or hand over judgment with little proof except words on a page? This confused her at first. She was too young for that power but she grew into it, taking less and less delight in looking into their eyes and seeing the fear.

A weapon to right wrongs, that's me.

As time went by, she understood there were consequences to her actions. Everything wasn't black and white as seen through a child's viewpoint. Worse, she didn't always have control. When you've never learned how to drive, there's a great chance you'll make a mistake, cause an accident.

Sometimes she'd injured others beyond what they deserved. Sometimes even good people died. This was the price for delivering justice to those who did evil. Like Alan West. There was no guilt over him and she bet her mom smiled down with pride. After all, her mom did a little vigilante work herself. If she'd only shared the secret with her daughter before her murder, she may have lived. Perhaps secrets were the reason she died.

As Greg stood and grasped her hands, his face like an expectant puppy awaiting his reward, her heart shimmered with pain. How could she do this to him, to her, to them? When she opened her mouth to say "no, I can't," she felt as though a wind blew through her mind, stealing away her will.

She heard her answer as if it had been spoken by someone else, and thought, *I'm going to regret this for the rest of my life.*

32

When Morris turned to face him, his appearance made William gasp. He couldn't have been more surprised if the man, who he'd once considered one of his greatest allies, had grown fangs and cat-slit eyes. Copious tears ran down his face and he looked desperate, like a trapped, startled animal. Then at seeing William his mouth fell wide open as his head cocked backward in obvious surprise.

"Morris? Are you okay?"

His ex-agent continued to stare at him as if processing this new scenario only to find he kept arriving at the wrong answer. William wondered if he should reach out and pull the man away from the water's edge in case he jumped right there and then.

Morris still hadn't said a word. Odd, as he was never short of an opinion. The whole scene felt surreal. The dark river, the lamplight, Morris acting like a zombie. And the tears. Now that was bizarre.

The agent half-turned and looked back across the water, then as if finally coming to a decision, he swung to face him. If he attempted to kill himself at this moment, big trouble would come looking for him. Big, big, you-have-motive trouble. So William began to talk, saying anything that sprung to mind.

They did that in the action films when someone took a one-way walk on a ledge. His thoughts wandered as he considered if many people really died jumping from a height. Certainly, you didn't see it in the news. Guns, pills, razor blades, yes. Not so much step-into-the-air-and-bye-bye suicides. So why did they feature so much in movies?

Oh, where was his mind? He was all over the place, but he snapped his attention back to Morris, his once-sworn enemy whom he now wanted to help. For a very good reason. This man kept a secret. And that secret might hold the answer to lifting the Orelia Mason curse from his life. He needed to win his confidence and that was all he cared about at this strange, Twilight Zone second in time.

"Morris, I saw your talk. I'm sorry... I... I wanted to say something to you. Need to apologize for, I guess, not doing a better job with my books. I've been..."

Morris shook his head once, as if in agreement, while holding up a palm, seeming to indicate William should stop talking. The same hand swiped across his eyes and cheeks to wipe away the tears.

"William... I'm surprised to see you. And, ah, I should be the one saying sorry. I have been sitting here thinking. Going over it. You and her. Me. I've learned a few truths lately. Seen things I can't explain. I had considered telling you but if I did, you'd think I'm crazy."

He waved a hand toward the trees, toward the festival area. "That person on stage back there, he's me on auto-pilot. This began two days ago, and my head's been a complete mess since. Not even sure how it started."

William remembered when they first met, and the growth of their friendship, as Morris helped him achieve the wild dream of publishing his novels. Then, for no reason he could find, that relationship ended. Sure his book had bombed, but did that fully explain his attitude change? This Morris wasn't the friend of years ago and he also wasn't the callous, arrogant man, who in recent times, had hung up on him. This Morris had lost all bravado and appeared broken and even desperate around the edges.

This close, he saw his disheveled appearance; his messed hair through which agitated fingers stroked; his crumpled suit with a stain near his loosely pulled tie which drooped like a necklace. Had he been sick on himself? He looked remarkably different from his stage persona or the outraged Morris at Orelia's sabotaged bookstore talk.

"I don't understand Morris. Are you ill?"

"What can I tell you? If I say more, I'll be in danger. So many have ended up damaged, ruined. We, we, shit, we argued..."

His voice trailed off as he looked around, his head twisting side to side, as if he feared being overheard.

"My suggestion is to get away, forget me, forget... please, you don't want to mess with her."

A winding thread of worry slithered in William's stomach. If his ex-agent meant Orelia—and who else could he mean—he was already messing with her.

"Listen William, she knows what you're doing. She's not somebody to play with and she's unforgiving. And dangerous."

An idea entered William's head. Orelia might be behind this, a predator literally hiding in the tree line, she and Morris in cahoots. This could be a trap. Could his ex-agent be wearing a wire as part of a plan to discover everything he'd done?

Then again, how would they have known his plans, that he'd be here at the festival, and now by the river? No, he had to believe the desperate Morris Usher standing before him, was as afraid as he appeared to be.

William took a step with his hands out, mindful that in body language open arms meant nothing to hide. He instinctively felt that this man wanted his help; that he was being honest. They'd both somehow been caught in something bigger than themselves. That wicked joker Serendipity had brought them here to this riverbank park at this moment for a reason.

"Morris, I don't know what you mean, but let's talk. If you are talking about Orelia being dangerous, then I'm with you pal."

"No, Shhh," he replied, holding a finger to his lips, glancing around as if he expected a wild animal to spring from the trees and tear him to pieces.

"Listen buddy, okay, you need to calm down. Whatever's happening, together we might figure it out, right?"

William took another step forward, but he didn't like the way Morris' eyes flickered back and forth from him to the river to the trees. He tried to put a smile on his face to say *you can trust me*, while reaching out with the intention of placing a hand upon the terrified man's shoulder.

But Morris extended his palms, indicating he should stay back, as if he was contagious.

"Calm down? Impossible, because..."

What happened next played out in slow motion, even in his memories later. William always pondered that to be within inches and to have failed was crazy bad luck or timing, or maybe just stubborn destiny. He might as well have been a mile away, for the good it did in preventing what followed.

William's hands briefly connected with Morris' body and he'd thought, *good, now I've got him.* His ex-agent though, at the exact same time, moved several steps back. It felt as if William's touch had, instead of saving him, put terrible things into motion.

In his frantic frame of mind, instead of giving in to William's offer and suggestion of calming down, Morris took one step back too many and missed the bank's edge. This misstep was enough to topple Morris backward, his arms flailing in the air like helicopter blades.

William reacted, rushing forward to grab hold of one of those helicopter arms. His mind blank except for the one thought that he must save Morris. He couldn't lose his only chance to discover the truth. Not this way. Not when he'd finally found a possible ally. But nothing would stop Morris from falling. His foot was already off the edge and he was gone into the river below.

William heard a giant splash in the darkness and made it to the edge in time to see Morris already dragged several yards along by the strong current. Even then he thought there was a chance he might be okay, until he saw his head duck under the surface and his arms splash madly about him. That's when he understood Morris couldn't swim. And neither could he.

This left him with no alternative but to watch helplessly as his only chance of discovering more answers had been dragged away fighting for his life. If it wasn't such a terrible tragedy, he may have found humor in the thought his amateur, aborted homicide might have ended in a perfect murder.

33

*A*ccepting no for an answer was not Greg's way. When Nem said "I'll think about it" to his marriage proposal, he simply kept on asking.

Every single day.

Nem thought he probably adhered to the *Star Wars* mantra too seriously. All that force stuff made him believe in his invincibility and that everything would work out in the end.

Nem knew differently, but she wanted to believe in a happy future too. She wanted a normal life with a husband and kids like in the movies and the books she loved to read. Her real life was sometimes closer to a horror story. Life with a partner who loved her was, in reality, a fantasy tale.

Children were a problem. What if the power of the diary was genetic? What if she bred half a dozen more like her; all destined to own their own special green book?

What if you don't? she told herself. *What if everything works out just fine and you're happy forever?* These were the constant arguments running through her head. It was enough to put her in a bad mood, and she couldn't have that either with Greg around. She needed to decide before a disaster happened.

After a week of his determined badgering, which included flowers, cards and chocolates, she'd begun to laugh and joke with him.

"Careful, I might say yes, and you don't know what you're getting in this package."

"I know exactly," he replied, pulling her body into him and kissing her. For a moment, within his embrace, she dreamed of a warm and wonderful future.

He didn't have a clue about her or the diary and that was a problem because he wouldn't know not to make her angry. If she lost her temper, there was a possibility he would be hurt. Your average couple fought, made-up and lived on to fight another day. A natural relationship. How would she avoid the you're-getting-on-my-nerves arguments if they lived together? He might even change for the worse, like Alan did with her mom.

Then if children came along, what then? She'd heard pregnancy hormones spread your emotions all over the place. Babies keep you up at night, and sleep deprivation wouldn't work well with her self-control.

No, no, absolutely not, she told herself, for every which way her romantic self argued for a *yes*. Marriage, in her case, was a thumbs down. The vision of her mom, blood everywhere on the floor as she mouthed *sorry,* was enough to strengthen her resolve.

Greg though wasn't making it easy. The more he talked about their future and his love for her, the more Nem warmed to the idea. Damn him, somehow he'd begun to make her believe she could do this. His arguments were hard to contest because she couldn't tell him the truth.

She began to strategize how to avoid becoming overwhelmed with emotion if they did marry. If she felt her anger growing, she could leave and go for a walk. *What if it's snowing or raining?* Well, she could lock herself in the bathroom. Or slip on a headset with calming music. She'd discovered beautiful pictures of art masterpieces helped, and she'd bought several coffee table books which included photos of the work of Monet, Van Gogh and others.

Hadn't she also managed to live with Peg and Ray bringing them amazing luck? So why not Greg? They might end up enjoying the best marriage in the world, with her being the perfect wife who didn't fight back or fly off the handle.

No children though. She'd make up something if the discussion arose. Over the years, she'd become good at lying or bending the truth as a matter of self-preservation.

Was she really thinking this now? The idea frightened and excited her and the more she thought about it, the more she began to believe she deserved it all and she could control it all. Love will do that to you. She only discovered later, love can also break your heart, but her life had been filled with harsh lessons. What was one more?

When she said her *I do* to Greg, it was a small ceremony on a beach on a tropical island destination that someone at her work had recommended. "It's like Bali," they'd said, "but quieter and with fewer tourists." Peg and Ray were there. They insisted, even though Nem told them they were eloping.

Peg insisted. "Sweetheart, you brought us incredible joy and luck over the years. Everything changed when you entered our lives. So, flying off to an island destination for a few days to see your daughter married, does not require much thought. We'll take off after the ceremony so we don't invade your honeymoon."

The day was perfect.

Their honeymoon was perfect.

The first three months of their marriage was perfect.

Until the day when it wasn't. The day she'd hoped wouldn't come but deep in her heart knew had always been on its way. You can wish away destiny, but, like the song says, hoping and dreaming just won't get the job done.

When she looked back on that wretched day and the weeks that followed, she came to think this heartbreak was her punishment for everything she'd done. All the lives she'd taken accidentally and those taken not so accidentally.

She thought she had it all under control. Maybe when she first discovered her pregnancy she was too thrilled and that pushed all caution from her mind. Greg was beside himself with concern because of the stupid lie she'd told him. Not wanting to discuss her reasons for not having children, she'd told him her chances of becoming pregnant were hopeless to none. After researching an illness and deciding on Endometriosis, she told him the scarring of her uterus was so bad, doctors had told her conceiving was next to impossible.

She'd showed him an article explaining in detail that women who experienced scarring of their reproductive system had low prospects of pregnancy. Greg had scanned the page, kissed her on the forehead and said, "I don't care. If I have you, that's all I need. You're my princess Leia and I'm your Han Solo."

"But I think they had children," Nem said, proud she'd paid attention in the reboot film Greg made her watch.

"Well, we didn't know that until later, so let's pretend that doesn't count."

"This isn't something that we're going to find out later Greg. I'm not going to have children, okay?"

She put her palms on his cheeks and stared into his eyes. Nem wanted to be certain he understood what he would give up being with her. "Do you hear me?"

"Yes, I do my princess. And I'm good, okay."

Now Nem knew she couldn't lie to him about this. The guilt of that lie, knowing how happy a baby would make him, would destroy her. She held out the pregnancy test with the thin blue line showing in the white results window.

"Oh my God!" His face lit up, before a furrow appeared on his forehead. "But you said you couldn't get pregnant. Will the baby be okay?"

She put a finger to his lips and said, "Shhh, yes, I think it'll be okay. I've done some research. Let's get some tests and see."

"I don't want to risk you, Princess," Greg said, kissing her face and her hands as if she really was royalty. In her mind, she prayed that the force would be with her.

.   .   .

Dr. Lillis was a forty-something man with a soft chin and manner to match. She'd found him from a local business search. He confirmed matter-of-factly that she was indeed pregnant and the tiny, magnificent tadpole on the ultrasound screen was alive and well. She just hoped he wouldn't reveal that she'd always been perfectly healthy, and this was not the miracle conception her husband believed.

Greg of course insisted on coming with her to the appointment and asking about her fictitious endometriosis. Her stomach was knotted at the thought that in the next few minutes, this could all unravel.

"You're very, very lucky," said the doctor.

Here it comes, she thought, hoping whatever he would say about her cure would sound credible.

"I know you said you suffered from endometriosis, but I don't understand why you were given that diagnosis. In fact, after my examination, I'm puzzled—"

"Thanks doctor," Nem interrupted, looking at her phone, pretending to notice the time. "We've got to get going. I have to get back to work."

She'd intentionally made this appointment close to the end of her lunch break for just this reason. To have an excuse to get away.

"Oh, okay, well congratulations on both counts," he said.

"Both counts?" said Greg.

Dr. Lillis finished writing something on Nem's card before looking up and smiling at him. "Yes, becoming pregnant for one. And Nem's recovery, which is quite the miracle."

He nodded at Nem and gave her a look that might have meant that he understood her subterfuge, or he knew but didn't care. She just hoped Greg hadn't seen it. If he knew she'd deceived him, well, that might start something, and with this first hurdle out of the way, she felt as though maybe this might all end up perfectly.

.   .   .

Later in bed, Nem snuggled into Greg as he slept, listening to his breathing and the rhythm of his heartbeat. Warmth and happiness blanketed her, and she assured herself everything would be fine. The minute she saw the little baby inside her on the ultrasound, she realized how much less her life might have been without this pregnancy. And without Greg. She deserved her happiness and decided it was a stroke of luck her secret birth control had failed.

This day would stay with her for a long time, and in her darker moments she'd recall the pine-needle smell of her husband's aftershave, his gentle breath across her cheek and the luxuriant warmth of his skin. Her last truly happy moment.

In her dreams she'd sometimes visit this memory, but awake with her pillow wet with tears, knowing she'd never be that person again. She'd tell herself for a long while that what happened between her and Greg was hell, and she wondered why she ever thought she could live a normal life; that this was payment for her arrogance. But, in hindsight, like most bad luck, it would turn out to suit her just as well as any good luck that had come her way.

To William the world grayed, growing ever fainter, and the lights on the other side of the river faded to a peephole of glowing silver. He heard the rushing water but for a moment none of it made sense. What was he doing here by the river?

"Morris," he whispered, as everything came back into focus and he remembered the last few minutes. A sharp pain flashed inside his heart as if a firecracker had exploded. He leaned as far out from the bank as was safe and tried to make out any movement in the water besides the natural peaking waves of the flow. His hope was he would see Morris climbing back up from the eddying mass, which for a moment, he thought of as a hungry monster.

"Morris," he shouted and waited for a reply.

He searched for a head bobbing in the current or a waving hand. For seconds he stayed silent, listening for cries of help that didn't come.

"MOHHH-RIIIS! Mohh-ris!" This time louder.

How did he disappear in such a short time? Or was it that quick? How long had he been fazed out?

He scanned the river again, as the panic climbed up into his throat, but there was no Morris saving himself. If he couldn't swim, and even if he could, that current at night was a death trap.

William stepped back from the edge, dizziness trying to grasp hold of his consciousness. He knew he was in shock and that he needed to clear his head and make some decisions. If he couldn't save Morris, he needed to work out how to save himself.

His legs felt wobbly and uncertain. God, this was ridiculous. He'd come here to kill the man, but he *had* changed his mind. How could the cursed man die by a stupid accident? This was black humor at its worst. If it was a dinner story he'd laugh. When it was happening to him he found no humor.

You need to get away from here. You look guilty.

Well, at least the demanding voice was back, and for once, talking sense. Before he did follow the advice, he took one more look at the place Morris had fallen. Shoe skid marks on the high bank's soft soil, near a small mud slide, told the story of a scuffle more than an accident. He looked around and saw security cameras on one of the light poles nearby.

That's when it hit him. He'd reached out to Morris. That could have looked as though he pushed him. Then he hadn't done anything when he'd blanked out for how long he didn't know. Anyone watching would look at him and put two and two together and come up with him as a killer. That was funny and ironic.

No, not funny. Terrible.

Should the police discover his escapades around Orelia, that he'd been at two of her talks, one easy to prove because he'd been carted off to the hospital, there was their case delivered on a platter.

He told himself he was being overly extreme. Nothing really happened that was in his control. His innocence would shine through.

The voice disagreed.

Nope, you look guilty and that'll be the verdict.

He imagined the detectives going through Morris' business contacts. *Who had a reason to kill him?* Ah, William Barnes. Top of the list. Ironic he'd be number one again.

She knows what you're doing, Morris had said just before he fell.

Could she know about him and his pranks? Come on, that's what they were really. Just nuisance games. Could this whole thing have something to do with her? Had she somehow willed this god-awful scenario onto him? If only Morris had given him more with which to work.

Get away, forget me, forget... please, you don't want to mess with her, wasn't much help. In fact, he was now in a worse position than before he came down to the river.

He decided he'd heed one piece of Morris' advice: *to get away.* As he thought that, he felt a mass in his pocket. With everything, he'd forgotten he'd even had the damn gun. God, he really had lost his marbles carrying that thing around like he was Clint make-my-day Eastwood.

His thoughts were clearing now though. Keeping his back turned from the camera on the path light, he pulled out the gun, stared at the weapon, before flinging it as far as he could into the river. It flew in a graceful arc to plop into the water; ripples shimmered outward from the entry point to be gobbled up by the swirls.

Tomorrow he'd decide on the next move. Maybe he'd dodged a bullet or the arrow of destiny (my, he was poetic at times). All he knew was Orelia was somehow involved. Morris had said so, and William knew too because until she'd entered his life, nothing even close to these disasters had ever happened to him. He should take his very-ex-agent's advice and get as far away from Orelia as possible.

As he hurried into the welcome darkness of the tree-lined path, mindful of the security cameras, he thought of the onslaught of bad luck she'd sent him. Maybe nowhere on Earth was far enough. Maybe his misfortune was a heat-seeking missile of doom, already targeted and on its way.

35

The argument began as arguments do, over something so small and inconsequential that Nem couldn't remember the exact beginning, even a week later.

One minute she and Greg were by the river, walking, laughing and talking, taking in the beautiful, graceful swans sailing along the surface as if blown by a gentle wind. In the next, emotional heat swelled in her chest as he made the mistake of asking her the wrong question.

"How do you think it happened?" Greg had asked as he gripped her hand and squeezed.

Suddenly she felt sick again even though she'd felt miraculously better today after weeks of morning sickness. The nausea was more precise than an alarm clock. The mornings she'd be awoken by a tight clench in her tummy, and she'd be forced to bolt to the bathroom. The instant she vomited, the queasiness disappeared. This respite lasted thirty minutes to several hours before the sick waves returned. By eleven am, the feeling was gone and other than tiredness, bordering on fall-down exhaustion, she was herself again.

When she awoke nausea-free today, she'd suggested they take advantage of the beautiful Saturday weather and walk to the nearby river. Every moment of wellness and energy had become precious. Pregnancy flicked an internal switch for Nem. She was more than herself, and sometimes, with the illness less. Her sense of smell had morphed into a super-power, and she could almost taste peaches being cut three rooms away through a closed door. But the important thing was that she had maintained control of her emotions.

When Greg asked the question, at first she wondered what he meant. He had a habit of sprouting random ideas which popped into his head, then he'd jump from one topic to another. Nem tried to keep up but found his train of thought at times difficult to follow. In the end she would give up with a nod and a smile, mindful she couldn't afford to let anything rile her.

"How do I think *what* happened?" she replied, suspecting she already knew his answer.

"The pregnancy."

Nem brought their entwined hands up and tapped them against Greg's chest as if to chastise him.

"I'm pretty sure you know how that works. When a girl and boy get together..."

"Not the physical part, Miss Silly Jar Jar Binks."

She shook her head at the *Star Wars* reference to the long eared, dopy character from the first film *Phantom Menace*. Even as the title came to mind, she felt a prideful thrill she remembered the film's name.

She replied with a mock frown. "Hey, that's not a nice reference. Are you saying I'm stupid and clumsy? You're the one asking the silly question. Which I still don't understand, by the way."

"I. Aaam. Saay-yiing..." Greg stretched the syllables as if her first language wasn't English. "... howw. Diiid. Yoou... get preg-a-nant with all the girl-health problems?"

Then more directly he added, "You told me having kids was impossible."

The question was now not the only problem. His condescending tone annoyed her. She instigated her usual and reliable calming techniques; she imagined herself dipping the hand, currently holding

Greg's, into cold water. The ice crystals traveled through her finger-tips into her veins, traveling where anger seeded in her heart. If she could halt the emotion there and not allow it to expand, she had a chance of remaining calm.

Nem stopped walking and pulled her husband to a halt.

"Greg, this baby is a miracle, that's all. The force was strong with us, right?" She squeezed his hand to emphasize her belief.

His expression had changed though. He seemed to stand taller and frowned as if he knew something she did not. The hairs on the back of her neck stood up in warning. Something wasn't right.

"You see, I mentioned this to Gail at work. Remember you met her at the Christmas get-together? She said, if someone has severe endometriosis, like you had told me, then they can't just miraculously be healed. If it was that serious, I would know because you'd be in pain every month. But you don't have *any* problems, do you? Not the same time each month or any other days. She asked me if I was sure endometriosis was the problem."

A winding hot tentacle snaked in Nem's stomach, and she wondered if the nausea had returned. Why must he ruin a perfectly nice morning? She didn't want to argue with him because he might see the guilt in her eyes.

She decided to call his bluff with a nonchalant reply.

"Well, let's visit the doctor and see what he says." She was about to ask if they could go home because she felt sick again (which was partially true because this was upsetting her) but he continued.

"So I wasn't sure if I'd understood everything you told me and if whether Gail was right. I Googled, and know what I discovered? Gail was right, you can't have children with that disease. No chance of healing, not even fifty percent chance. Not even two. So, now I'm asking. Did you lie to me? I love you, but this is a big thing for me. I was fine not having kids because I had you. I'm not fine with you making a decision like this without me and lying about it, Nem."

The heat in her belly growled as if an awakening monster had stirred. His accusations, though correct, annoyed her, and she didn't appreciate the way he spat her name as if she'd committed a crime.

Who was this Gail? He'd mentioned her a few times but she hadn't paid attention. Who was she to tell her husband anything? She didn't know Nem and should mind her own business.

Perhaps she could meet Gail again and the woman might find her luck suddenly transformed. She'd be too busy worrying about her own misfortunes to discuss her and Greg.

And that was the thought that sent her over. *A woman she didn't know and her husband.* The wild, hot monster inside, just waiting for this moment, tore through the protections around Nem's heart and escaped.

She tugged her hand back from Greg's, and said, "I don't like your tone. You'd listen to... some bitch at your work. Gail! Who is she anyway?"

Nem surprised herself. She didn't swear. Never. Ever. That was part of maintaining control, regulating words a solid step in staying calm. That one word was a catalyst, unseating a plug holding back fire now burning in her blood.

But, no, she couldn't do this. She loved Greg and they were having a baby. *Stop it, Nem, before it's too late.*

As she clung to reason, she knew she must get away from him and calm herself down. With every ounce of willpower left, she put several backward steps between them.

But the monster wouldn't be denied. The thing rose up and she was powerless to stop herself.

"Since you've brought it up, if I want to keep my personal health issues to myself, I will. Marriage doesn't guarantee I must disclose every little life detail to my husband."

"I don't think it's a little detail, is it? Children are a *big* detail."

His face was set hard but having said this, forcing what must have been troubling thoughts into the space between them, he seemed to deflate. Greg's shoulders drooped as he took a cautious step toward Nem.

"We're a team, you and I, aren't we?" He motioned between them with his hand. "And now we'll be parents. If there's ever a time to be honest and harness the Force, it's now."

He'd said this to reason with her, calm everything, but something about his reference to *Star Wars* yet again, rankled Nem. The silly made-up words were prickles catching in her gut. *Good Force, dark Force, light sabers, Jedi knights.* Ridiculous, senseless, and so far from the truth. Nem had experienced real horror. Her mom's murder, deaths of friends and enemies. She'd enacted her own power on the dark force.

This Good Force belief was a joke.

She stared at Greg without replying, her lips clamped tight, the anger humming inside and around her, a swarming hive of mounting fury. He seemed to think he'd diffused the situation, that his *Star Wars* reference was an apology. But the crazy little switch had been flicked and set to full steam, no emergency failsafe in place. Then a determined thought whooshed through her mind and she reached for it as a drowning man or woman clutches a lifeline.

Nem wanted out of this charade.

She didn't need a husband nosing around in her business. She hadn't wanted a child. Her desire was a quiet life, which seemed impossible in a marriage.

Nem wanted to be on her own again.

But she had no out. The trap had sprung on her during a weak moment. Now here she was married, pregnant and her husband standing before her unaware of the danger for him. This made her even angrier.

If he was sorry, well too late. He should have considered that before accusing her of lying and before he started talking to Gail; Gail who knew so much about ovaries and Nem's health.

But you did lie! a tiny voice said in her head, to which she replied, *For everyone's own good.*

A vision of her life stretched before her, with this same conversation repeated and never being resolved. The deception would always surface and bring pain. Damn it, she wasn't normal, so why pretend to be anything other than herself. She'd tried, and that was enough. Always her mother's fate lingered in the back of her mind, a warning beacon.

The words breathed from her mouth, came as barely a whisper. Greg must have thought all had calmed because at first a smile flicked at his lips. He took another step closer before realizing he might have misread her and something was still wrong.

He stopped, and said, "Wait, what did you say?"

"I said," she replied with a faint smile, "I hope you and Gail will be very happy. I'm leaving you."

"Nem, what? No. Come on now."

He reached out and grasped both her arms to prevent her from backing away. She threw them off, his touch feeling condescending and somehow inflaming her emotions even more.

"Stop looking at me. The poor pregnant, stupid woman. I don't want to be married anymore. I'm not your Princess Leia and you're not a Jedi knight from anywhere."

"No, no. Stop this Nem. You're carrying our child. This is the hormones. It says that in every pregnancy manual. Come on, let's go home and talk through this and…"

"I'm going home alright. But to pack."

His expression had changed in an instant to one of fear and confusion. His eyes broke her heart, but she'd come this far, and she wouldn't go back. Couldn't go back.

She turned and walked away, to put distance between them before she changed her mind. Her emotions *were* out of control. Maybe hormones. Maybe worry that he'd discover her secret. And that made her angry all over again, because he shouldn't have put her in this position where she had to worry about him and the diary and what might happen.

A little cog moved inside, just a small innocuous turn.

Oh no, what did that mean?

Now she was more frightened than she'd ever been. As angry as she felt in this moment, she couldn't bear if something terrible happened to him. She did love him and this baby, more than anything in the world.

With that thought her emotions calmed enough for her to see his point of view. He wasn't having an affair with Gail, and Nem *had* misled him. And, she loved the goofy *Star Wars* stuff. He was right, pregnancy had played havoc with her. She wasn't thinking straight.

Go back. Apologize and you'll work it out.

But what about the diary? She was sure she felt the cog move.

You're a team. You'll work it out, she repeated to herself.

She swung about to return to him and fix this mess. The extra baby weight and skipping breakfast this morning, which for a moment made her feel faint, threw her off balance. And she was falling before she even realized.

The path rose up to greet her; she saw it as if she was riding a roller coaster and heading for a dip. She tried to extend her palms to stop her fall but there was no time. A crack sounded—she hoped it wasn't a bone—just before everything went black. Her last thoughts were of the baby, then a why—*Why did Greg push her?*

Later she would understand the crack was the sound of her life switching from one path to another. This new one a journey taking her far away from her one chance at real happiness.

*W*hat am I to do! What am I to do! Really, what am I to do?

As William hurried away from the park, racing along the sidewalk, dodging pedestrians as if he was in a video game, those words blew through his mind like a tornado. They never stopped coming even when he arrived safely back at his apartment.

He had tried to sleep. Tried to eat. Nothing helped. They came at him in a hundred different voices, most of them hysterical screams echoing in his head.

Morris had fallen by himself. He hadn't touched the man. So could he be blamed? For a moment, he'd even picked up his cell to dial the police, his finger hovering over the *send* key after inputting the number. Then he reminded himself of how many innocents now served life sentences.

Phil Spector, the famous sixties music producer, for one. Lana Clarkson had been found collapsed on an antique chair in his home, dead from a gunshot wound. He claimed she'd committed suicide by accident. After viewing a documentary on the story, William agreed. Nineteen years he got for nothing. So celebrity and innocence didn't help you a bit when fate came after you.

He bet Mr. Spector wondered what he should do on that night

too, that things wouldn't go his way probably never occurred to him. The more William considered his predicament, the more he understood things would never go his way. Not while he wore Orelia's curse.

What am I to do? interrupted his mind's meandering.

Here we are, death by madness, he thought.

Okay, to solve this, he needed to be logical.

First, if she had placed a hex on him, then Morris' demise was connected to that. Just before he fell into the river, he'd alluded to her doing something to both of them. What that was and how she'd done it, he couldn't imagine.

Hopefully he wasn't seen.

Okay, decision made. He wouldn't call anyone.

Next, how to get this bad luck monkey off his back.

Think William. Think.

What am I to do? came around again, smashing through his mind, wrecking-ball style. The Miley Cyrus video flashed before his eyes, her sitting on top of an actual wrecking-ball, swinging to and fro. His heart pulsed in panic—not because of the exhibitionist singer's image, but because he hadn't a clue what to do next.

Focus William. For God's sake, focus.

Okay, focused.

His life was a mess, his actions due to crazy envy that had grown out of hand. The negative reviews, canceling events, stalking her and Morris, were small potatoes which had failed anyway. And contemplating murder? Was that his writer's mind working overtime? Did he have it in him?

If you were a story protagonist, what would you do? he asked himself.

First, confront her.

And that would achieve what?

William did not appreciate his devil's advocate's snark-filled tone. Even his mind seemed against him.

Well look where you are, writer boy? Smart people don't end up with careers in the toilet and implicated in murder.

There was no reply to that, so instead, he worked through the conversation he might have with Orelia if he was to reason with her.

Orelia, you've placed a curse on me. Morris is dead, I look guilty and my career is finished. My writer's block is the size of a mountain and my life is pretty much destroyed. What did I do to you?

Oh, are you hearing yourself? That's a touch... insane? interrupted Snark Voice, instead of his imaginary Orelia.

He thought to answer, *Any better suggestions? I'm all ears, buddy,* when he realized this thought process was unhinged. While thinking to yourself was normal, carrying on a board meeting in his head was not. He'd gone from being confident William, imagining he might bring that woman down through sabotage, to victim William, pleading for his life.

No, that wouldn't do. No groveling.

I agree, chimed in Snark Voice.

He saw her face in his hospital room as she sat across from him. She knew exactly what that would do.

"So terrible what happened to you," he heard her say in his mind. *"Darling man, you've been so forgiving, here's your reward. You relax now while I read an excerpt from my new book."*

Yeah, right, Orelia. A reward!

You can't go off half-cocked, Snark Voice added.

It seemed now on his side and was absolutely correct. He needed to be smarter than her.

First, was understanding what he was dealing with here, and he had to hurry. If someone saw him with Morris or recalled him from the festival, how long before there was a knock at his door? Then, no doubt, Phil Spector and he'd be spending bunk-time together.

What William must do was prove his innocence. He had to verify Orelia possessed abilities like in one of those SyFy channel shows. How he'd achieve this, he didn't know. And from Snark Voice's silence, neither did he.

For now, the important goal was to act normally to throw off any suspicion. While he was at it, the idea of hand balling that suspicion in Orelia's direction could be a solution and solve most of his problems. Somehow she had orchestrated all this.

Snark Voice chimed in. *You know, you do sound crazy. A lot crazy.*

William smiled, his confidence back, as he replied aloud, "Crazy? No, Orelia planned this whole thing. That doesn't make me mad. That makes me smart for realizing it."

A young couple approaching him, walking in the opposite direction, stared as if something was wrong. They laughed like he was a comedy act, or insane, as Snark Voice had suggested.

He wasn't crazy.

He was cursed by that woman who had come after him for no reason. Though he didn't know yet how he'd save himself, he would find a way to send that curse right back at her. Even if it killed him.

37

When Nem opened her eyes, the first thing she noted was a light in the distance. Her next thought was of Greg and their argument, and that he'd be sorry she had died.

She remembered the force of his hands on her body, and falling, and wondered why he would pounce on her. He hadn't been physical before, so why this now? Perhaps her husband would celebrate her death.

Before she traveled into the light, there had been time to consider everything. Why, when they were by the river, had her anger become all-consuming? That wasn't the Nem persona she'd cultivated over the years, the calm, consistent girl always aware of her emotions. To behave otherwise presented a danger for Greg and their unborn child.

Oh, the baby.

The poor thing would have died with her. She felt angry again. One thing to kill her but another to take this precious darling's life.

What was that light?

The brightness hurt, causing her to squint. How long before she entered the glow? She tried to pull her hand up to shield her face, but her arms no longer responded. That made sense. After all, she probably only imagined she still possessed a body. Damn, the light annoyed her though.

She couldn't think about Greg anymore, or the baby; a pain in her head above her eyebrows (which she couldn't possess if she had no body) kept distracting her.

Wait though, she wanted to keep thinking about him.

This wasn't adding up to make any kind of sense. Would he have killed her on purpose? No, now she thought about it, this must have been an accident. She recalled his hands on her, a heaving, pushing but that didn't mean... oh, she'd never know now because that glow kept pulling at her. People coming back from death said loved ones awaited to show you the way.

This was not great news because she was short on loved ones who had passed over. Only her mom. She wasn't sure though, after the way she'd used the diary, if it might be a happy reunion. That's if Nem even ended up in heaven.

She had tried to be fair to those whose names appeared in the diary, but there'd been mistakes. Innocent errors, yes, but people had died or gotten sick or terrible things had happened to them and their families. This was why, after she'd left school, she used the book less. This might be the reason her mother hid the book—too easily misused.

Why isn't the light doing anything?

She hadn't moved an inch and the sharp, white rays still stretched toward her. Was she meant to do something? Her legs weren't responding, neither were her arms. So what was going on?

If Greg was here, he'd know how to help. Since they'd met, his love and calmness had inspired her. At that thought, her heart twinged, the heart that no longer beat. Talk about bad luck. But her spirit lifted at the thought of seeing her mom again. She'd apologize for bringing the kitten home and creating a tragedy.

In the distance, to the light's left, she detected strange sounds. Voices maybe? A banging, clanging. A bell ringing. Survivors of death never mentioned banging and bells. Just light. That had changed too. The crispness had dulled, and the edges blurred, as shadowed objects took shape, creeping out of the darkness. A pale blue haze hung over everything, as if each nameless outline wore a fluffy coat.

Nem tried to move her head again but a hot, sharp, needle-like pain pierced her neck. Her arm moved to touch the tender spot. But she didn't have an arm, did she? Panic swamped her. This was wrong. The edges of the dark shapes sharpened. She'd made a mistake. She wasn't dead at all.

Her breath caught in her throat, stopping a scream she couldn't control. Again, she attempted to move her arm. Yes, now she felt her fingers wiggle, but a pressure held her hand back.

Through the gray, a darkness moved toward her and she screwed shut her eyes. The light had disappeared, and a warm breath traveled across her cheek. Her first instinct was to fight, with every fiber of energy left. She focused on her throat, her mouth, her tongue, in an attempt to call out. Wherever she was, she needed...

"He... help!"

There, she'd gotten it out, but her voice sounded weak and thin.

"Heeell-p."

She opened her eyes but the dark shape remained, and her hand still felt imprisoned. The response that came was nearby and she shook with relief.

"Nem, Nem, oh my God."

She tried to turn toward the person who'd spoken but again pain shot into her neck; this time, traveling through her arms into her spine. A moan escaped her lips, and she closed her eyes again willing this not to be a dream. She wasn't ready yet to see her mom or leave Greg. Or the baby.

She wanted to have this child, to love and give them what she'd never had until Peg. Safety and a childhood free from horror.

"Nem, can you hear me?"

"Gre-eg?" she said.

The pressure on her hand released, and now a gentle touch swept over her cheek. A palm. Lips. The relief flooded through her as she moved her arm to reach for him. Her limb felt encased in concrete, but she found the strength to find his hand, resting so gently across the top of her chest. She squeezed a recognition.

Her eyes fluttered open to see the shadows nearly gone. Greg's face glowed with a faint light and an excitement gripped her that at least she survived.

I'm so lucky danced in her mind.

They'd still be a family, and she'd make it work. First thing, the diary must go. Bury it. Throw it off the bow of a ship. Burn it. Get the thing out of their lives once and for all.

"Sorry," she said, meaning it for so many things. Her mouth felt grit-dry and her tongue swollen but she needed to share her feelings. She wanted to reassure him she'd never be so foolish again. Her mind fought past the fogginess and forced the words out between them, so their relationship could heal.

"You... and the baby are the most important... You're everything."

His face was inches from hers and she expected his response to be a smile. But he wasn't smiling. Or talking. Tears ran down his cheeks, tiny rivulets that hung from his chin for a moment before dropping onto the bedcover.

"Greg?" she questioned, now afraid.

"Nem, there's something I have to tell you."

But she already knew.

38

The police hadn't contacted William yet. Countless times, he'd run the scenario of what he'd say if they knocked on his door , so much so he felt it had happened. Each time he thought about it his heart pounded and the urge to visit the bathroom came over him.

A week later he remained free but continually on guard, but his anxiety grew less as each day passed. He hadn't left his house in days, except to grab necessities: milk, bread, eggs, and the big need, bottles of wine. The latter certainly helped.

News of Morris' demise appeared in the papers after four days. As the agent to one of the current biggest best sellers, he was far more newsworthy in death than in life, after such a grisly end. His body washed up on a bank, three miles from where William last saw him. Though discovered within a day, identification took longer because something had gotten to him and taken a leg and savaged his face.

Nobody reported him missing, proving him less indispensable than he imagined. His secretary had been quoted as saying she believed he was away on a trip.

"He travels all the time," she said. "So I wasn't worried. When the police contacted me, I was shocked. I thought they had the wrong person."

Of course Orelia made it into the news. "Devastated," was her word. She must have repeated it in five different articles and three TV stories. Apparently, the promotion for her latest book was about to begin and they were preparing to embark on a country-wide tour. William noted she managed to include the name of the new novel and the previous one enough times in shameless self-promotion.

He felt satisfaction in knowing Morris' passing disrupted her promotional plans. Then he reminded himself the man's death might *disrupt* his own life. According to the reporter, the police were contacting his known associates to assist the coroner.

He presumed they'd get to him at some point. That they hadn't already, showed how much water had flowed under the bridge between the two (excuse the pun). After the time he'd spent with the man, he felt insulted his name didn't factor near the top of the list. Most likely, his file lay shoved at the back of a cabinet, where Morris must have hidden it away and hoped it would stay.

After suffering through Orelia's appearances in the news, he got to thinking how bizarre to find himself in this position. He'd blamed her for everything, then decided she couldn't be responsible. Now as he watched her performance, he returned to his first belief. Something wasn't right with her.

Morris' last words about her played through his mind again.

Get away, forget me, forget... please, you don't want to mess with her.

What did he mean? What did she do to the man? Kind of obvious, really. If she distributed misfortune, then falling in a river and drowning pretty much trumped most bad luck. He wondered what the agent did to deserve his fate. Then again, what had he? A simple argument amid the tremendous support he'd given her. This hole in which he found himself was so far from where he'd seen himself only three short years ago. He saw the headlines:

One hit wonder best selling author convicted of murdering his agent.

That's what lay in his future if he did not take the initiative and fight back. He saw destiny coming toward him like a freight train through the fog. Someone could place him at the river and they'd trace the reviews and phone calls and everything else he'd done. Then bang-bang, his life would explode as surely as if she'd pulled a trigger or hired a hitman.

No, he wouldn't wait for that to happen. He'd be the one to act first. Go on the offensive.

One problem though. How to do that without drawing any suspicion to himself for Morris' murder. So maybe he should do the thing at which he'd always considered himself a superb talent.

Watching. Waiting. Remaining patient. The necessary qualities of an author. You must be a keen observer and maintain the fire of curiosity, even when you'd seen most everything. A person's movement or expression said more than their words. As a writer, it was his job to find those words.

He needed to follow, watch and work out exactly what was happening and why Morris feared his star client. He was no private detective, but he'd run out of ideas. In fact, he couldn't think of any others. He had to do something to solve this because he couldn't write, he barely slept, and his life now involved looking over his shoulder for the police, or her, or something coming for him.

He'd never publish again unless he reversed the curse which weighed on his shoulders as surely as if he wore an oxen brace. Orelia Mason might think she'd killed two birds with one stone with Morris' death but she figured wrong. Whether she was a witch or a clever fraud, so far she had played this game well. William had certainly been taken unaware, but no more. He had no life at all since she'd entered it, so what did he have to lose?

39

*N*em realized now the bright light was only sunshine streaming through the hospital window. A tube ran from a small band-aid just above her wrist to an IV bag. Greg, sitting on the edge of her bed, looked sadder than she'd ever seen him.

"Don't say it," she said, moving her hand from his to the covers above her stomach.

He leaned to her and kissed her lips. His breath smelled minty and was warm against her skin. While his eyes never left hers, Nem's mind traveled to the place before this, where everything was wonderful. That would change the minute he said the words. If only she could stay there in that moment where her future held potential. The safe, undamaged moment. Maybe she brought this upon herself. Bad fortune bouncing back at her.

You can do this, she told herself. *You've survived so much. Learned so much.*

She swallowed a deep breath to fill not just her lungs, but her soul, to prepare herself. Then she asked, "What happened?"

He found her hand again and squeezed.

"You fell. So sorry baby. So completely my fault. I ran after you and somehow, well, I don't know how, I tripped. Then, as if a giant hand pushed me, I landed on you. The momentum I guess. I'm ashamed."

Greg's tears broke Nem's heart. She knew he hadn't purposely hurt her. This was just an accident, a mere twist of fate. And if that twist came from the diary, if his name was there when she checked later, then she'd tell him about the diary's power. Make him believe her because she didn't want him blaming himself for something over which he had no control.

As she began to speak, her own tears spilled down her cheeks. Greg brushed them aside with a curled finger, but the drops were immediately replaced.

"I'm sorry too. I started the argument. Don't be ashamed. You were reacting to me. I promise no more flare-ups. Period. I'll count to ten, first. I think it's just the pregnancy hormones."

It was then she remembered what he had begun to say. The yet unspoken thing. The question on her lips needed to be asked because once she knew everything then she could begin to rebuild. She was no coward, but she realized in this second that the baby had meant more to her than she had imagined.

"Greg, tell me."

Her husband's posture stiffened as their eyes found each other. He squeezed her hands as he bowed his head to stare at their clutched palms.

He didn't want to say it either.

"The baby?" she whispered.

He simply nodded.

"You hit your head. Hard. There was a bleed on your brain. So the doctors had to operate to relieve the pressure. You've been in an induced coma for six days." He looked lost for a moment. "I thought I'd lost you both."

And there it was, hanging in the air, wrenching at them. A mistake that couldn't be reversed; the one time in years in which she'd failed at restraining her emotions, and this was her punishment?

"I know, it's like a knife to your... to your, your heart." His words came out in a strangled whisper through the tears and pain.

Nem struggled to breathe; her chest tight. There wasn't adequate oxygen for her lungs. She panicked, opening her mouth, gasping and sucking in air. Still, she couldn't find her breath. Her head spun as a dizzy wave invaded her body. She felt invaded by something dark and terrifying she couldn't ignore and couldn't fight.

Her eyes closed against her will as if they'd decided enough was enough. She wanted to escape this room. Escape the hospital. Escape her life. Nem needed to run away somewhere where nobody knew her, and she knew nobody. She wanted to hide.

A river of emotion dragged her along. A current pulled her savagely toward a deadly waterfall, with nothing to be done but wait until she reached the edge. Then she felt herself falling and tumbling, the wind and the crashing of the water loud in her ears, so deafening she couldn't hear her own scream. When she hit the white, churning foam below, the blackness sucked her down to the bottom where she knew she'd drown. They'd never find her body and she wanted that, she wanted cold anonymity.

Greg's voice called to her in the deep, with indistinguishable words that came to her jumbled and confused. Though she fought against returning, she surfaced, gasping for air and trying to speak. She opened her eyes, ready to tell her husband, the man she loved, that she'd never be whole again.

But Greg was gone.

She didn't recognize the woman standing over her who stared at her watch as she held Nem's wrist. The nurse wasn't looking at her and hadn't even noticed she'd awoken. She had a pleasant but no-nonsense face.

But Nem had no time to consider her visitor any further. A pain tore through her breast as though her organs had been crushed. Her soul ached. Her body ached as if a giant hand held her in its grip. This was her pain from now on, forever. Her penance delivered to endure every waking moment.

She tried to close her eyes, close out the world and return to sleep, when the nurse spoke in such a matter-of-fact tone that Nem wondered if the woman was aware she'd lost her baby.

"You're awake. Good. You gave your husband quite a fright. How're you feeling? My name's Belinda and I'll be here on shift for another four hours."

After completing taking her pulse, Belinda moved around the bed to check the fluid bag hanging at the side. After seeming to satisfy herself that the drip fed into Nem's body as it should, the woman stopped and touched her arm. Nem felt a jolt and she suddenly thought, *is this a dream*? The woman acted as though nothing was wrong. She *was* in the hospital and her baby had died.

"You nauseous at all? Headache? Hungry?"

Though difficult, Nem managed to shake her head, which made a scratchy loud noise on the pillow. The uncaring way the nurse looked at her made her uncomfortable. She didn't know why but the woman seemed strange to her and she wished someone else would come into the room.

"Shall I tell your husband to come back in? Your man is worried about you. Hasn't left your side more than an hour or two since you came in. He's just gone to the canteen to grab a bite to eat. I can call him if you like."

Nem wanted to say, *yes, I need my husband.* I need my mom. I need something to keep me sane, to help take this pain away. But a strange sensation stopped her. She detected a wrongness around her as if thick molecules of heavy moisture filled the air. She relived the weight of Greg's hands on her shoulders. The pushing. The moment of falling and the ground coming up to meet her. The blackness, the water, and sliding deeper into the abyss of cold, overwhelming emptiness.

A memory of long ago rushed in.

A click.

The satisfying clunk of the cog of fate nestling into place.

This wasn't a random event created by an innocent couple's argument. This was a message telling her she'd chosen the wrong path. A life filled with love and children and happiness was not her destiny. Hers was another future. This very scenario of love and trust had been her mother's undoing. Her murder, the result of not choosing wisely, or not noticing signs and listening to fate's whispers.

When first awakening, she'd presumed this was her punishment, her baby's death the sacrifice for everything the diary had taken from others. Instead though, she saw this was her lesson, just as her mom's murder was another chapter in her education.

She thought of Greg and their fight, and how quickly the anger had arisen within her. To believe she could live her life with caution, controlling her emotions, was a foolish gambit. An impossible task. For she had no more guarantee she could control her feelings better than any other person did. She might control the power of serendipity but that did not mean she controlled herself.

The nurse's voice interrupted her thoughts, and she turned her head to look in her direction. The pain caused her to wince, but compared to the ache when she thought of what she must do, this was nothing.

"So, do you want me to call your husband to come back?"

When Nem spoke, to her the voice she heard came from a distance, an echo of someone else. Perhaps this was her doubt. Could she really move her lips and say what was needed? Did she truly desire what would come from those simple words? Words to change her life; once spoken, that's what they'd be.

She must speak them, because she loved Greg and didn't want to have him hurt by her ever again. He deserved better than what she could offer.

"No, I'm tired. I need to sleep. Tell him something for me? Please?"

"You've been through a lot. Course. What do you need?"

The nurse smiled, possibly expecting her to make a declaration of love a la all the romantic, completely fantastical films. Well, Nem would deliver part of the fantasy in her first line but here would be no happy ending.

"Can you let him know I love him? That I'll always love him."

Belinda stroked her arm and smiled. Everyone loved a happy ending, didn't they?

"And something else please."

"Sure," she said, running her hand across Nem's forehead. "Whatever you want."

Nem paused, thinking what these words would mean, knowing once she'd spoken them she couldn't take them back, no matter how much she desired them to be erased. This was her line in the sand for her life. She exhaled, long and slow, wishing the waterfall had been real. Why didn't it take her deeper to drown, so she wouldn't endure the coming pain?

You can do this. You must do this. And she thought of her mom and the look in her eyes when she'd screamed, "I'm sorry. Run, gooo..."

Yes, mom, I'll run. And I'll go. You won't have died in vain.

Nem grabbed the nurse's hand and squeezed, so she would understand this wasn't a whim or a sick woman's fancy. She felt a tingle that caused her to pause for a moment. The nurse gave her a strange look as if she knew something was about to happen.

Their hands seemed locked in a moment of odd connection, but she had no time to ponder the feeling, as she said, "Can you please tell him that I hope he understands. Everything's how it should be. This was just bad luck. But you mustn't let him in this room again, no matter what."

Belinda's brows furrowed and then she seemed to catch herself. "Oh you can't mean that. After you take a nap, you'll feel differently."

"I'm sure," said Nem, her heart breaking, as she spoke the terrible words to a stranger she sensed didn't seem to care, who had probably seen too much heartache every day.

"A nap won't change my mind."

She closed her eyes and sank away into the swirling waters of another dream, and entered her new life. Without Greg.

40

Four days now he'd followed Orelia, and she did nothing which he perceived as unusual. She attended Morris' funeral, the event which had put a halt to her tour. He thanked his luck—whatever she'd left him—that she wasn't doing interstate publicity because he could hardly follow her onto a plane and around a strange city. He wouldn't know the streets well and he couldn't afford the cost these days. So for a change, thank you Lady Luck.

Since Orelia's publishing success, she'd moved to a large house in a suburb in the very outer reaches of the town. The property was in a development of stylish, five-bedroom, multiple bathroom homes sitting on well-groomed acre blocks.

He'd done some research on a real estate website and learned the place set her back $1.6 million. Not much of a setback he imagined. One or two royalty checks from her first book. Fox Studios had optioned her romance series despite only the first book released so far, and he guessed the compensation for that would cover furnishings and a pool.

By the look of the outlying boundary, which he'd walked several times trying to view the house, he surmised she enjoyed her privacy.

The fence was high and the trees alongside thick, providing a perfect screen, so that from the road nothing of her home was visible. The ridges of broken glass cemented along the top of the barrier said more than a *Do Not Enter* sign.

Had she something to hide? Or did she simply want to be alone in a peaceful, forest setting? When they'd met, she seemed a genuine, outgoing, enthusiastic woman with a passion for books. This home shouted overkill for one person, no family and, as far as he knew, not even a dog.

The first night he walked the boundary looking for a vantage point well-concealed from the road. At first, he imagined he'd climb over and get a close look at the house. He considered returning with a thick rug or canvas and a hammer, and use that to bypass the crude security. However, scaling the eight feet would require a ladder, and that became all too complicated.

If protection was her priority (and that's what he imagined), then she no doubt had cameras. So scaling the wall would gain him little except the chance of an embarrassing discovery.

What Orelia had done to him wasn't something you could see. You felt the threat as a breath on the back of your neck, and then only after she discarded you. He was certain she continued to use her misfortune-inflicting ability on others. Look at Morris. To prove his theory, he would need to catch her in the act.

The details of how to do this were like an outline of a novel, sketchy. Every time his confidence wavered, or he imagined he was just a little crazy, he reminded himself he had nothing to lose, and Morris was a reminder of how bad this could go.

He became vigilant and dedicated. Every day by 6am, William would park fifty yards away in a wooded area off-road and walk back to his surveillance position. He'd found a roadside clump of trees and bushes that concealed him from passing cars. From this vantage he could watch her gate unnoticed.

What he discovered after watching her house for days puzzled him. She could be in mourning, but she didn't engage in what he considered normal-people activities. Didn't visit the grocery store, have coffee with friends or go for walks. In the first few days, only once did she leave her home; for a lunch date with a man, whom he recognized as a big-brand thriller writer, David Place. Oh, how high and mighty was she now? Thanks to William. Yet he wasn't good enough for her to do lunch, breakfast, or even a hot dog.

Gratitude thy name is not Orelia.

Four long days he'd watched, and boredom had descended as surely as each long evening. He wondered if his sanity had slipped away over the past few months; to stalk a rival author on nothing more than a hunch was crazy by any rational measure.

Finally, though, on the sixth morning, things got interesting. Orelia drove out through her gates at ten fifteen, and William almost killed himself sprinting to his car. He took off, speeding well above the limit to catch her, which he managed a mile down the road. She traveled only another few blocks, to park in a suburban street, where she left and locked her car. Then she walked to a nearby bus stop and waited for several minutes before climbing aboard a bus.

William followed, allowing one car separation, in case she might glance out a window and see him at the wheel.

Where the heck was she going?

After forty minutes, she alighted within the North Park area, which was well on the other side of town. At this, his curiosity intensified. *What the hell was she doing here?*

He drove past the bus and found a space in a loading zone. No doubt his reward would be a parking ticket, but he had no choice if he was to stay with her.

In the mid-twentieth century, North Park had been a delightful part of the city, situated around several acres of forested land fashioned into a groomed park. Developers built dozens of cheap apartment blocks to cater for a growing population who wanted to live in a pleasant, tree-lined suburb. But progress edged back the park's boundaries each decade, to make way for higher density living, and when communal accommodation isn't maintained, rents drop. They then attract a lower socio-economic demographic; this attracts crime and the entire area becomes unfashionable, run-down and even dangerous. North Park was not yet a slum but not a place for a New York Times best seller to visit. Unless she was researching a book. That could be her only intention, and if so William had wasted his time.

She stood out as if white on black, although she'd toned down her usual *aren't-I-quirky* Orelia style, with dark pants and a dull-gray shirt. The olive-green Fedora hat covered her red hair well, but still stray wisps peeked out.

He stayed to the opposite side of the street about twenty yards back, following her as he'd seen done in so many movies. Ducking into doorways; intermingling into a group of people as he moved forward; pretending to stare into a window if he caught up to her.

They passed several bus stops and a train station after a good mile, and he wondered why she wouldn't have remained on board until further. Orelia didn't stop, nor waver in her choice of streets, as if she knew exactly where she was headed.

Twice, she paused at an alleyway's entrance. She looked down each side-street, even taking a few steps inside before returning to the street. On one occasion, William had to turn away quickly in case she noticed him. Each time he crossed to her side to check the lanes, but he saw nothing. What was Orelia doing? It made no sense.

Just when he'd thought this was a wild author chase, she came to a standstill at a main intersection. Here the crowds grew in density as they approached the main shopping and business area. The mid-morning coffee rush was in full swing. The surrounding businesses were a mix of diners, twenty-four-hour lenders, a cash-and-carry, and a jewelry store that doubled as a pawn-broker.

Something across the street had appeared to catch her attention as she waited, near motionless, despite the crosswalk lights changing several times. William shuffled back and forth to keep her in view as pedestrians bustled by him. He followed her stare, but he couldn't see anything that would be of such interest.

The supermarket on the corner looked like every other mid-sized outlet he'd ever seen. Security screens covered the store's windows.

Customers entered and left; six people in the minutes they had waited.

To the door's right, a bearded, disheveled lost-looking fellow sat on a flattened cardboard box. Wedged between a green duffle bag and a plastic ice-cream container was a hand-written sign on a small white board. People walked by, ignoring him as if he was a ghost.

PLEASE HELP! NO JOB! NO FOOD!

William looked toward Orelia, then back across the street. Was she staring at this man or the building behind him?

A woman walking by, with a little fellow of around five in tow, paused before the vagrant and handed her son coins. The boy spoke to the man before placing the money into the container. He nodded and smiled and waved as the pair continued on their way.

When William's focus returned to Orelia, she was already halfway across the road. He stepped back, moving closer to the large sand-stone building in case she turned around. Many people moved between them, which would help conceal his presence, but he didn't need her to notice him through a lapse of concentration and carelessness.

Orelia continued along the pavement after crossing the road, and ended up exactly where the woman and her son had stood only moments before. She fumbled in her wallet and withdrew multiple notes; he was too far away to see the denominations.

Then she squatted down, staying there for a few minutes in what appeared to be a conversation with the man. William couldn't figure out if she knew him or if he was just a random person on whom she'd decided to bestow charity.

Before arising, she placed the money in the container. As she did, his face lit up and William presumed it must have been a sizable amount. Another grand gesture by the amazing Orelia Mason. Helping the homeless. Where were the cameras to capture such an altruistic act?

Don't judge yet, he told himself. This was certainly peculiar behavior to travel this far, seemingly on a Mother Teresa mission. Then again nothing made sense with Orelia. He needed to keep watching, be patient, and hope for a breakthrough.

If he believed in God, he would have prayed the revelation came soon. Rising at dawn to camp outside her house all day had worn him down already. How many days he could keep this up, he didn't know. Headaches had become his constant companion, and he lived on painkillers that did little, except upset his stomach.

William expected Orelia to now move away from the man, like the woman and her child had done after their donation. Orelia though stood above the man as if waiting for something, before she reached inside her bag again. He wondered if she was about to give him a copy of an Orelia Mason novel? That would be a great joke.

And she did pull out a book, but the green hardcover looked too small for a novel, or at least a standard fiction. The man stared up at her as she flipped through the pages. She stopped, seemed to be looking for a specific place, then nodded as if she'd found it. Reaching in her bag again, she pulled out a spiral notepad, in which she wrote before tearing out a page. Then she bent to the container and deposited the slip of paper on top of her money.

The vagrant spoke to her, a few words, nothing more; William presumed a thank you. Without a second glance, she then turned and retraced her steps across the intersection. William swung about so his back was to her and stared into the window of the secondhand store he now faced. The interior was a hodgepodge of people's unwanted trash; old typewriters, odd assortments of bowls and glassware, electrical drills, ugly plastic dolls and more. Just the kind of shop he enjoyed browsing because it gave him ideas for stories. Right now, he didn't have time, as he watched Orelia's reflection as she walked in the direction she had traveled only five minutes prior.

Now he had a choice.

He could follow her and see if she went somewhere else, or cross over the intersection to the man and question him on his recent benefactor. For a few dollars he might discover the reason behind Orelia's trip to *fabulous* North Park. Once she'd passed by, his head swung from her as she moved along the street, to looking back to the beggar. He ran the argument in his mind, and as the seconds ticked away, he made a quick decision.

The vagrant didn't appear to be going anywhere soon. So, Orelia-hunting it would be.

here life would lead her next, Nem didn't know. Greg was her true love; she knew this because two people finding each other who fit like puzzle pieces, came down to serendipity. And serendipity, she understood better than most.

When she refused to see him again, it hurt; nearly killed her. Hurt almost as much as the day her mom died. Every time he called, texted or knocked at the door, her heart crumpled. Once when he called out to her, she stood there waiting on the other side with her hand so close to turning the lock.

To answer questions, give him reasons and argue their differences, was a slippery slope that could lead easily into reconciliation. Her decision would make no sense to him. Here, *it's not you, it's me* was the truest of clichés. Although her reasons were no cliché, but hid a dark twist.

How could she tell him that in leaving, she'd saved his life?

Greg stopped trying after six weeks and three days, but who was counting? Time drifted on and the grief of her loss faded, as do most scars. Her troubled nightmares of her ex-husband discovering her secret, or dying, or taking from her their child, who had never been born, lessened.

During waking hours, she grew adept at leading her mind to other things to avoid traveling down the river of life's regrets. She'd never become a mom; the only person she'd grow old with, would be the girl in the mirror. Big deal! A destiny with anybody was a fool's wish for her and, according to divorce statistics, most people. All she need do was to imagine her mom and what came from her death, to convince her she was right.

If her mom had made this same choice, she may never have been born. Her mom might have survived though. Alan, Dr. Shepherd, Lacy, those whose paths had crossed hers, might have lived too.

As dark as these thoughts were, that crept and crawled through her heart, there was an upside to her decision. If there was no love and no children for her, then Nem would take compensation in everything else life offered.

First order was to move to another city to avoid bumping into Greg or his friends. This place held too many sad memories, anyway.

Her working life had been as a freelance data entry operator, which took her to various companies. Temporary suited her. No need to connect because she wouldn't stay long enough to be noticed. The repetitive nature of keying information became a good place to lose herself. Now she wanted a fresh start, and that included a change of career.

After studying a map of the country, she decided Deering, only a two-hour drive north, was a good city, with 1.2 million inhabitants, every one of them strangers. This time she'd keep them all strangers. No need to worry if luck smiled upon her in finding an apartment or employment. Things always worked out for her.

She found a smart, two-bedroom place, a thirty-minute commute into the city, with a lovely view of a small park. The neighborhood had a nice mix of cafes, shops and happy people. As they passed each other in the foyer, neighbors said *hello*, and so she said *hello*. And that was enough.

Job hunting proved more of a challenge. As she cast an eye over the classifieds, she realized the advertisements didn't give her the important facts. Did their employees mind their own business?

Would they leave her alone? Could she be ignored and still find satis-faction in her work?

Disappointment had begun to filter in to her thoughts, until a job's headline caught her attention. She put down her coffee and began to read, growing more excited with each line.

Do you love books?

Yes, she did. To escape into other worlds gave her a chance to experience a normal life. Within the pages, she stepped into other lives and enjoyed the freedom to connect on a human level, without fear some terrible event might occur.

She read further, growing more excited with each sentence.

Help us make our little bookstore the city's favorite. We are looking for a sales clerk to help with inventory, stocking shelves, pricing and, when needed, assisting customers. You will start in the stockroom but not for long, with the right attitude. Contact Diane at (301) 754 3014.

To talk books as part of your job sounded fun, in fact, perfect. She practically bounced in her chair at the thought, but a niggling worry tugged at her. The interaction with a store filled with people might prove difficult, even dangerous. What if she landed an angry customer? Or the boss annoyed her? Or she awoke in a bad mood and...? What if? What, damn well if?

She rolled the thoughts around in her mind, pushing and pulling at them, and an unlikely answer came to her. For too many years she'd worried about hurting others by mistake, by taking a person's luck, who didn't deserve misfortune. She realized now that the expe-rience of losing the baby and leaving Greg had changed a part deep inside. Where once guilt and apprehension resided, now lived only mild concern.

Her heart had been remolded into something tough and gnarly; a shooter root from a young tree hardened by its push through stony ground. She wouldn't go out of her way to hurt someone but if things needed doing for the greater good, so what? She wasn't Mother Teresa, Princess Diana or the Dalai Lama. She was just a person trying to find her way through life, and why shouldn't she take every advantage given her?

Life was life. Bad things happened to good people; good things happened to bad people. Sometimes the good luck didn't just transfer to her; others benefited too. Look at Peg and Lacy's parents and those in need whom she'd helped.

She put down the paper to stare out the window through the wrought iron balcony to the little park, five stories below. She enjoyed walking there in the early evening, taking in the cooler night air and watching the locals pass by. These new experiences in this city came from having the courage to change her life.

In going forward, she decided she would always look on serendipity's bright side. If she hadn't left Greg she wouldn't be here. If she hadn't taken a walk yesterday in the park, she'd never have met *the mother*.

The woman had sat next to her on the bench by the wonderful old oak and chatted to her first. If that meeting hadn't happened, who would have taught her not to slap her little girl or call the child a *stupid brat*? The accident the woman would receive might remind her that words can wreak incalculable damage on a child.

To switch with those who deserved their misfortune meant everybody won. She now had a good luck swap all ready to go.

She picked up her coffee, closed the paper, and walked to the window to stare at the people passing by on the sidewalk below. A mother pushing a stroller; a couple walking arm in arm; a group of teens talking animatedly; another couple holding hands; a man in a business suit carrying a satchel.

They all headed somewhere without giving a second thought to whether the futures of which they dreamed and planned didn't belong to them. Now she headed somewhere too, but her destiny was as assured as if etched in the lines of her palm. Her fate, not random, but by choice. She decided that she gained nothing by feeling guilt or apologizing for the gift of the diary and the luck thing arising from within its pages.

She'd earned this through her mother's death and everything that had come since. For anyone who thought of her as undeserving, well, they could shove their opinion and go to hell. And Nem would gladly send them there.

42

By the time William rounded the corner around which Orelia had disappeared, she was a good twenty yards ahead. He dodged and weaved past pedestrians as he tried to catch up to her. A writer's life is sedentary, so he was not fit, and he soon found himself panting with the exertion. Rivulets of sweat trickled down the side of his face, and he wished he'd worn a short sleeve shirt. A foot race was the last thing he'd expected. Then again, nothing was as he expected when it came to Orelia.

The lack of hesitation in her stride suggested she seemed to know her destination. The same crowd of zombie walkers who blocked William's maneuvers weren't as much a hindrance to her. Orelia was nimble on her feet, as she appeared to be returning via the exact route she had come. When she reached the bus stop, the same one at which she'd alighted, she stopped and waited with a small group of commuters. Her demeanor was one of calm as if returning from nothing more than a job or an outing.

William dashed to his car, which, thank God, hadn't been towed. He'd expected to find it gone, but that was at least a piece of luck in his favor, a sign to him he could be doing the right thing. Fortune's kindness though, didn't extend to protecting him from a parking fine.

He tore the offending slip from beneath his wiper and threw it on to the passenger seat.

Who was he kidding? What the hell was he doing? Following a woman for no good reason except that he believed she'd taken his luck and, in doing so, his career. His embarrassing obsession was why he was on his own in this wild goose chase. Yet, so was she. Orelia didn't appear to have any allies or partners.

As he turned the key and heard the engine chug alive, he envisioned the image of the beggar, and Orelia placing the money in his container. So she comes all this way to donate to a stranger? Why does she spend her days inside her protected mansion, only coming out for a meaningless charitable act? Yeah, that made so little sense, his brain felt fried even thinking about it.

He steered the car around the corner in time to see her boarding the bus. His best move was to follow and discover what other sidewalk friends she might visit. He'd return later and check on the recipient of her good nature; maybe the man held a clue.

Wrong decision as he discovered. For she didn't go anywhere except home. Midday turned into late afternoon, and the hours outside The Fortress, as he'd named the place, passed with him anticipating something eventful. But she never ventured out again that day.

By eight he was hungry, tired and frustrated, and he imagined the vagrant had quit his begging spot or been moved on to another destination. The idea of returning to North Park in the evening didn't appeal either. It was time to call this quits and re-evaluate his whole strategy. A day which began with promise of discovering something to solve the puzzle of Orelia Mason had become a pointless waste of precious hours. He could have been writing today and all these past days.

No, you wouldn't, he told himself. *You'd just be sitting there plotting against Orelia. Obsessing like a lunatic.*

But he couldn't give up now because he'd invested too much time already. Quitting now meant nothing would change. He'd still be a has-been writer with no contract, beaten by her, the woman who had taken his generosity and repaid him with hell.

Oh and don't forget, you'll probably end up in jail when the cops work out you were the last person to see your ex-agent alive.

Yes, and there was that too. He must work out her connection to Morris' death.

Okay, he must be smarter than this. He *was* smarter than this. How the heck did he write an award-winning novel if he didn't have a little brain-power happening up there?

Think like a mystery thriller writer, William. What would a detective do?

He'd visit the scene of the crime and interview witnesses.

Right, good idea in theory but no crime scene in his case. Just the results. His career, murdered before his very eyes, ex-agent deceased, and who knew who or what else damaged or destroyed.

So Morris, what happened?

No interviewing a dead guy. His lips are sealed.

He pulled out his *Orelia* notepad. So named because he only used it to jot down his thoughts on her. (If anyone ever found it, he'd be incarcerated in either a prison or an asylum.)

Where was the page of the last words poor Morris made before he went for his final swim?

The flipping of the pages sounded loud and alien in the peaceful woods. William looked around for a moment, wondering if this simple act had alerted her to his whereabouts. He was tired, jumpy and thinking like a scared, afraid-of-the-dark teenager.

He cast his gaze around, imagining something green and terrifying loping toward him out of the tree line. Goosebumps rose on his arms. But nope, no creature to tear him to pieces, just trees and bush and goddamn ants that seemed attracted to him as if he was a rotting corpse. Maybe they knew something he didn't. Dead-man-walking scenario.

He finally found the page and began to read Morris' words he'd jotted down.

"I'm afraid if I say more, I'll be in danger. So many have ended up damaged, ruined. We, we, shit, we argued..."

"She knows what you're doing. She's unforgiving. And dangerous."

"We argued," sprang at him as if written in fluorescent bold red.

Morris and she fought too. Just like he and Orelia. What disagreement was so enormous as to end his life? That's if he believed in the theory Orelia was somehow behind his death.

And did he?

Yes, crazy as that sounded, he did.

Why did he keep questioning himself?

Because if he told anyone about any of this, they'd be making an appointment for him with a shrink. He just knew things though. Feelings that simmered in his blood, in the air around him. Something about her had always been off, as if invisible, energy waves surrounded her, and he wondered why others didn't see or feel it.

Could it be only him? Could he have a special ability to pick up...?

Pick up what, crazy boy? Vibrations as if you're psychic? Ooh, you could star in a Stephen King novel.

He heard a maniacal laugh in his head as if one of the King crazies had taken up residence with the other annoying voices that kept talking at him.

Then he thought back to his own argument with her. So long ago, but fresh in his mind as if they'd squabbled this morning. He wished it had been this morning because he now knew he should have apologized at once. He'd happily eat humble pie to have his life returned and to have never seen the look in Morris' eyes just before he died.

That was scary as hell because he could empathize with that cursed feeling. To be defenseless, waiting for that bus to hit, unable to get your feet to move.

His argument with her was when this whole shebang began. He'd felt a shift in the energy in the air about him, as if a wave had rolled in and wrapped around him. Then, as quickly as it came over him, it receded leaving him doubting it was only his over-active imagination.

A writer's mind is a tool and a writer has an innate ability to focus thoughts and mold any person or event into a whole other entity.

And that's what he'd do. Focus his sharp concentration on every step he had taken to bring him here. He'd make notes as if writing a novel's outline and, just like his books, as he wrote he imagined the answer would reveal itself. This was to be no book though. This was the recounting of his downfall and, hopefully, the road map of his survival.

He raced back to his car as the sun began to set, turning the surrounding trees into a crowd of giants looking upon him in judgment. After everything, that he could now handle; they were nothing compared to literary critics.

A clasp of hope now fastened about his heart. Where his energy had begun to fade, his mind and body felt supercharged. And determined. *How determined was he?*

More than ever before in his life. He could do this. Nobody had stopped her until now, but he would find a way to solve the mystery of Orelia Mason. He'd be the lone warrior who faces the invincible monster and frees the world from a terrible curse.

No more second-guessing. No more worrying about his past career or where he'd end up if he failed. He didn't care anymore. Just knowing how and why she preyed on others was enough reward. Stopping her would be a bonus. Getting his life back the ultimate reward. If the God of fortune looked down upon him at this moment, William hoped he saw the makings of a fearless hero. He'd never been one before, but who knew? Maybe he could become one now.

43

The morning of the interview at Bountiful Books began as every other day since Nem had moved to this city. Her entire being was filled with the anticipation of an exciting adventure. Greg, and what he was doing at any given moment whenever he entered her thoughts, hadn't happened at all today. A great sign that her new life had begun the untangling process of her future from her past. This gave her strength in the belief she could do this. If she could recover so easily from a miscarriage and her marriage break-down, then she had little to fear of the future.

She focused her thoughts on the interview; her earlier concerns of complications from surrounding herself daily with strangers had left her. She wanted this job and could have easily used the luck thing to be assured of securing it.

A quiet hope inside wanted the diary to ignore her desire and not use its power to simply hand her this. She wanted to win, fair and square, like the Bewitched character Samantha. She desired to live as an average person, failing and succeeding on her own merit.

She noticed since she hadn't always used the accrued power, that it worked like a bank account, allowing her to build a type of equity of bad fortune. When it needed to be spent, the good fortune was inserted in a line beneath the last misfortune notation.

The diary, while playing a balancing act with fate, seemed okay with being in debt either way. It hadn't seemed to work like this for the previous owners but for her, things appeared different. She wondered if this was because she'd tried so many times not to use it, or if she had used it on occasion to help others and not just herself. In the end, she told herself, however it worked, it didn't do her a scrap of good to worry about the mechanics. The diary did what it did, and she lived how she lived. Sometimes they were partners, and sometimes not.

She wanted, needed to know, that when it came to this job, if her own personality and smarts sufficed. Maybe that's what her mom had imagined she was doing with Alan. Had she wanted love to find her on its own and to work out her problems without magical assistance?

She wondered if these thoughts occupied the minds of a billionaire's children. Did they decline their parents' financial assistance in order to grow their own confidence in their abilities?

Probably not. Why would you? She laughed at her answer and hoped she might be stronger than that, but if in the end, she gave in and used the diary, or it just interceded, then so be it.

Nem had decided to walk to the store, using the opportunity to familiarize herself with the neighborhood. She'd chosen well and delighted in glancing at the smattering of coffee shops amid the apartment blocks and funky, designer stores. She made a mental note to visit a different one each day and explore this new world.

The sun shone and the warmth on her skin infused her with a deep sense of happiness and contentment. She very nearly skipped along the pavement. This was where she belonged. She'd trusted her instincts to come to this city and she had been right. She wouldn't doubt herself ever again.

When the man stepped in front of her, the sudden movement took her by surprise. She gasped and nearly fell sideways.

"Repent you sinner. Yooooou, bringer of evil and darkness. Look to God to forgive you."

He was dressed in a long white shirt in need of cleaning and his knotted, shoulder-length hair hung over his eyes, making her wonder how he even saw her. And he smelled. It wasn't only his clothes needing a wash.

Spittle exploded from his mouth as he spat out, "You, daughter of Erebus have strayed. No longer do you dispense justice. You are a shameful shrew."

He reached out and grabbed her wrist.

"Get away from me," she said, tearing her hand back, shocked and offended not just by his touch but the words. They seemed too close to the truth. Not that he could know anything about her. He was obviously insane.

What right did he have to threaten her or anyone minding their own business walking past? As if God would use a filthy man like him to contact his subjects on earth. How ridiculous.

But what he'd said did catch her attention. She had researched her name upon discovering Nem was short for Nemesis. This was news to her as her mom had only ever called her Nem. Goddess Nemesis dispensed justice to those who had grown arrogant before the gods. Even the Greek version of the word *némein* was translated to *deliver what was due.* Upon reading that, she felt even more certain she had been born to do this work and was the true heir to the diary.

But he was just a sick, mad man, who harassed everyone who walked past. Although he did appear to be solely focused on her. She managed to dodge around him but still felt his stare burn into her back as she continued away. Her heart beat against her chest as his words rattled in her head. He certainly shouldn't annoy innocent people, and she could do something about it. If anybody needed to be delivered their *due,* that guy sure did.

She stopped and turned to stare back at him. A creeping feeling came over her, for he now stood in the middle of the sidewalk glaring after her. Unmoving, as if he was a stone statue amid Greek ruins. People ignored him but moved around quickly. *Was he challenging her to return?*

Well, she'd take him up on that and teach him not to accost young women, especially this one.

Nem returned and stood before him. She noted the alcohol smell on his breath and realized what devil really possessed him. He was a drunk and nothing more. His dark brown eyes continued to bore into hers in defiance.

"What's your name?"

"She speaks," he replied, circling his hand between them as though swiping a window between them to the side.

Flecks of white spit hung from his lips and chin. He disgusted her, but she wanted to understand why he had chosen her to accost.

"What did you mean before? Why did you say those things?"

"You need to repent for your evil doings. God has sent me to warn you that you must stop and change yourself."

Nem sniggered.

"And if I don't?"

"The Kingdom has abandoned you and your doom is assured. Halt now and you may be forgiven."

"And your name is?"

"My name I will not reveal. I know what becomes of names. But you, daughter of Erebus... you cannot hide. You are found."

She smiled at him, a half-smile that didn't reach her eyes.

You know what, this man annoyed her, and on a day when she felt so good. She imagined he'd experienced his fair share of tragedy in life but that was no excuse for accosting her and saying such terrible things. At that thought, the little wheel of fate turned and locked into place. The metallic echo in her head as loud as if she stood inside a bank vault, locks turning slowly with a clunk at the close of day.

His name was unnecessary. The diary knew everybody's name; no doubt it had already recorded him and his coming misfortune.

"Okay, well thanks for the warning. I'll be sure to keep a lookout for my punishment coming for me. You might want to watch out too."

He looked puzzled for a moment. Then his eyes widened, and she wondered if he realized the mistake he'd made. Instead of delivering a message from his stupid God, his nonsense annoyed the heck out of someone he should have ignored.

"I forgive you," she said as she turned and walked away. "I don't think my gods will do the same."

She'd traveled only five yards before she heard his reply, but she never looked back or acknowledged his words. Why argue with a crazy man who didn't have long to live? In fact, death was just around the corner for him she imagined. Living on the street could be so dangerous.

"He is coming and he knows you. Your evil shall be avenged."

He'd learn soon enough about vengeance. Nem smiled as she returned her focus to the next step in her life. Her job interview. She felt good that she experienced no guilt or concern for the man or his fate.

He probably didn't have a life worth living, anyway. He should have found himself work and made different choices, so he wasn't left hurling weird accusations at strangers.

Nem turned the next corner onto the street of Bountiful Books. Her mind had traveled five minutes ahead; to meeting her boss-to-be and seeing the place where her career would begin. For she was positive great things would come from today and her new job.

When she heard the screech of brakes, followed by a loud bang, a gruesome crack, then the blare of a car horn, she didn't look back or wonder what had happened. She already knew.

Payback was a bitch.

44

The bored-looking assistant behind the register had one of those black circle things in his ear, which always freaked out William. What happened when they got sick of a hole there? And could he have any more tattoos on his arms? And that metal jewelry in his lip. God, the thing had a nasty point that could draw blood. What are these people thinking?

He'd returned early in the morning to the corner where Orelia had given the money and note to the homeless man. Upon arrival, he'd been disappointed to see he was no longer there. After walking up and down several blocks and even searching in dark, rancid smelling alleys, he returned to the store where he'd last seen him.

"A man was here. Yesterday... outside," said William

"Like a cud-omer?" replied Spear Lip. "How do I know who ya mean? We get hundred'd every day."

William didn't appreciate the way the guy looked at him as if he was stupid. He wasn't the one who'd mutilated his body in the name of fashion.

"I mean, the vagrant by your door yesterday."

"Oh, the Captain? Long hair, kind-a cradey 'round the eye'd?"

"Yes," said William thinking, *the pot calling the kettle black about crazy eyes.*

"Yeah, man, that dude wad okay. U'ed to throw him a roll and a drink when the bod'd wad-n't looking."

The disgusting metal shard in his lip, upon which William could not help focusing, caused him to pronounce his S's as D's. *Why would you do that to yourself?*

"Cop'd move him on but he'd alway'd come back. Good begging out-tide here he told me."

"Yes, yes, that'll be him. *The Captain.* Where is he? When will he return do you think?"

Spear Lip shook his head.

"Nope, he'd not coming back any time. Poor guy. Kinda ironic. D'aid hid last name was the s'dame as that fella in 'Tar Trek. You know, the Captain."

"Kirk. Are you talking about James T. Kirk?"

"Yeah. Kirk. That's why he called him'elf Captain. Bad luck for him he wadn't the real one and the crew could have teleported him away."

He vibrated his hands in the air and then flicked them upward to demonstrate dematerialization as in the beaming-up process made famous in the sci-fi series.

"What do you mean? What happened to him?"

"He came in here, all happy, midday yed-terday. Had a chunk of change he d'aid a woman gave him. If not for dat dollars, he'd-a been here today, begging away."

The clerk laughed and then stopped himself.

"D'um peopled'd just don't have no luck. I bet he wis'ded he'd 'tayed put, but he had that money and came in here, bought a pack of deegs."

"Cigarettes, you mean?"

"Yeah man, like I said, he had that windfall, and he wad happy-happy. I asked him, *Hey Captain, ya taking flight early?* And he said, *Yeah, I'm getting a hot meal and a room.* He held up that Benjamin like a winning lottery ticket. Good for him, I thought. He de'derve a break.

Hour later, 'n almighty bang.Like a ten-ton truck dropped from a plane. And that'd it. The Captain dematerialyded forever. Turned out, a pickup hit a building two block'd over. Corner of the whole thing collap-ded. You didn't cop a look at it? The fucked-up building? The rubble? It's a war d-zone."

"No," replied William, "And the Captain?"

"Of all the room'd the poor guy could have taken to d'pend his Ben. That wad the place. They pulled him outta there and well ya don't walk away from that. We heard thid morning. I hope he laid zees and never knew what hit him. If that woman—he called her an angel—hadn't given him the dollar'd, he'd be out front now. Talk 'bout *I'dn't It Ironic*? You know that d'ong?"

William nodded to the clerk about the song, then shook his head about the bizarre news. Words eluded him he was so stunned. He muttered a quick thank you and headed for the door.

He found the wrecked hotel within moments. Spear Lip was correct. The place indeed was a war zone, the front corner of the three-story building in ruins. A mountain of collapsed bricks lay piled high as if dumped there ready for construction. Crushed by a still intact portion of wall was a lone car.

Several men in hard hats and orange vests climbed among the remains, moving methodically and with caution. A temporary nine-foot fence erected to protect against voyeurs held back a swarm of pedestrians who'd stopped to examine the destruction.

William stood by the barrier, his hand clenched tight around the mesh. What an unholy mess. He wondered what the poor fellow had done to deserve this fate. Orelia couldn't have known him before yesterday, could she? No, that wasn't possible, but what did he truly know? Was she now targeting complete strangers? If so, why? Or was The Captain just unlucky?

Isn't It Ironic? played in his head. He'd always liked that song; kind of reminded him of his own life and the wrong decision made to follow Orelia instead of talking to the Captain. The answer to many of his questions may have lain only ten yards away yesterday, in the note in the vagrant's collection container.

Another person dead connected to her, even if only for a moment of contact. How many more had died? Would die?

The Alanis Morisette melody drifted through his head as he turned from the devastation, wondering at the power that could have created this.

Isn't it ironic? he sang under his breath, thinking nothing when it came to Orelia was random irony.

45

*B*ountiful Books' manager, Diane Lynch, looked like an escapee from the punk rock eighties. Her pink-wash hair, streaked with blonde, fit far better in an alternative designer clothes store than selling bookmarks, magazines and classic novels. She wore a Rolling Stones' *'Get off my cloud'* attitude and did not hold back her opinions.

"Out with the old, white thriller guys. In with the fresh voices. King, Koontz and Child have got one foot in the graves they write about in their books." This was her explanation as to why she only stacked piles of new authors in the coveted front table display.

"They're given enough shelf space in the big book barns and nobody else gets a fair chance. And none of these ridiculous YA apocalyptic books either. If the only person to save us is Jennifer Lawrence with a bow, I'll hand myself over to the zombies."

Nem attempted pointing out there were no zombies in *Hunger Games*, thinking this might be a test of her literary knowledge. It wasn't. She would learn that mixed metaphors, and crazy but somehow still reasonable ideas, populated Diane's quips.

"Well, that's the problem right there. The undead always improve a storyline."

When Nem discovered they were both Jane Austen fans, she decided to break her *no friends* rule this once, just for a moment to indulge her passion for discussing books.

"I've read Fifty Shades of Gray. I'll kill you if you tell anyone," she whispered. "And I wouldn't say *no* to Mr. Darcy if I met him at a dance and discovered he enjoyed using a horsewhip. I'd have no *pride* or *prejudice* with him."

By the end of the interview, Nem knew the job was hers. Even without the diary's help, the click of meshing kindred spirits was as loud as the green book's turning cogs of fate.

Work began the following Monday and she had spent the time barely containing her excitement. She avoided traveling via the preacher's street on her first day. He wouldn't be there anymore. Misfortune would find him without her as a witness. She also didn't want anyone to remember her from their meeting. Most likely nobody would recall them together, but she still remained cautious.

Her new boss' company was too much fun. She foresaw a friendship growing between them, despite her determination to stick to her golden rule. Diane made it near impossible to not like her. Her zany, multi-colored leggings alone was enough reason to adore her.

That wasn't the only rule she ignored. She'd begun to use the diary again. Removing the pavement preacher had lit something inside and she'd decided why not dabble in a little vigilante work. Maybe she'd need her store of luck one day.

She'd become even more cautious though, in that she would now venture to distant parts of the city, never visiting the same place twice. With this new *hobby*, along with working in the same location every day, she didn't want her habits noticed. Chances were remote that her secret would be discovered. Why tempt fate though?

Nem had never been keen on crossing paths again with any of the strangers whose names appeared in the diary. That had happened to her once with an elderly man, Mr. Bentley, who lived on her street. A crotchety old guy who repeatedly complained that living his life wasn't worth a damn. She didn't enjoy witnessing his face grow haggard as illness devoured his body, but she did feel a certain satisfaction she'd delivered his wish (whether he'd been serious or not).

With the unknowns she met, she also didn't care to know whether they survived accidents which befell them. Though she had banished guilt from her conscience, she didn't need reminding that every good piece of luck delivered, demanded that an equal tragedy befall another. She simply enjoyed totting up the lines filled with minuses like scalps worn by warriors.

The one challenge with her *don't-get-involved* rule was that she couldn't tell if somebody deserved their misfortune. After giving the quandary thought, she had decided simply to guess who'd been *naughty or nice*. Thinking of it as similar to the clichéd Christmas legend made the diary's acts seem less malevolent.

Thanks to the pavement preacher, she'd hit upon the notion to use people whom life had already kicked in the teeth, the populace of vagrants who lived on the sidewalks. She told herself her good deed was in helping them escape a terrible life and rid the world of people who didn't contribute. They had no future, and she rescued them as well as delivering a happy last few hours or days with a large donation.

Thanks to their gifts of luck, Nem thrived in her job and Bountiful Books' business increased in the weeks after she began her employment.

She loved the place and her work, just as she predicted. Several others worked in the store; Suzi, the assistant manager, and Cheryl were kind and friendly to her. When you love books, you never run out of conversation. Her fear of difficult customers disappeared because fate's blessings were on her side. Always.

She was no longer concerned there may be a disagreement with anyone. Her continued supply of luck took care of that. Shame she didn't think of using the diary during her marriage. Still, she harbored no regrets because after everything that happened with Greg, she was able to live in freedom to choose her future.

Within a few weeks, Diane promoted her to assistant manager.

Suzi's child suddenly grew ill with a disease which the doctors were unable to diagnose. With hospital stays and tests, she couldn't cope, and until her son recovered, she couldn't continue in her role.

"I hope his recovery will be swift," Nem had told her, knowing it wouldn't.

She hadn't yet dared expand her good fortune to include money. Though she'd helped Peg and Ray those years ago, she imagined winning the lottery would bring undue attention. She didn't need that or the questions about how her adoptive parents and she could be so lucky. Lightning striking twice was news and she didn't want to be news.

Besides, everything she needed for happiness was hers for the moment. A comfortable apartment, an enjoyable job, a friend with pink hair (who'd have thought?) and a sense of belonging somewhere. Happy days.

Until that Friday. For the six months she'd worked at the store, Diane had invited her for a meal or a drink or a movie every Friday on their payday.

"Pizza tonight?" she said this time. "Red wine. A discussion on why Stephen King writes five hundred adjectives too many on each page. Then maybe hit a karaoke bar if we've drunk enough. Come on Nem. You need to let your hair down—in fact mess it up honey—and meet someone."

"I've got a Skype call with my mom. But thanks for asking."

"Your mom. Brother. Hamster. Invisible friend. They can wait. I know family is the most important thing but so is hanging out and letting off steam and drinking with your boss. Especially drinking with your boss."

Nem laughed and hoped she sounded sincere. She'd used most of the excuses she had in her armory and was now on repeats.

Friends, lovers, anyone or anything could not be allowed to grow too close. For their sake. After Greg, her mother, and her school mates, she couldn't say she didn't understand the risks. Her control and power had grown, yes, but relationships were always a wonky one-way road with a destination of which she couldn't be sure.

Diane persisted this time. Well, she usually persisted but she was far more fervent.

"When are you going to say, 'count me in,' Miss? You need to get out. You're young and pretty. Something I aspire to but for some damn reason each birthday I keep getting older. I won't stop asking because I care about you."

And there was the problem, all wrapped up in that one sentence.

The woman did care, and while Nem thought the world of Diane, in her world that wasn't healthy. A sudden realization hit her: things needed to stop right here. She loved working with books and had begun to value Diane's friendship, against her better judgment. But she didn't need anyone caring about her ever again. The thought of leaving very nearly broke her heart, the heart she'd tried to harden and encase in steel for just this reason.

"Is it a yes or pester-me-next-week no?"

Diane's vibrant pink do, backlit by the store's internal lights, glowed angelic-like with a glistening, wonderful sparkle. She was a good person and Nem felt gratitude for her kindness and making her laugh with her smart quips on customers and authors. Now she had a decision to make and she knew, even before she considered it, which way she must go.

"I'll take the we'll-get-back-to-you box, okay?"

Diane folded her arms and waggled her head side-to-side. "Listen, if I didn't know better, I'd think you're keeping a deep dark secret. You know you can tell me, honey. My lips are sealed."

She ran a hand with her fingers pressed together across her mouth.

"Nothing to hide," Nem said, with a limp smile, already realizing the time at Bountiful Books and her friendship with Diane were nearly at an end. "I'm an open book."

"I wouldn't say that," replied Diane. "You're more a mystery."

46

William had learned many things watching Orelia; much of it left him wondering what the hell he had actually discovered. Along with this slight progress with events surrounding the Captain's death, his enthusiasm for amateur detective work had returned. Three days more of surveillance and he felt he was drawing closer to something. What that something was exactly, he couldn't tell yet, but a pattern had emerged.

Each day now she followed the same morning routine. (She must have been taking a vacation after Morris' water mishap.) Travel to a new part of the city—well, new to him. Who knew with her? The trip was at least forty minutes from her house by bus or train.

Each time she'd visit a homeless person, man or woman, didn't appear to matter. All they shared was that they begged from the pavement or roadside. Orelia gave them money and then departed to return to her home without stopping anywhere else on the way.

He'd follow her to her destination and back to her residence to ensure there was no deviation. There wasn't.

Unlike the first trip to the Captain, she hadn't yet left another written note. She only stopped for a few minutes to deliver a bill or two. She then returned to her beautiful residence with the high *walls* and remained holed up inside until the next day.

With only small variations on distance and times, her outings appeared to achieve little and the people with whom she interacted shared nothing in common except they lived on the street. *Odd, peculiar, and downright baffling.*

Until today, he had decided not to approach any of the beneficiaries of her kindness. Instead, he waited to see what became of them without interference or contact from himself. He also worried Orelia may return out of the blue and discover him there. He wasn't sure what might happen if she learned that her movements were under surveillance. Morris, struggling in the water before sinking under, always traveled in the back of his mind.

What he did learn from his spying blew his mind. Each time she displayed generosity, by helping her fellow man or woman hard up on their luck, that person didn't enjoy her gift for long. Each met a bizarre fate in the form of an accident. Thanks to a brilliant idea of his, he learned of each event once they occurred.

He only needed a police scanner for a hundred bucks—delivered within four hours by Amazon. This, along with Google and scouring news outlets on his phone, saw his journal fill with notes. He'd recorded times, events and tragic accidents far too co-incidental to her visits to be considered normal bad luck.

Case in point, Jerome Rapid.

Homeless guy number two, Mr. Rapid, hitched a ride on the front of a train car the same night following his happy visit from Orelia. Later that night, as he crossed a train line, he slipped and fell onto the tracks. Somehow, he managed to escape the moving carriages and landed to the side, unharmed. What he didn't see though was the other oncoming locomotive, which grabbed him by the feet, devoured his legs and dragged him thirty yards. The wheels had entangled Rapid's entire lower half. One leg had been torn away, with the remaining attached by a thread of muscle. Despite this, he survived. A lucky circumstance, or maybe not from his perspective.

Number three spent his windfall on a bottle of scotch. No real surprise there. Then rolled out of bed and died a terrible death. In his inebriated state, he'd used a ledge seventeen-feet above a highway intersection as a place to rest his weary head. His blood alcohol level was point two nine.

Today she'd helped a woman who'd been walking along the sidewalk, pushing a shopping cart overburdened with plastic bags filled with clothes, cans and bottles. A wide-brimmed red hat covered her face that if worn by a svelte young lady would be fashionable. Matched with her baggy trousers and stained purple t-shirt it delivered the correct impression, that her wardrobe was from a thrift shop or the trash.

He wanted to cross the road and warn her, but he was uncertain if his interference might have any effect. His first duty was to save his own life. He reasoned that only by continuing his surveillance could he put a permanent stop to whatever black magic Orelia wielded.

This Orelia was a different person to the one he'd first met. Maybe she'd changed. Maybe she had become the world's most charitable author, infatuated with society's underdogs. But he knew better. She had an agenda and today had become his lucky day because he had discovered something. Correction, today he'd remembered something he had forgotten. And that something seemed important.

Funny how inconsequential details become large beacons in hindsight. Thank goodness too, because he couldn't keep following her forever. His car had earned three parking fines and yesterday he'd narrowly missed being towed.

As usual, she had led him to a disheveled man leaning against the wall of an ornately decorated building of the early previous century. A pair of carved lions the size of large dogs sat guarding the curved-arched entrance. One half of the beast's snout, eaten away by the decades, made the carving of the animal appear to suffer leprosy. Ten etched columns ran along its façade overlooking a small open hallway running behind and the length of the frontage. The structure had seen better days but must have been elegant and imposing in its heyday. The irony that this place was a library, announced by the sign above the entrance, was not lost on him.

Two authors stood outside a library and one said to the other... he recited below his breath, then couldn't think of a punch line.

The man's makeshift home, a flattened cardboard box, had been placed to the side of the door. Protected by the alcove, he'd spread out his meager creature comforts of a thermos, mug, rug, and surprisingly a book (maybe borrowed from within).

William positioned himself nearby, three columns away, out of sight, but close enough to hear, he hoped. If he was somewhere in Europe, he might have imagined himself as John le Carré's espionage hero George Smiley. He wished he possessed a tenth of the fictional character's spy craft skills, but he'd feel safer if he possessed Lee Child's Jack Reacher's aggression. He'd even take just mastering his glare.

As with the other homeless, this man's appearance told a sad story of a tragic life lived on streets and in back alleys. His matted hair, lined face, and at this distance the slumping of his shoulders, painted a picture of lost hope.

Orelia approached the man with reverence, smiling and relaxed. Why wouldn't she feel confident and comfortable? She'd done this every day since he'd shadowed her. She might have done it a hundred times for all he knew. Now he wondered about every freak accident he read in the news.

She leaned down to him and said something William couldn't hear. The poor fellow looked up with empty eyes devoid of emotion and replied, but his words too were unintelligible. Forget spy craft and Jiu-jitsu skills, he'd take lip reading right now.

Orelia handed over several bills, and from the way the man bowed and nodded his head, William presumed as with previous contributions, they must be high denominations. Then she stood back, reached into her over-shoulder gray bag and pulled out a book. This he recognized as the same green volume in which she'd made a notation after giving money to the Captain.

This was the nearest he'd been to Orelia on one of her *missions*.

He was so close he could see the shade of her bright-pink nail varnish —fairy-floss sprang to mind—as she flipped through the book's pages. After a moment, she found whatever she'd been seeking, stopped and stared at the contents. After satisfying herself on something within, she returned it to her bag.

At this range, he now saw in detail the decorative, gold swirl markings on the cover, and that's what tugged and pulled at his memory. Because he knew that book. The image of it in her hands transported him back a few years ago, to the coffee shop and the argument which ended their friendship.

Back then, he recalled thinking it was a diary of sorts because of the size and leather binding. He hadn't seen the pages and didn't note it as being of any importance. His impression had been of a beautiful item, the craftsmanship of which was rare these days. An old but unremarkable journal.

The way she now stared at the book evoked such a strong response, he recalled every detail from then, as if someone had hit play on an old DVD.

Yes, there it was, all the same. The tilt of her head, the self-satisfied smile, as if whatever was written inside pleased her. Her demeanor, identical to that day three years ago.

In that second, he no longer stood mere yards from his nemesis, but he was now in that café on that afternoon. A flashback of immense value because—drum roll, please—there was something about the diary. Something important. This might just be the missing piece.

What had she said before walking away, leaving his life to the destruction that lay ahead?

"You'll be sorry William Barnes. Very sorry."

And he had been sorry. Not straight away, but yes, since he'd recognized her curse on his career, regret had walked beside him every hour of every day.

So what was in that book? Now he'd realized this connection, what other detail had been filed in his brain from that meeting?

What clue? What inconsequential words or behavior might reveal who or what Orelia Mason was, and what her true plans were?

He allowed the memory to flood his mind and realized almost at once he'd missed an extraordinary and important clue.

47

*N*em began looking for a new job at once. She checked online and in the papers on Friday night, instead of going out with Diane. This was a better use of her time. As she scanned the available positions, she considered returning to temporary work. Even if it wasn't data entry, she could do temp secretarial work in offices, insurance companies or any business really.

When she looked back on this moment later, she laughed at the irony of her concern. Her new career was coming for her as surely as sunshine followed rain. It took a series of events to deliver her to the path, each one appearing meaningless until viewed from the distance of time.

A rainy day.

A chance meeting with a stranger.

The discovery of a gift within herself.

A risk taken that altered her destiny.

They were just around the corner, waiting to direct her, a sign-posted walkway with each event leading to the next.

The first nudge arrived on the following Sunday morning. The weather was face-tingling cold and wet, and too nasty a day to go outside. The best plan Nem decided was to hibernate inside and read one of the multitude of books piled by her bedside. Her bookcase, filled to falling with advance reader copies, could hold no more. The publishers' sales agents delivered these copies prior to release, so staff could sample upcoming books. They hoped the staff would consider making recommendations to their customers. There were so many scattered around her apartment, she'd never read every one of them.

A writer she'd discovered in recent months, Caroline Kepnes, had a new novel which sounded good. Her debut *You* was a best seller and a heck of a read. But as she lifted the novel to study the cover, she noticed *Gone with the Wind* near the bottom of the ten-high stack.

At heart, she was a romance reader. If she couldn't enjoy love in her life, then she could live through the characters. She loved Scarlett and her dogged determination; when nobody believed in her, she kept going. That girl didn't break into a million little pieces because Rhett left her. Tough stuff was her middle name. Just like Nem.

She stared through the window, watching as the drizzle trickled down the pane, reminding her of captured tears. That was what she needed, a book with drama and heartbreak but with an ultimate happy ending. Not *Gone with the Wind*. No, she knew what she was in the mood to read as she made her way to the bookshelf in her living room.

"There you are," she said, pulling out her well-worn copy of Jane Austen's *Pride and Prejudice*. Another strong female character, but Elizabeth Bennett gets her man, and on her terms.

After making herself a cup of coffee and loading a plate with chocolate chip cookies and a token piece of healthy fruit, she settled herself on the sofa. Curled beside her, as if this was her idea, was Emily.

The spoiled black and white kitten had circumvented Nem's rule of no relationships when she'd spied her in the window of a pet store. She resembled Patch and so how could Nem leave her there mewling at passersby?

She'd considered calling her P-Two but decided she didn't need a reminder of that day two decades ago. Instead, inspired by one of her favorite authors, she named her Emily. As in *Wuthering Heights* Bronte, Emily.

Fifty pages in, and despite as usual enjoying Austen's Regency era world, her mind had wandered to mundane activities. Shopping for a new coat. Whether she should eat Chinese or Italian for dinner. And career ideas, because giving up her job bothered her. She'd miss Diane. Hey, that was the point, to distance herself from friendships.

Nem glanced at her empty plate and cup and attempted to convince herself to go make another. She would, after she finished this chapter. She returned to the story and, as she continued, wondered what happened to Austen's characters, Elizabeth and Darcy, after they married? And what might have become of the intelligent, witty young woman if she hadn't won his heart? Might she have started a business, or met a warmer man, or remained a spinster but a contented one?

She enjoyed the happy endings, but they weren't realistic. The prince and princess didn't always live happily ever after. *Now that makes for a far more interesting story.* More so, if written well, than conclusions wrapped up in clichés. No matter how many times she reread this book and other favorites, they traveled the same paths to similar destinations. She wanted a different ending.

She ran a hand over Emily's head and mused on the top-selling authors' books she'd read in recent months. The spoiled cat purred and rolled over to expose her stomach and Nem obliged her desires, scratching and cooing to her.

A strange thought entered her mind like a swooping bird, surprising her from overhead. In an I'm-talking-to-a-cute-fluffy-creature tone, she addressed Emily.

"Hey, my little friend, what if instead of reading someone else's novel, you and I write our own story?"

There, the idea was out. Nem sat in silence, staring at the ceiling; she saw herself hunched over a blank sheet of paper. Her curiosity chased after the image for a moment, and she laughed, thinking, *that's ridiculous.*

She caught the little dream and turned it over in her mind, seeing herself holding her own book against her chest, proud of accomplishing such a thing. Then she threw away the thought for its complete silliness.

Her an author? Yeah, right.

In an instant, a question flew at her with such force she felt as if struck by a big, fluffy ball.

What's so ridiculous?

Nem leaned down to the purring Emily and lifted her friend to eye height.

"Crazy, right?" she said meeting the cat's stare.

Her purrs sounded as if they were a reply, *No-thring. No-thring. No-thrrring. No-thing.*

"Is that your true opinion or are you smart enough not to bite the hand that feeds you?"

She pulled the kitten in and nuzzled her soft head beneath her chin.

"That's it Miss. I'm done with daydreaming and reading."

As if in agreement, Emily leaped from her lap to the floor and curled around her legs.

Nem picked up *Pride and Prejudice* with one hand while balancing her empty coffee cup on her plate in the other as she walked to the kitchen.

As much as writing a book was a daunting thought, impossible and even foolish, the idea wended its way into a recess in her imagination and stuck like a prickle. Prod as she might, she couldn't dislodge it.

Nem glanced over her shoulder as she placed the crockery into the sink. "You want lunch?"

A hungry kitten looked up at her in grateful acknowledgement. She pulled open the fridge door but quickly realized there was no cat food. Darn. She didn't love the idea of facing that weather.

A glance out the window told her the rain had eased at least. That worked even if it was cold. A walk in the chilly air was a good way to shake silly thoughts and little Emily needed her lunch. She put on her jacket, wrapped a scarf around her neck and pulled a beanie over her ears before opening the door.

Emily continued to follow her every movement as if she knew this somehow involved her.

As she pulled the door closed behind her, Nem caught sight of the kitchen table and again saw herself in a fantasy future sitting there reading over her finished manuscript. This idea sure was as stubborn as Scarlett O'Hara. She paused for a second enjoying the flight of fancy.

"When I come back, we'll start on our best seller. You come up with a story idea," she said to Emily.

The creature meowed an acknowledgement, then turned, tail whipping behind her, and walked toward the sofa.

"No, you're right. That's just plain stupid. Maybe crazy. Your namesake would tell me, *Sorry, being great at reading books doesn't make you great at writing them.*"

And the diary? flashed through her mind.

No, that couldn't help. Its power was in delivering good luck not the ability to write a good book. She had no experience and no education in writing.

No, she wasn't an author. She wouldn't know how to begin a novel. Nem couldn't even imagine selling a single copy if she wrote one, no matter if she had all the luck in the world on her side. She a famous author? Now that was a laugh.

48

The diary was a significant discovery. That day in the café three years ago, he recalled it in her possession. Even before that time. His attention wasn't focused on such an inconsequential detail. Why would you note an everyday item like a book unless you had foresight? He thought Orelia had written something inside, but that was his first mistake. He'd made so many with her.

He recalled now she'd used the book the same way as she had with the homeless man. That poor guy was him, a sitting *unlucky* duck, unknowing, naïve.

The other odd thing he also remembered from their argument was the way she looked. She had delved into her bag to retrieve the diary, and he'd seen anger flash in her eyes. Her mouth stretched into a mocking, knowing smile. Back then, he'd imagined she was the one making a mistake.

The disagreement at first seemed nothing more than a simple conflict of ideas. Once he'd calmed down hours later, he didn't give it another thought. In hindsight, he understood this was a crucial life moment, the beginning of the end for him.

He'd admit that he wore partial blame for the upset. In the

middle of her unreasonableness, with emotions fanned and flaring, he couldn't forgive her. But mulling over the events in the following hours after he'd calmed down, he saw it from her point of view. A writer's forte was insight into others perspectives. She didn't know how hard he'd worked on her behalf.

Of course, she couldn't have known how he'd put his reputation on the line. Morris needed more than gentle persuasion to convince him to read the manuscript. His agent had been adamant he had no time, didn't care, and wasn't interested in representing another author.

She'd been excited the last time they had met too, telling him how, after many scrubbed attempts, she had decided to go with the pen-name Orelia Mason. He'd told her to keep her name because he found it unusual. She said she wanted to keep the one she'd used when she first introduced herself to him. Something about distancing herself from her past. Starting afresh.

He'd laughed, thinking why bother, but he hadn't told her this. Okay, so the nom de plume had a certain sophisticated ring. Still, he cautioned her to walk before she ran. But hey, let her play the dream game. What writer didn't hope for success?

"No, call me Orelia from now on," she said, when he questioned her decision. "It'll keep me in the right frame of mind."

He should have realized then, with the resistance, that this meeting wasn't going to go well. Everything went downhill from there, an out of control sled, skidding and sliding until it ended in a ditch shattered, the damage irreparable.

Prior to this day, Miss Wannabe Orelia had proved a worthy mentee. She had listened with great attention and took every suggestion with enthusiasm. He recalled more than once how he'd challenged her to disagree with his opinion, so he might teach her a valuable lesson.

"Authors must trust their instincts. Have confidence. Reject an editor's corrections when you know you're right. This is your work not theirs. Your story to tell."

The finessing of her novel took months because William had

been in the middle of promotional activity for his new book. This involved travel for several weeks to festivals and so many interviews he felt like a wind-up toy. Despite this, he made time to speak to her by email or Messenger.

How generous had he been? Yet, ingratitude was his reward.

Once he returned home, they'd meet every Wednesday for an hour in a small out-of-the-way café. He wanted her to learn to work anywhere, surrounded by distractions. So he insisted she spend time, after he left her at these places alone, working on his suggestions.

Her first book was as much his as hers.

On the day their partnership died, exploded, disintegrated, William had been excited and filled with anticipation of sharing his news. He hadn't experienced euphoria such as this since his own novel hit the New York Times bestseller list. He surprised himself by how thrilled he was for someone other than himself.

It didn't occur to him to think of her as a friend. If he was being honest with himself, he wasn't helping her for only her sake. Every time they met, or he returned a message with a suggestion or idea, he helped himself. These interactions were akin to papering extra layers of confidence over his ego. And a writer needed his or her ego stroked often.

The way she looked at him, the admiration he saw in her eyes for his *genius*, as she called it, filled him with bravado. This in turn, transferred to his ability to tackle his own writing.

On that day, he recalled his anticipation, the warmth of the air, the smell of the coffee and freshly baked cakes, as he dodged around chairs and other café patrons. His stomach skipped, imagining her happiness when he delivered the best news any writer could receive.

She would be expecting this to be just another meeting to discuss improvements to her manuscript. His plan though was to tease her. He'd say something like, *We have a long way to go. Getting there, but plenty more work needed.*

This wasn't true. Not even close. What he hadn't yet shared was that four weeks ago it became obvious they were close enough to good that Morris might bite. And bite he did. Into the poisoned apple.

Ain't hindsight a smack in the head? When it came to Orelia Mason, even back then, it was more a knife sliced across your throat. Sharp, clean and deadly.

_a_gainst every _forget it_ thought Nem threw at the notion of trying to write a book, another voice fought back with two simple words.

Why not?

By the time she'd turned on to her street carrying Emily's food, multiple questions had already fired through her mind. How would she do this? Should she first attend a course to learn the craft? When should she begin? What story might she tell?

Thriller? She didn't think she could write about murders; death being too close to reality.

Ditto for horror.

Mystery? She wasn't sure she possessed the mind to create twists, turns and red herrings. Possibly though.

Science Fiction. Uh-uh. She'd failed science at school.

Romance? Hmm, potential there. She loved romances and happy endings, but she could put a twist on that. Darken up the storytelling.

What about _Mystery Romance_? Hmm, getting closer. Definite maybe.

Answers flew back without her even thinking, as if a helpful mentor or assistant had taken up residence inside her head. They seemed to have an answer for everything, their enthusiasm contagious. Was this the arrival of a muse?

It occurred to her that the other benefit would be an activity into which she could funnel her emotions. If she expressed herself through words and storytelling, she might gain another level of control over her feelings. This might be the key to controlling the luck thing, once and for all.

By the time she'd reached her door, the helpful voice in her head had generated the kernel of a story idea. She even had a wisp of an opening and closing chapter, phrases whirling in an eddy of crazy, incredible concepts that might just work. All she needed was to fill in everything between.

Easier said than done. But, hey, why not? The worst she could do was fail and nobody would know except her.

Nem happy-skipped into the apartment, her heart as light as her step. Emily had already arisen from her favorite sleeping spot on the couch to greet her sitting, waiting, a few feet from the door. She bent to pick up her furry friend, the psychic animal who had an uncanny knack of knowing exactly when she would arrive home.

"Hey there, can you extend your psychic skills to connecting me with your namesake? I'll take any help you got."

Emily's only reply, a deep purr, as Nem carried her into her study. Study being an exaggeration. There wasn't enough room to swing Emily, as per the cliché. She laughed at the evil, little thought, scratching the cat's head and hugging her as she turned on the spot surveying the area.

"Don't worry, I'd never do that to you. I wouldn't swing any animal."

She'd read enough author bios to know having a peaceful space in which to work was important. Writers always talked about their routines and places where they connected with their inner voice and imagination. This, many had commented, taught your mind it was time to write when you sat at your desk.

Yes, this might do as her own little creativity zone. Where her neatly stacked storage boxes stood she'd place a small desk. Move her coat wardrobe away from the window and perhaps add a bookshelf filled with her favorites. Then she would have ample light. *It was a bit bare,* she thought. What of inspiration?

A thought came back from the helpful muse-assistant. Hang a framed portrait of a quote like *"Writing is the painting of the voice."* — *Voltaire*

Hmm, perfect. Books, quotes, a desk and natural light. Yes, she saw herself sitting here. Creating. Making worlds. Conjuring a love story. *She. Could. Do. This.*

Who was there to tell her no? She had the advantage of being well-read and knowing exactly what did and didn't work. This, thanks to her work and noting what sold. It might mean nothing, but she'd picked two mega best sellers from reading the early review copies. This, well before their releases to the public, and both by unknown authors who nobody expected would create hits.

So she knew something of the mysterious and random formula for publishing success. Besides, writers who visited the store to promote their books seemed ordinary, at best. A few didn't even seem that, and they left her wondering how they conjured such magical worlds.

But, come on Nem, she told herself as she dropped Emily to the floor and pulled at the boxes against the wall, *you are flying too close to the sun.* Already, here she was, calculating the possibility of success and she hadn't even written a word.

She calmed herself, deciding the only thing upon which she could and should focus was to start the process. To write, perchance to dream with a smidgeon of hope. Build her courage too, which after everything in her life, she possessed in barrels, cartons and baskets full.

Should she manage to complete a whole novel, she might use the luck. The diary didn't have the power to help her create a master-piece, but it might aid finding an agent or with selling the finished product to a publishing house. That's if she decided to use its power. She kept coming back to the desire to discover if she had what it took to succeed on her own. No magical energy, just her.

Her hands trembled as she covered her mouth in surprise at her final decision. She was really going to do this. In that moment, everything seemed colored with a lens of hope and excitement. Who knew? If she was lucky she might write something special that the world would love.

And with little expectation, she began.

orris had said, "I don't see what you see."

This was after his first read through of Orelia's manuscript. After the work he'd done with her though, he let Morris give his opinion, but William wasn't taking no for an answer.

"We are both busy. Not much spare time to nurture another author." Morris continued. "I can barely keep up with the opportunities flooding in on your books. With the second releasing soon, we've got a tour in place to promote the hell out of you."

Three years later and William still remembered the thrill of the attention afforded by the success of his first book. The giddy sensation of walking on air, feeling he'd made it and this would be his life forever.

"How am I meant to finish my third manuscript and meet my deadline when I'm never home?" he had said to Morris, his face serious, affected modesty in place.

"You're the one who wanted a bestseller. That genie is not fitting back in the bottle. No complaining or you'll anger the Best Seller gods."

How true that had been, although he hadn't thought it had anything to do with gods or heavenly entities.

He gave his agent a frustrated look and mouthed "Please." He recalled a desperation to be right about her, to show Morris he understood the publishing industry as well as anyone, that he could back a winner.

Morris had tapped the top of the manuscript pages, then shook his head, his face serious. He crooked his elbow and pointed a finger at his temple insinuating William had held a gun to his head.

"Okay, I'll send it out to a few publishers who owe me a favor. Is that good enough?"

With that, Orelia's future as an author was on its way. *A Star is Born* but with words, not acting or music. He'd loved both the films with Judy Garland and James Mason, and Barbra Streisand and Kris Kristofferson. Something about an unknown making it against all odds was the age-old fairytale that captured everyone's heart. He was not immune to becoming part of the story. Of course, he never thought he would be the loser like Mason and Kristofferson's characters.

William wished he'd paid more attention to the storyline instead of thinking it was the men's fault for envying their wives' success. He wasn't married to Orelia, but it sure felt they were a pair, their lives tangled reeds in a river.

Turned out he was right and Morris wrong. The publishers expressed great interest, albeit with one very serious modification. She'd been receptive to most of his ideas along the way, so this meeting, *the meeting,* hadn't concerned him. He'd hoped the thrill of an agent's *Offer to Represent,* along with a publisher considering her manuscript, would overshadow the negative part of his news.

Until that day Orelia had been a keen student hanging on his every word. He became in his mind a guru of literature, a kindred of Hemingway, Steinbeck, Fitzgerald, all the greats. That's how she looked at him. While she was a diversion chewing up valuable time, someone as smart as her listening in rapt attention filled his soul with an emotional charge.

In his silliness at the time, their interaction, so enjoyable, even seeded an idea he might teach in the future at a prestigious university. Perhaps he'd receive an honorary doctorate as had J.K. Rowling and Bill Gates. For the love of what's-wrong-with-the-world, P. Diddy and Kanye West scored one. If they could, he deserved an award already.

After he'd spent years honing his skills and awaiting his book's publication, why shouldn't he now reap the rewards? Certainly the money hadn't flowed in as expected with a *six-figure deal.*

When they print that in the papers and trade magazines, they don't mention where the number fell in the six-figures. His was low sixes, like 150 thousand low for the first manuscript. He'd signed a three-book contract, which meant the publisher held fifty percent until he delivered the third novel.

The contracts had always confused him. He was a writer, not an accountant or a business entrepreneur. Back then, nobody explained royalty payments only came every six months, and that you didn't receive all your money. Publishers kept a percentage to cover returns —books the retailers returned that hadn't sold.

The first year after *Flying Toward the Sun,* having a novel in stores and sitting on best seller lists was a thrill. But the excitement took only eighteen months to fade. He grew desperate, wondering quietly to himself if something was wrong. He wasn't landlord-beating-at-his-door desperate, but he wasn't dining out at five-star restaurants either. Unless the publishers paid, and that happened less often after the second book. In fact, within five months of its release, he stopped wondering anymore if something was wrong.

The public, his fans, were unaware because you had to play your part in the media. Look successful, walk successful, dress and talk successful, and sell the work. *Sell. The. Book.* Man, that got banged in your head once you had that miraculous deal.

"You get the big money when the second sells well," Morris had told him. William bet he'd never have guessed it would sit on the shelves as if super-glued.

"Plus movie rights are valuable," his agent added, the said rights sold for two novels. "When they make the films, the book will sell like crazy. Look at Harry Potter."

But the films had stalled after the third book died a death. Nobody wanted to dance with a loser. Nobody. That hadn't happened yet when he sat across from Orelia in the bustling café, the name of which escaped him now. *Buttered Toast* or *Buttered Bread Roll*. Something to do with bread. Subliminal sales tactic, he remembered thinking.

She'd chosen the place. In hindsight, he understood in part why she had picked a new café and suburb each time. He still didn't understand the complete reason, but the pattern matched her random bus travels to donate to homeless folk.

He had hesitated to share his news, starting with the bad. The suggested amendments. Then to cheer her up, he'd tell her Morris wanted to represent her, thought he could do something with her work.

Things went wrong from the moment he opened his mouth. She flinched at the minor advice, and fidgeted and sighed, something she'd never done before with his suggestions. As he continued, he realized they were on different pages. Wildly different chapters even. Instead of understanding how fragile her ego might be—after all he knew how easily criticism had impacted him in the beginning—he thought this was an opportunity to *toughen* her up.

He might have handled the whole thing much better, but things weren't going great for him that day. He'd suffered through an unexpected, contentious conversation with Morris in the morning. The publishers hadn't liked his third novel's manuscript. *Details to come* it seemed.

He became annoyed with the process. Cranky like a toddler who'd lost a toy. Didn't anyone understand the fragility of an author's ego? He told himself he must take it as part of the game. If he must, he'd thought, so should Orelia. In fact, she had no standing yet, so what was with the quibbling? Yes, he'd advised her to fight for her manuscript, but not at this stage of her career.

"I don't get it," she'd said, through pouting lips, one brow raised in rebellion against the other. "They want my main character to be changed to male? That makes no sense. You told me you had good news. That's not good news. I'm happy they're interested but they're nuts. *Fight for my beliefs,* you said. Why are you now urging me to do this?"

Her focus on the negative and not the thrilling news that a publisher might sign her, rankled him, got right under his skin and twisted and turned. He should have ignored the comments, her attitude, her extreme ungratefulness. She was new to this. He was the experienced author accustomed to the vagaries of editors and the publishing world.

Today though, her words were molehills on a perfect lawn, well not so perfect thanks to the *details to come* news. They did ruin the positive thought process which he had been careful to maintain.

He tried to smile, make light of the whole thing. What he wanted really was to flatten those molehills; hammer the hell out of them and the creature who made them. At that thought, he'd stopped himself, thinking he was losing a little control.

It was his mind's fault, it kept traveling back to his conversation with Morris regarding his own manuscript. He'd expected to hear high praise, not "They require you to make drastic cuts. A ghostwriter possibly to help."

A ghostwriter! He'd won awards, for God's sake!

Heat, prickly and dark, shot from his gut to wrap around his chest and squeeze off his breath. Then he calmed himself and breathed out, digging his fingernails into his palm to remind him, this was a test maybe to teach him control.

He wondered why the hell he even sat here with her when he had problems of his own. The audacity of a novice to question them, him, Morris, the way of the industry. In his case it was different; he could wrestle with editors because he was an experienced professional. She was a nobody.

"No, my dear," he had said. He'd admit the *dear* had sounded a touch patronizing. "They're the experts and they have to sell the product. They know what sells in the stores. Think of this as a collaboration between you and the editor, the marketing department, and probably the girl who makes the coffee in their luxurious offices. If they tell you to jump over your laptop, you say how high and in what direction?"

He had thought at the time that she didn't appear to be listening, that his words weren't just falling on deaf ears but being swatted away by a determined hand. She wasn't asking how high or even taking a single foot off the ground.

"What do *you do* when they ask you to make big changes in your work?" she asked, with now the other eyebrow raised to meet its partner.

"I do what they say. They don't call a publisher's author list a stable of writers for nothing. You can fight inconsequential things, but this sounds pretty much a deal breaker. You're a new writer. This was a favor from Morris. From me. I didn't want you to get your hopes up. That's why I hadn't let you know I'd asked him to shop your book to publishers."

For a moment, he thought she might be about to cry, so he softened his tone, realizing this news had really hurt her.

"Here's my advice. You don't have a contract yet, so don't look a gift horse in the mouth. I know this isn't what you'd hoped, but sometimes you must sell a piece of your soul. Not all, but that little sliver on the edge you won't miss. Change the damn character and see what happens."

The pouty lips were back, joined by the frown. At least the eyebrows had lowered. They had annoyed him, and while he was being annoyed, he didn't like the way the glistening eyes had suddenly stopped looking teary, transforming to fierce.

"No," she said.

"No, as in you'll think about it?"

"No, as in this story is mine. I don't know this editor or your agent. You shock me, seriously shock me after everything. I'm not selling pieces of my soul to achieve this... this publishing *success thing*."

Well, that wasn't even a nod toward compromise. She sounded as if she imagined herself an artist and he a hack. He tried to keep the annoyance out of his voice and had widened his smile, to convey a fatherly concern. As he spoke, he felt the ire rise in him that he even had to explain this.

"What you're trying to achieve is not a *success thing*. You're chasing every author's dream. Publication. Handed to you on a silver platter, I might add. My mentoring. Feedback from a Big Five publisher. I referred you to my agent, who wasn't interested, but I insisted, so he tried. Where would you be without my help? Wishing and hoping."

The Dusty Springfield song flipped into his head. *Wishin' and hopin' and thinkin' and prayin', plannin' and dreamin'.*

He recalled making a mental note to download that song when he got home. It was one of those songs requiring repeated plays to repel the annoyance from your subconscious otherwise you'd suffer for days with a catchy melody invading every thought.

Somewhere during his speech, his smile had disappeared, and he found it difficult to recover while focused on her. He had tried, but when he spoke next, he may have sounded harsher than he intended. He'd meant to make a joke of the tension, for he still had the upbeat Springfield song floating through his mind. The problem was he couldn't bring that wishin' and hopin' zing to his words.

"Listen, Orelia, you're new to this, and if you care for advice from someone with a smidgeon—" He pincered his thumb and forefinger together and shook it near his face. "more experience. Just suck this up and move on."

The color her face turned at his words was as vibrant now as then. An unripe peach, mottled-pink. William realized he'd gone a little too far. Even looking back now, he saw himself as if he competed on a reality TV show. This interaction would have cast him as the evil character everyone loved to hate.

That wouldn't be the truth though. He wasn't mean. He was helpful. He thought of himself as the endearing, I'll-help-you-in-any-way-I-can competitor. That's the way they should cut his segments. If he was on a show, they should realize this was just a bad, frustrating day and this other person, Orelia the wannabe, wasn't helping his cause.

Only a week before this, his patience with her might have been better controlled, but the real issue that he couldn't get past was the few dreadful, bristling-nasty early reviews appearing for *Hidden in the Shadows*. He'd been doing a little thinin' and prayin' himself these last few days, hoping they'd disappear by some miracle. Or stop appearing. Morris had assured him they would, but they kept coming, an avalanche of disrespectful abuse. His temper grew shorter with each new one.

Not his fault on that day, in that claustrophobic café with the noise and her pinched face, that he wasn't able to keep himself in the land of tolerance.

His time had been no longer his own. His contract had demanded delivery of his third manuscript in four weeks—the progress of which hadn't been going so well. He had been still trying to stay on top of promoting his *brand*, as Morris called his novels and him. Thanks to this mission, ridiculous bloggers had littered his inbox with so many invites for interviews, he struggled to invent original answers.

And what was a *v-logger*, anyway?

How do they help sell books?

And if someone asked again, *Are you worried you won't repeat the success of the first book?,* murderer would be the next addition to the description of skills in his bio. He'd begun imagining a knife sticking out from interviewers' chests, same size as the one they now twisted into his career.

He felt entitled to be a tad tired of stupid.

Tired of stupid! Hmm, that was a good phrase which he'd noted for future use in his writing.

He never used the phrase, except in his head because he'd forgotten it until now. What he remembered, in vivid color though, was looking at his mentee and thinking that as a hobby she'd become a tiresome project. If she couldn't respect the publishing rules, then as far as he was concerned this was game over. She could make her own way and see where she'd end up without his sage counsel.

"That's not helpful, William," she had said, interrupting his musings about her.

She stared with those big, arrogant eyes as if he'd spoken in a foreign language she didn't speak. Maybe he did. Now that his hobby had rebelled, she'd become a liability. He had heard a whisper of warning his response might be an overreaction, but he had batted that away as if it was an insect with no rights to land upon him.

Then the dam of emotion burst. Every little thing that had gone wrong fueled the next words which erupted from his mouth.

"Of course, you know everything about publishing, do you Miss Wannabe? Let's get real here. You worked in a bookstore. That's it. No-brainer job as a sales clerk. On my side there is experience, unique creativity and what some have labeled *genius*."

He cringed a touch at *genius,* the harsher critical comments for his second book overlaying the title with *tedious, uninspired, clichéd.* Too late to stop though. Once a train is a runaway, not a hell of a lot halts its momentum. Until it crashes. And crash it did.

William cringed as he recalled what came next, wondering now what had gotten into him because being cruel was, up to that point, never part of his nature. How success must have changed him.

He fixed her with a haughty stare—one he only dragged out when he'd decided he didn't like someone—and said, "Writing is for the most part, hard work and compromise. Something you will need to learn."

It was then he really noted a change in Orelia's face, but the look wasn't what he had expected. The frown had disappeared, replaced instead by a neutral expression. Even years later that look angered him. She should have by now been sorry and submissive. A few tears wouldn't have hurt either. Now he understood of course, but then he was wound up and kept going, hellbent and foolish, nailing away at that coffin, which ultimately would be his.

He continued his lecture. "And that includes not arguing with somebody who's climbed the ladder before you. You're on the bottom rung. The bottom, just above the dirty floor. Imagine every author above you and that's a good place to start. You'll be lucky to ever be published. Luck does not favor arrogance."

William had immediately regretted the last words (not as much as right now), but he couldn't take them back. Not holding to his carefully crafted advice would destroy the image he'd sculpted of a successful man who knew his stuff. Instead he picked up his coffee cup and took a large swig, indifferent to any damage he'd caused the fledgling author.

He told himself then he was doing her a favor and that she needed to grow alligator skin. The terrible early reviews of his second book flashed in his mind and reminded him he should work on his own skin.

But he'd thought, if Orelia didn't like his news that was her problem not his. He'd decided he felt comfortable with his stance as he sat admiring the detail in his coiffed cappuccino. Now there was creativity, forming little animals, trees and patterns with milk.

William hesitated to look up because he already had known he'd gone too far. He thought he'd just sit and await her apology. But as the seconds ticked his uneasiness grew, until her lack of response forced him to change his plans, raise his head and glance across to her.

Okay, two points for forcing him to meet her gaze.

When he did, his first response had been of frustration that she hadn't heard a word he'd said. Then a spark of precariousness, akin to the feeling you have when looking over a cliff, came over him, unsettling his confidence.

He recalled watching her for a few seconds, lost for words, actually wondering what to say next. She did not behave as anyone would in that situation. Now he understood but back then all he could think was, what in the world was Orelia doing?

—————

51

*N*em's usual modus operandi was to prepare with care. Before she'd written a single word, she readied her *nook,* as she called her writing space. Here, for better or for worse, she would allow her imagination to roam and see where this adventure might take her.

She'd filled the bookcase with her favorite authors; classics, historical and modern, as well as every Jane Austen novel. Along the shelves sat photos of flowers, her favorite authors, and in the center the one photo she still had of her mother and herself when she was eight.

On the wall hung two prints of what she called her calming paintings. Monet's *Edge of the Cliff* and Paul Gauguin's *Rocks and Sea.* The colors and beauty they portrayed helped her keep her emotions in check. Just looking at them soothed her. She hoped they would also allow her mind to drift away to wonderful scenes.

In the corner sat a small, potted palm, which she hoped would survive (she'd never looked after a plant).

A desk she'd picked up in a thrift store sat against the opposite wall to the bookcase, with a comfortable chair, well-cushioned in a deep, rich shamrock green. Absent though was a computer, laptop or even a tablet.

Despite a world filled with technology, she wanted to begin the old-fashioned way, creating a story as did her heroes of centuries past. She would use a pencil and write on a lined pad. The simple movement of a hand to reveal letters, words, then paragraphs, made her feel closer to the spirit of those classic, great writers; Daphne Du Maurier, O. Henry, Emily Bronte, Oscar Wilde and Edgar Allen Poe.

On an early Wednesday evening following an after-dinner walk to settle her mind, she began. What happened next surprised her. She'd always believed writers faced difficult challenges, that writer's block, inexperience and lack of inspiration would greet her from the first paragraph.

Not so. Writing came as naturally to Nem as breathing or using the diary.

As she finished each page, she placed it on top of a growing neat pile at the corner of the desk. Other than looking up while moving the completed sheet to the stack, she didn't stop. Even when Emily complained of a lack of attention, mewling and swiping at her feet, she nudged the feline with her hand and replied, "Not now Miss. I'm on a roll."

Nem only stopped when her wrists and hands screamed at her, insisting while she might be enjoying herself, they, so unaccustomed to this spontaneous workout, were not.

She interlinked her fingers, cracking her knuckles as she stretched her arms in front of her body. Twisting her neck from side-to-side, she stared at her work and at once an immense sense of pride swelled in her chest.

She pulled the bundle over and counted the sheets, flipping each one onto a new heap with reverence, as if they were delicate lace.

When she'd finished she sat back and shook her head in disbelief. *Twenty-seven pages of story.* Wow! Twenty-seven pages with characters that hadn't existed until tonight. Until she ran her pencil across the paper and made them come alive.

Not discouraging at all for her first stroll around the block as a writer. If it weren't for her complaining hands and the growl of her stomach, reminding her she hadn't eaten in hours, she'd continue. Nem gathered her pages together and made her way to the kitchen where she placed them on the bench next to the stove.

As she ate the quickest meal she could find in the cupboard—instant chicken noodles—her gut tightened in anticipation as she picked up the first page to read back what she expected to be a mess.

With each sentence though, the dancing, stomach butterflies replaced her fear with a wonder. She could be mistaken, but this wasn't half-bad. Rough, but still a fine start. The character had talked to her as if sitting on her shoulder and she'd whispered a fascinating story. A girl with a secret.

Write what you know, she'd heard told. Secrets were part of her DNA and she could weave a tale around that without even thinking.

Writing seemed far less challenging than suggested by visiting writers who'd traveled through the store on promotional tours. Many had said they *bled over their keyboards;* the quote stolen from Hemingway, although he said *typewriter.* If she had a dollar for every time someone quoted him, she'd be rich. Perhaps they shouldn't be using a keyboard. Her pencil appeared to work just fine with not a drop of blood to be seen.

After reading through everything written so far, her excitement had built to bursting. She skipped like a child back to the nook; the story already engulfing her imagination to the point where she had to put that pencil on the paper.

The instant she did, her mind traveled away from her apartment and she hovered beside her heroine, climbing aboard a train where she'd meet her "true love." This winsome girl would enjoy success of the heart, except for the twist—

Which she'd work out later. Somehow.

She thought of Scarlett O'Hara's famous line in Gone with the Wind. *I'll think about it tomorrow. After all tomorrow is another day.* That's how she'd deal with the plot parts that stumped her. She'd just think about them tomorrow.

For the second time that night, Nem's fingers began to ache, and she glanced up to the wall clock to check the hour.

For a crazy, shimmering second, she imagined she'd time-traveled. It was one in the morning. She'd been at this for more than four hours and there sat the results of her labors. An even greater mass of pages sat on the desk beside the original stack.

She couldn't stop. *Just thirty minutes more,* she begged herself.

Her imagination set sail again, expanding with each paragraph, like clouds merging and separating to form unique images. The exhilaration so incredible that she felt a euphoria close to that of when she'd learned of her pregnancy. Maybe the book was the baby who would never be born to her.

Now, now. I won't think about the past ever again.

That part of her life no longer existed. This was the new, improved Nem and she wanted to draw a final line in the sand so that she would never go back there. She would build a barricade around her heart and only face forward.

"Change my name," she said, resting the end of the pencil on her lips. "That's what I'll do. To something sounding more like an author."

Orelia popped into her head from nowhere. She'd never met anyone by that name. The rhythm of the syllable sounded pleasing. A pure white flower sprung to mind, open and glistening with dew.

"Orelia. What do you think?" she asked Emily, who didn't answer because one, she was a cat, and two, she had been fast asleep for hours.

Then she tried a few surnames.

Eastgate. No, too long.

Smith. Too plain.

McCarthy. Too many syllables.

Then *Mason* soared in, attaching itself, a carriage connecting to a train engine, fitting perfectly as if the two names were reserved for her.

"Orelia Mason," she said to the room, and repeated her name to the bookcase, the prints and to Emily, who'd begun to stir.

"Orelia Mason, best-selling author."

Now that had a catchy ring. She saw it written across the cover of a novel. Yes. Yes. That was the name!

Orelia Mason was not just her new name. It would become the signature for a new beginning.

In this life she'd sail as far from her past as possible. In this life, she'd become a great writer and find a path to success with this growing mound of pages. Her heart swelled as she thought about the future which lay ahead. Nothing and nobody would stand in her way.

She smiled, confident she possessed everything she needed to achieve this dream. She had courage and maybe a little talent, and if things became too difficult, she had the diary.

Bye-bye *Nem Stratton*. Hello *Orelia Mason*.

52

*W*illiam stood still, not a muscle flinching, as he watched Orelia stand over the bedraggled man. He recalled the same image of her hunching over the small, green book as their relationship ended three years ago.

The homeless man looked up at her in gratitude, but in the café, while he attempted to stare her into submission, she hadn't even looked at him; in fact, her behavior was as though she'd forgotten he existed.

Her smile was what worried him; lips pursed, so sweet and demure, as if butter wouldn't melt in her mouth (such a hackneyed cliché but so apt).

Off with the fairies, sprung to mind. She was smarter than that though, and her self-control—which he hadn't known she possessed in such abundance—seemed to be serving her well.

He remembered thinking that perhaps she did have what it took to be a professional author. Discipline, infused into every pore to keep going on those days when your confidence is lost. Tenacity, so even if you're stuck or exhausted to the point of not thinking straight, you keep going. Crocodile skin, which he'd told her she needed, and seemed to be shielding her right then.

What could be so important in that book to draw her attention away after what he'd just said in the heated argument? Well, he knew now of course.

All he did then was follow her gaze, noting the open pages absorbing her attention. They seemed divided into two columns but from this upside-down view the words were unreadable. Orelia's arm partially covered the opposite page as though she protected answers given in a test.

She noted down a few words which he still couldn't read. He was about to ask her what the hell she found so mesmerizing, when an odd sensation came over him.

A buzz in the air. A distant vibration like an eighteen-wheeler traveling at speed on a gravel stretch, coming closer. Bearing down on him where he sat, wondering what was going on. The sound so distinct and overwhelming, he looked up and toward the door facing the road.

He tensed and gripped the edge of the table, imagining any minute now a wall would shatter with an ear-splitting explosion. Tables and screaming patrons would be sent flying as something large and terrible crashed into the room.

Orelia though, appeared unaware of any change in the atmosphere around them; her complete attention remained on the book. William couldn't tell how long they'd even sat there, with her gaze cast downward, and he swiveling his head around trying to figure from where the noise came.

No marauding vehicle appeared, and as the seconds ticked by, William began to relax enough to return his concentration to Orelia.

This wasn't weird. No not at all.

This was kooky with a double serve of *One Flew Over the Cuckoo's Nest* crazy.

He was about to ask her, *Can you hear that?* when she looked up at him, staring. Not at his eyes. No, it was as if she peeled back his skin and the layers of his soul with that long, unwelcome look.

In that instant, the buzzing, of which he heard every tone even now, stopped. What followed was an eerie quiet, the intensity of the silence as overwhelming as the hum. Despite being surrounded by a bustling café, filled with people in conversation, along with cutlery carving food on plates, and glasses and cups being replaced on tables, the cone of silence had descended.

He wasn't just rattled, he felt his heart kick up a notch, and the sound of his hesitant breathing enclosed him. She had somehow gained the upper hand, despite his maturity and experience. Whatever was happening, hard as he tried, he couldn't find a reasonable explanation; except that maybe she'd put something in his coffee. Or he was having a nervous breakdown.

Their gazes finally met, he with eyebrows arched in surprise despite his attempts to conceal his thoughts, and she with a Mona Lisa smile, which gave him no clue to what swirled within her head. It dawned on him at that odd moment, that she might be playing the pretend game too. Somehow, he was in a poker playoff and he didn't understand the stakes.

Then, just when he thought he was going to have to break the stare and allow her to win, she returned to her book. Yes, he'd won, he thought at the time, until she expelled a half-breath and smile in that way which conveys *yes, that's good. I have a great hand.*

He had nothing. Not a clue, so when she began to speak, without looking at him, her words took him by surprise. Of course, he couldn't see this future or understand that a war had begun; that he now sat across from an enemy. All he thought was their silly argument over a small difference of opinion was about to come to an end.

Orelia tapped the book's page before closing the covers and bending sideways to place it in her tote.

She cocked her head back and smiled a proper smile, not the fake smile she'd just worn to freak him out. Of course he relaxed a little. When she said "William, I'm sorry," he expected this little thing would become something they'd laugh about in the years ahead.

You should be, he'd thought, nestling himself into the chair, preparing for the lecture he would enjoy delivering to her. *She now understood who was the boss.* He opened his mouth to accept her apology and add, *you need to go away and think about your attitude Miss.*

When she spoke again, he realized he'd mistaken her words for a truce. His moment of pride in standing his ground was an underestimation of the person he had come to know. He'd even thought then, you never truly knew anyone or their capabilities. Now of course, he understood completely he hadn't a clue who sat across from him that day.

"You aren't helping me out of the goodness of your heart," she said. "You're helping you. Hubris and vanity fill your heart. Your mentoring is an act of selfish gain, not generosity."

An odd clicking noise filled the air around him, a frog's mating sound that belonged in a pond and not inside his head.

What was she talking about? Hubris? Him? She was the one bucking the system in arrogance, defying his experience, the editor's expertise. *Vanity, selfish!* How the hell could she say that of him after everything?

The clicking intensified, the clatter rising like a killer wave on the horizon, making him feel trapped as the inescapable bore down on him. The tics echoed and multiplied, smashing against his skull, until a twinge of nausea swam over him.

He must have drunk too much coffee; while wasting considerable precious time with a spoiled brat who imagined she was a best seller in the making.

He'd had enough of her. No number of apologies, even ones accompanied by chocolate, would ever convince him to grant her a second chance. This was it! No going back.

He tried to speak, to answer her accusations, but his skull vibrated so that he felt as if in the next ten seconds his brain would liquify.

He did manage to stammer, "I'm trying to... help you. Don't listen —at your peril."

She smiled a demure, cotton-candy smile and he recognized the woman he'd first met back in the Bountiful Books store. This was the woman, grateful for his guidance, enthusiastic and childlike in her wonder of his experience.

Recalling this moment these years later, he tensed, then relaxed, as he did back then. He remembered how it was that moment when the buzz, the clicking-hum annoyance waned, allowing him to gather his thoughts. That was when it hit him then, and even more so now in hindsight.

She wasn't smiling because she understood his kindness or because she realized her mistake and that he was right and she wrong. Orelia Mason smiled because she'd done something to him and she enjoyed what she'd done.

Her reply to his weak threat was to reach for her bag at her feet and rise. As she did, she slung the handles in a casual fashion over her shoulder as if she couldn't care less for his opinion. He stared in disbelief that she would walk out and leave him sitting in this place like a jilted lover.

In his mind, he had already begun to dismiss her, thinking *saves me from telling her to take a hike; get on her bike; start walking, sweetheart.* With that kind of attitude he had correctly assumed at that point, this little thing they had would never have worked.

"I'm disappointed in you," she said, standing behind her chair.

Was she waiting for an apology?

William held his hand across his heart, feigning surprise and hurt, although those at the time were about as far from his emotions as winter snow and spring sunshine.

He'd foolishly thought, what a godsend the hum had gone because he could now enjoy turning up the heat, that he'd have the last word. He'd imagined he deserved the last word, and even if he did, that was in a different world where normal rules applied.

He interlinked his hands behind his head and leaned back to stare up at the woman who'd surprised, angered and puzzled him, all in less than ten minutes. And how was he to know, when he addressed her next, though he spoke to her, he should have listened himself.

"You have just made the worst mistake of your life. You're about to lose any chance you have at success in this business. Going, going —gone."

She took several deep breaths but still kept that damn, stupid smile on her face as if she knew something he didn't.

"The mistake I made was in thinking I could do it your way. That I needed any help at all. I don't need you. I don't need anybody because I have something more powerful."

"Oh yeah," he replied, sarcasm wrapped in every syllable. "Is that your own self-belief? Good luck with that."

"No," she came right back to him. "I don't need your luck. It's already on my side."

Without another word or off-beat smile, she turned and walked away through the maze of tables and patrons. His stare followed her to the exit; he watched with amusement as the door swung closed behind her.

His mind instantly ran through the sudden turn of events as he took a gulp of coffee which had cooled to an unpalatable temperature.

"Yuk," he said, flicking his tongue between his lips to remove the taste of not just the drink but the remnants of their confrontation.

Who the hell did she imagine she was?

Bravo to him for keeping his cool. Nothing like removing ungrateful weeds before they seed and infect the whole damn lawn. *Hmm, that was a good analogy.* He told himself to jot that one down for use one day.

The waitress must have wanted their table and correctly assumed he was about to leave, for she swung past and delivered the bill. He couldn't remember her face anymore, but he did recall thinking she probably possessed more writing talent in her order-taking hand than Orelia had in her whole body.

He reached for his wallet to grab his Amex when he detected a movement in his peripheral vision, someone standing beside him. *Ah, she'd seen the error in her ways and come back to beg his forgiveness.*

When he looked up, a self-satisfied smile on his face, it baffled him to see he'd been wrong and nobody was there. The barest whisper of a *whomp-whomp* filtered through the back of his head and he suspected now a migraine might be on the way.

The image of Orelia staring at him as if he had a problem niggled the hell out of him; just the thought of her, a splinter in his psyche needing to be tweezed. If she called later, begging his forgiveness, he'd give it because that would give him the power to demand they move forward on his terms. He'd tell her that without hesitation.

Hubris!

Really? What a joke. She was Miss Hubris, imagining she'd ever scale the heights he'd achieved with his works of literature, not romance trash like she wrote.

The buzz and whomp-whomp played a tune in his skull, and as he saw himself in the café those years ago, even now he reached for his own temple and pressed. Then he'd thought it was serious, a brain tumor perhaps expanding, morphing into a killer; this sound the warning beacon something was wrong, and he needed to prepare.

He picked up the check, holding the slip and his card in one hand while pushing his other palm against his head to stem the pain.

This was her fault. Orelia Mason, the ungrateful bitch had made a serious mistake.

Good riddance to bad writers, he remembered thinking, *they'll be the death of any professional like himself.*

How prophetic he thought as he watched her stand over the poor homeless man and pull out what looked to be the same green book from her bag. The poor loser didn't have a clue, just like he hadn't that day. The guy just looked happy as can be to receive a few bucks. A small token, an unfair exchange paid to destroy his life.

You just made the worst mistake of your life, she'd said, no doubt believing she held the best cards. Kudos to her because for all these years she had been winning in a magnificent way. He was quite certain she had wished he'd go away and die, kill himself with an addiction or sleeping pills, or fall foul of an inexplicable accident.

Morris' last words had been, *she's not somebody to play with and she's unforgiving. And dangerous.*

Well ditto, she'd picked the wrong opponent and he wasn't in a forgiving mood either.

"Oh no," he whispered, "You played well, but I see you Orelia Mason, whoever you are, whatever you've become, I'll raise you."

He didn't have a full house yet, but he did know what he needed to do next.

53

*N*em enjoyed her writing time so much that even while she was at work her mind always drifted to her nook space. She could barely get through the day without the story racing ahead, and her, despairing she wasn't at home writing it down.

She had decided to continue working at Bountiful Books because now she had a perfect excuse to not take up Diane on her offers to *come out and light up the evening.*

Her boss remained as friendly and kind as always, but once Nem explained her determination to write her novel, she immediately offered her understanding and support.

Nem's life became a rhythm of living, working and writing and that gave her a sense of contentment. Every lunch break, she headed straight to a nearby café. In using pencil and paper, writing anywhere, anytime proved easy and uncomplicated.

It crossed her mind occasionally that the diary offered her the opportunity to win enough money to leave her job and write full time. Every time she began to lean that way, her concern that her personal luck might be limited prevented her from trying. She worried too, that granting herself a wish so large, might she be unable to stop? Then there was the desire to experience the satisfaction which would only come from achieving through her own endeavors.

While commuting in the evening, she spent the journey plotting and anticipating the joy of returning to her fantasy world. Her nightly routine was a quick meal before heading to the *nook*, where she'd write until her hand ached. Within a week though, her muscles grew accustomed to the workout, and the sessions lasted longer.

She'd take a break then and watch a little TV and be back at her desk until midnight when, with eyes gritty and sore, she'd collapse into bed. Quite often she wouldn't sleep because her mind still zigged and zagged with ideas. When sleep claimed her, many nights she would still dream of her characters. She saw herself talking to them as if they were alive and breathing. Sometimes to her they seemed even more real than the people she met in the store.

This is so easy, she told herself, as the days turned into weeks and the paper stack of pages grew taller. She rarely threw anything away because the characters whispered to her and she trusted they wouldn't lead her astray.

How many times had representatives from big publishing houses, Harper Collins, Random House and all the others, visited the store to sell books which supposedly took years to complete. That amused her. Maybe she was more of a writer than their authors. Regardless of whether her manuscript became a masterpiece or trash, Nem was comfortable in this world at last.

Nem stared at the page in speechless shock. She couldn't even open her mouth to whisper to Emily, who'd been her steadfast companion through the whole thing. Her lungs strained for air and she could barely move. A tear traveled down her cheek and tickled her face.

There it was, the impossible two words she could never have imagined only two months ago. She ran her fingers over them expecting to feel an energy travel from the page to her body. All she felt was a deep sense of satisfaction and joy. There it was—

The End.

Twenty-seven days after she'd written the first line on that fateful evening, those words appeared like a miracle. She took a deep breath and exhaled a long sigh as she patted the huge stack of four hundred and forty-nine pages. The happiness in her heart morphed into a smile she felt in every cell of her being.

"I'm done!" she shouted, leaning back and waving her arms in the air.

Emily, who'd taken up residence beneath her desk where Nem had placed a blanket for her, jumped up into her lap. Perhaps sensing Nem's excitement, she purred like a motorboat.

"My heart's in this story, Em. Your namesake would understand that. If I never do another thing in my life, I can die happy."

Later in the kitchen as she sipped her coffee, her gaze fixed on the pile of papers. She sensed a magic had happened without the diary but now she faced another challenge.

"Okay, now what to do with you?"

This whole adventure hadn't begun with any real thoughts of publishing the book. Yes, she'd jokingly dreamed of seeing her name up there on a best sellers' list, but she had never felt confident she possessed the ability to finish it. She hadn't truly dared to dream this far.

She would admit though, as the manuscript's completion loomed, she had begun to imagine her book sitting alongside novels on the Bountiful Books best sellers' shelf. The thought of readers entering her world awakened a real desire deep inside to see that happen.

As she lay sleepless in bed that night, Nem saw herself seated at a desk between shelves, pens in a pot, with a line of fans stretching out through the doors. All had come for her and her book. There she was too, interviewed on TV and radio, witty, amusing and charming. And traveling on tours, staying in luxury hotels, visiting bookstores where she would read from her novel, glancing up every few sentences at the hushed audience.

She told herself this mega-success was rare, one in a million. Didn't they always say the final ingredient of a successful best seller came down to luck?

The diary flashed into her mind and even though she wanted to make herself go to sleep, she sat up and leaned over to her bedside table. Her hand fumbled with the lamp switch, but she found it and then opened the drawer. She reached inside and pulled out the book, then laid back, resting it on her chest and pressed against her heart.

"Dream a little dream," she whispered.

No. Absolutely not.

She'd made a promise to herself to never use the power for anything like this. And she wouldn't. There might be no need. Everything had been going well, so who was to say that wouldn't continue.

Nem turned off the light and settled back under the bedclothes, still clutching the diary. She imagined herself standing on a high platform above a crowd. Beneath her fingertips, the green book hummed and grew warm, but she didn't feel the sweet sensation.

She had already sunk into a world where she stood before an old, large, wooden door, locked shut.

As hard as she tried to force it open, it remained determined to keep her outside—outside of what she didn't know and that frightened her even in her dream. Then she remembered she held the diary. Lifting the book, she held it against the portal, and in an instant, the door swung away, creaking and angry at being disturbed. What lay beyond was wonderful, and even before she entered she knew this was a place she would never want to leave.

But leave Nem did, when she awoke, though she only recalled the door. She remembered the diary and pulled back the covers to check the bed but found nothing. For a moment her heart erupted in a gallop and she couldn't move quick enough to check her bedside table.

There it was, back in the drawer, nestled away—safe, thank goodness—and she could breathe again. During the night she must have returned her magical partner to its usual place. It could stay there for the moment because she had no plans to use it anytime soon.

Serendipity could take care of her now. For she simply knew, no matter how many doors stood in her way, she would find a key, and that key would not be in the shape of a little green book.

54

*M*any questions crossed William's mind as he stood there observing Orelia with the vagrant. The book was of significance; he'd worked that out. His mind whisked a multitude of ideas around inside his head.

Why was Orelia giving money to people like this man? Was the book like a genie in the bottle granting wishes to its owner? If this was true, why did she wish him such a career disaster? Why not just wish for her own success and leave him out of it? What happened to live and let live? An argument over creative differences was all their disagreement had been.

Had he lost his sanity? That thought occurred to him every day since this had begun. Each idea his brain presented felt fanciful and wild, but he argued with himself quoting *Occam's Razor*: all things being equal, the simple answer was more likely to be correct than the complex ones.

So the answer here was she'd taken his successful career and swapped his out for hers. And it had something to do with that book.

William noted how Orelia examined the beggars as if she was a zoologist studying a wild animal. She paused, tilting her head sideways, as if considering an object. Then she wrote on a small notepad (not the green book) and tore off the page before returning the pad to her bag.

She leaned in and nodded to the man as she placed money and the note into his collection can. The beggar considered this donation, then looked up at her, his face visibly brightened. Without speaking to him again, Orelia turned and walked away in the direction from which she had arrived.

William side-shuffled around the concrete pillar as Orelia walked by. The whole interaction between her and the homeless man had taken two minutes. Yet, she'd spent forty-five minutes to get here, making this a ninety-minute round trip journey. *Why*? Not for a moment did he believe her actions were of altruism.

He had never approached a recipient of her generosity, although he'd thought to do that before, but now this was the opportunity. What did Orelia Mason, best selling author, say to a person she'd condemned?

With a glance up the street to be certain she'd gone, he advanced toward the man. Now standing before the poor creature, the tang of alcohol and stale tobacco wafted over him. The man's fingertips, filthy and yellow-stained, picked at his face as if invisible insects crawled across his skin.

Poor guy, what a terrible way to live. For a moment William imagined himself in his place. He shivered and pushed the thought aside. No, he would never allow that to happen.

More questions. Why was Orelia giving money to people such as him? What criteria did she use to choose?

The man clasped a large can in his hand which he waved toward William. William needed to get his hands into the tin and onto that note. He even considered walking away and waiting for the homeless guy to fall asleep, or maybe grabbing it while he was distracted by someone else giving him pennies.

Giving him pennies!

An idea hit him. From a side pocket he retrieved his wallet and extricated a twenty, brandishing it in the air in an exaggerated gesture.

"What's your name buddy?" he said, still holding out the money as if it was a bribe. Which it was.

Red, sunken eyes appraised him. "Who'shh asking?"

"Will's my name, and what's yours? Would a twenty buy a good meal?"

"Oh, shorry. Yeah, name's Jan. No joksh about a girl's name. My mom's Danish." He stared at the note. "Hey, thank you man."

Jan! Poor guy, that must have made for tough school years. *Jan* held up his tin and shook. Out of habit no doubt, to encourage William's generosity. Orelia's donation sat on the top.

Wow! A Benjamin. So that's the going rate for a man's life.

A paperclip held together the money and torn note. He couldn't read it from here, but he recognized Orelia's handwriting, having seen her scrawled writing enough times with her manuscripts.

He pulled another twenty from his wallet and grabbed the proffered tin. By twisting away to his left, he hoped this action would hide his thievery from Jan's view. His hope was in that moment, the man might turn away, embarrassed to receive two large donations within a few minutes.

It worked. Jan looked off into the distance, his eyes fixed with a faraway look, no doubt dreaming of a delicious meal and a soft bed for the night. William slipped his fingers inside the tin, pushing the twenties deep. With a pickpocket skill he didn't know he possessed, he separated the note from its partner as if he did this skullduggery for a living. When he withdrew his hand, secreted in his palm was Orelia's message.

"There you are. Enjoy, my friend," he said, handing back the container. Jan grabbed it and studied the contents, pushing the money further in as if it might fly out in the slightest breeze. His demeanor did not scream *I'm thrilled with my windfall.* Maybe this was a profitable begging spot. Or in living on the street he'd become cynical. Or he was too drunk to realize. There was Occam's Razor again. He probably did it out of habit.

"Thankssh. You'reAGooshOne. BleshYou."

"Take care of yourself. Really be careful."

William thought to warn him of the danger he might be in but that would take too long, and no doubt be pointless. He would die or be injured and possibly nothing William said could change that outcome. So he hurried away, desperate to read the message.

Once around the corner, he figured he was safe and he stopped to read the note. His curiosity wouldn't allow him to take another step.

"What the hell?" he whispered.

The noted contained just five words. *What did they mean?* As he thought about them, and ran a million ideas through his head, he realized the answer was obvious. Yes, yes, *Occam's Razor* was just a non-scientific concept when you couldn't think of a reasonable answer to a puzzling question. Yet, he couldn't argue with this. Occam's concept was right. Those five simple words explained a hell of a lot.

55

The day after Nem finished the manuscript, she brought it with her to work and presented the folder and the loose papers to Diane. It surprised her how filled with trepidation she felt, and yet proud as if she shared a newborn.

The conversation didn't begin as she'd hoped. Her boss appeared unimpressed. Although the sentiment wasn't conveyed by her demeanor; she was friendly as always. The questions she asked caused Nem to suspect she had reservations about the book even before reading it. Confused, Nem wondered why the usually enthusiastic woman wasn't at least happy for her?

"Congrats," Diane said. "Ooh, I can't wait to read it but... that was *quick*. Too quick to write a *whole* book, don't you think?"

She smiled as she spoke, but the emphasis on *quick* made Nem doubt her sincerity.

"A month, but I worked on it every spare moment."

"Wow. Edited too?"

"Umm, not yet."

"Well, there's a problem."

Why was she already talking about problems?

"You can't give a first draft to an agent or a publisher. They won't even read it."

Nem's white glow of excitement faded to gray drab disappointment. She had hoped for more encouraging words. What was wrong with Diane?

A creeping doubt slithered into her mind, but she fought it off.

No! Whatever bothered Diane she must ignore that response. She'd learned to be tough from the best. *Gone with the Wind's* Scarlett O'Hara, *Pride and Prejudice's* Elizabeth Bennett, Sofia from *The Color Purple* and so many others.

Nem took a deep breath and did something she rarely, if ever, did. Swallowed any pride lingering from the achievement of writing the book and asked for help.

"If that's the next step," she said in the brightest tone she could muster. "and how do I find an editor? Can you recommend one? I'd hoped you might help because—well, look at the first page. I've written a dedication."

Diane opened the folder and read. Her manner altered at once. The faux smile left her face replaced by a sad-clown frown, her lips pushed out in an exaggerated pout. She shook her head as she spoke.

"To Diane, for being there at the right moment in my life."

She looked up at Nem.

"Oh, heck, what was I thinking? Shame on me. I'm sorry honey, I didn't want you to get your hopes up. It's a heart-breaking business. Been in this game fourteen years. You know how many books of unknown authors we return, unsold, each month?"

Nem could hazard a guess after working here for five months. *A lot!*

"Unless you're King, Nora Roberts or James Patterson, well you're writing for peanuts. Every successful author I've ever heard quoted says they owe it to hard work and a small ration of talent. Then they add the biggest factor. *Luck.* Even if it's amazing. You'll need that luck too, sweetheart."

Nem relaxed, realizing Diane wasn't against her, that her heart was in the right place. That dedication, written because she knew she'd need help, had worked. She didn't know anyone else well enough to ask. One day, she might even have the diary reward Diane if she helped enough.

Diane must have seen the flicker of disappointment Nem had tried to conceal.

"Hey, don't you listen to me," she added, her voice and manner softer. "I'm old and over-cautious and I should just mind my business. How do I know who'll be the next big thing? Someone has to break through, right? Why shouldn't it be you?"

Diane reached out and rubbed a gentle hand up and down Nem's arm.

"You're smart. You'll work it out. Or not, because these things are in the lap of the gods most of the time. You've got my help. Whatever you need. What about a mentor? Enough authors come through the store that we might find one for you. We can only try, right?"

A grin spread across Nem's face. What a great idea. A mentor was a perfect idea, and she could do more than try.

"Yes, I like that plan," Nem said, the glow of excitement returning to her. "Perhaps I'll get lucky."

56

Thank you for the luck.

That's what the note said. The words made no sense at first, and William had stood hunched against the building surrounded by the bustle of pedestrians and the busy street. His mind wasn't there though. He didn't even notice when a long-haired teenager hurrying past bumped his shoulder and caused him to take a step to rebalance.

He had stared at the paper taken from poor Jan, who wanted everyone to be assured he was a man—soon he'd be a tragic accident news story.

The words had circled in his head. He even spoke the sentence aloud as if that would help decipher the cryptic message.

"Thank you for the luck."

Yes, it had made no sense.

As if anything about Orelia made sense. He had a good imagination; came with the job. Or necessary for the job. Or both.

Stay focused, he had reminded himself, staring at the puzzling phrase until the writing almost blurred.

Another part of the job, staying focused.

William. Focus! He repeated this to himself as his mind ran off on a tangent involving the necessities of a writer's life.

Doing the writing would be one, but he hadn't done that for months. *Was he even a writer anymore?*

His thoughts always wandered when the plotting grew difficult. He believed it was his subconscious seeking answers by distracting itself with meaningless concepts. In traveling through circles of connected ideas he found solutions to plot issues, or the exact word he needed to make a sentence sing.

Okay, back with the note, he'd told himself.

Thank you for the luck.

He knew the book affected people. They became accident prone. *Mega* accident prone.

Why strangers though?

How did it all fit together? Because fit it did. Somehow.

He ran through the memories of the other times he'd seen her with the diary. Their argument in the café was the other event. They had a real relationship though, whereas he doubted she had any connection to these itinerant people.

Another recollection filtered through his mind like a piece of trash in the wind traveling across a supermarket lot. He tried to grab at it, but the *thing* glided away. Something important knocked on his subconscious. The cloudy memory lodged against the barrier, a rolling ball of, of... something... green.

Green flashed, an exploding firework. Her book flying before his eyes trying to garner his attention.

Yes, he knew about that. But what was new? He didn't need his mind to keep reminding him how little he understood of Orelia's abilities.

Then a snatch of an idea came. The time when he'd not only seen the book but touched it. He hadn't realized its importance back then when their relationship had still been amicable. Who'd notice such an innocuous item?

She'd dropped the book.

No. It fell out of her bag when she reached for her wallet, insisting on paying the check at one of their catch-ups. His instinct was to lunge and, and... make a joke. *That's right!*

He'd picked the thing up, chivalrous but feeling playful. His third novel's manuscript just delivered to his publisher that morning. Euphoria had filled him with giddy happiness and relief. His arm snapped backward, holding the book behind his head with a hand and—

She'd said, "Give it back."

Her face was twisted, no, pinched. *Flustered? Worried?* A strange smile he'd never seen from her. *Gritted teeth.* He saw that look as if she stood before him this second. The grin of a painted doll. Plastic and not real. In that silly moment, he only saw an opportunity to have some fun and tease her.

As she reached across the table, he held her book to the side, waving it up and down.

"Must be valuable. Maybe I'll sell it. All your secrets in here?"

He'd even half-chuckled, thinking she seemed so cross it might be *that time of the month.* It was just a book. He'd leaned away to the right, ensuring it was out of her reach, and made out he would open the cover and read the contents.

"Noo," she had said, far too loud. Two girls at the next table had looked over toward them.

"It's personal. Records. A diary. Sort of. Please."

Her palm unfurled toward him. "Give it to me."

She appeared distressed and he instantly regretted the joke. Without hesitation, he returned the book to her hand, and realized he didn't know her well enough. He hadn't taken her to be a person who was easily upset. Right now though, she appeared on the verge of tears.

"Sorry."

He hoped his apology demonstrated his regret. "Must be important records."

"No, not important. Just a balance sheet of sorts. It's just personal."

She placed the *balance sheet of sorts* inside her bag and pulled the zipper closed. The awkwardness of how she balanced the tote on her lap for the rest of the meeting told a different story.

Simple records?

Yeah sure, he'd thought even then. The way they used to meet at out-of-way spots should have set off alarm bells. That's what she did now. Traveled to distant destinations in the city.

Ding-ding William. Pay attention.

She'd claimed, when he'd asked her, that she enjoyed *soaking up the atmosphere of new places* and *observing people from different walks of life.*

He understood this as a writer. A little extreme, he had thought.

When thinking about obscure meeting places, the first time he'd seen her with the book was a real *ding-ding* moment. Well, it was in hindsight. Not long after he began helping her, she'd organized a work session at a greasy spoon. The place was down an alley and up two flights of darkened stairs where he didn't even order for fear he risked food poisoning.

She had been waiting for him outside on the street, and he was across from her when the accident happened. Only a few yards away, hell had broken loose. He scoured his memory, pulling at the threads of the event. How important were those five minutes? With every-thing he now knew, *very,* with a capital *V.*

His initial thought upon seeing the arguing couple so near Orelia was that she might be in danger. The man's appearance matched their surroundings, rundown and beaten-up. His girlfriend or wife, who didn't look much better, cried and begged him to "please stop." She added *asshole* and *fuck off* enough times to those words, William presumed she wasn't such a sweet, innocent thing. Still, nothing justified his behavior.

"You're a bitch," the creep said, grabbing hold of the woman's arm and twisting. "I told you if you texted that dirty cheat again, you'd pay with fucking skin."

William considered intervening before reminding himself of multiple news reports of good Samaritans losing their lives for their trouble. He wrote about heroes, but he was definitely not one.

The man had continued to shove the woman. Her resistance didn't free her but only served to antagonize him further. The good news was, in the scuffle, they had moved away in the opposite direction of Orelia. William arrived by her side at the same time they paused at the curb waiting to cross the street.

Mr. Gallantry shook the woman none too gently as she begged him to leave her alone. "You fucking idiot, Barry," she said, slapping at him.

She wasn't doing much to calm the situation. Barry's response was a slap across her cheek, which stopped her struggling and for a moment hushed them both.

Others on the street watched too, but they must have all seen the same news bulletins because nobody made a move other than to watch with hands over their mouths or wrapped around their bodies. Some even just hustled past.

The girlfriend—he hoped not a wife because that was a marriage of hell hounds—raised her free hand to her tear-streaked face. He had laughed inside at *hell hounds*. What a great description.

Why keep a witty quote to himself? So, with his gaze still fixed on the couple, William repeated to Orelia, "That's a marriage of hell hounds."

When she gave no reply, he turned to her to see why, imagining the drama mesmerized her as much as it had captured him. But she wasn't looking at them. In her hand she held the green book, this the first time he'd ever seen it. A diary maybe, he'd thought.

When he had interrupted with his quip—which didn't sound so funny spoken aloud—she'd been jotting something on a page. Seeing him looking at her, she abruptly closed the covers and shoved it without reference into her bag. Only then did she acknowledge him with a nod. Odder, she made no comment on the Hell Hounds who'd now entered the crosswalk and seemed calmer. *How could she miss seeing them?*

"Hi William. Sorry, I was in another world. What did you say?"

"Just commenting on that charming couple."

"Oh?"

"Mr. and Mrs. Hound on the corner? You couldn't miss them? They were loud enough. The guy hit her with everyone watching. We can only imagine what goes on behind closed doors."

Orelia shook her head.

"Poor woman. I hope he gets what he deserves."

William thought to reply *let's hope,* but the screech of brakes interrupted. As he had still been facing in the couple's direction he caught every moment of the collision between the car and the man. He wondered at the perfect arc Barry made as he flew over the hood to land on the road. William pondered if using physics, you could calculate the curve of his flight based on speed, weight and other variables?

That was shock talking of course, because as much as the guy was an asshole, witnessing a human being assaulted by a vehicle was a distressing experience. Later, he'd think, despite the horror, he might have use for this scenario in a future novel. A writer never wastes any event in life. Everything was inspiration.

The woman who minutes ago had been crying, begging and calling Barry every terrible name in the world, preceded by a cuss word, ran around the car to fall at his side. The crowd surrounded him within seconds. Before he disappeared behind the wall of people, William caught sight of his body, still as a fallen tree on the black road surface. From the angle of his legs, in relation to his waist, he imagined if Barry survived, he wouldn't be dragging anyone down a street for a very long time.

"Oh my God," William said, looking at once to Orelia to offer comfort. But she didn't appear upset. In fact, she smiled. He'd thought then this was her behavior when in shock. Some people laugh when they're scared or worried, but smiling was an incongruent response to this unfolding horror. And that's why his memory had failed him on the book.

Her odd smile, the unsettling Hell Hounds fight, Barry the

asshole flying over the car's roof to land with a clunk, these images stayed with him for days. No doubt his brain's way of protecting him from trauma.

But he remembered now as he stared at those words.

Thank you for the luck.

She had worn the same expression on her face as she did after their argument, when she'd told him he'd be sorry. Others might describe her smile as one of satisfaction. He saw more. That smile, was one of wicked triumph.

Thank you for the luck.

Yes, things had become clearer. The puzzle pieces still didn't fit, but at least he believed that he knew roughly where they should go. Around her and her *balance sheet of sorts* book, people came into unforeseen bad fortune. His next move was obvious. He must get his hands on that book.

He slipped the note into his pants' pocket and walked back to where he'd parked the car, more assured than he'd felt in a long time.

57

The day Nem was to meet the person who would change her life had been heading toward her like a bullet. She sensed this as she always did when she used the book. It seemed a small decision to make use of the *luck thing* to find someone with experience to guide her. This, she thought, would still not muddy the waters of the question of her talent.

Since the timing of fortune's arrival was never certain, she kept a vigilant lookout for signs of the final ingredient to assure her future as an author. Luck delivered them to her two days after she'd jotted her request in the diary.

If you asked whose luck she'd swapped for this, Nem couldn't say, because over the months she'd built a backlog of entries marked with a minus. This was her security against an unknown future and she'd possibly also become a little too enthusiastic at dishing out punishment. Bad luck names now filled a full page with no coinciding balance of good fortune entries marked with a plus sign.

What she had noted with these was that each entry was followed by a spare line. What happened to the giver, as she called them, was no longer important to her and she didn't bother to look anymore to see what fate they were allotted.

Some must deserve their fate she figured. The idea of using the homeless hit after the preacher accosted her. They'd surely wronged many to end up where she found them. Most were alcoholics, which she supposed meant they abandoned a family, a spouse or an employer. They had decided their destiny when they gave into their addiction.

Nem gave no credence to the "disease" excuse. She overcame tragedy herself, so she carried little sympathy for their stories of misfortune. So many autobiographies of the famous, which they sold at Bountiful Books, told the opposite tale; celebrity or business identities who overcame terrible events to follow their path to success.

The morning of the day Nem met him, Diane hadn't a clue the role she'd play when she agreed to help an agent and an author. How could she suspect a thing because what occurred was unusual, but sounded plausible? Nem knew though, the minute Diane shared the news.

"Hey Lady Writer, when you're done with tidying the front displays, you can set up for the author presentation tonight. I'm expecting a full house. And hurry it up."

She said it in her usual drill-sergeant manner and Nem gave her a military-style salute in reply. Not that she was being bossy for real. That's how Diane talked. According to her, everyone in her home town of New York spoke that way or were accustomed to being spoken to that way.

"Why? There's nothing scheduled. I only checked yesterday."

"Yeah, and you would be right until this morning. Seems a fire damaged the original venue. Barnes and Noble three blocks over was due to host but there was a fire last night. The real crazy thing was the only part damaged was where they held the book talks. Can you believe that? His agent was desperate. He's talked here a few times. Actually, before everything took off for him. They told me he himself suggested us for tonight. Nice guy. A touch cerebral but polite and good with the audience. Least he was before he became a best seller. Steinbeck of our generation, they've called him. Let's hope it hasn't gone to his head. His latest book hasn't been selling so well but probably just waiting to take off."

"Who? *Who?* Have I read him?"

"Oh, didn't I say? William Barnes. You know, *Suffer Them to Come to Light?* Won all the awards? He's promoting the next release *Hidden in the Shadows*. Haven't got to that one."

Nem's interest piqued in an instant. The fire sounded suspiciously like fate stepping in to steer this William Barnes in her direction. She'd recalled reading and enjoying his novel too; that was handy. The writing was smart and poetic, but his prose probed intellectual depths she rarely enjoyed. He did it so well, he impressed her. She'd only taken a chance because everyone had been talking about the book, the word-of-mouth incredible.

"I read the first," Nem said, "but not his second. I saw a review saying it was disappointing."

"You shouldn't listen to the critics. Those who can't do, criticize."

"You're right. I hope if I'm ever published they'll give me a chance," she replied, thinking Mr. Barnes sounded perfect for her.

He didn't write in her genre, but she wanted to discover if she possessed a natural writing ability. Diane assured her, after reading her manuscript, that the story was *"good but just needed polishing."* How, though, could she decipher if her boss' words were empty kindness or if this was a genuine compliment? She needed another opinion.

"I'm staying for his talk then," Nem said. "I might learn something."

As she busied herself preparing the store for Barnes' visit, Nem found her mind drifting, wondering about him. Whether she'd like him instantly or his personality would grow on her. She was uncertain what role fate required her to play in the serendipity of their meeting. All she knew was that he was being sent here for her and she should be ready.

On her lunch break, she picked up *Hidden in the Shadows* from the front table where she'd just made a display of his books. She turned the novel over and scanned the synopsis. The story didn't sound interesting at all, and it occurred to her this might be the reason for the negative reviews. Wrong subject maybe?

She decided to read a few pages before he arrived, so she could at least open a conversation with him around his latest work, flatter him a little. Couldn't hurt.

She flipped it over again to stare at the cover. A big gold emblem sat on the right-hand corner.

New York Times Bestseller

How amazing! Her pen name *Orelia Mason* with that same moniker planted on her book. Maybe she'd even take her pseudonym out tonight when she met him. Play the role, so to speak.

"Hello, my name is Orelia Mason," she said under her breath to his book. "Pleased to meet you."

The click-click-click of the cogs turning as the evening drew closer sounded in her head. They whirred and busied themselves aligning happenstance and all the sliding doors between her and William Barnes.

She had no doubt that *New York Times Bestseller* would appear on her book one day too. With her mentor on the way, the hours flew. Destiny was coming for her and she was ready.

As she settled herself in the lunch room and opened the cover of Barnes' novel, a rush of excitement traveled through her. Tonight she'd meet the man who would change everything. Someone to teach her, be a friend and support. The last ingredient to set her sailing forward with the momentum to really make something of this book. He would be the stepping stone to the next stage of her life.

Her finger gently followed across the first line of the page as she began to read. "This is going to be amazing," she said, smiling to herself, as she saw her and the author shaking hands as they met.

Deep in her head, she heard the faintest of whirring, the little jagged-tooth wheels spinning and vibrating as they worked on her luck. *William Barnes,* she thought, as she began to read, *I know we will become good friends. Very good friends.*

58

Nine days straight William had arisen early to return late in the evening so exhausted he couldn't sleep. Accustomed to a quiet, solitary life, an absolute necessity for a writer, the constant navigation of public transport and crowded streets drained him.

Despite Orelia's penchant for crisscrossing town on her travels, there was one habit of hers she'd changed since poor Jan. Here he saw his perfect chance to get the book. He didn't like to think of anything anymore as chance because if he didn't get his hands on it, then he had nothing. Since realizing the importance of the journal, he'd become resolute in his determination to stop this woman and free himself from her curse.

Her early morning travels in the last two days had altered. Instead of taking a bus to distant, random suburbs, each morning she now drove to the same café, not far from her home. She also visited a bank twice.

To count her money and jewels perhaps?

Sometimes he was facetious because it made this whole thing seem normal, as if following a rival author was the most natural thing in the world, and joking made it so.

Outside the eatery, two small barriers cordoned off a section of pavement. Metal hurdles sprung to mind. Eight tables with shade umbrellas filled the space, along with potted ferns and several long flower boxes filled with red and white blooms.

William settled himself across the road in a diner with a perfect window view. He was grateful that this phase of surveillance offered food, drink and a comfortable seat. As he watched, he could almost enjoy himself, if he didn't feel a nudge of anger at her sitting there enjoying the sunshine without a care in the world.

She'd created a makeshift writing space. He'd read the *incredible* Orelia Mason was working on the fourth book in her series. The original was the one which had cemented her success, not the one he'd helped her with but the next. Although by the time the series began, she was already well on her way.

She released three books a year and that mystified him. Most writers weren't permitted more than the one, with limited available publishing slots each month due to marketing and printing schedules, and full author lists. How did her publisher—the same one who'd dumped him—accommodate so many releases? He'd never heard of it happening before, except maybe with Nora Roberts or Stephen King; but they'd been around forever. She was a newbie starting out, and yet she had been treated like a star right from the beginning.

Alongside a glass of water and a pitcher on the table, she had placed pencils and paper taken from her bag. What a nice set-up; a comfortable office with a view and coffee only a hand wave away.

He noted after two days, her habit was to drink three coffees and eat toast with a side-bowl of cereal and fruit. This was now the third day she'd missed her donation runs, foregoing them to write at the café in the morning. On the prior two days she'd returned home before lunch. The only time she rose in the hours she sat there was to go inside; he presumed to use the bathroom.

She must have a deadline William decided. *How nice for her.*

The thing he hoped to see was the green book. He was disappointed though because despite settling herself in, it hadn't extended to her putting *all her books on the table.* He laughed at his own wit but then realized it was only witty if someone was there to hear. And who in the world would listen to his crazy theories?

Not crazy he told himself.

If she would only bring the thing out and place it in an easily accessible spot—which would really help him out—then he could try a daring snatch-and-run. Or what about a swap-in identical copy for the original?

There's an idea. An idea, he dismissed almost at once because finding a similar book, when the only close look he'd gotten was three years ago while playing around, was, at best, impossible.

The point was moot anyway, and a waste of his time thinking up harebrained schemes, because she never once brought the journal out except during the moments with homeless people.

So if she wasn't making it easy on him, then he must use that imagination of his and hatch a good plan, one that was possible and not filled with holes. He wished he could find some luck and have the book fall out of her tote at his feet as it had done that time in the café.

Ah, then he saw it. The answer right before his eyes for two days.

The bag.

He'd been focused on the book but what he needed was to get his hands on the damn bag. Or even a hand inside.

William, sadly, or probably with good reason because he hadn't planned to be a criminal, wasn't skilled in pickpocketing. So, the concept of sneaking up behind her to carry out such a daring theft seemed doomed due to his lack of experience.

Practice would take time, time he felt slipping away, thanks to Morris managing to drown himself. It could only be a matter of days, if not hours, before the police knocked on his door. His embroilment in that sad mishap would play well into her curse on his life. Maybe an arrest would even happen here, with him being handcuffed, an entertaining spectacle while she sipped her morning coffee.

Another frustrating day of nothing gained, came and went but even when William arrived home, the bag snatching idea continued to nag him. Even though he couldn't see how he'd make it happen, he took the action in which he had become an expert.

Research.

He sat at his computer and googled *how to steal a handbag.*

Thousands of articles appeared on the subject as if it was a necessary piece of information the world needed to possess.

Kind of outrageous, this is out there in the public domain for anyone to use, he thought. *That's what's wrong with the world.*

Lucky for him though because he needed to become a student of the art of theft, and he needed to do it with speed.

The first article listing several ways to relieve a person of their wallet already gave him some ideas and proved interesting. The writer suggested distracting a person with their bag by their feet, by dropping something near them. In those seconds, their attention would be diverted as they reached for the item. This would allow you, *the wonderful thief,* to foot-shuffle the bag to the next table. Then easy as pie, you pick it up and make your escape with the victim none the wiser.

Another approach for a *talented criminal*, if they spied a tote strap hung over the chair's back, was what the author called *a cheeky grab* as you walked past the table. The bag owner wouldn't realize their loss until *Elvis had left the building.*

A safer way, the article instructed (as if there was ever a way to be a safe criminal) was to pickpocket them while walking alongside *the mark* on the street. In an almost gleeful writing style, the expert informed that this was a reliable option if you had developed the skill, but would require an accomplice. No suggestion on how to locate said partner, leaving William wondering if there were people on Fiverr who offered this. In a fit of stupidity, he ran a search on the site because he *would* be happy to pay but of course pickpockets don't advertise.

His biggest problem was that Orelia would recognize him if he got anywhere near her. So pretending to fall, drop something, foot-move her bag, or use the snatch-and-grab technique were useless suggestions. Thanks for nothing, *Mr. Assistant to Thievery* article writer.

What he needed was a more ingenious plan. There had to be one out there. He was a writer and all he needed was a spark of an idea to kickstart his imagination, so he continued to scan articles. As he opened and scanned each page though, he grew more frustrated. Until he came upon one paragraph which caught his attention. The instant he read the details he knew it might just work.

He did wonder if he had the courage to commit to such a bold plan. Not to mention, all things being equal, his little ducks needed to not just line up but all quack at the right time. With the way she'd sabotaged him, who knew if every negative variable wasn't already lying in wait to trip him.

In saying this, the plan did offer minimal risk of being seen; time to abort if things didn't feel right; and a higher success rate, in his opinion, than anything else he'd read, even with his undeveloped skills. Finally, he had nothing else and just maybe, he could pull this off.

The one thing it didn't grant him was the chance to see the look on her face when she discovered it gone. That would be amusing, but a price he'd happily pay to beat her. Now all he had to do was hope that tomorrow she followed the same routine and revisited the café. And be patient. He went to Google *how to be patient?* and realized in amusement, patience had become his new super power.

59

*N*em leaned against the wall at the back of the room they called *Author's Hangout*, a large space where the store held author talks and workshop events. She looked across the standing-room-only crowd toward the small, low stage she'd set up earlier. A majority of the audience clutched books on their laps or against their chest, if they were forced to stand. An excited hum of voices buzzed through the room as everyone awaited one man's arrival.

Seven pm on the dot, the noise descended to an instant hush. In the silence, Nem could hear her own rhythmic breath. She felt as though she was part of something incredible, but her excitement wasn't because she was a fangirl; it was because this evening was going to change her life.

William Barnes had appeared in the doorway and now made his way to the stage at a talking-pace with Diane. Her boss appeared animated and kept touching the man's arm. Too many times Nem thought. She'd clipped back her hair with an oversized black and red-polka-dotted, sparkling bow; her attempt at an evening look.

Both nodded and smiled at each other as they stopped at the small steps to the stage. Diane placed a hand on his arm, yet again, and leaned in to whisper something before motioning for him to continue forward. He stepped up and walked to the waiting lectern where he tapped the microphone with a finger.

The sound echoed around the room and ignited a smattering of excited, pre-emptive clapping from a group of women seated at the front. One even squealed as if he was a rock star.

Barnes looked at them, clasped his fingers together as if in grateful prayer and mouthed a *thank you* smile. At this, the entire audience erupted in applause which lasted a good thirty seconds. When the clapping didn't show any sign of dying down, he raised his hands and patted the air as if to say, *right, that's enough. Quiet down.* He shrugged his shoulders and pulled a face to convey he felt embarrassed by the overwhelming response.

Humble. That was good, thought Nem.

Still there was a smattering of applause, but he began to speak over it.

"Thank you for coming to listen to my blathering about my new book *Hidden in the Shadows*. I'm grateful for your support. We'll have question time afterward. Ask anything, okay? I'll sign books too, but my agent over there, Morris the Ogre as I call him, has me on a strict timeline. Ninety minutes is all I'll have in total, I'm afraid."

Nem began to analyze him. He seemed different from other authors she'd met. His confidence, as though born a best selling author, appealed. During his speech, which was fascinating, his charisma was obvious. He had an easy manner and wit which had the audience laughing and clapping. Then an instant later they were hushed, mesmerized by his fascinating stories of inspiration for his book.

Does being that good take practice?

The more he talked, the more Nem knew he had to be the one. His four-year struggle to write his first book meant he would empathize with her challenges. That is, of course, if she brought him into her confidence. She'd have to see.

His debut *Suffer Them to Come to Light* turned out to be a seven-year marathon. He had *some* patience. She wouldn't need the same, thanks to him and his help. Once they met, she was certain her path would be smoothed.

After forty-five minutes of his talk, he was true to his word, answering questions for another fifteen minutes, with amusing quips and an endearing sincerity.

While he was on stage, as well as after, Nem glanced at his agent every now and then. The man barely looked at his client, seeming over-preoccupied with his phone. He reminded her of an aging surfer with his sandy, a touch unkempt, collar-length hair. His constant frowning, despite the excitement in the room, made him appear the complete antithesis to William, who seemed to be enjoying himself.

Despite this, she wondered if he might represent her too. That would come later, she reminded herself. First, she had to get this book ship-shape. To do this, the next step had to happen. She must meet William Barnes.

As he finished question time, Diane appeared next to him to thank and escort the author to a desk to the side of the stage, which Nem had also helped set up for the signing.

William had said he could only stay for thirty minutes for signing books, but he managed to extend that to forty. Those who missed out received autographed bookmarks he'd left with the store. Once his agent motioned to him that he *had* to stop, he rose to follow the man who, Moses-like, parted the crowd of fans, still waiting and hoping to talk to the author.

Nem's pulse quickened as she realized the crucial moment now approached quicker than she had imagined. What to do exactly though? She hadn't thought this far ahead, she'd been fascinated by his stories and journey, and this evoked her own daydreams. She hadn't made solid plans and was caught off guard as the author disappeared through the room's exit. Many of the audience had left, but more than twenty avid fans, including the screaming one from earlier, remained and blocked her way. She pushed through the group, excusing herself, until she exited into the store showroom, her trepidation mounting that she had missed him.

"Please don't let him be gone," she whispered under her breath.

As she scanned the store, she spied him and his agent by the door, no doubt saying their goodbyes to Diane. *Forget playing it cool.* Still without an idea of what she might say, she rushed toward them.

The men had their backs to her approach, but Diane saw her. As Nem came up beside them, her boss reached over and grabbed her arm, pulling her into the huddle.

"Hey there, I thought you'd left already," she said, now holding Nem's hand as if she might run away.

William Barnes turned to face her, and her legs weakened, instant uncontrollable jellification. She was grateful Diane had hold of her hand or she may have stumbled.

"William. Morris. I'd like to introduce you to Nem, who set up everything for you tonight. Nem, meet William and his agent."

The author smiled that confident, wry smile she'd seen repeatedly over the last forty-five minutes. Her cheeks reddened as he said, "Thanks for saving our bacon. And considering you had no warning, amazing."

Okay, well here goes. Now she was here, she threw off her nerves. Fate would want her to contribute, she was certain.

"Oh my gosh, I'm so excited to meet you. Pinching myself. I loved *Suffer Them to Come to Light.* Extraordinary. Inspirational."

He cocked his head and stared at her for a long moment as if observing an interesting picture. Nem felt exposed as if he knew she'd chosen him, that he held a suspicion she instigated the events which brought him here.

Then he replied, and she saw he hadn't thought that at all; it was just her imagination. Or guilt.

"Thanks. You have great taste. Really, you're too kind."

Even in that small exchange she sensed an intrinsic connection with him. The cogs squeaking to life, click-clacking; the fate train traveling surely along the track.

"No, I've understood. Mr. Barnes your writing is wonderful. The rhythm of the sentences. The melody of the words, like a beautiful sonata. You're the Beethoven of literature. Your first book has transformed my view of writing."

She stopped there. Maybe she'd gushed too much. It wasn't completely true either. The novel had been a good read despite the flowery prose, but she had never understood why it had been such a mega best seller. Still, this was the reason she needed him. To understand how he'd managed that kind of success. What was the trick?

He seemed to blush, and as he did he rubbed at his chin with a perplexed look in his eyes.

How easy was this? she thought. Then again, luck *was* on her side. *Click-click. Clack-clack. Fate train coming down the track.*

"Wow!" he said, shaking his head. "That's ah, got to be one of the most amazing things anyone's said about my books. Can I clone you?"

"I mean it. I just felt compelled to talk to you. A voice in my head. I know this might sound crazy, but it was as if I *needed* to meet you. You might have altered the course of my life."

She might have occasionally thought about it, but she'd never believed, deep-down, a hundred-feet down, that she could become an author. The idea of thousands, if not millions of fans was too big a leap. Now though, a seed had been sown, a rope thrown down that hundred feet, and she dearly wanted to grab hold and climb up there. This desire even more powerful than having a child or a husband or her mom alive again.

She understood this as she stood there with William Barnes, at the same moment that she also noticed he'd begun to turn from her.

"I'm sorry, we have to go. Dinner with this one," he said, gesturing with his thumb in his agent's direction. He paused, half-turned from her, ready to leave her behind. Their lives not yet knitted together.

Something was wrong!

He smiled at her. "Excuse me, your name again?"

"Me? Oh, Orelia Mason."

She stopped.

What was she saying?

"Well, sorry, no, that's not right."

He gave her that quizzical raised-eyebrow look again.

"What I mean is, that's my writer's name. I think. I'm not set on it, but—I kind of thought if I use it in my real life for a few weeks I could see if it sounded good. As a full-time name, I mean."

He chuckled as he rubbed straightened fingers across his mouth.

Yes, she had his attention back.

"Have I read anything of yours?"

Click-click, clack-clack. Destiny on the track. Here she comes rolling into the station. All aboard for the Success Express.

Not yet, she thought. To him: "Can I ask a favor? Please."

The rest of their conversation was a formality of fate because the deed had been done. William Barnes was, from this moment, in her life. Her dream, which she didn't know until now meant everything to her, would come true.

She had already decided she'd reward him too, just as soon as he helped her with her book. If he did the right thing, all would end amazingly for them both. If not, well, as Scarlett O'Hara said, she wouldn't think about that today. That was for a tomorrow that might not come.

60

William's short-lived career as a thief began in inauspicious surroundings. He hoped nobody he knew would ever discover what he did and where; the embarrassment would be mortifying.

Another morning stretching toward lunch, watching and waiting until—

Orelia finally stood up, hung her bag over her shoulder and left her table. She'd just downed her second coffee after finishing her breakfast an hour previous and had just called over a passing waiter. The young man stopped next to her and made a note on his pad before retreating inside the café.

He hoped this meant she intended to come back, and if this was the case logic told him this had to be a bathroom break. *Perfect.* A relief too because William also required a bathroom break. *Urgently.* But he'd decided he wouldn't risk leaving his post and had begun to calculate how much success he might have relieving himself into a cup.

She entered the shadowed interior, dodging past a departing customer, and this was William's signal to move. He pulled down the baseball cap he'd taken to wearing, threw a ten-dollar bill on the table and bolted from the diner. No traffic in sight meant he would be inside her café within twenty seconds. The sprint across the road had him panting as he pushed open the door, keeping his head bowed but his eyes scanning the room with urgency.

His heart thudded into his ribs when he spied her where he hadn't expected. He thought she'd be in the bathroom, where he wanted her. But there she stood at the counter near the back wall.

William skidded to a halt, sliding sideways, to plonk himself into a chair at an empty table. Head still down, he picked up and opened a menu, which he held above his face to gather his thoughts. With the slowest of movements he lowered it to peep over the top. Orelia pointed into a cabinet filled with colorful cakes and cookies.

Oh damn it to hell, she hadn't come inside for the bathroom; she was ordering dessert. Now he needed to decide whether to stay and risk being seen or turn and flee back to his vantage spot. He hated the thought because it had taken him all morning to build the courage to act the minute he saw an opportunity. He wasn't sure how much longer his bravado would last.

Her voice and a tinkling laughter drifted over to him, but the distance prevented him from overhearing the conversation. Easy for her to nod and smile when she controlled everything. If the wait staff knew what became of those poor souls who received money from her —like Jan, it's not a woman's name—they wouldn't be quite so friendly.

The server leaned down to the sweets cabinet and pulled out a large chocolate torte. She nodded, and he turned away, probably to cut her a slice. William prepared himself to get up and get out the door. But luck was on his side today.

Orelia didn't walk his way, but instead disappeared behind a wall back of the counter. *Yes, yes, yes!* She had to be heading to the bathroom.

Just thinking the thought sent William's bladder a message that he too needed to visit the men's. No time for that; he'd just have to wear the ache a few minutes longer. He'd come so far, he had to keep going.

A final glance around the room to confirm he hadn't attracted any patron's attention, and he was on his feet and in moments at the wall behind the counter.

He snuck his head around the corner and saw an empty—*oh mercy*—hallway, only wide enough for one person. Milk crates lay stacked against one side and on the other barrels of flour. Beyond them above two doors, hung the men's and lady's bathroom signs; cartoon pictures of a cow and a bull. *Cute and stupid.*

As he navigated around the obstacles, he continued assuring himself he could do this, even though he felt at the pace his heart beat, it had other ideas. His imagination wasn't helping either. He saw his body lying prone in the hallway as Orelia exited the bathroom, shaking her wet hands and stepping over him with an amused expression.

Five steps was all it took to bring him facing the door to the lady's bathroom; the male's lay to the right.

Okay, so he was doing this. He was going to grow some balls and get the job done.

He took three gulps of air that tasted like rotten milk, which didn't say a lot for the hygiene of the place. The smell was foul. He wondered why Orelia would choose a place like this to frequent, where you'd more likely suffer food poisoning than gain inspiration.

Well, here goes.

He stepped to the men's entrance and swung open the door, waiting for just a second, before backing out and moving to the left.

With his hand pressed against the lady's bathroom door, he pushed it open with caution, prepared to jump backward in a flash. If caught he had his excuse ready. *The symbols confused him. A simple mistake.* Why he'd be in the same café as her, that he hadn't worked out yet.

Again luck was with him, and as he held the door half-opened he saw that nobody was at the basins. The gray-tiled room contained four stalls; three were empty. His gut churned like a milkshake maker as he placed his first step inside the room.

The smell-taste of the hallway lingered on his tongue, and at the thought of any kind of milk, nausea rose in him. He wiped the back of his hand across his mouth hoping to subdue the feeling. This worked but his bladder twinged, reminding him again he had a physical time countdown which couldn't be ignored. In fact, his apprehension seemed to make his need to pee worse.

He moved to the basin and opened the faucet, splashing his face with the fresh and invigorating cold water. It helped. The nausea faded a little. He pulled a handful of paper towels from the dispenser and wiped the moistness clinging to his skin.

Calm down. What's the worst that can happen?

Ah, death. Remember Morris?

He couldn't do this yet again. Arguing with himself at this point was no help; he needed to focus. *William,* he told himself, *hurry the hell up. Now or never.*

The annoying voice was correct. Only seconds must remain to execute this part of the plan. Succeed or fail, he was here now. Do or die! *Hopefully not die.* That was the point of everything he'd done so far.

If she saw him, she'd guess he knew something, if she didn't already suspect. What would someone like her do to a person who'd learned her secret? He shut down that line of thought pronto. He'd find out soon if he didn't move.

William turned toward the occupied stall. From inside came the sound of movement; paper rolled from the holder and shoes shuffling.

To back out now was impossible.

Seconds were all he had. *Left to live.*

No. Left to do what must be done. To get his hands on that book.

He took a deep breath and dropped to his knees to peer beneath the door.

Luck, luck, luck was his partner today. Protect me luck.

A pair of feet in expensive, designer boots were planted on the floor and there between them, her bag. All he need do was stretch his arm through and grab.

And be quick. No time to think.

Just go!

He lowered himself, so he now lay flat—an unpleasant thought considering his location—and crab-crawled himself to within arm's reach of the large tote.

Breathe. Breathe, breathe out. But quietly. I'm a thief. A stealth spy. Suck in that air and...

Strike!

William's arm shot out at a speed he never imagined he possessed. His hand arched, followed by a striking-snake move. As his fingers enclosed the bag's handles adrenaline kicked in with an explosion of energy. If his swiftness going in was impressive, his withdrawal with the bag was remarkable. He leaped to his feet, marveling at agility he had only developed in the last thirty seconds. His heart threatened to blow a gasket, but he'd heard that's good with athletes, and right now he could sprint a mile.

A scream roared from the cubicle as he bolted for the door.

"Noooo!"

It was definitely her. He'd heard her voice in his nightmares too many times, but it still made him jump and froze his body for half a second. And then he was through the door, sprinting along the hallway, running through the café (not caring anymore who saw him) and outside into the street before he'd even taken two breaths.

Would someone follow him? If not Orelia, possibly one of the staff who came to investigate the scream and would give chase.

Get out of sight.

A French pastry shop, two doors along, presented the next open doorway. As a hiding place it sucked. The windows were floor-to-ceiling with a brightly lit interior but, yes, the *get out of sight* command demanded he take the first opportunity to do just that.

The shop's bell chimed a merry hello as he entered. In his mind, he imagined the damn thing calling out his guilt in a high-pitched voice.

Thief! Thief! Thief in here!

He gave the too-blond, too-sweet, smiling young thing at the counter an *I'm-just-looking* headshake, while moving the hand with the bag well behind his back.

"Well, you let me know if I can help you sir."

Nope, nothing you can do to help. In fact, nobody, nowhere can help me.

"Our cinnamon rolls have just come out of the oven. We're famous for them," she said, as she pulled a tray from a nearby shelf and stacked the delightfully spiced cakes into the display cabinet.

"Ah, maybe, thank you. Let me just look around."

William pretended to examine the bread rack by the door. In the meantime, he slid the bag around to the front of his body, holding it close to his skin like a magnet, covering it as best he could with his arms to make it less noticeable.

The window was a big, big problem. If Orelia came looking and spied him in here, she'd know in an instant who had taken her bag. And the book. He toyed with asking the girl if he might use the store's bathroom to hide, but he didn't want to be too memorable.

As he examined the baked goods, pretending to be a customer, he noticed a space between a metal bread rack in the customer area and the front counter. He took a few steps to there and angled his body into the spot, making out he was examining bread rolls stacked on the tiered shelf behind the serving area. In this position he felt fairly protected and hidden from street view.

Miss Sweetness kept glancing over at him and smiling. If she'd known what he'd just done, her smile might not be so wide. He pulled out his phone and pretended to make a call, speaking in a lowered but animated voice. As he continued the fake conversation, he nodded and turned, bending to look out to the street through the bread shelves.

Any moment now he expected Orelia or an ally—possibly the waiter who appeared so charmed—to run by in hunt of him. Minutes passed, maybe five or six, and nobody came. He continued talking and nodding during his fake call, until his bladder punched him in the gut. He couldn't stall any longer; he had to leave this safety and get farther away. She could just as easily check in nearby stores. Like this one. That had nowhere to hide.

"I'll see you in a minute," he said to conclude his fake call.

Now to get out.

"Thanks," he called to the girl who'd finished with her rolls and now rearranged bread loaves into groups. He wished he did have time to grab a cinnamon roll. They smelled delicious, but what self-respecting thief eats on the job? He almost chuckled out loud at the stupid thought. Sometimes his wit appeared at ridiculous moments.

Without looking back, he moved to the exit, muscles tensed, his body ready to spin on a heel should Orelia appear at the window. The sound of traffic seemed too loud, as he pushed open the door and found himself again exposed on the street. He snuck a look toward the café but the crowd of pedestrians traveling along the pavement obstructed a complete view.

He had only one thing he could do, and that was run and hope like hell he ran *from* her and not toward capture. Holding the bag against his chest, his legs pumped as he raced along, dodging between the strollers, who were, at this speed, an obstacle course.

The bag made his gait awkward and he misjudged a sidestep around a couple—inconsiderate twosome, walking side-by-side—and glanced off the bear-like man. Two more staggering steps, and he'd lost his footing. Unable to recover his balance he came down hard, ending up sprawled on the pavement.

"You okay?" said the bear, whose shoulder had been his downfall.

In the spill, Orelia's bag flew from his arms and now lay a yard away out of reach.

After everything he'd just survived, had luck just left him like that? Here on the street, where the risk of being found compounded with each moment. He could cry, if he wasn't so terrified that when he looked up Orelia's smiling face would look down upon him.

A hand appeared at eye view, and he gasped thinking it was her. But the fingers had hair, as did the arm, and he felt himself breathe again.

"Here, let me help you."

Beefy fingers grasped his arm and half-lifted his body. He pushed up with his other palm and found himself facing a man with deep-blue eyes and a pleasant face, wearing concern.

"Thanks," he said, bending to look around him to locate the bag. That's when he very nearly collapsed back to the ground.

It was gone!

Oh my God, the bag he'd worked so hard to possess was gone.

She'd won again. His troubles now bigger than before because she must have followed him and taken it and now she would know that he knew. *Now she would know.* And then she'd come for him. Before the police, before anyone who could help, she would come and—

"You don't look so good. Maybe we'll get you to a doctor. You need help?"

Yes, I need help! Nothing you can do though. And thanks for being so huge and knocking me over and sealing my fate.

He fought to regain his composure and instead replied, "Oh my God, I've dropped my wife's bag, and someone's stolen it. It's lost."

"No, no, not lost," a female voice said behind him. "I picked it up."

He rotated with the speed of a discus thrower to face the man's companion. In her outstretched hand she held Orelia's bag.

"Thank you. Thank you," he said, snatching the bag as he checked behind her for signs of pursuit. Then he threw the handles of the gray tote over his shoulder. Ignoring the couple, he swung his head from side-to-side as he scanned the street.

He had to get away, and quick.

"Luck, you fabulous friend," he whispered beneath his breath, when he saw his escape arrive as if on cue.

A bus pulled into a stop within ten yards of him. The destination didn't matter if it carried him far from here. He felt Bear and the girl stare at his back as he took off in another Olympic speed sprint.

He bounded onto the bus through the open middle door and headed for a window seat facing the pavement side. If someone had seen him and followed him aboard he wanted to know so he could at least attempt to run.

He slumped into the double bench, but he didn't relax for a second as he positioned himself on the outside to prevent anyone from sitting beside him. The last thing he needed was a nosy person noting he carried a woman's handbag.

Now to catch his breath, which came in ragged gasps that showed how unfit he had become from sitting writing for years. With each breath, oxygen filled his lungs and the nausea which had crept back from, he imagined, over-exertion, began to subside.

He still needed to pee but perhaps the adrenaline from his escape had lessened the urge. Thank god for that. It must be part of the fight or flight response. *Don't suppose you can do battle or run while crossing your legs.*

The bus seemed to take hours to move, but eventually it did, and with each yard it traveled his heart began to slow; and he felt himself start to believe he'd actually succeeded. He'd gotten his hands on the green book.

After several blocks, he cast a glance around the interior, still careful to keep his head lowered so the baseball cap covered his face. Nobody came toward him with menace or any intent. Orelia was not on board, nor any pursuers. He sighed and shuffled himself across to lean against the window. Exhaustion overwhelmed him as the adrenaline left his system. He could almost fall asleep, there in the middle of his escape. So not a seasoned international spy response.

After the bus had traveled several stops, he figured he could now take the chance to check inside the tote. He placed it on his lap and stared at the fastened zipper, proud of himself that his plan had worked. Now he would have answers to his questions. He hoped.

The unzipping sounded loud and accusatory as if the bag objected to its own theft. He checked around again, but nobody had noticed him. He returned to his prize and peered in, slipping a hand inside to push around the contents. A wallet, makeup case, two notepads, a novel by Dean Koontz, a pen and pencil, gum and keys.

No green book. Where was it?

He darted his hand between the items again, checking, moving, growing more puzzled as the seconds ticked by.

Then he noticed the zippered section in the lining on one side.

Ah, of course. She would keep it hidden away.

He couldn't get that pocket zip open quick enough. Or his hand inside quick enough.

That was the moment when his euphoria evaporated like drops of water on a hot rock. His luck had left him—if he'd ever really possessed it—fizzled away it had, after he'd risked so much.

The book was not inside.

He returned to the Dean Koontz novel, flicking through the pages in a frantic thumbing of the edges, in case inserted inside the covers of the horror author's thriller was the green book's contents.

Nope. No. Negative. Nada.

He slid to the aisle seat and systematically pulled out everything, placing the bits and pieces beside himself, pushing and grouping them together. His disbelief so high he kept imagining he'd see it in the empty spaces. But there was no book, journal, balance sheet notepad, whatever the damn thing was according to her.

His excitement from the earlier moment had gone and been replaced by a gooey, black mess of thick disappointment. Orelia's luck continued, while his took the same old course of *fail, fail, fail.*

When would he catch a break?

He thought to give up right now, throw the contents back in the bag, leave the thing on the bus and await his fate. Something stopped him, and it wasn't his own fear. The image of poor Jan, hopeless, homeless, and Morris, idiot, terrible agent, and the others whose lives she'd destroyed, hovered over the scattered belongings.

For some reason only known to Fate, he was the only person who knew about Orelia and her callous use of a terrible power. The *only person* able to stop her. That was his challenge and his burden because there was nothing else in his life anymore.

So William, we just need another plan.

Yup, like I'm so full of them.

As his hopes crashed about as low as they could go, waddya know, an idea sprung at him as he stared at her things.

He just might have one more play. Fortune just wanted him to work a little harder.

The saying, *the best luck is the luck you make for yourself,* was very true. He felt infused with a determination as if the entire world depended on him, even though he was more an out of shape, hopelessly out-gunned super hero. From where this new William Barnes had evolved he couldn't say, but he was beginning to like him and his ability to bounce back, tiring as that might be.

Yes, he was beginning to like him a lot. And though he wouldn't back him in a race to win, he'd certainly put a bet both ways.

61

*N*em flung open the stall door but the person who'd stolen her bag had already gotten away. She ran down the hall to arrive at the café counter where only moments before she'd chosen and looked forward to eating a delicious cake. She wouldn't be eating that now.

As she came to a stop she took a deep breath to calm herself then she addressed Benny, the waiter who'd served her earlier. He apologized for not noticing anyone suspicious near the bathroom area, but he didn't seem to understand. His assurance that they'd thoroughly check everywhere later while cleaning in case the bag was misplaced, gave her no confidence.

"I'm telling you it wasn't left in here. Someone reached under the cubicle and stole it away, bold as brass."

"Shall we call the cops?" he asked.

"No. Not much cash in my wallet and I have another set of keys. I'll cancel the cards. Just disconcerting how brazen they were."

She didn't need any more attention focused on her by notifying the police. Thanks to Morris' death, she'd already had to deal with them and there was more to come. Despite the diary entry supposedly meant to protect her against people like Morris, it hadn't.

She wondered if she'd asked for too much over the last three years. Nothing good came when she acted with high emotion. After all this time, she still struggled on the odd occasion. In his case, with his drowning, she'd created a mini disaster for herself. Now, thanks to his death, there'd be months, even years, of unraveling business contracts.

William Barnes was to blame. He was the reason for this mess.

He'd have to be the most resilient person she'd met. She didn't understand why he didn't go away and leave her alone. She stopped short of asking for worse consequences for him because his was a minor transgression. And he had helped her considerably with her good fortune.

He'd murdered nobody and wasn't in the same league as Alan or that kid shrink. Morris' fate was possibly overkill, but the diary's power was at times an inaccurate process.

She didn't know when her agent had decided her money was his. Once she realized he had his hand not only in her cookie jar but other authors, what else could she do? It wasn't hard to work out with her statements. She'd always been good with numbers and with just a little investigation his legal but dishonorable deceit became clear. It all came down to wording.

She warned him bad things would come his way. Without revealing how or when, she simply quoted him the cliché: *what comes around, goes around.*

His *go around* would hurt.

He didn't get it though, and in a smug, self-righteous manner, he proceeded to explain the contract she had signed gave him every right, and her not so much.

That made her bristle. Everything she had worked toward had been blackened by his betrayal. It wasn't the money. It was his hubris in believing he could take advantage of her naïveté.

She wanted out of her contract, but he wouldn't agree. The arrogance of him, in that he believed his contribution created her best seller status.

Small warnings, accidents too regular to be random, had been sent Morris' way to persuade him he shouldn't fool with her. Several bouts of food-poisoning; nothing like constant days of diarrhea to humble you. Bumping into doors in the middle of the night. A minor car accident. Falling down stairs. Cutting his finger with a knife which required stitches.

The whole thing made even more amusing when he told her he had hired a psychic to come to his home and office with magical charms (including burning a foul-smelling cowpat) to ward off *evil spirits*.

He thought she'd be scared off when he told her he had organized protection. The fool actually laughed and mocked her, saying an ungrateful prima donna could easily find her sales declining and head in the same direction as an ex-client.

"Where do think William Barnes is these days?" he'd said.

When he added, *"William Barnes was right. You are a witch,"* that surprised her.

She'd taken a moment to think through the William mess. In all the months of the man's mentorship, he had seemed harmless. Conceited and arrogant. Yes. Confident his answers were the only ones. Yes. But other than a talent for writing prose, he hadn't appeared to be as great a genius as she'd first thought.

His comment concerned her though. She'd never had anyone sense she had been responsible for good or bad luck that came their way. It had occurred to her that some recipients of either might recognize that more than serendipity twisted around them.

Barnes' appearance at the canceled bookstore presentation, albeit collapsed on the pavement, had aroused her suspicion. She did consider that he had followed her there and had something to do with the mix-up. Morris seemed convinced that he did but by then she couldn't believe anything that sprang from the agent's mouth.

When the police interviewed her after Morris' body was discovered, they'd shown her grainy park surveillance footage. She suspected then what had happened. If she hadn't visited William in the hospital and seen his thin and disheveled appearance, she might not have recognized him in the video. Though the angle was only from behind as he approached Morris, she knew.

She didn't tell the detectives because she wanted to see what would happen. He didn't scare her, and she needed to know what he knew. Nem had all the time in the world.

The best theory she could come up with was that two people whose names were in the diary coming together created a collision of misfortune. Perhaps the diary wasn't infallible. The entries held no clues either. The line after their argument for William was the same as last time she checked.

William Barnes ... *writing career decay.*

Morris's fate was there but not his death. She'd wanted him alive to recover her money, and not become involved in a suspected murder. Something had gone very wrong.

His original fate had appeared in the flowery handwriting, which over the years became closer and closer to her own. A phantom hand forging her style. But it had changed on its own.

All this had become a growing concern. William somewhere out there worried her. This had forced her to create extra protection, in the way of continuous good fortune channeled into her life. This though disrupted her routine, forcing her to venture out nearly every day to seek new sources to feed the minus side, so she could use the positive.

Somehow Barnes had entwined himself in her business and even created chaos, aka Morris' death. This was more than a minor annoyance. Now another unlikely misfortune. Her bag gone.

"Ma'am, if you leave your number, we'll call you."

She looked up at Benny the waiter who'd interrupted her thoughts and smiled. "Thank you, that's very kind."

Nem practiced caution with any connections or contacts, so she gave out her cell to few people. Even old friends such as Diane, or Peg and Ray didn't have it. Nobody suspected anything about her or the diary for all these years because once she walked through one life door, she locked it and her past firmly behind her.

She hesitated to give Benny her number, and so she transposed three digits before handing a piece of note pad upon which she'd scrawled her details back to him. The bag's return was of no concern as her most valuable possession was still safe. Things going wrong for her though wasn't normal and she wanted to understand why. When she arrived home, she'd go over everything out of the norm which had occurred over the past few weeks. See if anything stood out to her.

But wait, what if her bag was found? Then that may give her some connection to the thief and their name could just appear in her book and they'd receive their reward.

"One moment," she said, holding out a hand to Benny. "Give me that back. I think with all the stress I've given you the wrong number."

He returned it to her and she quickly corrected her intentional mistake and then passed the slip back to him, hoping this wouldn't come back to haunt her.

As she left the café she headed for the bank only twenty minutes' walk away. There, she kept a spare set of house and car keys in a safe deposit box, along with the diary and a large sum, which she never bothered to count. The diary was always able to create more in various ways. These were her escape supplies if ever needed.

She wanted to check for new entries which might explain these events. If her mother had been more vigilant in checking the journal she may have foreseen her own murder. It occurred to Nem that owning the book was a double-edged sword, the equivalent of simultaneously holding a genie's lamp in one hand and a ticking bomb in the other.

A quote she'd read somewhere came to mind.

There is frequently a poison in fortune's gifts.

Of course that only applied if you didn't own the key to the gift maker.

62

$\mathcal{W}$illiam returned to Orelia's house, a pit in his stomach, uncertain whether she'd arrived before him. From this vantage the thick foliage around the property protected her home from view. The only way he would know was if he saw her come or go. So he settled down to perform the activity in which he was now an expert.

He waited. And watched for nearly six hours. Every twenty minutes he'd check his phone to just fill in time, but he couldn't become too absorbed as he needed to watch the gate.

He would read Google news, glancing up every few lines, or visit her Amazon page to check her books' rankings—old habits die hard.

Now and then, it would occur to him he may have overlooked a way to gain access. Then he would stroll the perimeter for the umpteenth time, only to decide yet again the high, brick walls were impassable. At least to him.

The only entrance appeared to be through the front double driveway gate. The wrought iron metalwork with vines and dozens of flowers, entwined between thick, black bars, wouldn't look misplaced guarding a gothic mansion. The pointed stakes of the gate, though climbable, still presented the problem of visibility from the road. He'd noted security cameras too.

Despite morphing into a far more agile version of himself in the café bathroom, this transformation did not stretch to scaling challenging walls, barehanded. Forget traveling at flash speed over a gate; he was too old he thought.

In his possession were the keys to her house but not the front entrance. The gate clicker must have been in her car. If he could only find a way onto the grounds, he had a chance of gaining access to her home and finding the book. That's if it was inside. It had to be, he told himself, if only to stay positive.

But he needed to know if she was in the house, and then if she left, he must be assured she'd be out long enough for him to search. His first thought was that he'd simply wait for her to leave, then take the risk on timing. Then it occurred to him Orelia would do what any wise person would: change her locks. So the time remaining for using the keys might run out.

Becoming a thief so far had only half-worked, and half wasn't good enough. His moment of criminal glory continued to replay in his mind. The hand reaching out as if it didn't belong to him. The feel of the bag straps as he pulled it toward himself, disbelieving he was doing this. Her scream of surprise. Boy, did he love that sound. Even a small win was wonderful.

Yet here he was, stuck. He reminded himself he, at least, could forever be proud he had Googled a daring plan, carried it out and succeeded. He would take his victories against her, no matter how small.

Google.

His imagination pushed at him—more like shoved—hinting there was a forgotten *something*. His experience at crafting plots was to never ignore his tapping subconscious. At times, it could be a cognitive super power. The several articles he'd found on stealing a bag floated in his mind. So he had used the best of them for his snatch-and-grab at the café, but what else had he missed? Or what did he need to recall?

Five clever ways to burgle settled in the forefront of his mind.

He recalled the article because each of the five suggestions fascinated him. People were ingenious and *so* dishonest. One was as amusing as it was simple, and he'd taken note in case scammers ever tried something like that on him.

"Ahh," he said, slowly nodding his head at the thought. *In case scammers ever tried something like that on him.*

There lay his answer, where it had been all the time, right in front of him. Hours wasted sitting here when this might have been over so quickly. Whether she was inside or not, he could have gained access, found the book and been on his way.

Even a quarter-good idea he would have taken, but this was genius with a solid chance of success. Though it required him to do the one thing he hoped to never do again. Speak to Orelia.

He scanned the ground, his head moving about in search of the right size and perfect shaped—

And there he spied his necessary accomplice, standing out as if it glowed with a supernatural power.

He leaned over and picked up the smooth, grape-sized pebble, brushing the surface with his fingers to remove any grains of dirt. Popping an unsanitized stone into his mouth appealed about as much as eating oysters, which he hated with a vengeance. *Slimy, disgusting, blobs of phlegm. Yuk!*

The image of Morris' face contorted as he fell into the river though, was all it took to overcome his distaste. Hell, he'd down a bowl of oysters, plus shells, if that got him inside her house.

He gave the pebble a final polish on his shirt and popped it in his mouth. The cold, hard object felt unbearably large, and he fought the urge to spit it straight back out. As he rolled the stone around with his tongue, pushing it to one side, then the other, his panic lessened. After a minute, he settled it between the inside of his cheek and teeth and practiced saying a few words out loud.

He didn't have time to make it perfect because his gag reflex had already reminded him this was never going to be a comfortable feeling.

"Okay, I'll do this now. And it will work," he said, as practice.

William picked up his cell and thumbed her number, which fortunately he still had in his contacts. She'd been so cautious when they'd first met, not wanting to share her details. He'd argued, how was he meant to contact her if he needed to change an arrangement? He imagined she'd had a difficult history which created a suspicious nature.

Since beginning his Orelia campaign, he had blocked her number. This, an unnecessary move, as she had never tried to call him, anyway. Her details remained in his contact list just in case he climbed back on his publishing feet; one day he might send a *gloat* text.

He punched the code to block his number in case she had still kept his number. As the ringtone sounded in his ear, he practiced his *hello* in various tones. He thought it sounded good. Convincing. Yes, this just might work.

The taunt of *sticks and stones might break my bones, but names will never hurt me* singsonged in his head.

Maybe, maybe not, but one small pebble might just break his bad luck and even give him his life back. A step at a time though, because right now he needed to focus on the task at hand.

When Orelia answered with a quiet "hello, who's this?" his heart plummeted into his stomach. He'd been so unprepared to hear her voice again, he almost sucked the stone down his throat. What gave him strength and returned his calm was how absent she sounded. Her mind seemed somewhere else; this was not the voice of the woman he'd come to despise.

William inhaled through his nose and pushed the pebble into his cheek with his tongue, holding it firmly in place on the side of his mouth with his teeth.

"Hello? Hello? she said.

The person you thought you'd destroyed, he replied in his head.

If there was a way to reach through the phone, grab her by the throat and strangle her until her eyes bulged and her tongue hung limp, he would.

For now, he'd settle for one more step toward what he believed would be his freedom. Freedom to live his life however it turned out, to dream again, write, to exist without her curse. Succeed or fail, he'd take all fate's twists on the chin because that was natural and real.

A funny clicking noise filled his head, the rotating of little wheels so loud that for a moment the sound drowned out his thoughts. This meant something, didn't it? What, he couldn't work out, his mind already filled with the challenge at hand. Did it mean this journey had neared its end and he just might make it home? He would put his heart into this.

He took a quick breath, pushed at the pebble and forced his lips to move. Let the charade begin.

63

*S*omething felt out of balance.

The shock of such a personal invasion was bad enough but the feelings of vulnerability shook her to the core. Nem was appalled at how close the thief came to getting their hands on her diary. She only carried it with her when needed. Today, thank goodness, was one of those times when she hadn't needed it.

When she'd arrived home, after collecting it from the bank, she'd paged through her book to look at the latest entry. Disappointment filtered through her body to discover there was nothing new. She'd hoped the luck thing offered her protection, that on the recent page a line might appear for the thief.

But it was empty. She wondered why. She'd always assumed the power would encompass everybody who wronged her. That's how it had seemed to work in the past.

There were plenty of entries related to the dirty homeless people, but she'd swapped most of those to protect herself and continue with her most recent hobby, obsession if she was being frank.

At least the police hadn't come back. They'd said they would be in touch. Two detectives questioned her on the contract dispute with

Morris. This surprised her with the issue only being in the early stages of legal discussion. A pest to the end, her agent must have something in his files, or his assistant had said something.

To the officers, she downplayed her anger at what he'd done, brushing it off as nothing when measured with her success. They appeared satisfied, but she needed to give that a brushstroke of luck to ensure they didn't return.

She needed to find another agent. Thanks to the diary or the publishing industry grapevine, two well-known managers had made contact since the news of Morris' death.

Right now though, her main worry was William Barnes. His image in the CCTV video from the river park caused a throb of concern in her mind. Nobody ever came back at her. That was because she'd been careful after high school to not create bad luck entries for people she knew. She'd been good. Careful. Until William.

That's where the growing art collection—the obsession—fit in her life. Her careful purchases went a long way in helping to control her feelings. When she stared at a magnificent picture, she became lost, transported into a realm filled with color and dazzling beauty. This serenity entered her core, her subconscious, and took her on a journey to a happy place. Emotions kept in check, the beast soothed by the poetry of color.

This is another reason she lived in seclusion and ensured everything in her home pleased her, as if placating a troubled child with a myriad of desired toys. The more she owned, the more she saw her purchases as a necessity.

She lay on the bed and stared at the stunning pastel of a woman with a parasol by Jose Trujillo; his work captured the texture of a Monet with the esthetic of more modern scenes. The gallery owner assured her the artist's fame was on the rise and his pieces were a solid investment. Each artist she'd chosen to collect bore similar strokes and style to the masters, Van Gogh, Matisse, even Da Vinci.

To find a talent awaiting discovery thrilled her because this was her own experience. Throughout her life she had possessed a hidden gift for telling stories; it just needed to be discovered. So these artists were kindred spirits.

Trujillo and the others in her collection only required a line in the journal for her investment to bear fruit.

As she stared up at the woman in the picture, she felt drawn in, her breath becoming slower, the tension in her body releasing. The affront of the boldness of someone taking her property melted away. She wondered if the brunette with the loose-pulled bun, wearing the crisp, white dress had been happy in that moment. She looked contented.

Maybe one day that peaceful place in her heart might become her permanent residence. She just needed to clean up a loose end named William Barnes.

He was trouble. The how and why she was yet to understand. Every time she thought of him the *click-click-clack* sounded in her head. She put the diary in the drawer by her bed and closed her eyes.

Just for a moment.

The image of the glorious woman with dark hair and peach complexion floated through her mind. She drifted to sleep even though it was only mid-afternoon, and she hadn't felt tired.

When the telephone rang, for a split-second the disorientation caused her to be so dizzy she felt sick. Startled in that second, she'd imagined she had traveled back through time. Her mother stood before her, frowning, with a warning to be careful and not allow the sun to touch her skin.

"Don't be silly," came Nem's reply. "Here's my protection."

She twirled her parasol, confident her mother didn't understand the rules she'd created to protect herself and the book. Life was in her control because she lived with caution and care.

Shaking her head, she pulled herself enough awake to at least answer.

"Hello," she said, her brain still so sluggish, demanding she go back to sleep.

As she listened to the caller, she continued to stare at the painting. It really was a beautiful work of art, the colors, the look on the girl's face and the detail in her parasol.

Annoyance flickered inside her as the person spoke, but she pushed the emotion away as he continued talking. Within a few seconds a smile stretched across her face.

Plans for a nap had just been postponed. Luck was back on her side.

64

William's words sprung from his mouth as if he was an accomplished actor. For the next thirty seconds he would play a role. To make it authentic he imagined himself as a waiter standing behind the counter of the café, where he'd stolen Orelia's bag. He pretended he was happy to be contacting a customer who'd endured the injustice of a crime on their premises.

With the pebble in place in his mouth, his voice sounded as different as if he had rewired his vocal chords. He steadied his nerves by using his hands like an Italian as he spoke. In his mind, he saw Orelia believing everything he said.

"Hello? *Hello?*" she said.

"I'm Franco from Il Cucina. You leave yourrr num-berr with us. Your bag is stole this morning, yes?"

William added what he thought was a brilliant Italian accent, rolling his r's, adding to the pebble's vocal disguise. The Googled burglary story suggested to slow your speech but it was his idea to add the pebble and pronunciation.

Nervous beads of sweat spotted his brow. Though he'd talked himself into maintaining confidence, nothing stopped his heart thumping out of control at the sound of her voice.

"Yes, that's me. You found it?"

Orelia sounded surprised, then happy, the distant tone gone.

"Si, señora, we have fount your bag. I check and wallet ee-ssa there and credit cards. But scusi, no cash."

"No, don't be sorry. Thank you. Grazie."

"You come now? We close in an hour. We not have dinner service today. Only weekends."

"Let me think." Orelia hesitated.

William panicked at her hesitation. The thought of another day or night staked outside her house was not pleasant. He wanted that book and he wanted this over. An idea flipped into his mind.

"Okay, I take home and bring back tom-orrro to keepa safe for you señora."

William heard a sigh, then a long pause.

"No, no, I'll come now. Keep it there. Twenty minutes and I will be there."

Five minutes later, her car pulled through the gothic entrance, which looked so impassable only an hour ago. It took off at a high speed, turned the corner and disappeared. The gates swung closed behind her but that didn't matter.

Orelia's absence lowered the risk of discovery while he scaled the gates. Imposing as they might be, he'd sat here long enough to calculate the footholds in the design and had assessed that he could manage. He was no young monkey, but he was a man fighting for his life with a time disadvantage. That would add some pep to his muscles.

The Googled article, which he'd glossed over at first, suggested burglars stole bags not for their contents but for access to their victim's home. They had the keys and driver's license from the first part of the scam. Then through the *White Pages* they found the owner's address. Next challenge: how to organize for no-one to be home?

Simple. Call from the bar, eatery or business where they'd stolen the bag. Voila! Said burglars welcome to the pleasure of an empty target. They then need only calculate the round-trip travel time for the owner to return to the initial crime scene.

William figured he had forty minutes or so.

After waiting five precious minutes to be certain there'd be no surprise return, he moved to the entrance. He could be a ninja or CIA —watching TV crime shows had taught him a lot—in the way he smoothly side-crouched forward, checking up and down the road for passing cars.

Everything seemed clear for the climb. Now standing before the gates, up close they appeared far taller and more unscalable than they had from his hiding spot.

After several attempts to pull himself up by fitting his foot on an entwined metal vine running across one of the horizontal bars, he managed to somehow succeed. Once there, he found another foothold and scaled it with far less difficulty than he had expected.

Hey, he was getting good at this. If he ever got his life back and rebuilt his career, he might just write a spy story with his new experience. What about a horror tale? A man, his world destroyed through magic. There's a novel which required no research. Funny how he could joke about the mess of his life. He guessed it stopped him from panicking.

Within two minutes he was up the drive and inside the house. As he closed the door behind, he froze. He had just landed in humongous trouble. This almighty problem hadn't been mentioned in the Google article.

"Shit!"

He didn't like swearing, but, "Shit. Shit."

A shrill tone emitted from a wall panel, setting his heart racing and his mouth spewing vulgarities. Of course, she would have a security system.

He paused, his shoulders raised like a cat, a surprised cat ready to run.

Despite the noise, no tick-tick-tick of an alarm counting down sounded. He checked the panel, and though he was no expert on security, there appeared to be no green light glowing below the words *Alarm On*.

In her haste Orelia must have neglected to set it.

"Luck, you magnificent wonder," he said blowing a kiss to the air.

He relaxed but he felt like an alien in someone else's skin. This was not something he'd imagined he would ever do. The thick silence of the house folded in on him, condemning his invasion. He didn't belong here, that's what it whispered to him.

He told himself though, her claim on this lifestyle was questionable. An eye for an eye. A crime for a crime. If he must visit the dark side to end this battle, that's what he'd do. She had used another-world power against him. So if he had to break into her house, hey, that was ingenuity as far as he was concerned.

He checked his watch and noted the time. Four twenty-three. Thirty minutes is all he'd given himself as safe. If he didn't find the book by then, he had no choice but to leave and find another way.

He scanned the entry. To his left lay an enormous living room. He'd try that first. As he walked around, surveying the grandeur, a stab of envy bit him. Wow! This place was something. The house that books built. She certainly possessed sublime taste, or the person she'd hired to create the interior did.

The cream marble floor incorporated a black cross-diamond pattern and shouted expensive. A luxurious honey-toned rug broke the coolness of the stone. From the glamorous white lounges, the matching Queen-Anne dining chairs, to the crystal lamps, the artwork, everything combined to convey this person has money.

It was stunning, transported from the pages of *House Beautiful* magazine. The effect was elegant and peaceful. Considering his pumping over-excited heart, just standing here made him feel calmer, more relaxed. Quite a feat, considering the circumstance.

Time though did not allow him to play tourist. He had a book to find and a ticking clock hung over his head. In such an enormous building, locating it would prove difficult. The green cover should stand out though against the pale honey and white decor.

For some silly reason, or maybe thanks to wishful thinking, he felt as if luck walked with him in every step he'd taken these past few days. A quiet confidence imbued every move he made as he walked around the home. He was going to find that book because he was on the side of right. How he'd gotten to this side, after everything he'd done, he didn't know, but luck favored the brave and the good, and that's what he carried inside him.

He calculated that the journal, being of such value to Orelia, would be stored somewhere safe.

An entertainment area where visitors would access?

Ah-ha. She'd keep it in a more private place.

A bedroom or study.

To be absolutely certain, he still made a quick circuit around the kitchen, the living and dining areas, and a guest room and bathroom on the bottom floor. After opening doors and closets at lightning speed, he surmised his guess had been correct. The book didn't appear to be on this level.

As he moved through the house, he marveled at what a successful publishing career could buy. One thing was missing he noted. Despite the interior decoration perfection, where were her personal items?

No photographs of parents or summer vacations, friends, family. Nothing that told of a life story. If he hadn't seen Orelia come and go from this house over the last few days, he would question whether anyone lived here, or this was a vacant home simply for display. Not a single thing was out of place. No fridge notes, no cup in the sink, a scrap of paper that had missed the trash, or even dust.

He checked his watch.

Twelve minutes had passed and only the ground floor had been searched. He'd used extra seconds to return everything the way he had found it, so it would take her longer to realize someone had been here, if at all. Eighteen increments of a ticking time-bomb clock remained. Or twenty-five, thirty if he pushed his chances.

Now to move upstairs where he suspected lay the most likely hiding place. A worrying thought crossed his mind. What if she'd taken it with her and everything he was doing, the risk he now took, was wasted time?

No, no. He didn't believe she had, because he sensed it here as if he'd turned into a psychic endowed with a type of divining power. The book was meant to be found by him, so he could stop her.

It might all be in his head but believing was the first step to making it real. He'd read that somewhere and, true or not, he would use the belief to stay positive and focused on the task of being the best burglar in the history of man.

A wide, curved, grand Hollywood style staircase, complete with polished dark wooden steps and an iron balustrade, wound its way to the second floor. He stared up, placing one foot on the first step and sensed a hum in the air.

The book was up there. It called to him.

It made perfect sense to keep a valuable item in your bedroom or study, very nearby while you slept. Or plotted how to bring down a friend and destroy his life. Just the thought of what she'd done gave him courage to take another step, then another, until he reached the second level.

Upstairs, the décor and design stunned him even more. An enormous, magnificent lead-light circular window overlooked the stairs. The pattern of green stems and orange and yellow tulip heads, created a colored tapestry on the pristine, thick alabaster white carpet. No expense spared for Orelia's private living areas. This was something else. She had sold this many books? *Really?*

Glorious paintings lined the hallway, with glowing spotlights to emphasize their detailed splendor. William peered at one he thought he recognized. He knew enough of art to know a *Salvador Dali,* but when he looked closer at the signature, he saw it had been merely painted in his style. Still it was breathtaking.

As he walked along the corridor, he noted the paintings were of the same quality. He wondered how somebody seeming to have only simple taste a few years ago had transformed into a collector of such fine art pieces. Orelia was certainly an enigma.

William looked at his watch again. Fourteen minutes left until his absolute must-leave time. With a safety margin, even less. He had wasted too many precious seconds admiring the paintings and surroundings. So no more stopping to admire. He got the message anyway, loud and clear. She'd done well for herself.

Her bedroom lay behind two light honey-colored timber doors at the end of the corridor. He pushed them open and, despite his resolution to ignore the grandeur, paused to take in the scale and magnificence.

Wow! This *was* nice!

Intricately detailed French-oak floor-to-ceiling cabinetry framed an enormous king-size bed. Gold curtains, matching coverings, and pillows just as exquisite as the art. A chaise lounge positioned by extensive windows said no-expense spared. Even the fern-patterned taupe-cream carpet appeared custom designed to match the surroundings. The glorious crystal chandelier hanging above must have cost more than William's car.

While the level below spoke of a somewhat wealthy person, upstairs was straight out of an E! Channel documentary on lifestyles of the rich and famous. How could Orelia have accrued this in a few short years since her first novel? Unless she had amassed it before this started. Then why had she been working in a humble store?

Yet another mystery which required solving. *Or not,* he reminded himself. The only mystery needing to be uncovered was how she had cursed him and how to stop her. The book and unraveling its secret was his goal. The rest were just questions of curiosity.

He entered the room and roamed, scanning left-to-right. His fear of failing evaporated in an instant and his heart lifted. This was too easy. On the bedside table was the prize.

He rushed toward the bed, thanking luck for smiling on him. The innocent-looking volume lay open, and the pages he could see contained only a few hand-written sentences.

He wanted to read them right then, but a glance at his watch told him his time had disappeared. By his calculations, five to ten minutes remained before Orelia's return. He'd need every moment of them to escape and climb over the fence.

William scooped up the book, and as he did, an odd flow of air surrounded and coddled him in a physical embrace as if someone was there beside him. He swung to face the door, thinking the slight breeze was somebody entering the room. Excuses as to why he'd be here in her bedroom ran through his mind. Nothing sounded reasonable of course. He was in trouble. Big trouble. All he could do was run but—

... he was alone.

Yet the air sparked with an odd energy, the aftermath of lightning crackling, of the brush of an entity, causing the hairs to rise on his arms and the back of his neck.

He breathed a long sigh of relief, and whispered, "Oh my God, get a grip Barnes."

The sound of his voice echoed in Orelia's private boudoir as though the walls protected her sanctuary and railed against him, the intruder. His fear multiplied with each second, a building of hellish intensity that swarmed over him. This sanctuary didn't like the invader and wanted him gone.

A *ping-ping* startled him, and he jumped.

His watch alarm broke his focus and reminded him he must leave; and in a hurry. He had five minutes according to his calculations. Those precious moments were his overtime, so he may have none if she returned sooner.

William was out the bedroom doors, along the hallway, flying down the stairs and outside in the time he imagined her face and her voice arguing with the waiters, demanding to know who had played the prank. She might even realize it was him. The sweet and sunny disposition she carried so well, morphed into the wicked Witch of the West.

You're not in Kansas anymore William. You're in my land now. I own you and you dared to challenge me.

He peered through the window to the gate. No Orelia coming up the drive yet. Pulling at his waistband, he shoved his prize into the front of his pants and opened the door.

The alarm which, thank God, wouldn't go off but still made him jump. *Where you going buddy?* It was only a sensor noting a door had been opened.

Then he ran, his arms pumping as he bolted as if he had everything to lose, because he did.

The gate barrier stood tall but not insurmountable any longer, and he knew the footholds as if he'd trained for this. He was up and over like a monkey, even landing on the other side in a perfect squat.

No seconds to praise himself for his remarkable and surprisingly agile effort. He took off toward his car which was parked behind dense foliage and several large trees. His sentinels, as he thought of them.

His arm extended as he neared the vehicle, his thumb clicking crazily to unlock the doors. By the time he'd reached it, his breath was gone and his lungs strained to feed oxygen to his depleted body. His hands slammed against the car hood as he leaned over to gain balance; his legs angry at being pushed well beyond their usual pace. A stitch flared to the right of his stomach and he moved his hand to press against the pain. Though he still needed a few minutes more to recover, he didn't have time. He must get away because he now had her book.

He'd done it!

He reached in to his pants and pulled his prize from its hiding place. Whether from exhaustion or the greasy sweat slicking his palm, the journal tumbled from his grasp to land at his feet.

When he bent to pick it up, a sharp jolt moved through his fingers, flaring at his wrist and burning up his arm, as if he'd touched an electric fence.

What the—?

He stopped dead, staring at the object in his hand, thinking it seemed peculiar but he would almost say there was a green glow to it. Or was that just him and his delirium from fear and the physical exertion?

Just as quickly, the tingling disappeared, and all he held was a simple book. No spark or strange vibrations. A volume made from ordinary paper with what seemed to be only handwriting of a few names. No special spells or potion recipes for weaving magic on the populace.

"Don't want... to give up your... secrets?" he gasped, still trying to catch his breath. "Too late. I've got... you."

William opened the car door, threw the book on the passenger seat and climbed in behind the wheel. He'd done it. Her book was now his. Now he only needed to figure out where to go next.

65

*S*omebody had played Nem. Her bag wasn't found by a waiter at the café and nobody there had called her. The staff took a good ten minutes checking with each other to come back to her and swear none of them had seen her bag or anything it might have contained, like her wallet.

Her initial annoyance had been because the unknown caller had awoken her, while she wanted to sleep; needed to rest her mind and recover from everything seeming to go so awry in the past few weeks.

The bag and her wallet meant nothing to her. She had plenty more of those, and the cash was inconsequential. She had only roused herself and rushed back there because she figured by reuniting with her bag she might gain a connection to the thief. That in turn might affect the diary; start it up possibly by reminding it someone deserved to be punished.

As she drove home empty-handed, she wondered at the timing of the bag theft. The caller's voice sounded familiar. She'd told herself being tired and annoyed made her brain jump from one foolish notion to another and she was imagining things. Even the dream she'd been having just before the call had been odd.

Three miles from home was when the rush of emotion slammed

into her as if someone had not just walked over her grave but stomped on it with big, angry boots. Her hand waved around her face in an instinctive response to her first thought, which was that a bug or spider or creepy-crawly had clambered over her skin.

Nothing was there, and she relaxed. Then in that quiet moment, a flash of recognition told her what she'd felt was an imbalance; a disruption in the air, particles of something powerful filling the car's cabin; the feeling of fate, which until now she had controlled so well, suddenly shoved off course.

Tears slipped from the corners of her eyes as the sense of damage, of loss, and the vertigo from that, overwhelmed her. Not a physical blow to her but to her life, to every cell of her being, her existence.

She struggled to drive, keep control of the car, but her instincts told her she must get home, even as she knew as if whispered in her ear, that she was already too late.

As she pulled into the driveway and waited long, long seconds for the gates to roll open, she knew. The sobs came then as the feelings of nakedness and exposure swamped her heart.

Even before she ran inside, to leap the stairs two at a time and fling the bedroom door ajar, she knew. The diary was gone, and the person who had stolen it wasn't a stranger. He would be very, very sorry.

66

William's first plan was to find an out-of-the-way eatery, grab a bite and look over the book. He probably wouldn't be able to eat a thing, but, after the day he'd had, if he didn't force himself he'd probably faint at some point.

The farther he traveled from Orelia's house though, the more he found himself unable to wait. An itch to see what secrets the book held began the minute he'd turned the ignition key.

The café stop was necessary for two reasons. Refueling, and he didn't relish the thought of being alone with the thing.

Since picking it up from her bedside table, a peculiar pressure had settled over his body, as if a heavy blanket had been draped across his shoulders.

But as he drove past a neighborhood park with an oval expanse flanked by large trees of various species, his plans were changed again. He spied locals enjoying the surroundings; playing ball, walking their dogs, or strolling. This was perfect. He could eat later, takeout was just as easy. The burn to open the covers was greater than a niggling hunger.

He slowed and pulled alongside the curb. A minute later he'd found an empty bench under an oak and settled himself down. For a moment, he held the book pressed into his lap as he surveyed his surroundings.

A young boy ran through the open space between the trees, a kite trailing behind him, as he attempted to make it fly. He wasn't having any luck but still the kid continued to try. From the sideline, his father yelled encouragement.

Good for him; it reminded William of himself.

A group of power walking women went by on the path. Their chatter and laughter made everything seem normal. He could almost believe he didn't have a care in the world, that he'd imagined the last six months, heck the last two years.

The afternoon sun felt warm and heartening but with every minute a tinge of oncoming, cool night air reminded him darkness was on its way. He didn't want to be sitting anywhere dark with this book.

From his position, he had a good view of the park entrance. He feared Orelia would realize it was him who'd taken her book. In his mind she'd been imbued with super-tracking power like a terminator from those movies. His imagination had her running toward him, her hand morphing into some dreadful sharp weapon.

His focus returned to the book on his lap which he opened with care, as if he held an ancient, precious manuscript. It fell to a place bookmarked by an attached cream, satin ribbon. He stared at the two pages for long seconds trying to understand what he saw.

What had he expected? Certainly not the minimal jotted words with so little detail. One thing became clear after scanning a few more pages, this was no financial record. Nor anything related to money.

Yes, the dates made it appear a normal diary, but this was not a humble journal. His first impression was a record of observations of people, events and behaviors. Something else too that he didn't understand yet. Wishes for them? Prayers? The pages ruled in half like a balance sheet, revealed names and details of what seemed to be perceived *crimes*.

No, that was an overstatement, not criminal acts but more

personal wrongs and slights; some in his opinion, petty. They weren't only transgressions against her but observations of people mistreating others. Even misdeeds against society, such as the homeless men and women he'd seen her visiting.

Poor Jan—the man forever explaining he had a woman's name—was included in a notation. On the first line his supposed infraction and on the next his punishment.

Jan, vagrant, alcoholic
Subway accident

William picked up his phone and Googled the accident, but nothing had been in the news yet. Perhaps it lay in the future. He wondered if, because he now possessed the book, the power might spare Jan. The thought he could help the poor guy inspired him to work out this mystery. This wasn't just about him now, but many lives.

He worked his way backwards, flicking through several pages looking for his own name. The sheer number of people recorded astounded him. The oddity was that not all the people mentioned in the pages suffered misfortune. Some seemed to experience incredible good luck.

Orelia's name was in there many times, far more than anyone else. She appeared under her author name, and her birth name Nem. It seemed the names changed around the time they'd met. Funny he hadn't ever thought of her as Nem, although he did remember her being introduced to him. The name had stayed with him because he thought it was unique enough he might use it in a novel.

When he saw his name his blood chilled. Written in black and white lay the proof of what she'd done.

William Barnes, arrogant, hubristic, undeserving 11/13/15
William Barnes... writing career decay

Writing career decay? What the hell did that mean?

The listed date matched their argument in the café. He had

checked enough times in his own diary, even marking it as DL-Day (death of life-as-he-knew-it).

Perfect description too, of the dissolution of his career. The end crept up on him, a noxious vine, tendrils climbing the creative wall he'd built. Knotty suckers pried into cracks, pushing and prodding until the whole thing, meaning his life, weakened and collapsed.

Below his entry was another for her.

Oh, and how nice for Miss Orelia Mason. His orbit *decays* while hers *rockets.* She'd written:

Orelia Mason to write a best seller

A page later Morris' name appeared.

Morris Usher to represent and sell my book

So she *had* stolen his agent? He saw now how this possibly worked. He flipped forward looking for current dates seeking another entry noting his agent.

Stop thinking of him in that way William. He hasn't worked for you in a year. Now he's dead, and he won't be representing anyone ever again.

He soon found *Morris Usher* noted, with a minus next to his name. *Ah, so here was why the man met his maker.*

If the notation of *embezzled from clients* was true, possibly he'd been sent to meet the other guy in hell. Maybe he could swing a deal down there.

An obvious pattern emerged. Good luck. Bad luck. Wishes that came true, created by a genie in a book. Fascinating reading if it wasn't true and didn't tell the story of lives devastated.

His imagination required only a single line to visualize each victim's suffering or each winner's joy. No flights of fancy necessary to see Orelia's fortune and her wonderful life. He had enjoyed a front row seat for nearly three years, and the show was a horror story.

The sound of a child crying invaded his thoughts and caused him to look up. It was the boy with the kite, but now the kite was on the ground and his father ran toward him. The man picked up the toy and they walked away together.

As he watched, William noticed the light had begun to fade, and he knew he must move soon. A few more minutes he told himself. Nothing had settled in his mind on what he could do with the book. He still couldn't understand how it all worked.

He flipped backward, reading a few lines from each page. As he read notes from the past, he felt as though he'd climbed aboard a time machine. He traveled through Orelia's recent years, from a woman to a teenager, then back into her childhood to a girl named Nem Stratton. The further back he went the more her entries became childish scrawls covering only small infractions by other children or teachers.

Stick figures decorated the edges of this section. He smiled (before realizing he shouldn't) at a misshapen dog biting on a stick-boy's leg. This Jeremy's crime? Calling a young Nem *weirdo*. Poor Jeremy. William hoped the animal wasn't rabid. Ten points to the kid for getting it right about her; she was a weirdo.

Punishments distributed by her as a child were minor. Bikes stolen, bags lost, scraped knees, broken arms. Nothing serious until a girl called Lacy ended up sick. Very sick. He wondered if she survived. A tear drop drawn beside her entry suggested the young Nem regretted what she'd done. Back then she owned a conscience it seemed. He found other signs of remorse against several other names as if their misfortune might have even been a mistake.

When did she become the heartless creature of today?

He jumped forward again and found the name Alan West. His punishment listed was short and not so sweet.

Dead

His crime, if it was true, meant he probably deserved his fate.

Murderer

He picked up his phone and Googled *Alan West* along with *Nem*.

The answer came back in several news articles with interesting if not bizarre headlines like *The Unluckiest Killer*.

As he read he began to understand her a little better. This man who killed her mother and orphaned her when she was so young was a monster. As a convicted criminal, he survived a stem cell transplant in prison, only to die in a freak accident. There was the requested *death*.

He Googled information on another entry. Dr. Ken Shepherd who was titled as *child hurter*.

His punishment: *cancer*, along with the words *painful*.

A news article confirmed he died from the disease. *Prostate.* Kind of ironic if he was a pedophile. Three entries inscribed beside his name, looked to be appointments at the same time every week. Commentary on Shepherd's demeanor was also noted.

Watching me. Tricking. Thinks I don't know.

Was he her therapist? That would make sense after her mother's violent death.

His final entry: an underlined single word *justice* next to a date. He referred to the news article and saw this was the same day he died. This could be coincidence, and she might have added dates and details after events. Easy to believe Nem was a child who'd suffered a terrifying tragedy and afterward formed a morbid preoccupation with dying and misfortune.

That would be a reasonable supposition. It made more sense than a world where there existed a person who could inflict death-by-book. After the stress of the past months, had his imagination run wild? No, worse than that, embarked on a rampage.

He closed the book and reopened it at the first page. These earlier entries were oddly not in Orelia's hand writing, and they were dated from the early decades of the previous century.

His nervous fingers flipped to the first line, hoping to find the original owner's name. He found no ownership information and only two blank pages before the written records began. The names weren't known to him. Why would they be if the 1903 date was correct? A sense of nostalgia wafted from the pages as he scanned the inscriptions written in flowing fountain pen ink; the author's strokes typical of the era's precise, cursive style. The beauty of the writing did not soften the growing severity of the fate dispensed to the victims.

The bad luck entries told of illness, minor accidents and financial ruin. As with Orelia's section, they graduated into far more serious afflictions. Death appeared many times. Page after page of lives damaged and destroyed grew more cruel and dreadful as the logged entries traveled through the years.

The benefits to counter-balance these proved interesting in that they related to the desires of the era. Money featured often. In the late 1920s and early 30s, stock market wins, despite the collapse, horses recovering from severe injuries, and an amusing entry wishing for *no more children*.

Twenty pages in, the handwriting changed as if the book had fallen into another's ownership. The same pattern emerged. Small mishaps for many entries morphed into disasters. On and on it continued, and William counted the appearance of five different owners including Orelia.

It seemed to him that the diary influenced its owners. As they accessed its power, they experienced a one-way descent into indifference to others; even a decline into narcissism.

This reminded him of Oscar Wilde's novel *The Picture of Dorian Gray*. A charismatic teenage Gray is given a portrait by a sensitive artist named Basil Hallward, who had become obsessed with Dorian's beauty. Over eighteen years, Hallward's painting of Gray records every corruption and debauched act in which he participates. The image grows uglier and more distorted over time, until it becomes the face of a monster. Gray though, remains youthful and unchanged no matter how evil his behavior.

William had always thought the painting influenced its owner, that it was the evil character. Gray's story begins as an innocent youth, but he didn't pay for his crimes and so is changed; his own arrogance becomes his demise.

William reflected on his original offer of help to the fledgling writer Orelia. His generous gesture hadn't been for her sake but, if he was honest, came from his own vanity. Was that such a crime though? How many other people were charitable, good Samaritans because they wanted to brag or appear superior? If millionaires required no gain from altruistic pursuits, why were hospital or school wings named after them?

Each of the book's owners began with positive intentions. Nem, avenging her mother's murder or this Doctor Shepherd. Then they descended into Dorian Gray's contemptuous thinking where nobody else mattered.

Was it in their nature? Or did the power of the book change them? If the latter was true, he didn't want it in his possession any longer than necessary.

Orelia described this book once as a *balance sheet*, of sorts. Now he understood. It was a balance sheet of life, of justice, of serendipity. A book of luck.

Him possessing it may also mean he now had her power. Could he then swap back his luck? Recover what she'd taken from him?

He looked up and scanned the emptying park. The boy with the kite and his father had long gone. The walkers, their circuits completed, had left. An elderly couple, the only ones left in sight, played fetch with a small white dog named Ella, who chased after a ball but refused to return it to them no matter how many times they called her. Within moments they gave up and headed away, berating the animal for its disobedience.

He was now alone with his thoughts and a book he believed might help him recover his life. But was there a downside to even touching the thing? Like living near power transmission towers where your chances of cancer increase? Or working in a disease center where you must take heavy precautions to prevent your own infection?

Many questions and nobody to ask.

He checked his watch. Over an hour since he'd left her house. By now she could have learned of the theft, but would she realize it was him? Any of her victims could be the culprit. He wondered if she possessed a connection to the book, an invisible thread that could lead her to him. Sitting here in such peaceful surroundings he should feel happy and pleased with coming this far. He'd managed to get hold of the book, to discover more than he could have imagined. Instead, all he felt was fear.

With that thought, a shadowy feeling seeped into his subconscious. He felt as though the book knew him, wanted what he could offer. Fog drifted through his mind and pulled him toward a billowy cloud of gray nothingness. A dream-like, pleasant ambience settled over him and carried him to a wonderful calm place. This perhaps akin to a drug addict's experience with the first hit.

He fought the desire to open the book and continue looking at the pages. The most intelligent action would be to destroy the thing and forget it ever existed. Fate, luck, whatever force of nature it controlled, should be only at destiny's whim or God's, if he existed. This power did not belong in human hands and especially not hers. She'd proved herself a poor caretaker. Human nature might be such that nobody could ever be considered a wise custodian.

He sat for a minute, feeling as if his skin crawled with tiny invisible creatures, worrying that the power had contaminated him already.

In his mind's eye he saw her luxurious home, the paintings, the interviews on the morning shows. He recalled the pure jealousy and hatred which raged inside him at her good fortune. How he had wanted the same success. Look how he'd been transformed by his own uncontrolled emotions.

Everything he envied of hers had been achieved through using others. He had watched her star rise. Back then he'd have done anything to achieve the same success. But he couldn't allow himself to take that success from others, and he didn't want to tempt fate right now. So, no, he wouldn't keep the book.

But he would use it one time. To put things right. Surely, once wouldn't hurt?

An idea had settled in his mind after reading the entries, but he was concerned. He had seen the diary's owners slide down a dangerous path after a single use, slipping into a life of wronging neighbors for their own gain.

How would he execute this vague plan?

The six previous owners' entries flowed through his mind, the different writing styles, the names of those they'd besieged with this power. A strange notation, the only exchange like it in the writings, between one owner and the next. That kept bouncing around in his thoughts.

One name floated to the top as if the book suggested the answer he sought.

Nem's mother, the one person who seemed to resist the pull of the diary. There was something she'd written in her few entries. He'd thought it was another one of the good luck wishes but maybe it was something more. He hadn't paid attention at first because by the time her daughter had started school, it seemed she stopped using the book's power. He felt as if she spoke to him, whispered in his ear, gave him the final play.

A plop of rain landed on his nose and he looked up at the sky.

Out of nowhere heavy, dark clouds had gathered, a storm on its way. Another wet drop slopped on a page causing the ink to run. He dabbed at it with his palm attempting to soak up the moisture. Then he decided, what did it matter? He had no intention of keeping the thing, so if rain damaged it, good.

In that moment, as the raindrop slid down the paper, dragging a smear of ink with it, her mother's entries and that water speck collided in his mind and gave him the answer.

The only other question was, did he possess the courage to take the next step?

He told himself he had no choice.

He told himself he could do this.

He told himself he'd most likely fail, but it gave him a chance to end this.

An immense storm lay on the horizon and this time he would be the one bringing the thunder and lightning. He just hoped he'd live to see the sunshine again.

67

The panic rattled inside Nem in the way a train passing overhead can shake you to the core. If she didn't recover the book, what then? The thief had to be William Barnes, the splinter in her life now. He'd been following her for the past week and she'd done nothing. That was a mistake. She'd put it down to a crazed obsession and figured soon the police would arrest him over Morris' death. Even if he suspected anything, who'd listen to the ravings of a killer?

If he did take the diary because he knew about the power, then what might he do? What if he disappeared and she lost it forever? How would she continue? Even thinking about that scenario made her feel weak and sick in her stomach.

No, she couldn't let that happen. The book was hers, and he had no right to it. In the hands of anyone else the power was dangerous, not just to her if he used it for revenge, but to everyone. It had taken her years to master control of the luck thing. Even then, she'd struggled.

When her cell rang, she looked down and gasped, surprised by the caller ID.

She drew a calming breath and answered, keeping her voice cool, to hide her anger and outrage.

Nem didn't open with hello. They'd gone past niceties.

"I'll call the police," she said.

"I don't think you will," he replied.

"Why is that?"

"No need. You can have the book back. I just want to talk first. I'm thinking we work together like the good old days."

Now she saw his plan. She'd underestimated him in thinking he would try and stop her, embark on payback.

Okay, so he suspected something, and imagined he could use her. She would show him though. A partner? He wasn't as smart as he imagined. This was her game and she'd played it alone for a long time.

Her confidence that she would soon recover her diary and resume control instantly erased her anger. Barnes had little comprehension of the book's power; he was a fool if he thought he could beat her.

When he suggested where they were to meet, she paused before replying. For a single second her mind froze, as she puzzled what advantage he would gain by meeting at that place? Not to mention, one look at the skies told her a hell of a storm was on its way. And it was a two-hour drive.

What the devil are you thinking? she wanted to say. Instead she replied, "Of course, I know where that is."

68

$\mathcal{I}$f clouds could be conjured to create the tone for a breathless thriller scene for the finale to William's saga, these would win an Oscar for set design. Thick, gray and oppressive. Unforgiving. The heavens appeared complicit in creating light and atmosphere for the ant-sized author below who soon would face his enemy. With each crack of startling thunder, the gods shouted their displeasure, or perhaps their cheers.

Now that he'd arrived at his designated meeting spot, William worried he had presumed wrong. In fact, his presumptions were many, which meant failure was a real possibility.

First, would Orelia meet him where and when he'd stated? Or might she approach him in another way he hadn't considered?

Second, in a leap of faith or stupidity, he made the decision that this was the best place for their rendezvous. And it was wacky, to say the least.

Third, he dismissed the idea he had lost his sanity when clearly this whole plan was crazy. Dangerous. His mental faculties could indeed be compromised, and he had dragged himself out in this weather as a cry for help.

Fourth, he now gambled that inside Orelia, she still possessed remnants of humanity, small pieces of the little girl who'd set out to use the book's energy for good.

Why he thought any of these conjectures were correct, or the plan had any hope of working, since his experience with the paranormal was nil, came down to believing luck sat in his corner. This incredibly arrogant belief that the book wanted him to stop the misuse was his assurance. Pretty darn ridiculous.

He told himself he needed to quit personifying an imponderable power which had no explanation in science. It helped brace his courageous thinking with logic, he decided. Considering he held the proof in his hands that fate, as a tangible force existed, he was also avoiding a truth.

As he scanned across the rows of gravestones, he pondered why authors wrote horror and readers read it. Anyone desiring to be scared out of their skin only need visit here at night.

In a storm.

To meet with their enemy.

And stand amid the graves and contemplate that one day, maybe even today, you'll join the residents.

This landscape being the unavoidable, absolute proof of the real misfortune of life. That no matter what you did, your existence would bring you to a place like this, with a good chance of pain on the way.

William wondered what ironic twist placed him here, the hero in this story, the person trying to make everything right. His childhood reading diet of Enid Blyton classics *The Secret Seven* and *Famous Five* had characters, who even as children possess skills and smarts which far outweighed his abilities.

His arsenal lay empty. All he had was a hunch. Oh, and a weird magical book of which he only vaguely understood. His theories were only guesses.

But he need only remind himself she had stolen his hard-earned career to stiffen his resolve, reed-thin though it might be. Either way this turned out, he had nothing left to lose. Cliché as that sounded, his first love was writing, and that had gone too. He hadn't written a word of fiction in eighteen months.

He stared down at the grave before him and pondered if this woman knew the wheels which had been set in motion, the fates changed because of her. Dreams stolen, health destroyed, lives extinguished. Poor victims who survived, but spiraled downward, incorrectly blaming fate. They couldn't imagine the one responsible was a girl, and then the woman she became, who used her power with such wicked abandon.

Perhaps it wasn't all her fault. This insidious exploitation might be a generational disease. Someone empowered the pages, infused them with a spell. If not for this woman and the book, Nem might have become a good person?

In his first reading of the inscription which inspired this game plan, the words meant nothing to him. He was more taken by the *life accounting*, as he thought of the notations. The curses of many. The granting of dreams. But when he read the page again, he speculated who was the author and who the recipient?

Dearest Pat, may this bring you your desires. Be careful, be wise, and be kind, Love Aggie.

He realized at the park this was the only example he'd found of a passing on of ownership. Each time he noticed the handwriting change in the book, he presumed this signaled the passing to the next person.

Here, though, was something different. Between the old and new script, the dedication had been left.

This could mean something, he'd thought. Lucky he'd noticed it because a simple online search revealed Patricia was Nem's murdered mother, and Aggie had to be her older sister Agatha Jane. The elder fared no better than her sibling, having also suffered a violent death. This at the hands of her own father.

The time line of the two women fit, when he counted the years back from the time a young Nem began to use the book. Why Aggie gave the book to her sister before her death was a mystery, but there followed an entry regarding the father, which must have been the revenge via Patricia.

William peered into the foreboding dull-gray sky and wondered if the patriarch knew. If he saw the consequence of his daughter's use of the book, maybe conscience forced him to commit an unspeakable crime. Imagine a choice between hell and purgatory?

The other thing he'd noticed too, was that only women had owned it, or they seemed the only ones to use the power.

A droplet fell from the sky, followed by another. The sky had looked ominous before he made the call, but he couldn't help that. He realized he hadn't planned this whole thing so well. Not because of the storm; he needed the storm. At least, he hoped he *would* need it.

No, he hadn't left a farewell note in case this didn't go as he hoped. A warning is what he should have conveyed to someone. Or he should have found someone trustworthy as an ally. In the past year though, he'd abandoned the few relationships he'd enjoyed with friends. He tried to not think about family. That was a mess he didn't need in his head. So for him there was no-one. Alone and isolated was the description of his life, and he'd been good with that, until he found himself standing in a cemetery with storm clouds overhead.

At the least, he should have thought to bring an umbrella. The rain had begun to come down. It wasn't raining cats and dogs, but by the dark angry black and brown hues of the sky, someone was about to let them out. He pulled up the collar of his jacket and shivered. Not from the cold and wet, but from his imminent future.

Two hundred yards in the distance, headlights signaled a car heading along the private stretch of road leading to this section of the graveyard. It must be her. Who else dared venture here on a terrible night like this?

Now that the moment was near, his mind fled back to the notes in the book, focusing his attention away so he didn't think too hard about what might happen. Thinking about her written comments about him, he would admit the traits described were reasonably accurate.

He hadn't seen it of course, because you gradually slip into that hole of giving in to what is easy and feels good at the time. He *had* grown arrogant and careless, taking for granted the luck associated with his success. Nothing like losing everything to appreciate the precariousness of serendipity.

His hope was she would see this too. The solution of righting wrongs to create a clean slate and write a new story seemed to fit with the ethos of the book. If he never reclaimed his career, he could live with that.

The mistake made by Wilde's character, Dorian Gray, would not be his. He *was* truly sorry. Not for himself but for the way he had treated Orelia and others. His failure in his career—and maybe his books were lousy—and the magic wielded against him had done him a favor and shown him his error.

His envy. His anger. In hindsight, deserved, but then... really? If her success had been from her natural ability and not stolen, was that his business? Was anybody else's life his concern?

The car slowed and pulled to the curb only twenty yards away. A darkness descended across the landscape, and as the driver climbed out, lightning flashed, silhouetting the figure against the background of the gentle roll of hills filled with headstones and tombs.

A second flash lit the sky. William had a sense that these markers of lives long past were sentinels, observing and grading him on his performance.

Thunder reached his position two seconds later, crashing twice around him. He jumped and felt his heart leap as a hundred butterflies fluttered in his chest. Still, he returned his focus to the approaching figure.

The rain turned into torrents of water as the wind whipped up, buffeting him without mercy. The sound, a fury of whirling pressure beating him, daring him to leave, seek shelter.

His clothes were wet through, but the chill didn't touch him because he forced his mind to ignore everything except her. Every drop, he told himself, was a bead of energy, feeding focus, keeping his tense muscles warm, his heart brave.

The sky ignited again. It was a hell of a storm, one he would have enjoyed if he was inside safe, looking out. He smiled at that description. A *hell of storm* was what he'd hoped might arrive and, as if ordered, it had come.

Orelia was nearly here, picking through the graves as if this was an obstacle course, looking down every few steps to check her footing. She at least had prepared for the elements, her umbrella waving left and right as she moved.

She stopped only yards from him on the other side of the grave, so the patch of dirt and headstone separated them. He liked that analogy. It seemed fitting and even poetic. Something he'd write in a novel to show the unspoken chasm which lay between two characters.

He imagined this moment in the short hours he'd given himself to prepare. Each line he would now speak he had practiced as he drove here. So this felt surreal, another make-believe rehearsal. The butterflies beat against his ribs as his eyes met her.

As usual, she dressed in style in a tailored three-quarter length jacket. Despite the inclement weather, her grooming remained impeccable. Perfect pixie-styled, vibrant hair. Rich coral lipstick and mascaraed eyes. She could walk straight on to any stage or television set. He almost expected her to launch into a speech on *what it took to write a best seller* or *succeed in the tough publishing game or—how to destroy innocent lives.*

She swapped the umbrella from one hand to the other and peered at the grave. Her head cocked to the side, her face expressionless, as she read the inscription as if she'd never seen it before.

Moments ticked by. Long seconds filled with only the sound of the tumult of air, whistling through the stone-filled landscape. And the crashing rain beating against stone and soil. The water, ricocheted this way and that, mesmerizing until—

"Well, well, well. William," she shouted over the melee. "This is an intriguing surprise. I'd say nice to see you again, but that would be a lie."

She gave him a sweet smile as if she'd just said the opposite.

"I could say the same, Orelia."

He worked at maintaining his demeanor, thinking it was almost amusing that after everything the two of them were forced to shout at each other in such surroundings.

Don't be nervous, he told himself. *She's the one who needs what I now hold. She doesn't know what you have up your sleeve.*

If she doesn't listen, hear what he has to say, he'll move to the next part of his immaculate and well-crafted plan—of course, this being sarcasm to maintain his bravado.

He hadn't a clue what he was doing; just a hunch and a desperate desire to bring this to an end.

A sudden flash from above lit the smirk upon her face; then an almighty whip-crack an instant later followed. An angry rumble concluded the bone-shaking nearby lightning strike. The gods weren't just in a bad mood tonight. They sounded furious and wrathful. The storm had traveled at a gallop and was almost above them. Even through the rain the pungent zing of ozone assaulted his nose.

He wanted to wipe the water from his face but he didn't dare move a muscle in case his legs buckled and had him on his knees before her.

He returned her sneer with as much confidence as he could find.

"I wondered if you'd come. You couldn't say no though, could you?"

"I'm surprised you're still here in the city," she said, charming as a young Shirley Temple. "I mean you killed poor Morris? Pushed him in the river. The police have footage you know. Shouldn't you have run away? Saved your own life instead of interfering in mine?"

Another jagged line of white-yellow split the sky behind her, adding dramatic punctuation to her words. The thunder, so close overhead, growled as though two forces argued above the two mortals.

"Oh, I'm not worried about them anymore. I bet they'll discover Morris drowned all by himself. You know in those TV law shows where the innocent character says they have truth on their side? Well, I have a better partner than truth."

"Really." she said, tilting her head, as if patronizing a small child. "What does that mean?"

"The entry has gone."

She continued to smile but slowly as if she had lost all muscle control, her face drooped. Her eyes squinted at him and he felt as though he now faced an awakening enemy who suddenly realized they might not hold all the cards.

"I hope you haven't done something stupid William. I don't believe you know what you're playing with."

He allowed himself the hint of a smile as he said, "Oh, I think I do. My question is, do you?"

69

*T*his whole cat and mouse game annoyed Nem more than she would expect. She decided the second she had the diary it was *bye bye William Barnes*. How he'd figured out to bring her here, puzzled her for a moment until she realized he had foolishly decided this might spark something in her.

She laughed to herself. *Good try.* What did she care what he thought? He was no more a challenge than a mouse to a snake. The book had been passed down through multiple generations of her family. What did he think he could do?

She hadn't visited her mother's grave in a very long time though, so she took a moment to think about all these years she'd been gone, leaving Nem to fend for herself. She still hadn't decided if she blamed her mother or not for what had happened.

Sometimes the anger would bubble up when she considered what she speculated was the woman's selfishness in not preparing her young daughter for her inheritance. She even wondered why she wouldn't have protected her life at all costs, so she could be there for Nem.

On other occasions, she felt a deep, unrelenting despair. She even experienced moments of profound regret, but something heavy and thick wiped those away.

A darkness had seeped into her core and colored her world to an oddly crystal-clear sharpness, and she welcomed that clarity. The cool calmness made her feel untouchable. She enjoyed the sense of invulnerability and had grown comfortable with the hue of her life.

She looked across her mother's grave at the thorn which she should have picked from the stem and crushed long before now. Her one thought: *You are about to be very, very sorry.*

70

Her fading smile encouraged William's confidence even though the whipping rain now lashed him as if the elements were not on his side. He shivered but refused to wrap his arms about himself to maintain his inner warmth.

"Do I know what I'm doing?" she said, tilting her head as if she'd misheard him. She hunched her shoulders in an exaggerated movement. "Of course I do. Haven't you realized?"

"Realized what?"

"Once you write in the diary, there's no taking it back. It *will* happen. You'll be arrested for Morris' murder and enjoy years to consider the mistake you've made."

"Unlike the man who killed your mom."

"Unlike anyone who's dared to do wrong like that. *Violence begs violence.*"

As if on cue, so his words could be heard, the heavy rain stopped as suddenly as it had started. The dark clouds still hunkered over them, but a gap expanded allowing a shimmer of moonlight to shine through. The glow lit them and the grave between the two enemies. This break would not last long; wind threatened to blow more storm their way.

"Oh, we're quoting Martin Luther King. And the rest of his speech, you've forgotten that? *Returning violence for violence multiplies violence.* That book wasn't meant for you, was it? The entry made for your mother. That you wished her dead. Really? Because she wouldn't let you keep a kitten? An animal. The entries she'd written for you were only for good wishes. To see the light, be kind and enjoy happiness."

William moved to his left and forward, so he now stood beside the headstone. He placed a reverent hand on the slab as though the woman buried below still required his defense. His fingertips tingled as if her spirit imbued him with the energy of good.

"Your mother understood the dangers of the book. That it was not a power for most hands. She died trying to stop you from ever possessing it. She'd written that you might never own it. Twice. Hidden between a previous owner's entries. Your Aunt Aggie. Did she see traits in her own daughter that frightened her? Or the entry you'd put there condemning her to death? Maybe she never saw it because she was already dead."

Orelia's eyes grew wide. This close he saw her lips quiver as she shook her head in a slow, considered motion. William had sent her on a journey to her past.

"No, that's not the truth. I didn't know. She kept it from me. I was so angry that day. All I intended was to take it from the hiding place and use it to bargain. I'd keep the kitten and give her back the diary. I only discovered what happened when they gave me the book later. Her fault, not mine, for not telling me. That book was to be mine after her. She needed to explain what it did. What it could do."

She addressed her mother's resting place as if William was no longer there.

"Things might have been different if you'd trusted me. Maybe then I might have been able to live my life making pathetic, little wishes like yours. Health and happiness and love. Ha! Some of us face tougher stuff. Life forces us to make horrific decisions. If you had the courage to do what was necessary, you'd be alive. I could have grown up in sweetness and light. Become a different girl."

William thought about the words in the book, the varied hand-writing of the entries dating back over a century. The references to babies birthed healthy, diseased crops renewed by unseasonal rain, illness cured by a miracle, lives touched by love. Every owner had begun in goodness. Only Orelia had started with violence and anger from the first.

He'd hoped in making her face the past, her part in her mother's death, an epiphany might smack her in the conscience. She'd see the only way to free herself and make amends was to stop and be sorry for what she'd done. He would help her. That was his means to salvage his own soul.

"You're responsible for so much heartache. Your mother and your aunt didn't use the book the way you did. You can't just dream big. The energy to deliver your dreams must come from within you."

Orelia looked back at William. "Close, my friend."

She appeared unconcerned and he would admit, that worried him. A lot, if he was honest, which he wouldn't be with her. Did she know something he didn't? Still, he knew a little something himself and he still had his last card hidden. If this went south, he would play with his best poker face. So he would keep talking and keep the tremor from his voice, because he needed to keep her attention to buy time. How much time? Of that he was uncertain.

"So tell me," he said, "how does it work?"

"Oh, a history lesson, is that what this is? With atmosphere thrown in. Are you crazy? Okay, I'll bite. What the book can do might be described as spells or witchcraft, I guess, in the good old days. Before that, who knows? Divine intervention from gods. I'm sure somewhere in the future science will discover a flow of energy which influences nature and actions. A thread, a connection between every-body and everything. I think the special power of the diary is its ability to give focus to emotions and dreams."

She paused. "I must say, you've done well to work most of this out. Took me years."

"After what you did to me, you know I had no choice. You took my life for your own. Why, when I only tried to help?"

"You're a fool. You helped me for yourself. People help others for their own benefit. The longer I live the less I believe in those memes. Generosity. Chivalry. Selflessness. Yeah, nobody's all-wonderful. That's how we survive, by using each other to do what we can't or won't. It's the nature of society. Why we exist together."

Her eyes became black slits; the pixie look gone. Orelia's tightened mouth barely moved as she added without a pause, "Now I want the book. Do *not* make me angry. Do you know I don't need it in my hands for the exchange to work?"

No, that was news. The butterflies had turned into grasshoppers and begun to jump in a chaotic dance.

He had come prepared and that would be news to her. What he couldn't know was whether it would work.

"If you give back the diary, I promise you'll be okay."

"And what about everyone else you will hurt to continue living how you choose?"

She shrugged her shoulders and furrowed her brow. "What do you care?"

A thunderous bang along with a white-hot flash made William's heart jump. The air around them became super-charged, sizzling with the energy of the storm. This time the rain gave no warning. One moment dry, the next, the sky opened as if a hole had been wrenched above to send down hell.

William fought the desire to run, to escape the deluge and get away from her. He knew what was coming. Hoped he'd been right. Prayed his idea would work. So many presumptions but please let luck be on his side. Crazy as it might seem, as he stood here in the middle of a goddamn graveyard, talking about luck and magic, he prayed if there was any god looking down, that he liked William's side better than hers.

He hoped she had no clue, no inkling, even though he kept thinking she would guess. The weather. This scene. If she did suspect, was she telling the truth? Was she able to control the force without holding it in her possession?

He wasn't going to change her mind. He saw that now and he

didn't dare tempt fate much longer. His hand reached inside his jacket and pulled out the book.

The look on her face heartened him. Orelia had been caught off guard; maybe she had expected more of a fight. He noticed her perfect grooming had been unraveling courtesy of the elements. Despite the umbrella, her clothes were near soaked. A thin line of black mascara ran down one cheek; her hair, having absorbed the moisture, had lost its style and begun to turn to frizz. She didn't seem to care.

He'd imagined he still had time to stop this, that he had the choice to change the next moments after he heard her answers. He had hoped in bringing her to her mother's grave, this would remind her there were other paths to choose. He saw now that like Wilde's villain Dorian Gray her thinking had been colored. She had drunk from the cup of self-deceit, which can poison your soul so you never again see the truth.

"I care Orelia, because you've shown me what happens when you live only for yourself. I'm glad you did what you did to my life. I'd written one great novel. Big deal. I experienced the pull of that drug too. Success. Power. But you know, it's not winning if it comes at the expense of someone else. Success should come from giving not taking."

William surprised himself at how much he believed those words.

He stole a glance at a black cloud which seemed to fly across the sky in their direction. The storm must have understood the importance of timing.

She followed his look, her head tilting upward. A deep frown creased her forehead. He could see her mind ticking through what was happening, if there was something she had missed.

Yes, he thought. *You've underestimated me.*

"Why didn't we meet in a coffee shop and stay dry. This is overly dramatic, even for you."

She held out her hand, and raindrops hit her palm and bounced away as if repelled by her.

"I'd love to get out of this weather, if that's okay with you. I presume you've brought my diary as a bargaining chip. And, alright, you win. Whatever you want is yours. Money, your next book launched at number one, selling millions, a wonderful love life. Anything. Name it."

"Nothing. I want nothing. All I wanted was for you to stop. To see this was wrong."

"Okay, now you are being ridiculous. Let me rephrase that. Give it back."

William's hand shook as he held out the diary. He'd spent a good hour considering the words before he wrote them on the fresh page, untouched by any previous owner. The white ribbon bookmark dangled against his chest as he held the book close.

He looked up again to the sky, felt the rain on his face, maybe for the last time. The cloud hung above them now. Thick, black as hell. *Was that a gaping mouth embedded in its core?* His imagination ran away, on fire from the fear, the curiosity and from facing the knowledge that in the next few seconds he most likely would die.

"Be my guest," said William, opening to the bookmarked page as he stepped forward. He placed it in her hand as if bestowing an award.

She gave him a triumphant smile. He nodded toward the book, as if to say, *read it*. His focus didn't shift from the green cover as one hand rose to open the pages.

Then he smiled and waited, because he'd done everything he could and now it was out of his control and in fate's hands.

For a moment she looked down and he saw her chest contract in a sharp intake of air as she picked up the note he'd written so carefully before placing it inside the diary.

"What does this mean? What have you done?"

He thought he saw green, white and yellow sparks fly; that they exploded from her eyes, her head, her hands, but everything happened so quickly, within a split second that he was sure of nothing. His brain had no time to process the image only a few feet from him.

Weeks later those moments would remain a blur. Every time he tried to recall them, they slipped into a time-lapse movement of his surroundings as if someone had flicked a light on and off. Until later when they came to haunt him day after day, night after night.

What he imagined and what was the true reality, he'd never know.

The unexpected flare of brilliant white blinded him as the intensity of the explosion threw him to the ground. He thought he saw fire but his faculties had been sent into a spin with the impact. The graves, the grass, the sky and black clouds shook as though he was trapped inside a glass container and a giant had slapped the surface. The earth trembled from the force and caused him to imagine at any second, he would fall into a chasm and be crushed.

He tried to rise but he had nothing left inside. His breath, knocked from him as he fell, left him depleted of oxygen. He dragged at the air in ragged gasps; a fish out of water, straining to refill its lungs.

As though nature's sound and visual department had awaited its cue, a flash akin to a thousand light bulbs, and a roar like a jet, exploded around them for a second time.

William reached with both hands to cover his head, instinctively curling into a fetal position for protection. He wasn't sure which terrified him more. The light, the sound or that he couldn't move a muscle. His mind fumbled at this as if it was the most important question in the world, until the pain of a hundred million needles piercing his skin in a split second, wiped any thoughts from his brain.

Night, Night Mr. Best Seller, snapped into his mind, and he wasn't sure if it was Orelia's voice or just his imagination.

71

𝒩em felt her body become weightless. Her entire being became an empty balloon, free and floating. She tried to reach up to the sky, which had become the most incredible white she'd ever seen. Pure and sparkling, the way light glances off a lake in the early afternoon when the sun is high.

She reflected on William and how they'd once been friends. Well, working acquaintances, the only style of friendship she allowed herself. Or maybe that wasn't true. She had a vague feeling she had loved someone once and cared for others but that she couldn't stay with them because—

Why she had decided to only create those relationships, she couldn't fathom. When she tried to form an image of the one she loved, it flew out of reach.

Now he had the book, her mother's book, the one she shouldn't have touched; she hoped he might enjoy better luck with it. That idea made her want to laugh and she couldn't think why? It was as if there was an inside joke and she just didn't get it.

Confusion drifted into her thoughts, jumbling what she thought she knew, stretching memories away like elastic, so she didn't have time to understand and put the pieces together. Good fortune had been hers, but somehow it evaporated and left her for another place. Another person. A different life.

She tried to focus on that concept but found her mind straying to other unimportant ideas and then they faded and wafted into the air to disappear.

Her attention returned to the sky. An incredible, brilliant glow shone down upon her, warming her face, and she didn't want to miss the glorious vision. She wanted to remember this for the rest of her life as a reminder of beauty that money can't buy.

Despite being soaked from the rain and bone-chilled moments before, she now enjoyed the luxurious bath of incandescence, which radiated from the shining circle above.

She had just begun to wonder about the brilliance and why it was there, when the lightness reached for her, wrapping around her body like a glove of softest silk. A feeling of being lifted to the heavens and gliding on air overtook her. She gave herself to the sensation because this was the most wonderful experience of her life.

Even though, as she drew near the glow grew whiter and brighter, but it didn't hurt her eyes. That was strange because she didn't even blink, and she should have with all this vivid whiteness flooding over her.

Then the luminescence engulfed her, and she finally understood. For a millisecond, sorrow consumed her for what she'd done. The cruelness, the selfishness, the disregard for everyone and the anger she'd carried for so long toward her mom.

Someone called her name off in the distance.

She turned her body, her now strange light-as-air body, toward the sound. Maybe she could ask that voice what had happened. Where she had gone wrong? That seemed important to know, now she was here.

"Nem," the whisper came. She couldn't see anyone; the light engulfed everything. The white overwhelmed her senses and touched her but was softened by a far away streak of gold.

"Nem," it repeated in a hushed, breathless sigh.

She thought she recognized the voice. *Yes, she was sure now.*

Though she hadn't heard it in decades, the moments between then and now melted away.

"Mom? Mom?" she called.

She felt like a little girl again, her body returning to that moment as a child. She reached out her hand as the gold glow came toward her, gentle as a rolling wave. Quiet as a sigh.

"I'm sorry," Nem said before letting go of everything.

Everything had seemed so important. But now... nothing.

72

*W*hen William opened his eyes, his first thought was his killer headache was the least of his concerns. His arm had slammed against Orelia's mother's gravestone and he knew at once he'd broken the limb.

The sky had cleared by some miracle, and the moon shone bright, as if to say, *hey, now it's my turn*. The storm appeared to have traveled on at breakneck speed while he lay unconscious. He pulled himself up to a sitting position and looked toward the horizon. His math wasn't his strongest point, nor his visual perception, but he calculated the dark, treacherous clouds were a good five miles to the South.

"Ow," he cried, touching his left arm gently with his fingers to check if his first diagnosis was correct.

Yes, broken for sure, because arms don't normally sport an s-bend below the elbow. That wouldn't be of any use for a while. He might need to learn to dictate his work if he was to get anything done. Despite the throb threatening to explode in his head and the fire in his fractured arm, he felt strangely uplifted.

Anything to do with his craft, other than curses, hadn't entered his mind for months, so that alone made him... happy.

Happy.

Another emotion he hadn't experienced in recent times. Nothing like a massive bolt of electricity to realign your priorities.

But Orelia? The vision of her hand outstretched demanding the book, her black eyes staring with such hatred, flew at him. Where was she? She had said something about him *caring* or *why he cared* about the book. Then, then—oh, he couldn't remember.

He scanned his surroundings and realized why his change of heart; why he felt lighter, a weight lifted from him. Orelia lay ten yards away, unmoving. She must have taken a direct hit. The impact of the lightning strike had sent her backward where she'd landed on a gravestone.

Even from this sitting position on the ground, he saw her head had broken her fall. Skull versus stone is never a good contest, not for the skull, at least. In her case, it was a fait accompli.

William pushed himself up to standing, careful to move his arm as little as possible. Once upright, he nursed the injury with his other hand, and took small, cautious steps toward her body. Once there, he squatted beside her to check her pulse.

Blood flowed from a jagged crack near her temple. Not much to his surprise, but in the moonlight, white patches of bone shone through the wet, matted hair. She no longer reminded him of a youthful Audrey Hepburn.

There was no pulse. There was no life. She was gone.

Her eyes stared at him, wide, no longer creased in fury. He should feel sorry for her, but he felt nothing except relief and maybe even pride that he'd done this.

Using his good hand, he pushed back onto his haunches and leaned back to stare up into the night sky, dotted with a million stars; overseen by a gold moon. He looked back down at her wondering what she was looking at up there because her face carried the barest wisp of a smile.

Clutched in her clawed, stiff hand was the green book, or a better description, the remnants. The exterior had been blackened so that it was unrecognizable from the original handsome volume. Pages were now only jagged, crisped and curled edges. Small wisps of smoke curled up into the damp air as if the object had been recovered from a camp fire.

William wondered if even a few pieces of paper was still enough to hold the power? Or did it need anchoring in book form?

He crouched over her, pushing at her fingers, prying them away until he slipped it from her hands and pulled open the covers, stiff and flaking from the damage.

Even if a vestige of power remained in the unburnt paper, he was relieved to see the saved pages were close to mush, thanks to the rain.

He carefully stroked the pages open and looked for the place where he'd written the words. He found them on the page he'd sweated and puzzled over, as he tried to choose the perfect phrase.

It wasn't as if his life had depended on it, or anything, he'd thought sarcastically as he wrote.

His inscription, though only partial, remained visible but fading, as the moisture soaked into the fibers. The letters now runny and blurred were barely legible.

...ath. St.uck by lightn... twice.

All the notations which came before them, destroyed; the tragic stories they told, gone forever. Thank the God of Fortune—whoever that one was—because he didn't need reminding of the events which had set this in motion. Nor the terrible things he had contemplated doing to Orelia in the beginning. He hadn't been serious, not really, but he reminded himself to *be careful what you wish for William Barnes. Look where that took you.*

The note he had handed her, the moment before she had been struck by the bolt, lay in muddy grass, inches from a burned hand. At the moment she was hit, the paper must have fallen.

Though his injury throbbed as if a hammer had been taken to his forearm, he smiled. Shame descended just as quickly as it took him to admonish himself for feeling anything beyond remorse.

But, hey, he was a writer, and if that shredded, soggy scrap didn't contain the wittiest line ever penned, given the circumstances, he'd eat his keyboard. Despite this being a scene straight out of a horror film, he began to laugh.

Even as he reached for the note, he laughed. Even as his arm reminded him he had months of physical therapy ahead, he laughed. And as he considered, ruined as it was, that he might still frame the piece, he laughed. It would be a unique reminder to him that he should never forget the tenuous grasp any person has on their fate. That fate enjoyed delivering a constant stream of big, cosmic jokes.

The sheet tore into tiny, soggy shreds at his touch. The more he tried to save it, the more it dissolved in his hands, returning to its original pulped form. The words faded and became only smeared lines on the disintegrating paper. But he'd never forget them. He saw them in his mind as his hand trailed across the notepad only a few short hours ago.

The End. Goodbye.

He laughed again as he scrunched the mush and pressed it into the book before bending to Orelia to return her precious possession to her grasp.

73

*W*illiam slid his hand between the two books and pushed, so that he might gain a closer look at the novel to their left's cover. Yes, he was right! *Suffer Them to Come to Light*, an early edition. He hadn't seen it on a shelf—other than his own—in a long time. For a moment, he even considered asking for a pen and offering to sign the inside flap, then thought better of it.

That book was part of his past, along with the title *New York Times Bestseller*. This one, printed before he'd earned that moniker, only included his name in bold, white letters.

He was good with that, for the moment.

Plain old William Barnes. Copywriter.

Not such a bad job. To write blurbs for websites and make a little on the side hawking a few magazine pieces. This work paid the bills without the pressure of striving to top sales charts. The bonus being, he didn't need an agent or a publishing house with their deadlines and demands.

At night he still wrote fiction but now for his own pleasure. He no longer craved that others read his books. Reading his own work was enough. The pure pleasure of creating something from nothing was all he needed for the moment.

Somewhere amid the mad fury of those days of his early success, he'd lost his way. He had forgotten why he created stories. It had become about sales numbers, due dates, reviews and money.

As time distanced him from all that had happened, perhaps he might return to publishing, when he could tell himself that the events on that storm-filled night were just a bad dream. That a book conjuring good and bad luck, had never existed. To believe that it could seemed ridiculous.

In a surprise turnaround, he carried only warm feelings toward Orelia. She had gifted him the wisdom of viewing success and failure in the same light. He could easily have descended into hell following many other great wordsmiths like Fitzgerald, Hemingway and Salinger. The list of unhappy, alcoholic writers was long.

The greatest story was the one he would never tell, of two authors and a mysterious green book. Maybe he could write it as a parable, but after only six months, the emotions were still too fresh.

He replaced his novel among the other used volumes and hoped it would find a wonderful reader.

With no idea what he desired to read tonight, he strolled the aisles, trailing his fingers across spines, gently pulling the books into his palms. He checked the blurbs before returning them to the shelf and pushing them back into their place. None of them seemed a right fit for his contemplative mood.

A classic tonight perhaps? Something by a previous-century, troubled author. Anything by Oscar Wilde would work; he felt like a little comedic irony. Besides writing, reading was his great pleasure now. Avoiding people, his hobby. He was still a crumpled ball of paper, rolled into small nooks to hide away from life while he healed.

He was okay with that too.

William ended his search with F. Scott Fitzgerald's *The Great Gatsby*. He'd read it before, twice. As depressing as he'd found it, he admired the twist of Gatsby's innocence when he'd appeared so guilty. Like himself, if you'd followed his whole life story, which no one had since his *nobody* status became official a few years back thanks to magic.

For the hundredth time, the question crossed his mind. Was Orelia to blame or the diary?

He'd wonder that for the rest of his life. Might anyone succumb to the pull of such incredible power? Could he, if he'd kept the book instead of using it to destroy her?

He didn't regret what circumstance forced him to do. In this case, the end did justify the means—and they had been spectacular.

For the thousandth time he told himself to forget it. *What's done is done. Book closed. Epitaph written.*

Reading matter chosen, he moved to the counter, holding the novel, and nodded to the clerk. By the age of him, the man might have known Fitzgerald in person. White tufts stood out at interesting angles below a shiny dome of scalp. With so little hair, he wondered why the old guy didn't give up and go with bald.

The shopkeeper offered a genuine smile and picked up the book William had placed on the glass cabinet which doubled as a counter.

"Was that all, sir?"

He nodded and opened his mouth to reply, *thank you,* when something on a shelf below the clear surface captured his attention.

Every volume displayed therein appeared to be antique. Each leather cover adorned with the handsome, gold hand-lettering of a bygone era. The one which now caused his breath to stop in his throat lay off to one side. Its matte-green face and striking gold engraving seemed to catch the light in a strange, almost impercep- tible glow.

It couldn't be possible, but *wow, it sure looked similar.*

He bent down for a closer look, his head cocked to the side at the same height as the counter, as he peered through the glass.

A sudden jolt in his chest made him stand up and step back as if struck by a slap to the face.

Could it be?

No.

Impossible.

He stepped back and tapped a finger above the book, expecting a minute bolt of lightning to fly up and meet his touch, like those electrical balls they sold in gimmick shops that respond to your hand.

"This book here with the flowing design on the cover. It doesn't have a title."

The man's voice, croaky and weary: "Which one?"

"Green cover. Old looking."

"They're all old," said the man, stroking his gray-stubbled chin.

He slid open a cabinet door and reached in to retrieve the volume. Then he leaned sideways to pick up a pair of glasses perched on the cash register.

"Hmm. When did you arrive?" he said, examining the book, turning it over in his hands.

"How much?" asked William, as the man's gnarled and arthritic fingers handed the thing that couldn't exist to William.

"*Hmph*. Don't rightly know. Joe might-ta bought these from someone yesterday when I wasn't here."

William took the book and stared at the cover. His fingertips tingled, minute icy particles of energy feathered his skin, sweeping over his hands. He waited for the sensation to travel into the rest of his body, but nothing came. Instead the feeling faded, a detonation wick fizzling out.

It had disappeared, he told himself, because that was his imagination playing with him.

Had to be. Didn't it?

He sensed the man's gaze upon him as he opened the pages. For some reason, the action caused small beads of sweat to rise on the back of his neck as if a humidity switch had been flicked.

Ridiculous for him to react this way because it was impossible for this to be the book.

In the first few pages, in scrawled handwriting from a time before computers, a time before ballpoint pens, when someone with a feather and ink wrote by candlelight, were the lines of observations. And dates. And pluses and minuses and wishes and curses.

Whether the writers were related, a grandmother, great-great-grandmother, a great-aunt or a sister, he couldn't know. Many authors, was all he surmised from the different handwriting and notations.

Absolutely. Not. Possible.

But he believed he held in his possession another diary of *balance-sheet* luck. Orelia's face swam through his mind as she'd stood in the rain demanding he return what was hers, the one burned and turned to a pulp.

The last words she ever spoke: *What have you done?*

Now as he flipped through the pages of this beautiful and dangerous green book, he wondered too what he had actually done?

He placed the book on the counter for fear his shaking hands might drop it. With a slow, reverent touch he closed the covers and left his palm resting over it.

Not possible.

No doubt.

He stared at the innocent looking object, lying in wait, between himself and the shopkeeper. When he spoke, he felt uncertain whether the quaver in his voice would give away that his heart had become a battering ram inside his chest.

"How... how much?"

The old man was slow and took too long to retrieve the book. When he did, he spent an eternity flipping over a few pages as if they had all the time in the world.

"Now, let me see." He pushed his glasses further down on his nose.

"No," he said, checking the back.

"Nope," he said, opening the cover.

"Hmm. Hmm-hmm, that is a puzzle. Don't rightly know son. Normally we put the price on a sticker somewhere. Jeez, I'd better check with Joe. Can I take your number and call you? Okay?"

He smiled when he looked up, lowering his arm, the clutched book momentarily out of sight, below the counter.

William was in a panic. "What about I give you a hundred? Make that one-twenty."

The man arched his neck backward and tilted his head, examining William as if he'd just said, *hold up your hands; this is a robbery*. Then he scratched above an ear like he had a family of fleas living in the snatch of hair.

"Well, hell... I guess. Yeah. I doubt he paid *that* much for it."

He nodded and puckered his lips.

"Okay, okay. Tell you what, I'll throw in the *Gatsby* too. That'll pacify my guilt. Can probably close up for the rest of the afternoon from this sale. You a collector or somethun?"

He added in a thoughtful, quizzical tone. "You know something I don't, about this here book?"

"No, I know nothing, nothing, really. I just like the cover. Green. Yes, I like green."

He chuckled as William handed over his credit card.

"Must be my lucky day," he said, processing the payment. He stopped for a moment and looked up to add, "Or maybe it's yours, huh?"

"Maybe," replied William, shaking his head and giving a nervous chuckle. "But I'm not a big believer in luck."

74

The shopkeeper waited until the door closed behind the nervous young man. He gave him little further thought.

His hands ached a little today, his arthritis playing up again. Days such as this—warm with a chance of rain—always reminded him his youthful years were a long way behind in the rear-view mirror.

He should see his doctor soon for more medication. Someone told him to take Omega-3. He wasn't convinced, and fish didn't agree with him, anyway.

Besides, sometimes experiencing pain made him feel more alive. This was the circle of life and his decaying body was the reward for everything before, good and bad. That sucker of a wheel didn't care about him, or the fellow so intent on the book. It didn't care about anyone. The thing turned and around you went; a squeaking mouse pedaling like hell to keep up.

He shuffled through the door into the backroom where they kept the extra stock. Hundreds of books in a dozen groups stacked to near ceiling height greeted him. To one side, boxes rested on top of smaller book stacks.

Must get to those, he told himself.

Tomorrow.

Maybe.

If his knuckle joints loosened.

A table stood pressed against a wall with cracked and peeling, once-bright-yellow paint. Multiple dirty cups perched amid out-of-date magazines and more books on its surface. Best wash those tomorrow too. *Maybe he would.* If he couldn't find a clean one come coffee time.

A small window with a view to a side alley allowed enough light through to catch dust particles dancing in the air. Old paper made a lot of the stuff and it irritated his sinuses. Even after all these years.

What ya gonna do? Where else was he gonna work? And who'd have him? Wasn't as if he was skilled up like the young folk with their computers and tappy-tappy screens.

Nope, he'd probably die between science-fiction and the women's literary shelves. They'd find him smiling because he'd dropped off this mortal coil surrounded by what he loved.

Just Lord, please don't let him collapse anywhere near romance.

Now where was that carton?

He knew he put it somewhere out of the way yesterday. Or was it the day before?

Hmm, possibly even Monday.

And today was?

No, that was too much thinking.

Today was today. Good enough for this little mouse.

Then he remembered. He had pushed the box beneath the table. The contents had caught his attention, and he wanted to take a better look at his leisure. Joe hadn't mentioned to him where and when he got them.

He'd forgotten it was him who'd put the book out there on display. Sometimes this memory of his, it just went 'round and 'round and ended up nowhere.

Lucky he found the books and had the good sense to put that one out on display.

Hundred and twenty bucks! Woo-wee, that was something.

No way was that little thing worth that. No accounting for a collector's taste. Nope, there was not.

Yes! There she was, the carton as he remembered, now he'd got thinking. Still juice in this old brain yet.

He leaned down and his back reminded him he should bend at the knees. Easier said than done with his joints and tired, worn muscles. Some days he felt put together with tape and string, and spit and glue—more spit than anything else.

He pulled at the carton's edge and it obligingly slid toward him. His grizzled hands lifted the cardboard flaps, and he stared inside. They were all there. Joe had removed none of them yet. Thirteen left after he'd sold that one just now.

Pretty and green and... *strange.*

Because he'd already looked over a few of 'em and they seemed nothing special. A bunch of handwritten notes, that was all. Not worth what the guy paid, Mr. Collector, but who's gonna argue? *A fool and their money, right?*

His first impression of them was they belonged to a therapist or an artist, writer maybe. Thoughts noted down about lotsa folks. Private stuff. A lot of it nasty.

People oughta mind their business.

He learned a long time ago, no good comes of sticking your nose where it don't belong.

The books had an odd feel when he handled them. Kinda like someone glued rough sparkly stuff to the cover. Made his fingers tingle and the hairs on the back of his hand stand on end. Static electricity he figured, and over-sensitive, old nerves that lied.

After checking over a few, he decided he didn't want to know what the others contained. But hey, who was he to argue with profit? Paid his wages. *Yes, indeedy.*

He picked one up and sensed a tickle in his palm. *God damn.* When handling them next, he would use a cloth. The feeling was unpleasant. That static could give a nasty shock to his system. Who knew how the ol' ticker's wiring was these days?

He turned and shuffled from the room, past the cartons and stock, which he'd sort through when he *got to it*. At the counter he stopped and stooped.

Pushing open the glass door, he rearranged the books inside before placing the green volume beside the others. This time he gave the odd, little collectible pride of place in the center.

He might even hunt around for a stand to sit it upright. Better chance of catching another collector's attention.

"Woo-wee! Hundred and twenty bucks, my friend," he said to the book as he closed the cabinet. "That fella was a fool. Yes, siree, he didn't know much about nothing."

I don't believe in luck. That's what he'd said after paying enough to cover two days' wages.

Well, the books might be ancient like him, but if he could sell these others for even half that price, they sure seemed lucky to him.

February 22, 2018

Loved Best Seller?

Grab a starter library of **FREE** eBooks by Susan May
www.readerlinks.com/l/490258

After, please return here to turn the page and read Susan's popular *From the Imagination Vault*, where readers are taken behind the story to share in her inspiration for Best Seller and maybe you might discover where fiction and inspiration merge into another reality.

After the Thank You section keep reading to enjoy a preview of The Troubles Keeper.

IMAGINATION VAULT

When I typed *The End* after completing the last draft of this novel, I sobbed. This has been the toughest book I've written so far and at times I didn't believe I'd even finish. Three things fought me every step of the way: a character, technology and life balance.

Best Seller was conceived as a novella in June 2016. It was to be a one perspective stalker tale of an author driven by extreme jealousy. I never imagined it would grow into a novel with a complex inter-weaving of characters and a paranormal talisman.

My husband Franco loved the initial few pages of William's rantings, but he posed a question.

"Do you think you need another character as a break between the William chapters?"

"What about a few scenes of Orelia as a child?" I replied.

I saw the kitten in an alley and the trouble this might create for a young child. So Nem was born to add only a few chapters to compliment William's storyline.

Oh dear, little Nem didn't want *only a few chapters*. She wanted half a book. My one hundred page novella became a five-hundred-page novel to accommodate this prima-donna. The more I told her story, the more I saw a complex battle of wills with each character challenging their own demons as well as each other.

Then came *my* battle with technology. Halfway through the original draft I adopted a new program to store my story and notes. Instead of making things easier, I had chapters out of sequence, confusion galore and a huge mountain of re-arranging ahead which weighed on my mind. I'm now back to Microsoft *Word* which works just fine for me.

An interesting aside was my discovery of *Dragon Dictate*, a program which allows a user to narrate instead of typing. The second half of this book was written while driving, walking and even folding clothes. Pretty neat, right?

Now to the inspiration ...

Who doesn't occasionally look at someone's success, especially one who appears undeserving, and tell themselves *it must be luck* or *that's not fair*. This envy would not be unknown in the publishing industry, so I just ramped it up a notch.

Oscar Wilde's *The Picture of Dorian Gray* is a favorite of mine. Like the green diary, I loved the idea the portrait influenced Dorian as much as he transformed it.

Morris Usher's name is a nod to Edgar Allan Poe's 1839 short story *The Fall of the House of Usher*. I grew up reading Poe and he inspires my work. Secretly adding my heroes or something from their stories into my books is fun.

The good and bad reviews throughout this book are actual reviews of my own books on Amazon. Not the New York Times ones; those I delighted in writing.

The publishing details are based on truth. Authors stalking other authors happens. People on sites like *Fiverr* do offer to leave positive and negative reviews on any product you like. William's agent and publisher canceling his contract occurs more than you think. Writers whose books don't sell can find themselves looking for a new publisher. Countless blog posts attest to this and, as an example, author Boyd Morrison wrote about his terrible experience with his publisher. Do Google for the number of agents who dupe their clients. There's plenty.

Of William and Orelia's passion for writing… yes, that is how it feels to be a writer, at least for me. When readers share their enjoyment of my books I'm thrilled. Feel free to email me at susan-may@node1.com.au, and I'll always reply.

In my early twenties, while dreaming of writing for a living, I read a Stephen King quote which stuck. This was in the back of my mind while writing *Best Seller*. In 1981 in his non-fiction book *Danse Macabre*, he wrote:

> … *to be successful, the artist in any field has to be in the right place at the right time. The right time is in the lap of the gods, but any mother's son or daughter can work his/her way to the right place and wait.*
>
> *But what is the right place? That is one of the great, amiable mysteries of human experience.*

Finally, why do most of my stories delve into serendipity?

Well, the whim of fate is fascinating. I may not always believe in luck or curses but many life twists do feel touched by a greater hand.

Or, maybe it comes down to an old man stocking magical books on a shelf in a dark, dusty second-hand bookstore, hidden down a lane, in a large city in Somewhere Land.

You may have just read a non-fiction book, wrapped in a pretty cover with names changed to protect the innocent—or not so innocent.

I'll leave the answer to your imagination.

I wish you and yours good fortune in life. You must excuse me now though, as I need to check the notation in my little, green book for you. I'll be right back.

Happy nightmares!

Yours, Susan May

P.S. I bet you, curious reader, want to know who sold that carton of green diaries to the bookstore. And what William did with the book he bought.

Well, first up, I don't know. You'll need to ask the owner of the bookshop. With William, I don't know either. He will continue to get himself into trouble; that I do know. Join my mailing club and if he ever turns up in a story again with that book, you'll be the first to know. Join the Susan May Gang

LOVED THIS?

What's next?

Three things you can do right now.

1) Jump into another Susan May read! There's many more novels and story collections for you to enjoy. While Susan mostly writes stand alone novels, she's currently working on a trilogy for her most beloved book **The Troubles Keeper.** Explore all available books in order of most recent publication: **susanmaywriter.net/susan-may-books**

2) Do you have a moment to leave a review on Amazon? It's one of the most beneficial ways you can support an author. Every review helps —even just a few words! **You can leave one here.** Your help is appreciated. Thank you!

3) Join **Susan May's Readers' Club** and receive two FREE books to keep. **susanmaywriter.net/free-books**

Connect with Susan May

Join Susan May's Readers' Club and receive two Free books
susanmaywriter.net/free-books

plus

- *Behind the Story* access to fascinating details about the writing of Susan's books.
- Contests to enter with great prizes like Kindle readers and Audible books.
- Free and discounted book offers
- And much more (we're working on the *much more* all the time)

Find Susan May every day at her private Facebook group **The Mayhem Gang.** You are welcome to join a great bunch of people from around the world, discussing books, life and other fun topics.

Facebook Susan Mayhem Gang

Susan May would love to hear from you, so email her at
susanmay@node1.com.au

THANK YOU

My first thanks always goes to my incredible, supportive husband who was my shoulder to cry on over this darn book. He kept telling me, "You can do it." I didn't always believe him, but it sure helped, my love.

To my kids, Bailey and Harry; you are my lucky *clovers*. You've brought me my greatest wish in life: the lesson of loving unconditionally and experiencing the depth of love only a parent can understand.

Thank you to my parents, no longer with us but here in spirit with me every day. Their lessons are in my stories.

Thank you to Diane Desmarest Lynch for always being there. You made an awesome imaginary bookstore manager. She's also the real-life cheerful head moderator of my Facebook group Susan May's Mayhem Gang.

Thank you to Steve Marvel for another wonderful narration of **Best Seller** What a talent! He also narrated my book **The Troubles Keeper.**

Thank you Wonderful Reader, for giving your time to this story. I'm grateful you trusted me enough to come this far.

Finally, to all those who dream of writing or any endeavor dear to your heart...

You don't need a magic book or permission to do this. In your imagination put on a pretend coat with writer (or whatever) on the pocket. You never know what might happen after that.

Go be magical in whatever moves you. There's no telling where the lucky spot lies in your future. You just gotta believe it's there. Failing that, you can always hunt through a second-hand bookstore for a little green diary. As my dad would quote from Shakespeare whenever I'd ask if something magical such as fairies existed: *There are more things in heaven and earth than are dreamt of...*

Susan May

HAWK-EYES

As always, this manuscript was sent out to my early reader group. These are wonderful, clever people who have helped me root out those weed-like typos my eyes and my editor's can't see. Where's a superpower when you need it, right?

Special thanks to Diane Lybbert and Walter Scott, who went above and beyond the call of duty.

Diane Desmarest Lynch, Diane Lybbert, Shari Small, Bill Schmidt (Holy One), John Filar, Mike Rice, Lisa Ensign, Beth Baskett, Julie duChene, David Place Jr, Alicia Maryweather, Mad Wilson, John Filar, Maureen Scalia, Manie Kilian, Heather Hackett, Kenneth Lingenfelter, Christine Lowe, Beenish Siddiqui, Debora Hauser, Marty Whipple, Heather Rice, Paula Lopez, April Hughes, Richard Tamer, Cathy McTernan, Brandy Kistler, Barbara Harrison, Ren Drake, Shari Gross,Victoria Schwimley, Sherry Martin

THE TROUBLES KEEPER PREVIEW

Enjoy the opening opening chapters of Susan May's International best selling novel The Troubles Keeper.

HE SAVES OTHERS FROM THEIR TROUBLES. WHO WILL SAVE HIM?

Bus driver Rory Fine possesses a unique and wonderful gift. He has the power to relieve others of their troubles for real! With just the barest of touches the worries and woes weighing down the hearts of those he helps simply fade away. All are unaware why in being near him they feel happier and more able to face life's challenges.

Despite his special talent, Rory is shy and awkward. So much so he can't find the courage to utter more than a hello to one of his regular passengers, Mariana, whom he believes he might just love. That is, until, during an evening commute one stormy night, when he stops the bus and invites the sullen-looking passengers to play a little game. If they tap his palm as they step off the bus he'll take their troubles. Later he'll throw them in the river, freeing each person to face their evening in a better mood.

This moment might also be the perfect chance to finally speak to Mariana and maybe even ask her out. On board, though, lurks the Trepan Killer, a terror who has stalked the city for months. And he leaves behind something darker than everyday troubles. .

Can this sweet, simple bus driver discover the killer's identity and somehow stop this relentless evil? To do so, he'll need to face a harrowing past and overcome his greatest fear. But he'll need to find a way, because at stake is not just Mariana's life but the very fabric of the world.

From international best selling suspense author, Susan May, comes another page-turner keeping readers up way past their bedtime. Board The Troubles Keeper for a non-stop killer suspense ride you won't want to get off.

⭐⭐⭐⭐⭐ "Not since Dean Koontz's Odd Thomas have I enjoyed a character as much as I do Rory Fine!" Carolyn Werner

⭐⭐⭐⭐⭐ "Susan May seems to be following in the footsteps of **Stephen King.** I, for one, have already put her on my *'If she writes it, I will read it'* list." Madelon Wilson (*Good Reads Reviewer USA*)

★★★★★ "A unique take on a serial killer and the author is brilliant at creating a storyline that leaves the reader breathless." Maureen Ellis *(Good Reads reviewer UK)*

Now read the opening chapters of the book readers are saying they cannot put down ...

The Troubles Keeper

INTERNATIONAL BEST SELLING AUTHOR

SUSAN MAY

1

*H*e examines his work. Certainly not the best he's done but not the worst either. He's improving and becoming more artful. More certain and confident. There's magic in this moment; the *just after* moment when he can breathe again. *In. And out.* A drowning man reaching the surface to suck in pure air so he can survive.

Disappointment rushes in as he feels her last breath. He feels the failure like an ache inside ripping at his core. He felt so certain his search was over, but he was wrong.

He'd found her on the bus. Something had attracted him to *that* bus. Surely the girl, he'd thought. He'd sat behind her as they had traveled downtown. Pretending he'd dropped something, he'd leaned forward. In the closeness he smelled her hair like a bee smells nectar. Sweet. Enticing.

After the bus ride she'd met a friend. A girl just like her, unsuspecting and unaware. As she'd touched her friend, greeting her with a kiss, *there* was the glow, the shine of what lay beneath, inside, where only he could reach down.

At the cinema she was merely four rows away when he saw the shine. Surrounding her, glowing in the dark, a gentle halo of gold as she leaned to her friend to whisper something. They'd laughed, before returning their attention to shared popcorn and the film.

From the multiplex he'd followed, watching from a distance from doorways and shop fronts, pretending to peer into windows. She'd shouted a goodbye to the other—her final goodbye. She hadn't known, so certain there will always be just one more. Does anyone ever recognize their last of anything?

All hope is gone as she slumps. One leg stretched before her, the other bent back beneath the chair like a mannequin awaiting display. Moments before her hands gripped the chair's arms like claws. Now they lay unfurled and limp.

Blood flows in rivulets from the thin, white line carved in her forehead. Red against shiny white bone and pale, translucent skin. Shimmer-black hair falls about her face; strands caught in the blood. He considers brushing them aside to examine the incision, but he's lost his taste for her. He doesn't like the way the face muscles have slackened and her skin droops; how the eyes lay open, staring at him. Above those windows to the soul, white muscle and bone shine through.

As he studies his work he sees his mistake. The hole above her brows, slightly off center, not neat enough. Wrong. Or perhaps not wide enough. The pink-beige flecks of brain matter mingle with the blood. Wrong. The incision is also too deep.

Her fault.

She'd moved, even after he'd explained—in detail, always in detail—why she should be still. Usually they listened. Sometimes not. His concentration had wavered and allowed her to move. He grew stronger with each one though, and soon his control would be absolute and he wouldn't need to bind them.

A long sigh escapes his lips. The need remains, tearing again at him like a climax almost there, but fades away. He wanted, *so wanted* for this to be The One.

He sighs again. No matter, he tells himself—even though this does matter—The One is in this city somewhere out there. He senses her like a hum in the air.

He leans over her, the girl he thought, hoped, would open the door to home. From her brow, he wipes a drip of blood, which hangs like dew. Squeezing and smoothing the blood between his fingertips he thinks back to the bus ride. Something is there behind the curtain of his mind. A strange, little catching lingers, scratching at his awareness, crawling into his subconscious, seeking a memory, a very distant memory.

Now hovering there before him.

The redheaded bus driver.

Could this really be him?

What an ironic twist.

Maybe, *maybe,* this one now just blood and bone and empty flesh, is a sign, a glowing flashing marker. Not The One, but fate's message sent for him. He rolls the idea around inside his mind like the last peppermint in a packet, to be savored, considered.

In that slippery, sliding moment, his disappointment begins to heal. If the bus driver has appeared at this moment, this very day, then there *is* a reason. All he needs to discover is why. He'll take his time. He'll watch. Surely the reason will be revealed.

Reasons usually do.

2

*Y*ou could blame what happened on the weather.

If not for the sizzling and humid summer evening, the moisture hanging heavy in the air, clinging to everyone's skin, heralding a storm flying toward us, I might never have done what I did.

Rain or shine, storm or blue skies, everything was all fine by me. The weather might get other people down but never me. I knew better.

"Fine" was a great word.

My wonderful mama used to say: "*Fine* by name—Rory Fine, that is—and *fine* by nature."

She peppered my life with that word from the day I entered this world. Until she drew her last breath, haggard and weary, she still insisted *everything* was fine. Always had been and always would be, no matter how much Adversity knocked at her door she wouldn't allow those bad thoughts in.

According to her, my manners were fine enough for the President, should he ever come to visit. My friends, my quite average school results, my smile, my sandy, red hair—the butt of schoolyard jokes—

my stories, everything, was just fine. Nothing earned her reproach. Nada.

"You're the finest thing in my life," she'd say.

"And you're the finest in mine," I'd reply.

The day she left this earth was certainly Heaven's finest and the saddest day I'll ever live. Her last words, spoken in broken syllables and wisps of sound to me, her sobbing seventeen-year-old who'd kept vigil by her bed hoping for a miracle.

"Don't ... cry, my darling boy. God smiled the day you were born. Have a *fine* life my son. That is your destiny."

She may have revised her prediction if she'd known about this hell-hot day that awaited, nine years down the road. There was too much of what St. Alban folk call the Madness Air. The kind of hot that never helps anyone's mood. Or troubles.

A slight breeze blew in off the Dawson River, trying for all it was worth to cool things down just a little. Without that freshening whisper people'd be crawling up the walls by nightfall. Three days straight the heat had invaded our city and sure made my job all that much harder. At the end of a day, all the passengers wanted was to get to their air-conditioned or fan-cooled homes. You know how people look when they've had enough, their muscles stretched beyond capacity and energy on low flow? Well, this described my passengers today. Every single one of them.

I've been driving buses for five years now. A peculiar job for a young man, I know. I know. At twenty-six I should be exploring the world, making my mark, building some kind of résumé to show I've done something with my life and secured my future.

For me though, this job is perfect fitting like a glove with my other more important work. *Life Job*, as I think of my sideline business.

Probably what I do is a smaller scale version of solving global warming by switching off a single light bulb one lamp at a time. So a big job. *Big.* Yet, one by one, I switched off those bulbs, because who knew the effect that might have? Think of my intervention as saving one butterfly that might flap its wings in Bangkok and, in flapping those little wings averts a bushfire in Australia and saves a town. You know the Butterfly Effect, right? That's me, the Butterfly Effect guy. Except, I call this thing I do troubles keeping, which makes me a Troubles Keeper.

I love this job, both jobs, most days. Looking for greener pastures doesn't enter my mind. Even if those thoughts did, I couldn't leave, because in the last six months all had changed. I simply can't leave until everything plays out.

3

*M*ariana entered my life via the bus's front boarding steps. She delicately boarded the bus, gliding like a dream. Her smile, followed by a casual "hello," hit me like an electric spark that traveled up my spine and charged my soul. Think those zap things that restart hearts. Her smile did that to me. *Smile. Spark. Zap.* Now I'm magnetized to her. *Nope, I can't leave now.*

I'm in glorious, wonderful, very fine love.

The day she hit me with that warm smile was cold, wet, and nasty; not a day you'd expect love to come a knocking. She climbed aboard my bus, soaked and bedraggled, golden-blonde coils, dark with moisture, poking out from beneath her raincoat hood.

Mariana pushed back the hood of her green-with-pink roses patterned coat, looked down her front, then back at me.

"Sorry. I'm dripping. Raining crazy out there. Am I okay?"

Droplets ran down her jacket to puddle on the charcoal-colored steps as she stared at me through running-mascara-blackened eyes. A gentle, magical light switched on instantly brightening that cloud-darkened day.

I heard my Mama's voice whisper in my ear. *Rory, she's the finest,*

most beautiful natural woman in the world. I like her. I know Mama,
me too.

I remember that day like yesterday, remember I'd wanted to say
something smart, something flirty and light. Normally I'm good with
a quip. Witty Fine, some call me. Something happened to my brain or
my heart or whatever had joyfully twisted inside my chest. My voice
had been suddenly held hostage so the best I had managed was a nod
toward the back of the bus and a limp smile.

"Thank you," she'd said, pulling and pushing at her coat as
though removing a layer of skin. More drops flew about her. Then
she had moved down the aisle, her coat now over her arm. The last
glance I had snatched in my mirror was of her seating herself next to
Mr. Ogilvy (gray-haired, weary eyes and always missing his son).

Six months ago that had happened and still I hadn't worked up
anything close to enough courage to squeak more than a "hello" or
"have a nice day." I guess that's why today I became bold and took a
risk. On reflection, what possessed me?

Love. Unexpressed love.

On this stifling day, air sticky with invisible moisture, the high-
light was my anticipation of Mariana's stop. Nearly two years now, the
nine-zero-five was my regular route, traveling through City Central
with its towering buildings, bustle of shops and department stores,
clutter of lunch bars and cafes, and thousands of workers navigating
the streets, seemingly always in a rush. From the city we enjoyed a
picturesque two-mile drive along the wide and glistening-blue
Dawson River, the focal point of the city. Then, on to East Village
(doesn't every city have an East Village?). Here we passed the
ramshackle, no-longer-in-use, ancient cemetery. Then along
Ellsworth Road, the epicenter of the village, dotted with small
boutiques, sweet, fine eateries nestled beneath low-rise residential
apartment blocks, (sprung up like well-watered saplings since the
reinvigoration of the area).

The route terminated at East Village train station by Benedict
House, so named to conceal the building was really a halfway house
for addicts on the mend. Then the route reversed back the same way.

Three hours after I'd swung the bus out the gates, I drove back into the depot for a break, before repeating the journey all over again.

What most people would consider a mundane job—same streets, same view, same stops and starts—I enlivened by getting to know my regulars. In fact, I did more than get to know them, more than transport them from A to B. I helped them. I changed lives.

They never understood, of course, why on the odd occasion their commute left them happier, more content than when they'd boarded. Maybe they thought the change in mood was due to my friendly smile, or the chance to relax while someone else drove, or that anywhere was better than where they'd just left.

But the difference was me. My touch. My gift to them, delivered without a trace, without a sound, without anybody knowing why suddenly the world seemed a brighter place; the troubles they carried when they left their homes that morning now not so heavy.

I didn't need a thank you or to leave a florist's calling card: *Here's a gift because I can, because I want to make the world a better place.* I didn't need acknowledgment; all I needed were their smiles, their improved moods, and to see extra bounce in their steps as though they no longer toted that emotional backpack.

Troubles. They stick to skin like glue, like gum to the sole of a shoe. They slide into the crevices of your heart, slither into your veins, and tug at you from the inside until they become something dark and heavy and not so easy to shake.

The length of time you allow them to take up residence, that's what makes all the difference between the good, the bad, and the ugly days. Sure, you can brush them aside—and most good folk usually do—but what gets you is the sometimes; the sometimes when shrugging off troubles may not be so simple.

I took away the sometimes.

Dawson River was my favorite stretch. Some days the word *fine* just wasn't enough. The sun rising, yellow and pink, a present to those awake, and the sun setting over glistening water, warm gold, a splendid vista that made you believe in all things good. Some days the river didn't need the sun to shine. Rain splashing its surface,

urged small white-tipped waves to rise up like dancing handker-
chiefs. I knew this river like a friend. We shared a secret; in fact, we
were allies.

This five-fourteen afternoon run was my favorite. Not just
because of Mariana, either. My best work was done in these hours. If
people ever needed relief from their troubles, the time was after a
hard day's work. But, for whatever reason on that day, most passengers seemed to feel the weight of life more than usual. I guess that's
why I did what I did, before I'd thought the whole thing through.

4

*H*e peers through the bus window at the ominous clouds. The light drops of rain, quickly turn the gray of the sidewalk to a mottled black. He likes this dark brand of sky. People are less aware, far more concerned with getting to shelter, staying dry, worrying about plans made more difficult by the heavens spilling down.

Though he walks freely among them, beside these scurrying creatures of habit, there's always a risk he'll be recognized for his true self. Rain feels like an invisible cloak; the humidity like soft, protective fiber against his skin.

Until he found *him* on this bus in the late afternoon, he had spent the day traveling the bus routes, attempting to ascertain if what he felt yesterday was because of this bus, or this man, or a random connection to something else. *Now he knows.* He'd moved seats numerous times, reached out and brushed a few of those around him. *Nothing.* Just a nagging frustration growing within that he may have been mistaken.

Now as he watches him—yes, and the man *is* him—he understands like a faded memory reinvigorated by an old song or the whiff of an intangible scent. He *knows* his search is over.

With each stop he studies the driver, cobbles his memories together, and wonders why he hadn't sought him out before. Of course, he may help him to open the door. *Friend or enemy, though?*

The way he looks at the girl, all golden hair and a smile, as she climbs aboard and skims past the driver, reveals so much. This makes perfect sense; the two of them special lights in a world filled with half-opened doorways and empty rooms. They are both of the same design.

As she maneuvers down the aisle, the girl places a hand on the seat back in front of him. He reaches out nonchalantly to touch her. Electric fire, blue and sharp, rushes through his skin.

She could be The One.

He soaks in this knowledge, and the peace this thought brings. This long search could be over. Her brow lifts playfully as she looks down at his hand; surprise crosses her face. He smiles and withdraws the hand, feigning embarrassment. She smiles. Unsuspecting. No reason to fear. A random accident of physicality, a moving bus, an unbalanced body.

Now she is his and he can source her at will. A thrill plays through him and goosebumps rise on his skin. For the next fifteen minutes he slides between exhilaration and frustration that he must wait until tonight. He'll follow, but he's learned through experience that timing is everything.

Then the bus stops and the driver stands facing down the aisle. He introduces himself. *Rory Fine.* Has the man recognized him? Surely the bus driver cannot know or he would have noticed a reaction.

As the bus driver talks he begins to understand. This isn't a random chance meeting that he is here on this bus with her. Something grander is at play. He just needs to figure out exactly what that means.

Continue reading
for FREE with Kindle Unlimited or Kindle Prime

The Troubles Keeper

Available also in whisper-synched audible

The Troubles Keeper

ABOUT SUSAN MAY

Susan May has sold hundreds of thousands of books and is an Amazon best-selling author, ranked among the top one hundred horror authors in the USA since 2015.

Her growing number of fans from all over the world have likened her immersive and page turning style to Stephen King, Dean Koontz, Robert Mathieson, Gillian Flynn and Ray Bradford.

Susan was four when she decided she would become a writer and packed a bag to march down the road looking for a school. For forty-six years after, she suffered from life-gets-in-the-way-osis. Setting a goal to write just one page a day cured her in 2010. This discipline grew into an addictive habit, which has since born multiple best-selling dark thriller novels and dozens of short stories and novellas, many of which are published award-winners in Australia, the U.S.A and the U.K.

Passionate film lover since childhood, Susan is also a film critic with the dream job of reviewing films for a local radio station. You'll find her several times a week in a darkened cinema gobbling popcorn and enjoying the latest film. She sees 150 plus films a year on screen at the invitation of all the studios and, no, she never tires of them.

Susan lives in beautiful Perth, Western Australia with her two teenage sons and husband, while her mind constantly travels to dark, faraway places most would fear to visit. That though is where her inspiration lives, so go she must.

ALSO BY SUSAN MAY

Explore all available books in order of most recent publication:
susanmaywriter.net/susan-may-books

NOVELS

Destination Dark Zone

Best Seller

The Troubles Keeper

Deadly Messengers

Back Again

The Goodbye Giver (THE TROUBLES KEEPER 2)

(COMING MID-2020)

JOIN SUSAN MAY READERS CLUB FOR ALERT

NOVELLA

291

Behind the Fire

OMNIBUS

Happy Nightmares! Thriller Omnibus

SHORT STORY COLLECTIONS

Behind Dark Doors (one)

Behind Dark Doors (two)

Behind Dark Doors (three)

Behind Dark Doors (the complete collection)

(Includes one, two and three)

WHISPERSYNC AUDIBLE NARRATION

Behind Dark Doors (the complete collection)

Destination Dark Zone

Best Seller

The Troubles Keeper

Deadly Messengers

Back Again

291

Behind the Fire